Song of the Universe

Song of the Universe

A Novel

Robert Veres

iUniverse, Inc.
New York Lincoln Shanghai

Song of the Universe

Copyright © 2007 by Robert Neal Veres

All rights reserved. No part of this book may be used or reproduced by any means, graphic, electronic, or mechanical, including photocopying, recording, taping or by any information storage retrieval system without the written permission of the publisher except in the case of brief quotations embodied in critical articles and reviews.

iUniverse books may be ordered through booksellers or by contacting:

iUniverse
2021 Pine Lake Road, Suite 100
Lincoln, NE 68512
www.iuniverse.com
1-800-Authors (1-800-288-4677)

This is a work of fiction. All of the characters, names, incidents, organizations and dialogue in this novel are either the products of the author's imagination or are used fictitiously.

ISBN-13: 978-0-595-40227-4 (pbk)
ISBN-13: 978-0-595-84633-7 (cloth)
ISBN-13: 978-0-595-84604-7 (ebk)
ISBN-10: 0-595-40227-5 (pbk)
ISBN-10: 0-595-84633-5 (cloth)
ISBN-10: 0-595-84604-1 (ebk)

Printed in the United States of America

This book is for Barbara Frilen—and for all the people everywhere who know in their hearts that there's something more than meets the eye.

I

Something new is happening in the world. Listen carefully, and you can hear behind the background hum of the nightly news a quiet stirring of new questions, questions that have never been asked in quite this way before, questions about our lives, our health and our potential, about who we are and what we can become.

If you've ever thought that there must be more to life than what you experience with your five senses, more than what they teach in schools, and if you have ever dared believe it, then you are a part of this new thing, and it is a part of you.

—From *The Rutherfordton Spiritual Gazette*

My dearest Karen:

As you can see from the number of pages in this box I'm sending you, this is not a letter. It is, instead, a gift made especially for you.

If gifts were measured in time and effort spent, and by the love poured out in the spending of them, then this one would be too valuable to measure. But, as I have been reminded over and over these past few weeks, our world measures things very differently from the way the heart would. As it is, I just hope you will find the time to read my gift to the end.

The most important message here, which I want to come right out and tell you now, is that I love you. I have loved you deeply from the moment I held you in my arms at the foot of our bed. I held your head and shoulders even before you were fully out of your mother's body, and in the hour or two that I touched you on your mother's breast, and finally (after a lot of hints that perhaps you were not hungry any more), when I was finally able to hold you in my arms, I fell ever more deeply in love with you.

Over the years, when we cuddled on the couch in front of the television, when we played together outside and I pretended that I was a slow, hungry, easily-confused monster and chased you and your little friends around the house, whenever I watched you on the stage or from the sidelines, I would feel my soul touch yours with a force that gripped my heart and made me feel weak and strong at the same time.

Despite everything, that love has grown stronger over the years.

I know that this will surprise you. After your mother finally gave up fighting the terrible sickness that was eating her alive, you and I could have turned to each other for comfort. Instead, I felt overwhelmed. I allowed my anger at your mother's death to manifest as anger at you. In my pain, at my time of loss, fatherhood seemed like an obligation, rather than an opportunity to share your special journey to adulthood.

I can see now that your mother's end came at the worst possible time in our relationship. In every generation there is what my friend Apollo calls "the Battle of the Paths," and you and I fought it too. It is a simple thing, and yet it is also the never-ending story of parents with emerging adult children, going back to the earliest days of human life.

Karen, as you will learn, when parents take a journey through life, their experiences map out a difficult pathway, full of wrong turns and painful mistakes and hazards which, in retrospect, could have been avoided if we had only known more about the path beforehand. Always, as we see the next generation beginning its own journey, the parents hope and expect that their children will follow this route that we have learned to navigate, because this time it will be safe and well-mapped, and we can prepare our children to overcome the hazards and unpleasant surprises.

Of course, the children always, without exception, feel a powerful inner need to follow their own path—which is always defined, at first, as any path except the one that the parents are offering.

And so there is conflict, and the conflict makes it hard for either side to see the love of the other. The parents feel rejected, and ask God why no generation is ever able to accept the hard-won wisdom of the previous one, why the children they love should have to repeat the same mistakes over and over again on their own. The children growing to adulthood feel an overwhelming pressure, from people more powerful than they are, to move in this or that direction when everything inside is telling them to go somewhere else. They look to the sky and ask God why the inevitable road to independence has to have such painful obstacles, created by the very people who should be supporting them.

This is you and me and every other parent and every other child since the beginning of time. As you were growing up, you must have felt my expectations like bars around your soul.

But Karen, here is the wonderful thing about this. Today, I know the answer to those questions that every generation asks God about. Before long, you will see *how* I know, but for now I ask you to just hear the answer, and test within yourself the truth of it. When a butterfly emerges from its cocoon, it struggles terribly to free its beautiful wings from the confining structure that it has built around itself. The struggle can take hours, and if you were to see this fight to break free, you might feel inclined to have sympathy for the poor struggling butterfly and separate the last of the threads with your hands and let the butterfly go free.

But if you did this, Karen, the butterfly would drop to the ground and flutter its wings in a pitiful way, and you would see that it could not fly. Its wings become strong enough to fly only through this difficult struggle against the threads of the cocoon. And, in one more example of the amazing organization of the universe, the cocoon is built exactly strong enough to provide exactly the exercise needed for the wings to carry the butterfly into the air.

Now Karen, here is the secret. Every person—you, me, everybody—is a butterfly. We have to struggle to free the wings of our freedom in order to be strong enough to follow our own unique journey. Just like the cocoon, the Battle of the Paths—the repeated tragedy of every generation of people for as far back as people have been around—is a small but important part of the detailed master plan for our species. It is not a tragedy; it is a gift that we, poor mortals that we are, receive with anger.

So Karen, I am sorry, but at the same time, I am now able to forgive myself, and forgive you for struggling so bitterly against me. I can hope that as these things are understood, you, too, will be able to forgive me.

And most importantly, I want you to know that, despite my interference—despite the terrible execution of my best intentions—you have done something I never would have thought possible. You have exceeded my expectations.

I truly love who you are, and I love your journey, even if it has been harder and more painful than ever I would have wanted for you.

And so please know, first and before all else, that I love you three times over: once for the child who brightened my days. Once more for the person you are, and much more again for the remarkable person that you are becoming, who will brighten the world with her essence.

I could not leave without telling you this most important thing.

Your friends tell me that you are well, and they say firmly that you still do not want to see me. I knew this before I asked. But as you read this, please think about letting me visit with you one last time before I leave on my own journey. There is so much to tell you, much of it here, but more of it that will not fit on paper. I have seen so many things since you last saw me. I have seen the spiritual parasites that vex the lives of humanity. I have learned to read the rich, usually tragic life stories that are written in every detail on the delicate gossamer parchment of our spirits. I have conversed with the citizens of the maelstrom surface of a star like our Sun, befriended living clouds and raised my voice to the Song of the Universe, the chorus that is now spreading across a thousand times a thousand galaxies.

I want, now that I understand it myself, to show you who I am and what I have become. This is harder for me than most, because there is almost nothing remarkable about me to hold your interest, except for the fact that I love you and you, at your deepest core, love me.

But I think that will be enough.

Karen, I start this message to you with paper and pen graciously lent to me by my attorney, sitting on the hard bed of this jail cell, which was crowded a few hours ago, and where now I sit alone. I wonder where the others went. There were more than twenty of us, and everybody but me was peacefully asleep. Were they bailed out before dawn? It seems unlikely. But they have a history of vanishing in interesting ways, as you will see before long, as you perhaps have already read in the papers.

I also wonder what has happened to my life.

Many years ago, when I was in the second grade, my father was transferred from the only home I had ever known in New Jersey to Hendersonville, NC. I was moved to a new school in the middle of the year, and everything and everybody was new and unfamiliar and somewhat frightening. In that year, I formed an unusual habit, which I follow to this day. Every night before I allowed myself to fall asleep, I would try to recall everything that happened during the day, in as much detail as possible, trying to make sense out of it, but also trying not to lose the details.

And every night, I would be surprised all over again at how much had happened to me in my brief time of wakefulness, how many things I was already in danger of forgetting.

Last night, while the others slept, the images that came back to me were so vivid and confusing that I can hardly insert them into the narrative of my life. The fire. Falling down into the blackness below the floor. The awareness of watching my own body from somewhere outside of it. The arrest and the remarkable sight of the Master in his full glory. The visit to the Deva Community. How can I put these things into words that you can understand? It all seems to me now more dream than reality, even though I have already experienced things that are a million miles beyond my previous imagination.

And so I lay there in a state of anxiety and confusion, staring at the ceiling for what must have been hours.

Finally, I sat up and checked the time. It was 4:15 AM.

All around me in the room surrounded by concrete and bars, the followers of the Master were spread all over the floor in attitudes of slumber. Like children. I stared into my hands, and then back out at the tangle of bodies, feeling paternal in my concern for their welfare.

What was I going to do with them now? How had it come to this?

I spread my hands out and shut my eyes, trying to let it all be, trying to reconnect with creatures far, far away, to do what I had forgotten to do earlier in the evening, which was ask them for help and guidance. But my mind had become too jumpy, too full of worry for me to squeeze my awareness into that magical space between words.

As I tried to meditate, there was a sound in the corridor, footsteps and the loud jingle of many keys. At this hour?

Hoping to protect the sleep of my friends, I stood up and carefully picked my way across the obstacle course of bodies, keeping my feet from treading on anybody's hands or legs. Just as I reached the bars of the cell doorway, a police officer rounded the corner. I could not remember if he was one of the arresting officers, but I did not think he was. He seemed surprised to see me waiting at the door for his arrival.

"Can you tell me which of these people is Adam Zakar?" the officer asked me, speaking, I thought, quite a bit louder than necessary.

"I am," I said softly.

He looked me up and down, at my disgracefully-wrinkled business suit, and then past me at the unkempt jeans and shorts and torn T-shirts of the others on the crowded floor. "Yes, I might have guessed," he said with a hint of irony that I knew must have been an inside joke among jailers. I had to read the glow of his spirit to discover the meaning of this wry joke: that it is always the most well-dressed prisoner who has the services of an attorney.

The officer carefully opened the door, allowed me to step outside, and then locked it just as carefully, giving the bars a final tug before he looked me up and down.

"Follow me," he said finally.

I was led down the too-brightly-lit hall toward another doorway composed of thick metal bars. And then, just as I was certain we were going through this second door, the officer turned abruptly to the right, into a small room that was just as barren as any of the cells. The room was furnished with nothing but three chairs and a spare wooden table that was nicked and scratched with age and cigarette burns. In one of the chairs sat an older gentleman in a business suit, a man with a regal bearing and a shock of eminent white hair that made him look like a beneficent lion. I thought at first that he was here to interrogate me. But then he stood up, nodded that the officer could leave the room, and shook my hand warmly.

"Mr. Zakar, I'm Wes Bennett, of Bennett, Kleindeinst, Winnower and Brown. The House has asked me to come down and see what I can do for you. I'm just sorry I couldn't be here sooner."

"Please don't apologize," I said, feeling suddenly embarrassed. I found myself staring at a furry troll-like creature attached to the base of his neck, which opened its lazy eyes to look me over, and then gazed at me thoughtfully as I stared back. I could see that it was contemplating the interesting implications of the fact that I was able to see it, and knew that if I continued to stare, the creature would know where to insert its talons and influence its host to dislike me.

I averted my eyes, and found myself looking into the face of the attorney, who regarded me with intent curiosity.

"You will sit down?" he said finally, indicating the chair on the other side of the table.

"Yes."

"I have a summary of the charges here," he said, pulling a pile of papers out of a narrow briefcase. He put on his reading glasses and looked them over with an air of aloof distaste. "It is, as I'm sure you realize, quite an impressive list. Arson. Harboring fugitives who are facing a variety of charges. Insurance fraud. Assault. Resisting arrest. Here's my favorite: Possession of narcotics. That always gives you an excellent chance to win over the jury."

"It's called Soma," I said. "Fool says that it's made of mashed fly agaric mushrooms, natural ergot fungus and a milky extract of cannabis called bhang, but I'm never sure if I can believe him. It's the ancient ceremonial drink mentioned in the Hindu Vedic scriptures," I added helpfully.

"Yes, I'm sure." Wes Bennett and the furry creature attached to him both gave me a faintly quizzical smile. Finally the attorney pushed the paper aside and folded his hands on the table between us.

"As I said, I'm here to help you," he said. "But first you have to help me. I need to understand how a person of your…standing with The House could have been involved in any of this."

"It's a long story," I said.

I I

Historians can never say what age or era they are living in, any more than a fish can tell you how to drive to the lake it lives in. But when people look back at today, they might compare it to the early Renaissance.

They may conclude that the early 21st century was another special bend in the river of history, when people dared to step outside the accepted truths. A few brave people of the Renaissance questioned whether the church was authorized to sell tickets to heaven at a profit, and whether the medical professionals of the day could really heal people by attaching leeches to their bodies. The brave people of this era are questioning every small conception of the Almighty, and whether your body can ever be properly healed without restoring a healthy flow of energy into and through it.

—From The Rutherfordton Spiritual Gazette

On an unseasonably warm October morning that (somehow, I still wonder how) started me on my way to the jail cell, I arrived at the elegant regional office of our company, known, despite its real name, simply and familiarly as The Brokerage House, which most of us internally call *The House*. I normally walk in the doors an hour before anyone else. Karen, I think you know that this has been my habit ever since I joined The House, ever since I became a securities broker with one of the largest financial services companies in the world.

Why? Our building, a towering 16 stories high and set on top of the hill near the center of the city, offers some of the best mountain views this side of the Mount Mitchell summit. People don't believe me when I say that I can look out my window and see out to the mall on the eastern side of the tunnel, and if I lean forward far enough, make out the stone turrets of Asheville High School poking up through the trees on the far side of the other tunnel, over on McDowell Street next to the hospital complex.

Beyond the city buildings sprinkled around the valley, the western North Carolina hills roll out of sight in successive waves all the way to the horizon. If I get there early enough and the sun is warm, the morning moisture will be sublimating up into the air from the patches of ground between the trees, wisps of vapor rising slowly into the air above the forest, merging finally into low clouds. It looks as if the hills themselves are on fire.

Some early settler must have watched a scene very much like this when he named our local hills the "Smoky Mountains."

It is our treasure, this temperate rainforest that extends from the outskirts of Asheville all the way north past the Wolf Laurel ski resort and out over the Tennessee border, south past Hendersonville to the northern border of Greenville, South Carolina, and westward into the North Georgia hills out beyond Western Carolina University.

This view seldom failed to remind me that it really, truly is good to be alive, and that despite our daily challenges, we live on a beautiful planet. Then I would settle down and spend at least 30 minutes behind the computer, evaluating the mutual funds that I might consider recommending to my customers. With my own money, I subscribe to various databases, which tell me how much trading each fund does a year (the less the better), the size of their management fees (the less the better), and enough information on rolling monthly returns and comparison indices that I can almost imagine that I might, someday, be able to spot in advance one of those very rare managers who will be smart and lucky enough to beat the returns of the market itself.

I have to do this before anyone else arrives at the office because whenever the branch manager catches me, he is moved to anger approaching rage, and he tells me that "you don't need to know how a watch works in order to sell a watch." He's angry because if any of the younger brokers were to look carefully at the "watches" they're selling, they'd see that The House's in-house and recommended investment products are embarrassingly overpriced and consistently deliver below-average investment returns..

This particular morning, I had four appointments on my calendar, and I studied the first file carefully—the net worth statement of an extraordinary schoolteacher named Alice Gray.

When Alice came to me 20 years ago, she was standing on the edge of a financial abyss. She had no savings at all, and had gotten into the terrible, very common habit of spending a few dollars every month more than she made. None of the other brokers would let her near their offices, so I simply gave her budget guidance at first. Then, as she began to set money aside, I would periodically help her roll her money out of the horrible irresponsibly expensive annuities offered by the school's 403(b) plan into thrifty index funds.

Over the years, she got into the habit of consistently, steadily putting aside 10 percent of her paycheck every month, and the markets have been kind enough that she now has more than $1.7 million in her accounts, all of it saved the old-fashioned way, a dollar at a time. Now Alice is looking at retirement while the other teachers at the school are still working just to pay the bills.

Every so often, one of the other brokers will call her and try to steal her away so he can pick her clean. They don't know I did this, but I actually calculated, for Alice's benefit, how much she would have now if she had invested in one of the separate account programs that *they* recommend these days. Even I was startled by the result. Their excess (and often hidden) fees, chronic underperformance and tax inefficiency would have cost her more than $750,000 over her 20-year investment life.

"Come on back," I called out, leading Alice down the hall to the door of my little office. I cleared some papers off of the chair behind my cluttered desk and waved her to sit down.

"I was afraid you'd be too busy to see me," Alice said nervously.

"Busy doing what? This is what I *do* for a living."

"Oh, deals or something," she said vaguely. "I mean, there must be more important people than me who come in here all the time."

"I doubt even the ones who served with distinction on the battlefield would have the courage to face 35 fifth graders every weekday for a school year."

She laughed at that. "I think you may be right." Then Alice told me the story of an especially interesting young man who had a bad habit of bringing matches to school and setting fire to bathroom wastebaskets. "He just does it to upset the routine," she said. "Someday, he's going be a famous political activist."

"And he's in your class?" I said.

"He sits two chairs over from Nathaniel, who figured out how to bring the school's computer network down last week. He's going to be a hell of a programmer someday, if he stays out of jail. It's funny," she said, "how, if you watch them carefully and pay attention to what they do, you can see how they're going to contribute to the world. It's right there in the mischief they cause. Sometimes I encourage the girls to get out of their perfect behavior and cause a little trouble of their own. I want to see who they're going to become."

As she talked about the school, and the kids, and the other teachers, I studied the lines of worry on her face.

"So what's wrong?" I said finally. "I thought you were all ready to kick back as soon as final exams were over."

She twisted her hands in her lap. "I was," she said. "But—my sister, her husband…"

There was a long pause, and I let it run for as long as she needed.

Karen, I've learned, over the years, that it sometimes takes people a few seconds to figure out how to say whatever they need me to hear. Too many financial advisors are uncomfortable with these awkward silences, and feel compelled to jump in and say something. But my rule of thumb is that the people I work for should do at least two-thirds of the talking and I should do two-thirds of the listening.

"Faye called me a couple of nights ago," Alice told me at last. "She's remarried, and he seems like a nice man, but all his life he's bounced around from job to job, and now he wants to start a business."

"What kind?"

"Some kind of gourmet pet food. They want to collect garbage—the uneaten food off of customers' plates from all the local restaurants that are right there near her place. It's a very nice house in Walnut Creek, near San Francisco."

"Does *she* work?"

"Yes. She makes a wonderful living as an interior decorator."

"So if this new husband were to stay in the house and do nothing but drink beer all day, they'd have no trouble, because without him in the picture, she was doing fine financially."

"Yes—that's right."

I gave Alice a quizzical look. "So how, exactly, did her new husband become *your* financial obligation?"

"I—I guess I want to help Faye," she said, twisting her skirt in her hands. When I didn't say anything, she looked up. "Actually, what I think I mean is that I can't think of a way to say *no* to her without seeming selfish. I was hoping to take a short trip to Ireland this summer to celebrate my retirement. Now I might have to work a few more years."

"Does your sister know that this loan would postpone your retirement?"

"I'm sure she hasn't really thought about it. To her, I guess it seems like all the money in the world."

"How confident are you that the loan would be repaid?"

She looked at her hands. "Not very," she said in a small voice.

"It's never easy to say no to people you care about," I observed gently. "Now that you've put some money aside, you're going to get this kind of request more and more often. The question you have to answer is: are you going to give away what you worked so hard to acquire to whomever asks for it?"

Alice looked up at me for a long second.

"I didn't realize how hard it would be to have money," she said finally.

"It's hard both ways."

"Yes."

"But I don't think it would be wrong to give some of it away," I continued. "After all, a portion of it will have to go to taxes anyway, and I can help you redirect that tax obligation, if you want, to somebody who might be able to use it more efficiently than the government. What you have to figure out is where *you* want to give it, where *you* think it will do the most good."

Alice looked back at her hands and took a deep breath. "I actually was thinking about that," she said, the words coming more quickly now. "The library at the elementary school, they don't have many of the kind of books that the kids like to read, the kind of books that get them started reading for fun. Lately there's never been enough room in the budget to buy new books, and even if they had it, they wouldn't know what the kids really like, because nobody pays that much attention any more. Every free dollar goes to the reference books, even though all that stuff is on the Web now."

"I don't see why that's *your* problem, any more than your sister's new venture."

"It isn't really," she said. "And yet it is. There are only a few of us, the veteran teachers who would do this even if they didn't pay us anything, because we really care about making better kids—we know something that nobody else in the world seems to know."

"Which is?"

As she talked, I could see, from the light that was coming into her eyes, why Alice was so effective in the classroom. "Everything they spend money on, everything you see in the debates over making the schools better, is about learning the driest of the basics," she said. "But *we* know that all the magic is in the enrichment, in awakening the children's sense of their own potential. The relationship between a young person, where the idea of reading is still new, and a really well-written book is a precious and powerful thing. It has an enormous influence on who they become. And so I've been asking people, what *were* those books in their lives, and I have a list.

"And..." Alice hesitated. "You were on my list to ask."

"Wow! You're letting *me* put a book on your magic list?"

"I think something must have helped you become the person you are."

I sat back in my chair. Finally I said: "There was a book by a woman named Andre Norton called *Star Man's Son,* and later retitled *DayBreak 2025 AD,* which I think was her original title. That one book made me realize that I could strike out and be different and be right, that the herd was often wrong. And then there was a magical little book called *A Wrinkle in Time*. I don't think I could even tell you all the ways it changed the way I looked at the world."

She nodded. "Madeleine L'Engle. None of the kids are reading her any more, because it just isn't around."

"What else is on that list?" I asked, curious in spite of myself.

"Oh, it's a pretty eclectic mix. Nancy Drew and the Hardy Boys. Dr. Seuss. The Harry Potter books, of course. The Black Stallion books. *Catcher in the Rye. The Bell Jar. Charlotte's Web*, Lloyd Alexander's Prydain series. The Chronicles of Narnia. *The Phantom Tollbooth*. Sharon Creech. The entire Oz series, both the original books by L. Frank Baum and the later ones by Ruth Plumly Thompson. Some are out of print, but I've found copies on the web."

"This is an absolutely fantastic idea," I said.

"It's unbelievable that nobody else is thinking about it," Alice said,shaking the hair out of her eyes.

"How much do you think it would cost to buy the kind of books you're talking about?"

"Realistically? You'd need at least four copies of each, and the list is already up to 135—136 now with your book," she corrected herself. "You can get a discount through the library, but even so, I was thinking it could be as much as eight thousand dollars. Can I afford that?"

My inner voice of reason told me that this was an impossible enterprise, and that I would be foolish to encourage it. I took a deep breath.

"Yes," I said.

Karen, for half an hour, I and this schoolteacher who has given so much to the world looked over the funds in her portfolio. With the cost basis information in front of me, it was not hard to identify eight thousand dollars worth of highly-appreciated shares, going back to our early days together, which could be donated directly to the new library fund that I would set up for her. For a bottom line cost (counting all the various tax savings) of about $4,000, she would be able to put $8,000 into the charitable account and start buying books immediately.

The appointment time was just about up, but I promised to handle the details and talk with her again before I pulled the trigger on anything.

Alice stood up. "I still don't know what I'm going to tell my sister," she said.

"Send me her number and I'll offer them a business loan through The House," I suggested. "I'll tell them you arranged it with me, and we'll collateralize the loan with your sister's home in Walnut Creek. If the business makes money, she'll pay back the loan with interest and they can enjoy the profits. If it doesn't, she'll risk losing the place."

"Oh God. Her home means everything to her."

"It's always easier to take huge risks with somebody else's money," I said. "Of course, you can always invest later if the business gets up and running. But I don't think that's going to happen. Do you?"

She actually giggled. "No," she said. Then she added: "I feel like you're my guardian angel."

"You just call me any time," I said. "Nothing I do this week will be any more important than what we did here."

"Can I ask you something?" she asked as I walked her back down the hallway to the reception area.

"Business or personal?"

"Personal."

"Shoot," I said, holding my breath.

"Who takes care of *you*?" she asked.

"What do you mean?"

"I mean, I see you here taking care of everybody else. Some nights, I see the light on in your office when I'm driving by, and I know that you've given up a lot to do things the way you do."

"That's not true."

"We're not so stupid as you think we are," Alice said reproachfully. "You and I, we both have to fight against our various bosses in order to make this world a better place. Sometimes I wonder if it isn't that way everywhere in the world, that in every company and in government and every other organization, there is a small minority of people who never lose sight of the real goal, which is to bring a little goodness into the world. We'd be ridiculed and maybe even fired if our real intentions ever became clear. So we hide as if there was something shameful about it. It's a lonely fight, all the more so because nobody knows we're fighting it."

"It's the only way I know how to be," I said. "I can't help myself."

"I have you to help me," she said. "Who do *you* have to help *you*?"

As she said this, she looked directly into my eyes, and I realized that it was the first time she and I had really, truly connected, person to person. At this moment, she was offering to become something more than a customer. She and I could be friends.

Karen, I think a normal person would have felt validated or loved. But my primary feeling was discomfort. My inner voice of reason told me that it was safer, somehow, for me to be in the superior position of being her advisor, rather than an equal in a relationship where she and I would be each giving to the other. I wasn't sure how to bring this moment back to safety, and not totally sure I wanted to.

I looked down at my feet.

"I'd feel better if you didn't spend your time worrying about me," I said finally. "But it's wonderful of you to ask. If it makes you feel better, I'll think about your question."

"And you'll call me?"

"Yes."

"Either way?"

"Depends on how busy I get," I said, feeling suddenly back in control again. "Now get out of here, so I can get back to work."

I had three financial plans in various states of completion on my desk and I had to get an investment policy statement finished for another client meeting tomorrow afternoon. Plus I had another appointment later that morning, maybe the most important of my life. So I was unpleasantly startled when the senior broker we all referred to as Heavy Hitter followed me back to the office and poked his head in my door.

Heavy Hitter is the top-producing representative in our office, one of the superstars in the whole global system. The Branch Manager refers to him as a sales machine, and we are all envious of the $3 million in sales commissions he earned last year.

"Hey, Zakar," he called out heartily: "What do you call an Afghan virgin?"

I smiled weakly. "I have no idea."

"Never bin laid on!" he called out triumphantly. "How did Burger King get Diary Queen Pregnant?"

I shook my head.

"He forgot to wrap his whopper."

In our masculine environment, it is extremely impolite not to laugh at jokes like these. I did what I normally do: smile and snort a little as if I'm holding back a belly laugh. Even though it makes me uncomfortable, my sensible inner voice reminds me to be grateful that, no matter how low my sales production numbers—and, therefore, how low my status in the office—legendary producers like Heavy Hitter will still go out of their way to include me in their banter.

"So what do you need here?" I asked him curiously. It was very unusual for Heavy Hitter to waste his valuable time in my crowded little office.

"I need you in the conference room. We're closing an important deal."

"It will have to be without me," I said, reaching protectively across the desk to retrieve the estate planning documents for my morning appointment. If Heavy Hitter ever got wind of the kind of deal I was going to pull off today, he'd be figuring out a way to get a piece of it. "I have an appointment on the other side of town in twenty five minutes."

"Not any more," Heavy Hitter informed me cheerfully. "I had the secretaries cancel it."

"Who said you could do that?" I demanded, astonished that I was raising my voice at a person who could get me fired with nothing more than a wave of his hand. For a second, I considered getting up to tell Claire to call and uncancel the appointment, but then I realized how lame that would look to the people on the other end.

I sat down, feeling defeated and sick in my heart.

"Let's see..." Heavy Hitter examined his fingernails. "You were probably on your way to close a little hundred thousand dollar mutual fund sale, gross commission, about $4,000, less if there are break points involved. Net to your wallet, about $1,500. Am I right?"

I had no desire to let on how much the appointment could really bring me, so I nodded glumly in what I hoped was a convincing way.

"So what if I told you that I could get you a guaranteed six-figure return on an investment you don't even have to make? Would that make you want to follow me down the hall to where the papers need to be signed?"

"You're kidding, right?"

"Do I ever kid about money?"

"Do you ever get me involved in your deals?" I countered.

He waved the question away. "We're doing a favor for a customer of mine—actually my biggest customer, if you count him and his company together," he said. "His company isn't going to make its numbers this quarter, and we've already arranged for the sale of a lot of his stock options."

I nodded. In order to get a safe harbor on the insider trading rules with the regulators, senior executives typically have to pre-announce the sale of their options. Otherwise, they can be accused of knowing, with the benefit of inside information, when the stock price is going to drop, and selling before that happens. This would be so unfair to other stock investors that the Securities and Exchange Commission has created some fairly stringent rules that we all have to follow.

Our brokerage firm handles a great number of these option sales for senior executives, and a lucrative side business is helping these companies create phantom transactions which can magically transform liabilities into profits on the balance sheet—propping up the share price long enough for the options to be exercised and the executive to sell at a profit before the bottom drops out on the poor suckers who buy the executive's shares.

"And so he doesn't want the share price to go down for at least six months," I finished for him impatiently. "What I don't see is what that has to do with me."

"I'm arranging a series of private transactions," Heavy Hitter said, leaning into the room as if he was taking me into his confidence. "Malroy is going to buy $15 million worth of customer credit that is about to go into default, which they've agreed to buy back later in the year. The company will book the $15 million immediately, and then pay him and The House once the books are closed, plus a little extra profit for our trouble."

"How much profit?"

"$2 million total. I told them, if you want us to hide liabilities from the accountants, then we should get paid for taking on that kind of regulatory risk."

"You're screwing your own customer," I said.

"I think the company shareholders are the ones who are paying for all this," Heavy Hitter replied cheerfully. "And why should *they* complain? Over the next six months, the company will beat expectations by two cents a share, rather than missing by five. These days, that can mean the difference between a nice jump in the stock and a sickening drop."

"So what does this have to do with me?"

"To get that last two cents, we need another $2.5 million in profits booked by the end of this week." Heavy Hitter explained. "As it happens, the company has a warehouse that they've been carrying on the books at zero basis, part of a division that was closed down two years ago. So I told him you'd take it off their hands."

"Me?"

"It can't be me or Malroy or The House," Heavy Hitter explained with exaggerated patience. "Otherwise an SEC auditor is going to say that we're in some kind of collusion here, instead of a lot of completely separate transactions."

"What's this warehouse actually worth?" I asked. For some reason, I felt as if my body was sliding deeper into some kind of moral quicksand.

"It's worth what somebody pays for it, which just happens, by a remarkable coincidence, thanks to our negotiating here, to be $2.5 million." Heavy Hitter grinned at me, obviously expecting some kind of applause. "I've arranged for a very generous short-term loan from The House," he continued, his grin morphing into a happy smile. "We loan you the money, you come down the hall where the lawyers are probably just sitting down right now, with the papers already drawn up, and you also sign a contract that guarantees that my customer, personally, will buy back the property for $2.85 million a week and a day after the purchase date."

The math was not complicated. "And my share in all this is $350,000?"

"No. Your share is $150,000. The House takes $200,000 as interest on the loan."

I shook my head. "I don't think so," I said with what I hoped was a firm voice. "Your customer is president of this company? Surely he can buy the place for himself and not have me in the middle of this."

Heavy Hitter shook his head. "You know, that's the problem with you: you always have to look for somebody else to make the profits. Is it too much to ask that, just once, we put a little money in *your* pocket? Couldn't I see a little gratitude here?"

I didn't have a good answer for this, except that the deal smelled unpleasant. But much of what happened around the office smelled bad, so I didn't imagine that this would have been an argument Heavy Hitter—or the branch manager—would understand.

"What's your take in all this?" I asked. This was the question I had wanted to ask all along.

"I'm a shareholder too," Heavy Hitter said with a smile. "As soon as the numbers come in ahead of the analysts' projections, as soon as the stock spikes, I'm going to liquidate my own position. All of it. And I dare anybody to call that insider trading when I'm moving out *after* the earnings report instead of ahead of it."

"How much?"

Heavy Hitter reached across the desk, patted me on the shoulder, and then, without warning, grabbed my suit and pulled me to a stand. "Let's go, time's up, questions over," he said. "You do your part, and let me worry about my retirement fund. Besides, when we're finished, you're going to have some work to do."

"What kind of work?"

"This is why I canceled the rest of your appointments," he said. "My customer's son happens to be living in your new property with a bunch of religious nuts."

"So?"

"They're not paying rent," Heavy Hitter added with exaggerated patience. "Nobody can figure out how they even got *in* the place, since it's supposed to be locked up. As landlord, your job is to get them all out of there before you sell the building back to us next Tuesday. If you want to take the easy way out, just tip off the cops."

"Because—?" I said, feeling myself sink deeper into the quicksand.

"We think the people he has out there are on the run from the New York City police. But don't worry," he said, giving me a slap on the back that got me moving again toward the conference room. "We don't think they're dangerous."

I I I

People today often use the term "New Age" to describe beliefs which are too strange to be believed by sane, rational persons, just as they once used the term "heresy" for the ideas of madmen who suggested that the world was not flat, or that the Sun did not rotate around the Earth.

Perhaps the New Age idea that rational people find strangest is that our bodies are not just a physical structure, but also are composed of energy fields that define their health and vitality.

—From *The Rutherfordton Spiritual Gazette*

That afternoon, I turned my car off the 19/23 highway at the University of North Carolina/Asheville exit, executed a left turn toward the river and an immediate right, into one of those sections of town that most of the residents never see. The road followed the contours of the French Broad River past a series of industrial buildings, tobacco storage facilities and warehouses built alongside the railroad tracks on this side of the water.

As recently as the 1970s, trucks had carried booming loads of locally-manufactured furniture, locally-grown tobacco, electrical equipment and high-end clothing into these riverside warehouses, to be sent out by train to the rest of the world. But in the last 30 years, more and more of this manufacturing had moved to cheaper-labor places in Mexico and Asia, and a kind of dry rot had taken hold along River Road. I passed an abandoned building that might have been a warehouse or garment factory, then an auto salvage yard surrounded by high barbed wire, where illegally parked cars are towed for temporary storage. A busy grocery store warehouse with two dozen tractor-trailers parked against its bays was sandwiched between two more buildings in various stages of decay, marked with "for sale" signs that were so old they were hard to see behind overgrown weeds the size of bushes, and hard to read if you *did* see them because the paint had faded.

As I toured the neighborhood, I felt a queasy feeling of remorse. It actually felt as if, now that I'd signed my name to one of Heavy Hitter's deals, my soul needed to take a bath. Why couldn't I stand up for myself? Why did I let him bully me? Because, I told myself, he's one of the most important people in The House. Including me was actually an act of generosity. Wasn't it?

There was nothing to indicate which of the abandoned buildings I owned, no street addresses that I could find, so I pulled into the only occupied place on the river side of the road. This had once been a small office building, but, I saw now, from the collection of earthenware and clay in plastic bags scattered around the floor, that it had been converted into a pottery studio. Somebody had knocked out the far wall and installed a floor-to-ceiling bay window overlooking the water.

"Hello? Anybody here?" I walked further into the room and finally stood at the window, which offered an extraordinary view of the river, more than two hundred yards from shore to shore, wider than the Rio Grande through most of Texas.

I often wondered why such a great-looking body of water was so totally invisible to the residents of Asheville, when cities like San Antonio, Chicago and Savannah were able to turn the shores of *their* rivers into riverwalk shopping and dining areas.

"Hey! Who are you?" A woman's voice challenged me from behind.

"I'm lost," I said, turning to confront a dark-haired woman in a long white apron, hastily wiping clay off her hands with a white rag. Her face had all the crinkles of a habitual smile, but there was no sign of one now.

"The hell you are," she said with venom in her voice. "You get the hell out of here, and tell them I'm not going to get interested in selling, no matter how many suits they have in their army."

"I'm not here to make an offer," I protested. "I think you and I are neighbors, of a sort."

Her eyes narrowed. "What do you mean?"

"I own the building at 75 River Road," I said. "And I can't seem to find it."

"You bought it without looking at it first?" she demanded suspiciously.

Clearly I wasn't making a terrific impression on this woman. "Yes," I admitted.

"How much did you pay for it?"

"I'd rather not say."

"It's right next door," she said, giving her hands a final wipe and waving the mud-stained rag in the general direction of behind her. She held out her hand. "I'm Ellen Moore," she said, the face settling into a more gentle posture. "Now, you want some friendly advice?"

"I could always use some of that."

"You hang onto that property, and you watch your back," she said. "They're up to something, and if you find out what it is, I'd sure like to be the first person you tell. And while you're at it," she added as I headed toward the door.

"Yes?"

"You tell the kids that live over there that they should keep their clothes on when they take their baths in the river."

Leaving the car parked where it was, I walked across the property line toward a high chain-linked fence that surrounded an expanse of asphalt broad enough to park a hundred trucks at least. The warehouse at the heart of this empty paved space was a one-story structure made of ancient brick, so large that it covered the equivalent of a city block—at least twice the size of any building I had seen so far. A row of smoky windows just below the roof seemed to reflect more light than they allowed to enter. Many of them were broken.

The front gate was locked securely with a chain and padlock, both of them so rusted that I doubt a key would have helped, even had I been given one. I made my way slowly along the near side of the fence toward the river, looking for holes big enough to climb through, but the chain barrier appeared to be intact all the way back to the high bank overlooking the water.

Here, I entered a cool wilderness shaded by trees, where a path had been trampled through the weeds along the top of the bank. I followed the path until it stopped, unexpectedly, at a thick tangle of thorny bushes. Confused, I retraced my steps and found that about 15 feet back, the path branched down the embankment to a wide flat rock whose surface was damp with evidence of recent bathers, located right on the edge of the rushing water.

Looking up, I could see that this place was clearly visible from the bay windows of the pottery studio. I resisted the urge to wave.

Retracing my steps, I finally found what I was looking for: a washed out gully where the asphalt ended maybe 30 inches before the fence began. The dirt under the fence had eroded down enough that I was able, getting my suit disgracefully dirty, to lie on my back and squeeze up onto my new property.

Across the parking lot, weeds had pushed their way through cracks in the asphalt, and I could feel the heat of the morning sun on the pavement coming up through my shoes. The back of the building was made up of 20 cargo bays with large tractor trailer tires nailed directly into a 5-foot ledge where the trucks would have backed up, the floors of their vans flush with the floor of the warehouse, so fork-lifts carrying pallets full of containers could be driven directly from the warehouse floor into the back of the trailers.

None of the bay doors were open now; in fact, they looked as if they hadn't been moved in centuries. I felt as if I were walking through the ruins of an ancient civilization.

I finally located a side door along the wall toward the front of the building. There were muffled voices inside, and the echoes of voices.

I knocked timidly, waited a few minutes, and then knocked more loudly.

No response, although it seemed to me that the voices inside were louder now than they had been before.

I thought about knocking again, but then a bold idea came into my mind. Didn't I own the place? Shouldn't I be able to walk in unannounced?

I opened the door, and stopped abruptly and might even have backed up a little, my eyes blinded by an intense bright light, so bright that it blocked out everything behind it. The sight was so unexpected that I stumbled gracelessly across the threshold, the door slamming shut behind me.

"Abso-damn-lutely! Look at this! Right on cue; exactly what we need!" A woman's strangely melodic voice echoed impressively in that large empty space. I turned toward where I thought the voice was coming from and opened my mouth to say something about vacating the premises, and I think my mouth was still open as an extraordinarily beautiful young woman materialized out of the light. My awareness was momentarily lost in eyes the color of the sky on a perfect cloudless day. She was wearing a loose cotton shift and apparently nothing else underneath, because the strong backlighting rendered her clothing almost totally invisible.

"Come on; we need you over here," the woman said, taking firm possession of my arm and leading me forward.

"See?" she called out to somebody behind the lights. "This is the universe's way of telling us we're on the right track. Who says we aren't being watched over?"

"We need greater virtue to sustain good fortune than bad," called a voice from the back of the lights. "Duc de la Rochefoucauld. Let's not stand here gloating until we know what kind of Trojan horse it sent us."

I was led to a hard-backed chair, facing directly into the intense glare, and the woman brought those magical eyes close to mine.

"We're going to ask you some questions," she said, pushing me back into the chair. "All you have to do is answer honestly. That's all we're asking."

Karen, I sat there and stared at her face, and after staring for an embarrassingly long time, I realized that I had been in state of shock from the first second I had seen this extraordinary creature.

"I know you can hear me in there," she said finally with a toss of her hair.

"We don't have any evidence that he knows how to speak," a voice behind the lights pointed out.

"Tell me your name," I said, "and I'll answer any questions you want."

"You call me Venus and I'll call you Mr. Commuter. Are the cameras ready?" Venus called back over her shoulder. She stared at the place behind the lights, and then turned back to me.

"What do you think your spirit—the thing some people call your soul—is made of?" she asked.

"You might want to tell him there aren't any right or wrong answers," the voice called out from back of the lights.

"There are for us," another voice reminded him.

"But that's not relevant to *him*," Venus said impatiently. "Can we run the camera back and start over?"

"My spirit," I said, "is made up of everything I wish I could be and everything I am determined to become."

"That's actually not bad," said the voice behind the lights.

"What is karma?"

"It's the effect I have on the world that sticks with me."

"What makes the world so likely to disappoint our goals and dreams?"

"Us," I said.

"I like this guy," said the voice behind the lights.

"*Eyes are more accurate witnesses than ears,*" the second voice cautioned. "Heraclitus. To my eyes, he still looks as confused as any person we could randomly have selected. Ask him what he *means* by these things."

"Ask him who's going to win the World Series," suggested an altogether different voice.

The woman who called herself Venus abruptly turned back to me. "What is God?" she asked.

I considered this new question for a long second, although I couldn't imagine why a part of me insisted on taking this game seriously. "God is a projection of our hope, maybe a desperate hope, that there is perfection somewhere in the universe."

"Would you like to know God?"

"Who wouldn't?"

"Do you believe in life on other planets?"

"Of course. It's a big universe."

"Ohh; this isn't any good." The woman turned abruptly away, and something in my solar plexus was deeply sorry that I had lost her attention.

"None of those are totally correct answers," the voice behind the lights pointed out.

"But they aren't totally wrong either. I was hoping for *so* much less." Venus looked at me in exasperation with her hands on her slender hips. "Men are the only creatures in the world who can be completely arrogant and clueless at the same time," she said. "Was it too much to ask for you to live up to your species?"

"There is no worse lie than a truth misunderstood by those who hear it," the second voice rumbled with a note of vexation. "William James. It makes me wonder if our message isn't slipping through the chinks out there. If they *think* they have our wisdom, then it will be ten times as hard to give them the real thing."

"I'm not sure you understand who I am," I said again. "The truth is, I—"

"Abso-damn-lutely I know who you are," Venus said, turning her eyes back on my face so I would receive a full dose of her annoyance. "Before you were led here by holy spirit, we had just decided to go out and look for somebody whose place in the script is described as Mister Commuter, kind of an everyman, the Before, as in Before and After, the kind of person who is trapped in a reality he can't embrace and doesn't know how to change. Maybe we should talk about those things," she said suddenly to the men behind the lights. "I'll bet we could get some stupid answers out of him on *that* subject."

"I think *you're* the clueless one," I said in frustration.

As my voice echoed back to me, the buzz of discussion became instantly silent.

For a long second, Venus didn't move, and I noticed, oddly, that the hair that cascaded around her shoulders, reflected in the intense light, was the brightest object in the room. Then the hair shifted as Venus turned slowly around and looked me up and down, finally raising her cool gaze to my eyes and holding it there for a long, leisurely second.

I tried to maintain my anger and glare back, but everything about the scene told me that I had made the unbelievable mistake of giving her a reason to be annoyed with me.

Then she did something so peculiar that I forgot my anger and almost my fear. Her eyes glazed over. As they did, her face seemed to take on more, not less concentration.

"You're a stockbroker," Venus said, and at her words, a chill ran through my body, as if I had walked through a ghost. "You work in that building up near the center of town. Your wife released her spirit back into the universe thirteen months ago, leaving you with one grown daughter. You loved her to the end,"—and here the voice softened—"which means you rank comfortably in the upper one zillionth of one percent of all men in all history. The pretext that holy spirit employed to get you here isn't important, but if you really need me to—holy shit!" she cried out suddenly. "Apollo, take a look at this!"

All at once, a group of five or six younger men crowded past Venus, and they all had that strange look on their faces and they all looked at each other and nodded. Finally, another man stepped forward and the small group of strangers made an opening for him. He stood at least four inches taller than my six feet, with a full well-manicured blonde beard and a permanent network of creases across his forehead that made him seem intensely troubled about everything in his immediate surroundings. The calm intensity in his icy blue eyes told me he was accustomed to leading everyone else, and that he took these responsibilities no more seriously than he did those who looked to him for leadership.

At his cool leisure, the eyes glazed, and once again I experienced the peculiar sensation of being stared, not *at*, but *through*.

"*My candle burns at both ends;*
It will not last the night;
But ah, my foes, and oh, my friends—
It gives a lovely light," the man they called Apollo said at last. "Edna St. Vincent Millay. What can this mean?"

"The Master can tell us."

"The Master knew about this beforehand," someone said. "I'll bet it's a test."

"What about the movie?" one of the men with a camera on his shoulder asked impatiently.

"Screw the movie," said Venus. "Mister Commuter shows up here two weeks before the public seminar, with—*that*. It has to be some kind of omen. It could be a message from the universe."

"What rotten luck."

"*An adventure is only an inconvenience rightly considered. An inconvenience is only an adventure wrongly considered,*" Apollo said mildly, with a last oblique, bemused stare at my chest. "G.K. Chesterton," he said as an afterthought.

"Let's ask the Master exactly what this means. Turn those damn things off," Venus called out to the now-empty space behind the lights as she walked away toward the far side of the building.

"It looks...like...you've somehow guessed why I'm here," I called out, but nobody even turned around. The lights switched off, making it easier for me to see their retreating backs.

"I'm here to tell you that all of you have to leave this place and find some other place to live," I said, more to myself than them. "If that's a problem, then perhaps I could help—"

I took a step toward where they were going, and immediately ran into a young man with a large video camera in his arms. It was only a light bump, but with comic exaggeration, he flopped onto the ground and began moaning.

"Oh the pain! Get me an ambulance. I think I can feel the bone sticking through my leg."

"Well?" he demanded after a minute. "Are you just going to let me die here? Sure you are. That's the way they treat the mentally ill in this country. We never get the same respect as presidents of multinational corporations or movie executives, and now it's come to harsh denial of medical treatment."

"Come here; get up," I said, pulling him to his feet. He was an inch or so shorter than me, no more than 20 years old and light as a feather as I lifted him, landing on his feet with the grace of an acrobat. A thick goatee made his chin look impossibly long, and his shirtless upper body was so thin that you could see the detailed action of the hinges in the joints of his shoulders. I was startled to see that he had shaved his eyebrows and tattooed new ones in their place. In the darkness, the tattoos that encircled his arms looked like real snakes.

"You're not going to knock me down again, are you?"

"I promise," I said, smiling in spite of myself.

"Then you can hold the camera," he decided, placing the heavy object in my hands. "I'd show you how to work it, but the chances of another fool walking in here and screwing everything up by giving moderately intelligent answers seems too small to worry about right now."

I followed him toward the front of the building. It was my first opportunity to really look around, and I was surprised all over again at how enormous the place was. By the faint light coming in through the filthy windows overhead I could see that five picnic tables had been set end-to-end at the street side of the building, and beyond that an assortment of tables that looked as if they had been randomly selected from garage sales, covered with gas-powered Coleman stoves and an assortment of pots and pans and dishes and glasses and assorted mismatching silverware that might have been lifted from the same garage sales. There was no visible source of running water, but two large water jugs rested upside down on portable taps, and behind them, an old wooden bookshelf was stacked with canned food.

To my right, the building extended off for at least half the length of a football field. Covering most of the front third of this space were mattresses scattered around at random, and a few people on a few of them, reading by the light of a candle or sitting cross-legged in an attitude of deep meditation; further down, half a dozen others were being led by a yoga instructor. Kerosene-powered space heaters had been set here and there. We passed several people standing around two women, one who hung her arms limp at her side, the other holding the arms and asking questions, and I had the odd impression that she was reading the answers from the stiffness of the person's arms.

The young man led me to one of the tables in the kitchen area.

"Some palace, isn't it?" he asked. "We're trying not to get too spoiled by the luxury of it all."

"I think I should introduce myself—"

"Why? I think we've already decided we're going to call you Mister Commuter, so your real name is kind of irrelevant to us."

"And what do they call you, then?"

"Fool. As in, hey, Fool, get out of the way of that camera. Or: Fool, you're pointing it the wrong way. Or: Fool, we sent you out with twenty dollars to get lunch, and all you brought back was potato chips. Or—"

"I see," I said.

"They don't ever compare me with Albert Einstein or Roy Rogers or any of those other classical philosophers, but I try not to let it bother me too much. But now that I look at you, you must get *your* share of insults, if not for your looks then for the absolutely ineffective way that you handle these social situations."

"I'm not sure anybody notices," I said absently.

Fool huddled over a dark table, and then turned around. "Here, put that thing down and have a drink," he said, handing me a cup. "Sit down and tell me everything about yourself."

He swept the top of the table off with one hand, scattering paper plates with food still on them and plastic forks and cups into an untidy mess on the hard concrete floor. Slowly, I lowered the camera and drew the drink to my lips. It tasted very odd and very good, like a kind of milky-white sweet tea.

"I'm not really a commuter," I said.

"That's a brilliant way to start out," said Fool earnestly. "You talk about everything you are not, and then eventually, perhaps in a thousand years, I'll figure out what you *are*. Okay; my turn. I'm not really an international film star. Now it's your turn again. What else are you not?"

I looked at him for a long second. "I'm not always patient," I said meaningfully.

"I'm not always quick to catch on to what people are trying to tell me," Fool replied cheerfully.

For a few seconds, I didn't say anything. "I'm here to tell all of you that you have to leave this place," I said finally. "You, everybody, have to—move out and find someplace else to live."

The other nodded sagely, never taking his eyes off my face. "I see," he said after a moment. "Can you tell me why?"

I thought about this for a second. For some reason, my thoughts seemed to be coming very slowly. I rejected one answer after another as not quite the *real* reason, until finally I arrived back at the source of everything.

"Because Heavy Hitter says so," I said triumphantly.

"That's a *very* interesting reason."

"He told me that I have to get you people out before next Tuesday. That's when they buy the place back."

Fool slapped his leg and laughed. "What a perfectly funny answer!" he said. "Does that make sense even to you?"

"Not really," I admitted. "It's kind of hard to explain."

"But it is very important to these other people that we leave here."

"Yes."

"Why?"

That stopped me, and my cheerfulness evaporated. Shouldn't I have asked this question myself? "I really don't know," I said, feeling strangely ashamed of my own words. "I just do what I'm told."

"So if I told you that you should move in with us and quit working with these people who give you mysterious commands without explaining them, would you do that?"

"Of course not."

"You're quite selective about who can tell you what to do." The young man who called himself Fool nodded pleasantly. "You take direction from people who do not mean you well, and you refuse to be influenced by somebody who wants only good to happen to you."

I took another drink from the cup. This was not going quite as well as I'd hoped.

"All I really want to do is get this complication out of the way and get back to my life."

"Because your life is so wonderful?"

"My life stinks right now," I admitted glumly.

"And that's why you're in such a hurry to get back to it?"

"Well—"

"Tell me." Fool leaned forward earnestly. "What would happen if you went back to the office where you work, and told them that you were not going to do whatever it is that they tell you to do? What would happen in your life?"

"I don't think that's possible."

"They probably wouldn't fire you—at least not immediately. You have at least 20 or 30 customers that they'd want to reassign to other brokers first."

"What?" I said, startled.

"Two of them have more than four million invested with you, and none of the other brokers have ever even talked to them."

"I—don't understand how you could know that," I said, staring into this young man's face intently.

Fool waved his snake-entwined arm dismissively. "Suppose it's true. What would happen?"

"I'd lose my status. Except that I don't have any status. There probably isn't a working toilet in here, is there?"

"No," Fool told me cheerfully. "But so far that's about the only drawback I can see to life here in the palace. It's nice and gloomy, very hot in the summers and icy cold in the winter, because there's really no insulation to speak of, and every once in a while we see rats nosing around not far from where we sleep."

Suddenly, I felt impatient and very, very sleepy, even though I had done nothing more strenuous than try to make sense out of our conversation. Fool looked at me expectantly, but I just looked away and didn't say anything else. We sat together for a minute, watching people walking here and there and somewhere else around the far side of the building. I couldn't imagine what they were doing.

"I need to know something," I said finally.

"Yes."

"Please, in ordinary straight English, tell me how all of you know so much about me. Have we met somewhere before? Is this some kind of joke you're playing on me?"

"Yes it is," Fool assured me.

"Then tell me the joke."

"Are you sure you want to know?"

"Of course I want to know," I said in exasperation. "Why else would I have asked?"

"Sometimes asking the right question is the most dangerous thing a person can do," said Fool, slapping his leg as if this was the funniest thing in the world. "Here, finish your drink, and I'll explain everything, no matter how long it takes."

I took a long last gulp, and put the cup down. My head felt very strange, and my thoughts jumbled around at random. With a great effort, I focused my eyes on the darkened face of his young man who, more now than ever, reminded me of the devil.

"So tell me," I said.

"To understand everything, you're going to have to glim with us."

"Have to what?"

"Glim," Fool said impatiently. "If you're glum, you glim. That's the easy way to remember it. Come on. I don't think we'll be visiting the deva community today, so it shouldn't be too scary for you."

Having no idea what he was talking about, or even, for sure, what *language* he was using, I found myself following Fool to a place between the mattresses and the wall, where a group of people were gathering on the ground with their eyes closed, humming.

I looked at Fool suspiciously, but he simply motioned me to sit down.

"Look here at the wall," Fool instructed me, indicating a random place on the floor. "The answer is right there in front of you, but you have to know where to look."

I stared, but for some reason it was hard to focus my eyes. I shook my head and tried to see the features of the surface of the concrete block, but the light wasn't quite good enough to make them out clearly. "If it is, I can't see it."

"Of course not; not yet. What *do* you see?"

"The wall."

"Now don't stop looking at the wall, but at the same time, be aware of the air between your eyes and the wall."

"The air is invisible," I protested.

"Yes," Fool agreed. "It is not the air that you're noticing, but something else. For the first time in your life, pay attention to the sensory input from the eyes of your spirit body. There!" he added triumphantly after a minute, although I didn't see how anything had changed. "You don't see anything now?"

I was about to give him the obvious answer, but then I became aware that I *was* seeing something. Oddly enough, it was something that I'd *always* been able to see—only I'd never really looked at it before.

The texture of the space between my eyes and the wall was much more complicated than I had ever consciously realized. It was as if the air was filled with a very soft, heretofore invisible cloud, a collection of dim shimmering shadows in the air.

I concentrated my attention on the barely-visible cloud instead of the wall behind it, but the view was frustratingly unspecific. Finally, I thought I could see, among the shimmering shadows, what might have been elusive bits of light, tiny irregular dots, too small to detect individually, like pale dust. If I looked obliquely toward the wall, they became slightly clearer.

There was something about that oblique stare...I was suddenly carried off by an odd memory of the first time I'd been shown a painting with hidden 3-dimensional images embedded in the picture. Magic pictures, they called them; computer-generated portraits which, when you stared at them in a certain abstract way, suddenly revealed a three-dimensional image that was not visible to your ordinary vision.

Now, as I looked at the mysterious shapes and forms in the air, it felt as if I was seeing in an extra direction, into a place that was hidden from my normal perception. The thought made my head spin, and I had to redouble my concentration just to maintain my focus on the cloud and the dust between me and the wall.

From what seemed like very far away, I heard others gathering more closely around me, and a slight squeak of a wheelchair somewhere behind, and would have turned my head, except that the thing I was looking at was too interesting to take my eyes off of.

"Fool, what have you done here?" the unmistakable voice of Venus demanded somewhere behind me.

"Don't get on my case, Hag," he said. "I gave him taste of Soma. I thought it might calm him down."

"What?" I asked.

"It's an ancient recipe," Fool told me. "Very good for spiritual enlightenment."

"You bastard," I said without any emotion. I was too interested in the Brownian motion of the inverted shadows. The longer I stared, the more their brightness seemed to intensify. I could have sworn, at that moment, that they were alive.

Then another voice spoke, and there was magic in the sound of it.

"Draw them toward you," the voice advised me.

I had no idea how to do that. My eyes watched the sparks of bright dust helplessly.

"Clear your mind of words," the voice commanded, and somehow the sound caressed my mind, drawing me into the spaces between the incessant babble that constantly murmurs at the back of normal human awareness. I could feel...*guided* somehow, my attention led deeply into one of those spaces, where there was clarity, purity—and something else.

"What you see in the air around you is what the Hebrew sages called holy spirit," the voice told my unresisting awareness. "Mistranslated to this day as 'the' holy spirit. It is also inside of you. Give it your trust, and it will guide you where you want to go."

Slowly, as in a dream, I turned my eyes down toward my own abdomen, and as the voice had promised, I saw the same glow, more concentrated inside my body than in the outside air. I gave this interesting interplay of light my full attention, tried to connect what was inside me with the sparkles that filled the air.

In that instant, my awareness shifted from my physical body to...*something else*, something that was much more fluid and alive. For what might have been a hundred years, or a thousandth of a second, "I" was no longer simply my head and torso and legs, although all of those parts of me were still in the room. "I" was also the air that I was drawing in and out of my lungs, and the dark walls of the building around me. Then I was also the street outside, and the leaves shimmering in the trees, and the air that made them shimmer. I was the river that flowed over deep rocks and under a bridge and the wind that blew across the grass on the opposite shore.

This expanded awareness looked back and saw my physical body seated on the floor in the gloom of the warehouse, surrounded by others, our spirits pulsing beautifully inside. What was it that was doing the looking, if not *me*?

You are no longer responding to the universe with your mind. You are thinking, feeling, sensing with your spirit.

Was that *my* thought? Or did it come from somewhere else?

A cricket leaped across the floor near my feet, and I saw its spirit and the mind of its spirit. In that moment, I somehow knew with certainty that insects and birds and plants and animals all did much of their thinking via this invisible glowing extension of their bodies. This was what living creatures had in common: spirit minds all made of the same magical dust of holy spirit, all part of the awareness of the universe itself.

Yes, that's it. Now you recognize the next thing you must do.

Did I? Carefully, fearfully, I expanded my awareness to include the cricket.

Instantly, the room brightened into a chaos of images that overwhelmed my brain's ability to interpret them. All I could see at first was an interplay of colors that were all a mad exotic variation of brilliant purple, and I realized (or was I told?) that I was now seeing, through the eyes of this insect, deep into the ultraviolet end of the spectrum, seeing colors that cannot be processed by human eyes. My cricket body, armored, tense, always ready to explode into a joyful, triumphant leap, experienced the air and the temperature of the air, calibrating it to a precision that astonished the human part of my awareness.

Through this body, I felt the vibrations of the room. The voices of the human creatures was a subtle tickling in the back of my forelegs. When I was certain that I had properly evaluated the temperature of the air against my feelers, I scratched my wings in a comfortable, rapid rasp which sent out chirps, communicating intimately to a female partner-in-my-future what I had learned about the air in this place-near-the-crevasse-where-warmth-persists-even-in-cold.

Soon, soon the female cricket in the opposite wall will hear my song, recognize in herself the truth I am speaking about the temperature and the feeling in the air, that there is a hint and more than a hint that the time to mate is becoming urgent. For much of my life, I have communicated the warmth of summer, which crickets know is the lazy absence of urgency. But now we can both feel that the time is approaching.

When the last chirp has been counted and measured against the warmth of the air, I coil my legs. A single leap takes me up in the air 10 times the height of my own body, and I am anticipating my descent, landing with a grace that few mortal creatures will ever experience, and with a second burst from the unlimited power of my back legs I am up again, flying without wings toward the rough textured wall whose smoothness is an illusion for the humans and other giants, leaping toward the crevasse, toward the outside and the grass and the temperature of the grass which is calling me from the far side of the wall through a passage only I know about, and I will feed and talk once again to the female-partner-in-my-future as surely as my death in the cold to come...

I gave myself to the alien, perplexing vividness of the cricket's awareness, whose actual thinking—the processing of the data and the personality of its response—seemed to proceed almost completely from this invisible spirit body, rather than the tiny handful of nerve ganglia clustered behind the exoskeletal crania. Was my mind, too, simply the receptacle of thoughts that originated in my spirit? An imperfect interpreter of the purity of thought, a muddle of the clarity that I was experiencing now...

Yes. And—?

The powerful comfort of that voice, which seemed to be latent in each of the dots of holy spirit, led me to expand my awareness once more. Instead of withdrawing from the cricket, I allowed my awareness to incorporate other creatures, in the grass, under the ground, in the air, letting the strange, utterly-alien cacophony of sensory data wash over me and resolve itself into ever-larger patterns and relationships, of the symbiotic and loving interdependence between predators and their prey, of the gentle caress of the wind against the grass and the leaves, of the bright, highly-focused awareness of creatures above the ground and below, of the incomparable raw, generous energy flowing from the bright sun into and through the world.

I experienced from the inside the delicate, fragile web of life on my planet, and I was also the warm, nurturing planet that enveloped this fragile, ephemeral network of creatures large and microscopic in a protective embrace.

And then, gradually, as my awareness continued to expand out into the infinitude of places beyond my little world, I noticed something else. Just as the individual creatures were part of a planet-wide network, so too was the Earth itself a part of something greater.

I felt rather than saw the Thing-Which-Watched-It-All-From-The-Inside-Out, the Mind-Which-Was-Composed-Of-All-Holy-Spirit, the Awareness which exulted when the hawk found the mouse in its talons and which also bled from the mouse's wounds.

It was life and death, triumph and tragedy, it was both sides of the ledger in every transaction, and it extended out into a distance and beyond that distance to all the places where my mind was not prepared to follow. And yet I could sense its own pulse of awareness, and where I had expected a ponderous gravity and arrogant majesty that would make me feel as if I was nothing and less than nothing, it was instead quick and insightful, and I thought I detected amusement as it watched through me my own awareness of its presence.

It experienced with me the recognition that it was participating in my astonishment and awe, and through me it shared this wonderful delicacy of experience that traveled in endless circles and made my mind spin.

Out of that spinning, I landed gently on a realization.

This, thinking purely with the spirit, is the real, original, true goal of meditation. This is something the human species has temporarily forgotten, and now it must relearn.

Karen, I was so excited at this flash of understanding that I wanted to break the connection with my expanding consciousness and run out into the streets shouting this news to everyone who would listen. Everyone should know this!

At the same time, I wanted to deepen the connection and never let go, to live the rest of my life in meditation.

In that conflicted instant it seemed as if the connection would break. Yet I was able to watch my foolish impulsive contradictory reactions from outside myself, and as the moment passed, I participated in a vast, good-natured amusement with the Ancient Consciousness itself.

We, the mind of the universe and I, laughed together.

Somewhere during that laughter, out of that shared joy, in that communion with the Unthinkable, the tiny sparkles of holy spirit, finally, at long last, began flowing from the outside of me into my body. I watched in fascination and embraced them as they added to the glow inside me.

"Stand up." Fool's voice came to me from a thousand times a thousand miles away, a tiny insistent tug at my awareness that wouldn't let go. "It's time for me to show you around."

Reluctantly, I took my awareness off of the dancing brightness between the shadows of the air, and followed this young man back into the gloomy center of the warehouse.

I must have been meditating for quite some time, because the interior of the building was dark now. Only—amazing thing!—it was dark only to my conventional sight. I saw (with the eyes of my spirit?) that all of the people in my warehouse had a ghost living inside of them, and the ghosts were made up of the most beautiful, the strangest colors.

The individual sparks had seemed to my untrained eyes to be uniformly white, like diamonds. But when millions or billions of them were latticed together into these human spirits, they cycled through a fantastic array of colors, but—amazing thing!—all colors that I had never seen before.

If I had not seen the world through the eyes of the cricket, I probably wouldn't have been able to process this information. But now the answer came to me with a gentle breeze of recognition.

Karen, imagine that somebody reprogrammed your eyes, so that you could see beyond red or violet on the spectrum of light, and you could experience hues that have no human name and which have never been captured by a human retina. It was something like that, except that this was far, far distant along a very different spectrum, and so the colors were all the more alien and inexplicable, not red or green or yellow, but brilliant shades of black like Milton's *darkness visible*, ranging up the spectrum to a clear demarcation point, where suddenly the entire color scheme shifted to endless brilliant variations of white, each rainbow exploding with vivid brilliance and contrast that was far more extensive and varied and beautiful than the colors of our mere visible spectrum.

To define any of these colors, you would need a hundred words at least. And when this or that hue on the rainbow of white mixed with this or that pigment of black, the possibilities became endless and hypnotic.

The effect was so bizarre that as I walked among the people and their interior ghosts, my overwhelmed mind did what I later learned all minds do when confronted with the colors of the spirit; it began to automatically translate those otherworldly hues into familiar shades of the visible spectrum, and to make this translation so automatic that I began to actually see them as myriad subtle shades of red, green, blue, yellow, brown, and only with a great effort of the mind was I ever again able to see the untranslated reality of colors beyond definition.

There were at least a dozen souls in the warehouse, moving about in the gloom as if it were as bright as daylight. I turned to look back at the kitchen area, and saw that several people were now spoon-feeding a young man in a wheelchair, who seemed not to be aware of what they were doing, for they had to open his mouth with their fingers, insert the spoon, and then manually close his mouth and wait for whole minutes before giving him the next bite. It looked like very hard work, and I felt a wave of intense sympathy toward the poor cripple, and wondered how he had become so badly disabled.

Fool led me impatiently to a beautiful orange-colored glowing shadow inside of a young man with short light hair and glasses, who looked up from a laptop computer and, seeing me, shifted his spirit momentarily to an amused off-green color.

"Briareus, this is my best friend in all the world. Let me introduce— Actually I don't think I know your name, my friend," Fool said to me.

"Adam," I said. I reached out my hand and absently touched the chest of Briareus, trying to mingle the glow of my body with the glow of his. Where we touched, there was an interesting melange of colored light.

"Recruiting?" Briareus said to Fool over his shoulder, still watching his computer screen. "He seems unlikely."

"Look at his spirit."

Briareus glanced up and back, gave me the now-familiar abstract stare, and raised his eyebrows. "Oh my yes. Wherever did you find him?"

"He just sort of walked in."

"Even so, I'm not sure he totally belongs here."

"He's all right. A little uptight and rigid, but I'm fixing that."

"I can see."

"Is the network back up?"

"Another ten minutes. I think we've figured out how to tap into the wireless system at Bean Streets downtown."

"We?"

"I got some technical help from a creature that looks like a fish with feathers. I met him through the glim last night. Listen," he said, indicating me with a slight gesture of his head, "does he know anything about computers?"

"You are so beautiful," I blurted out, watching the orange color shift to a beautifully skeptical brown.

"I don't think he knows anything about anything."

"Around here, that's always a good start. Welcome to insanity," Briareus and the glow that was the real Briareus said to me, and my second sight experienced his warmth, his sincerity and then his disinterest as he turned back to the keyboard.

Fool pulled me reluctantly away from my new friend and steered me toward an intense collection of shifting glows, all moving around with evident purpose in the background darkness like a construction crew composed entirely of multicolored ghosts. Somewhere in the far back of my awareness, I was remembering scraps of information I had heard somewhere about the spiritually adept who were able to detect a faint colored aura about the human body, and even read these auras. I had never believed or paid attention to the stories, and if I had thought about them at all, imagined they were the false advertising of hucksters and crystal ball readers. But as I walked into the midst of the busy assortment of glows, this skepticism was a good deal harder to maintain.

"What are they doing?" I asked Fool.

"Setting up folding chairs in the center of the building, carrying wood and nails and stuff for the platform where we hope the Master will speak to the multitudes, getting the leaflets ready to distribute so people will know how to get here."

My daughter, some part of my mind recognized that I should have been alarmed to hear these words, but I couldn't quite bring to my memory why having some kind of a public meeting on these premises should affect me at all.

As Fool was talking, one of the ghosts stepped in front of me.

For some reason, looking at this person, my split perception was more confusing that it had been with the others. My physical eyes, peering into the gloom, saw a dark-skinned woman with a round cheerful face and impossibly dark eyes which seemed to be set just far enough behind the cheekbones that they could peek out of hiding or retreat from visibility altogether. Her figure, in a white peasant frock, emphasized strength over grace. Yet the spirit below her skin shimmered with the most complicated and intricate collection of patterns I had yet seen.

As I stared at this woman, her spirit body sparkled like diamonds and radiated a welcoming golden color that was beyond description.

She pulled a strange instrument out of her pocket and aimed it at me, running it slowly from my head down to my feet and back up again.

"Who's your new friend?" she asked Fool as she examined the instrument critically, her voice carrying the slow lilt of a Mexican accent.

"You like him? You can keep him if you want."

She laughed. "All I want to keep right now is his name."

"Why don't you ask him?"

"I'm Cassandra," the woman said, extending her hand. "Who are you?"

I stared at Cassandra's hand in fascination, admiring the way the golden glow inside it mirrored its physical structure, down to the tiny bones and the veins that interlaced between them.

"He's a little new," Fool explained helpfully. "In fact, he just walked in here four hours ago, so I kind of took him under my wing."

"The Master hasn't seen him yet?"

"They've talked, but He left before the journey was finished."

Suddenly I found my voice. "Who is the Master?" I asked, my tongue thick in my mouth.

"You haven't told him *anything*, have you?" Cassandra demanded with more than a hint of exasperation.

"I figured he'd find out soon enough."

"Tell me about the Master," I said to Cassandra, losing my gaze deep into the swirls of white color behind her strangely recessed eyes.

Cassandra looked at Fool, who offered an elaborate shrug of his shoulders. She looked at me again and pulled me backwards and down, and I was surprised and pleased to discover that, by some amazing coincidence, there was a chair under me at exactly the place where I was sitting down. Taking the gravity off my legs and feet made me realize how tired I was, and I began to feel instantly sleepy.

"Aren't you supposed to be helping them?" I asked her.

"It's pointless. I keep telling them that it doesn't make any sense to do all this work right before the building is going to burn down and mess up everything," she said, pouting a little. "But nobody here ever listens to me."

"Cassandra, I need you to help me," I said, fighting off the sleepiness. "Nobody is explaining anything to me, and I'm starting to get confused a little bit."

Cassandra pulled out her device again, and leveled it at a place just below my chest.

"You're in a state of spiritual shock," she said finally without taking her eyes off of the instrument. "What do you want to know?"

"How they know things about me."

"It's written on your spirit," she said, putting the device away. "Everything you do is incorporated into your spirit; it becomes a record of your life, a living embodiment of all your actions. Is there any chance that makes sense to you?"

"Karma," I said slowly, a trace of my connection with the extended mind still functioning.

"Yes," she said, and Cassandra's spirit glowed with happiness, a color toward the top of the white spectrum. I stared at this interesting new color for a long moment, and then I thought I saw something more, images, pictures, scenes, and these were endlessly fascinating until I ran across a few that I thought I recognized.

"You were going to tell me who the Master is," I said after a moment.

"Was I?"

"It's written right there on your spirit."

"It is *not*!"

"Right next to the place where it is written that you show extraordinary kindness to confused strangers."

Cassandra turned and took a chair out of the hands of a person who was carrying three or four of them. There were several odd things about this transaction that later puzzled me. First, she had turned and grabbed without looking. How had she known that somebody was walking past at that moment? And the man she took the chair from released it without even looking up at her, and I noticed that his spirit tinged momentarily with the dark yellow color of fear, which was near the top of the black spectrum, almost touching the bright yellow band of surprise-related colors toward the bottom of the white spectrum.

She unfolded the chair and sat down across from me, taking my hands in hers.

"What do you know about God?" she asked me.

"Nothing," I said.

"Try to imagine God," she said. "In fact, it helps if you don't use the word 'God,' but instead try to imagine the awareness that permeates the universe. What would that look like?"

"It would be made of holy spirit," I said. "It would have a wonderful sense of humor that I'm not sure I totally understand."

Cassandra laughed again, and her remarkable assortment of spiritual jewels shimmered like leaves in a strong wind. "I was really looking forward to this conversation with you; in fact, this is my favorite part, when I find out that Fool didn't *totally* neglect your education," she said, shifting colors in mesmerizing ways. "If you were that Awareness, you would be everywhere, a part of everything, and there would be an extraordinary balance and symmetry and connection between everything. Does that make sense to you?"

"Yes," I said, remembering my recent experience, which already seemed like a thousand years ago.

"Look at my spirit," she said, apparently unaware that I had been doing nothing *but* look at it for the entire time we had been talking. Something distracted my gaze, and I saw Venus walk by with an impatient flip of her beautiful hair, and for some reason I found myself comparing her lovely face and lithe figure with Cassandra's broader frame—and, at the same time, noticing that compared with the incomparable loveliness of Cassandra's spirit, the glow inside Venus was monochrome and simple. I looked back at Cassandra, and for some reason I found myself trying to sort out the individual sparks of holy spirit, to follow one out of trillions.

"That's good," she said. "Now pick out a dot of holy spirit, and imagine that this one spark is you, and imagine that my whole spirit is the Awareness of the Universe. Can you do that?"

"Yes," I said.

"Now imagine that the one spark somehow managed to convince itself that it was an individual creature separate from the spirit as a whole, and forgot that it was connected with the others."

"But it's not," I objected. "Anybody can see that."

"You and I, looking at the big picture, can see that," agreed Cassandra readily. "But that one spark has a different perspective. And it has this enormous handicap; all of the other sparks in its immediate neighborhood also believe they are separate. Of course, from the standpoint of the spirit, it really doesn't matter very much, because the spirit itself is always whole and intact."

"Are you saying that the one confused spark is me?" I asked, looking up into Cassandra's dark eyes intently.

"I'm saying that the Master is the only spark who *isn't* confused," Cassandra said, giving her hair a gentle shake that did interesting tricks with the spiritual hair that glowed through it. "Somehow, he found a way to reintegrate his spirit with the bigger whole that is God. And now he's teaching us how to do it. And it will be our job to teach the world."

"Whoa," I said, shaking my head, feeling sleepy all over again. "Can't *he* just teach the world and leave me out of it?"

"He's teaching as many of us as will listen," she answered sadly. "But there's a reason, which you'll eventually find out about, why people automatically fight against the truth, why they stubbornly fight for their limitations and do everything they can to kill the messenger. It is our ancient enemy, and also our ancient sin."

"The devil?" I said.

At this, Cassandra laughed, and beneath her skin, her laugh was a beautiful thing to see. "It's a great deal more complicated than that," she said. "But when you come back here tomorrow, you'll see it for yourself. And a few days from now, you'll see why the others here think you're remarkable."

"Can't you just tell me?"

"You wouldn't believe it if I did." Cassandra took my hand in a warm, impulsive gesture. Slowly, as if I were a child, she helped me lie down on the floor, where I felt the smooth, cool embrace of the concrete against my body.

"Soon, you will discover a wonderful greatness in you," she said, touching the back of my head gently. "In your future, you will travel further than any of us, even—" and here the voice and fingers hesitated, and her aura took on a beautiful green-yellow glow—"even further than the Master himself."

Cassandra looked at me quizzically for a long second while these words hung in the air between us. And then, with spontaneous affection that touched the core of my spirit, she turned my upraised head back down against the cold, unyielding, embracing floor and stroked my hair until I closed my eyes. I felt myself relaxing more completely than I ever had before.

"Don't worry," she said; "nobody ever listens to my predictions. Right now," she added with a beautiful note of sympathy in her voice, "you need to sleep off the Soma. In a few days, as soon as you really really don't want him to, the Master will call for you, and you will be in for the surprise of your life."

I V

What is the "New Age?" It is first of all an attempt to reach forward and backward at the same time, to recover the powerful knowledge given to this world by the founders of the great religious traditions, knowledge about the human spirit, about sin and karma and the illusion that we could be separate from the Universal Awareness that is sometimes, in some traditions, called God.

The New Age is defined by a faith that this wisdom can be recovered in all its glory, and that everything we learn can be used to create a new and better world going forward, to build this wisdom into ourselves, into a society that owes as much to our understanding of the spirit as to science and technology, into the health and happiness and effectiveness of all people, so that these practical lessons can never be lost again.

—From *The Rutherfordton Spiritual Gazette*

My dearest Karen:

I wonder now why I never told you this: that before I went to work for The House, I earned my living as a drummer in a small rock and roll band that played at the clubs in and around Asheville.

After your mother and I were married, our little band reached that point when everybody in town had heard us play, and we would need to find a wider audience. A friend of a friend convinced a record company executive to visit one of our club appearances. We talked with him on the phone a few times, but nothing ever came of it, and then your mother was pregnant with you. I gradually realized what she had felt all along: that my musical career was leading us into financial difficulty.

I looked in the paper for other kinds of work, and interviewed randomly all over town, took a job loading trucks and another as a typist with a medical transcription company, and the two jobs gave us enough money to buy a life insurance policy from a neighbor of ours who told me that he had recently joined The Brokerage House. Of course I asked him: were they hiring? They were always hiring, he said. All I needed, he told me, was a new suit and a willingness to help people become rich.

What a wonderful job description! At that time in my life, I had a strong, powerful desire to improve the world. If it would not be through my music, then I would express it this way! I felt as if I'd stumbled onto the perfect opportunity.

I believed everything this person said for my first three days on the job, while men with hard, cynical eyes trained me and a dozen others to call people on the telephone and offer them "financial opportunities" according to a very precise script. It seemed strange that one of the largest financial services organizations in the world would have to call people at mealtimes to convince them to become wealthy. I wondered why somebody like me, who didn't know an annuity from a zero coupon bond, should be chosen to offer The House's investment products. But for the first day and most of the second, as people on the other end of the phone told me (politely or not) that they could not be less interested, I told myself that they were missing a wonderful chance to live a better life.

At lunch, the other brokers were frankly boastful about how much money they were making off of this or that customer relationship. I listened intently, and in vain, for any boasting about how rich their customers were becoming as a result of their work. After another day of lunchtime banter, I realized with a sick horrible feeling that my real objective, as a representative of The House, was to attach myself to peoples' investments like a leech, and convert their life savings into trading commissions or management fees, which I would share unequally with The House—70% of someone else's money for them, 30% of someone else's money for me.

By then, I had sold a life insurance policy and a few stocks, and I returned home with a bowling ball in the pit of my stomach—and also with my first weekly commission check, which brought a cry of joy from your dear mother.

It was that happy exclamation that kept me working at The House these 21 years. It was a devil's bargain, and I knew it. But there are days when I think it is no worse than millions of other men and women who, with misgivings and an element of queasy fear, start careers with organizations that manufacture things like fizzy colas and cigarettes, beer and cosmetics, video games, junk snacks and faddish toys for children too young and trusting to know the difference between the powerful TV images and the reality of the actual item on the shelf.

We, I think, are the majority. We sacrifice away our sense of self-worth, and the companies we work for replace these inborn values with other, artificial value systems made up of promotions and reserved parking spaces and year-end bonuses, quarterly numbers and production figures, and our mission is to get lost in this new hierarchy of goals and forget what we are actually doing to the world.

What I did not know—what, I think, somebody should have told me, is that this sacrificial bargain would make me so very unattractive to you. I wish I had known that acclimating myself to The House's value system would make it impossible for me to switch my brain back far enough to build a real relationship with a bright young girl who sees the world with fresh and innocent eyes. You tried to talk to me about your friends at school; I tried to talk to you about making my numbers, but there was so little in common for us to build a friendship on.

And so I not only sacrificed my human values for a paycheck; I also, without realizing it, gave up a chance to participate in the wonderful discovery process that was your unfolding from infant to girlhood to womanhood.

At The House, this is considered a completely frivolous consideration, but I could never quite get over it. This is just one reason why I have never been held in high esteem by my supervisors.

When I woke up on the floor of the warehouse the next morning, and realized that my cell phone was ringing, I thought for a hopeful second that it might be you, calling to say you would like to talk to me once more. I had dreamed this, and in the dream, we were sitting on the edge of the stream, you and I, near the entrance to the campus, and you were telling me all the things that had happened in your life since last I saw you, and I was thinking that this wonderful coming together was the result of a single brave phone call.

And so you can understand why I was heartbroken when I heard a male voice on the other end.

"Mr. Zakar?" I recognized the voice as the Big Score's personal assistant.

"Yes, Zho."

"My employer wonders why you canceled yesterday. He says you would not have done this unless it was an extreme emergency."

"Yes," I said, rummaging in my unsteady mind for an excuse that would placate this man and the very important person he worked for. "Somebody in the office needed my help," I said, telling as much of the truth as I dared. Before he had a chance to ask more questions, I blurted out: "Can we meet later this week?"

There was silence on the other end. I could hear a rustling of pages. Obviously they kept the Old Man's schedule the old-fashioned way.

"He can meet not this Friday morning, but the following, if that is convenient." The tone of voice implied that it had better be convenient. I checked my Palm Pilot for the following week. The morning was full of appointments.

"I'll have to rearrange my schedule."

"He didn't cancel the appointment. You did."

I had no good answer for that. "I'll be there at ten o'clock," I said.

"He would prefer nine."

"Then so would I."

I lay back on the floor with my eyes open, staring obliquely at the ceiling. It was all metal supports festooned with lanterns, under what appeared to be heavy corrugated steel that allowed no hint of sunlight from the morning sky.

I stood up slowly and looked around. Overnight, a lot of chairs had been placed in orderly rows toward the center of the building, and some kind of enormous low wooden platform had been set up in front of them. Otherwise, the place seemed to be empty now. Where did everybody go?

I shook my head, trying to get my mind past the disjointed and disturbing memories so I could think clearly.

What happened to me last night? How could I have fallen asleep on the concrete floor?

On the drive back home, I happened to glance over as a car pulled up next to me, and looked at the driver as he passed. I noticed that there was a ghost living inside his body, and as I stared at this strange thing, there was a rumble under my tires which told me I had let the car drift into the corrugated shoulder of the road.

My attention snapped back to the steering wheel. I looked at the reassuring familiarity of the dashboard and seat. Had I really seen that? Or was I hallucinating?

I slowed down a bit, and other cars passed me, some with just a single driver, others with somebody in the passenger seat.

In every case, their bodies glowed with inner fire.

Karen, I would caution you against driving while you're trying to see through two sets of eyes at once. I think I probably endangered the lives of most of the people who were unlucky enough to be in nearby lanes of traffic on Interstate 26 between the warehouse and my home and, after I had showered, there were several more close calls between my home and the office.

In the lobby, and again in the elevator, I stared at the colorful essences of my fellow humans, the bands of twisted light that lived inside of them.

"Mr. Zakar?"

"Huh? What?" I had been staring at the mellow pinkish color that surrounded the face of Jill, the new receptionist, which turned to a light brownish confusion as she, in turn, wondered why it was so hard to get my attention when I was staring right at her. I could also see, from the unusually bright cluster of strange light near the center of her aura, that she was carrying new life in her womb.

"Congratulations," I said.

"For what?"

"For the baby."

"What baby?"

There was a moment of intense awkwardness. Then I leaned close to her. "If I were you," I said in a whisper, "I'd get a pregnancy test. I have a hunch," I added.

Jill gave me a long look, and her aura momentarily took on a darkly suspicious blue-black shade. "The branch manager has put you on his schedule for 20 minutes Thursday starting at nine," she said evenly. "He says don't be late this time."

"Great," I said absently, turning back to the waiting area. The fish in the goldfish tank had an interesting spirit sparkle to them. Then I spotted the ghosts of my first appointment: an older couple who I had worked with for nearly 20 years, who I call my squirrel clients. Harold and Francis Coddington had been married now for five and a half decades. I wondered what they had looked like when they were first together, because now they looked like the male and female versions of the same person.

"Hello," I said as they stood up. "Have you been waiting long?"

"About ten minutes," Francis said, looking to her husband for confirmation. He nodded, and she looked back at me, her face settling into its habitual anxious expression of crisscrossing wrinkles across her forehead. She was in her seventies, and you could see on her face that nothing had ever come easy for her. Looking at the dark mottled hues of her spirit, I could see that she would not have allowed anything to be easy; she would have been too suspicious of any shortcut or run of good luck to be able to pluck the low-hanging fruit of life.

Her husband, meanwhile, held his hat in his hand and waited for instructions. The colors of his spirit synchronized marvelously with hers, and I wondered now, not for the first time, how long it had taken her to train him to follow her lead.

"Please come on back," I said to them.

Karen, if you were to read the files on these wonderful people, you would think that they were more machine than human. In a world brimming full of temptations to spend and a million clever advertisements telling us that our lives will be fulfilled only if we purchase this car or that piece of jewelry, my squirrel clients have trading accounts which reflect monthly investments amounting to 15% of their income going back, without deviation, to the year 1970. They had set aside far more than they would ever need for the rest of their lives, and because I admire their tenacity and because it is my job, I had taken very good care of their money—far better care than their previous three brokers.

But now I was worried about them. It seemed like the more they accumulated, the less they spent. They would recycle the income from their investments back into their portfolio and live like church mice in the house that they had occupied since the Eisenhower Administration, drive a beat-up car until it collapsed on the side of the road, and dine out no more than once or twice a year.

They had a portfolio value north of $7 million, spent no more than $30,000 a year on all expenses, their mortgage had long since been paid off, and they were here to argue with me that they couldn't afford to retire quite yet.

When they were seated and each had a cup of tea, I gave them a quick summary of their money, where it was invested, and made a point of showing them that the income on the portfolio was almost exactly 11 times their yearly living expenses.

"Mr. Zakar," Francis said, coming, as was her habit, right to the point, "I think I speak for both of us when I thank you for all you've done for us." She looked to her husband for confirmation, and he nodded shortly. "We've talked about how risky it was to have all that money in stocks, but we trusted you, and over the years I think you've been right more often than not. But," she said, "I also remember when my Pa was out of work for almost three years during the Depression, and people today are too young to remember what it was like, and they say it can't happen again. But I say to you, what happened once can happen twice, and if it does, I don't want Harold and me to be caught unprepared."

"I understand perfectly," I said.

Karen, as an aside, I should tell you that despite all their apprehension, never was more than a fifth of their money in stocks, and that was always the safest of the blue chips. I had placed the bulk of their savings in laddered Treasury bonds—an investment strategy you don't see much of any more, which involves buying government bonds with zero default risk. I like to buy Treasuries that mature—which means gives you your money back—in ten years, eight years, six, four and two, so that every two years, roughly one-fifth of the bonds are giving you your original investment back. You live off the income and use the money coming back from the corpus of the bond, plus whatever has been saved in the interim, to buy more 10-year Treasuries in a beautiful cycle of never-ending retirement income from a portfolio that can never go down in value.

Of course, the bonds pay interest every six months, at a rate which is locked in when you buy them, and the Coddingtons would always put most of that money carefully aside and buy more Treasuries, which would generate more interest.

"So you're not ready to leave work," I said, looking into their faces with loving, exasperated amusement.

"We don't think it would be wise," Francis said, looking to Harold and receiving a nod of approval. "Not yet, at any rate."

"As you know, I'm here to give you advice, not to try to make any decisions for you," I said. "But in this case, I'm going to interfere, just a little."

They looked at each other, and then back at me.

"The problem," I said, "is that I don't think either of you know how to have fun. If you did, I think you'd be better able to understand some of the things I'm telling you about."

They looked at each other again.

"I'm not sure I understand," Harold spoke up for the first time.

"That's exactly the point," I said, leaning forward. "So here's what I'm going to do. I called over to the plant, and also had a talk with the people at the gift shop last week, and we coordinated your vacation schedule so you're both taking the same two weeks off next summer. And I've taken some of the dividend income from your stock investments, and offset it with some sales of stock, which created a taxable loss which will be worth, on next year's tax returns, about $3,000, all told. Last month, you remember, we wrote a covered call on two of your ETFs, and they expired out of the money, which added another $3,000 in essentially found income."

They looked at me blankly, and for a moment I wavered, as a voice inside told me how foolish this was, to risk my relationship with these people in this absurd way. Who was I to think I could change them after so many years?

"I've made arrangements with a local travel agency to use that money to give you a trip to Paris," I said, plunging ahead recklessly before my wiser half could talk me out of it. "Buying this early, we got an incredible deal. Fourteen days, the hotels, travel, food, everything is arranged."

I reached into my desk and took out the tickets and itinerary, handed them over and watched their faces, which, disappointingly, didn't change at all as they examined with unnecessary wariness the printed 14-day agenda that included wine tasting trips into the countryside and a six-day river cruise.

They looked back up from the tickets to me in a synchronized gesture. "And you're saying this won't cost us a cent?" Francis said, clearly incredulous.

"Your retirement portfolio will be exactly the same as it was before," I assured them.

Their faces didn't change expression as they looked back down at the materials I had handed over, but something else did. In the next few seconds, the glow emanating from their bodies shifted from that mottled blue color to something closer to purple, and then began to shimmer with yellow highlights. It felt like the whole room was much brighter, and I knew at that moment that when they returned from their trip, they would know, first-hand, what "fun" is.

Francis stood up, and I came around the table to walk them out. Then, unexpectedly, she embraced me, and I saw that there were tears in her eyes.

"Thank you," she whispered. "Thank you so very much."

I was midway through my last appointment of the day—a new customer—when Heavy Hitter put his head in the door.

We had been talking about creating a retirement plan when she suddenly blurted out that she'd had a terrible experience with her previous broker. Apparently, this other broker had done a lot of unauthorized trading in her account, and she'd filed an unsuccessful case through the arbitration system set up by the National Association of Securities Dealers.

Karen, before you're allowed to do business with a broker at any of the large firms, they require you to sign away your rights to a jury trial and agree to settle disputes through a legal process that is set up and managed by the brokerage industry itself. In any five year period, one branch brokerage office in three faces one of these legal disputes from an angry customer, usually either for recommending risky unsuitable investments, doing a lot of unauthorized trading in the customer account, or not disclosing the enormous fees that are siphoned off of those wrap-fee separately-managed accounts.

Most of the time, The House's legal team will delay and obfuscate and at worst end up giving back pennies on every dollar that was taken. In the really terrible cases, they'll make an offer to return all or almost of the ill-gotten dollars—and the settlement agreement will include a clause that says that if the customers reveal anything about the settlement to the press or anybody else, they forfeit the money. So nobody ever hears about the worst abuse, and consumers have no way to look up which brokers to avoid.

My goal was to win back this woman's confidence, and I knew it wouldn't be easy. I had just asked her if she'd consider trusting me for a short time on a trial basis when Heavy Hitter's face appeared in the doorway.

My new client stared up at him owlishly, and he winked at her.

"Have you evicted those kids yet?" Heavy Hitter asked me.

I made an apologetic gesture toward my new customer.

"I'm working on it," I said.

"Work harder. I have some good news for you."

"What's that?"

"My customer wants to close a day early, same time, same place. So instead of $18,750 a day, you'll be earning a little over $21,000 a day on this deal. How does that make you feel?"

My new customer stared at the two of us with an expression that was about twelve steps beyond mistrustful, and the glow around her body turned an unhappy bluish color bordering on bright black. I didn't have to imagine the impression this was making on her.

"Actually, I'm thinking that it might not be so easy—"

"Trust me, you'll get used to making some easy money once you've done it a few times," Heavy Hitter assured me. Hey, why is sex like riding a bike?"

"I'm not sure this is a great time to—"

"You have to keep pumping if you want to get anywhere!" Heavy Hitter chortled. He winked again at my guest and then ducked back into the hall.

The room grew very silent. The woman and I looked at each other. I was waiting for her to ask a question, and I think she was waiting for me to offer an explanation. I didn't know what, exactly, to say.

"Maybe I should come back," she said at last.

"That would be fine," I said quickly. "I'll—I'll call you for some numbers and do a quick financial plan before you decide who you want to work with."

She stood up, shook my hand and I never saw or heard from her again.

After she was gone, it suddenly occurred to me that I hadn't noticed Heavy Hitter's aura.

V

People say that energy fields don't exist in the human body because they can't see them—without realizing that you could make the same argument about electrons, magnetism, black holes and the air we breathe. But the truth is that your nervous system is powered by an amazingly subtle and complex interchange of electricity, and this electricity can be diverted or made to flow more freely by the ancient science—now accepted by modern physicians—of acupuncture.

Throughout the ages, all spiritual traditions describe the glow of this energy field. Mystics of the Kabbalah and the writers of the Vedic scriptures of Hinduism talked of seeing astral light projected from around peoples' bodies, and Christian religious tradition tells us that Jesus and his spiritual followers glowed with a radiance that we call a "halo."

In modern physics, we are discovering that all physical particles are ultimately made up of energy fields that interact with each other to create our visible reality. Our personal energy fields are part of the larger universal energy. The question is: are we in harmony with it or not?

—From *The Rutherfordton Spiritual Gazette*

My first two appointments for the following day canceled unexpectedly, so if I could manage to forget about the pile of other work on my desk, I could trick myself into believing that I was free to drive to the warehouse.

On the drive, I took a hard look at myself. I could not for the life of me figure out why I was feeling such divided loyalties—why, when I should have been thinking of good persuasive words that would convince everybody to leave, I was instead trying to think of plausible ways to stall the closing and let Fool and Venus and Cassandra and this Master person have the building for as long as they needed it. The sane, rational part of me wanted to get them out so

I could get my life back, but I had a dark suspicion that the sane, rational part of me was on the wrong side of the angels.

And so I was in a state of deep confusion as I pulled up to the front of the building.

As I followed the trail along the back of the fence, I heard sounds from below. It had rained hard last night, and the river was higher and noisier than usual, rushing in a white foam against the rocks along the edge of the bank. On impulse, I turned away from the narrow hole under the fence and walked to the edge of the embankment, leaning over so I could see down through the trees.

What I saw was a bunch of naked bodies taking turns submerging each other, and others sitting in little groups along the rocks. A man with a guitar was seated on the embankment about six feet down from where I was standing, fully unclothed, next to the wheelchair I had seen the night before. In the wheelchair, the young man they had been feeding the day before appeared now to be in a deep sleep, except that his eyes were open and lolled back toward the sky. As far as I could tell, they stared at nothing.

The man with the guitar cocked an eye at me as I scrambled past him.

"You were raised Baptist?" he inquired.

"Yes. Who are you?"

"Orpheus. I sing to peoples' spirits. Would you like to hear your song?"

"I'm not sure."

Without waiting for a more definitive assent, Orpheus bent over his guitar, picked a few chords and then, when the melody sorted itself out, he began singing in a voice that was at once very serious and mocking, drawing over-the-shoulder looks from people below, who moved out of the water to hear him better over the background roar of the river.

> *Let us raise a song to the jolly king*
> *and give Him what he craves.*
> *Once a week the faithful meet*
> *and feed Him churchly praise.*
> *Now it's time for Him to pay*
> *for the worship time we lend.*
> *We love the Lord, we love to pray*
> *for money we can spend.*
> *A miracle is what I need*
> *to liven up this place.*
> *Oh Super Santa, with stars about your face*
> *It's You I don't believe in now...*

The payback for our Sunday faith
is great prosperity.
A Lexus and a better job
would be just fine with me.
He's the cosmic force and easy touch
who answers all our prayers
Magic man we thank You much
for rallying up our shares.
Give us this day our daily bread
and co-sign every loan.
Oh Super Santa, with heaven for your throne
It's You I don't believe in now...

All we ask is all we want
from the Dad who has it all.
Let the Joneses envy all the stuff
we haul back from the mall.
You save our soul and credit score
and feed your sheep champagne.
'Our lives are good, but we want more,'
To You the saved complain.
We give you faith and all our prayers,
you make our lives so sweet.
Oh Super Santa, with angels at your feet,
It's You I don't believe in now...

With some difficulty, I managed to climb down to the flat rocks on the edge of the water. A different song floated down after me, but I couldn't make out more than a few words, and then only when the wind was right.

Let's go away
for a life and a day,
while the road goes on forever...

"Hello again," Fool called out to me from the water. "Come in and get chilled with the rest of us."
"Like this?"
"Take your clothes off first."
"Because it's part of the ritual?"
"Because you don't want them to get wet."

At least a dozen others were splashing some distance upriver, and I tried not to pay too much attention to the two women I had seen the night before. I recognized two of the men from the previous night, and wondered which of these people were lovers.

Slowly I undressed down to my boxer shorts, and then gingerly put my foot in the water. It was colder than I had imagined.

"Switch off your senses." Fool had to shout to be heard over the sound of the water.

"What?"

"I mean turn off the part of your mind that processes hot and cold," Fool called out. "Don't think about it; just do it. All it is, really, is an electronic message from your skin to your mind, telling your mind that you should experience discomfort. Turn off the part of your mind that processes the electrical impulse and translates it as beastly ice cold water that causes you to freeze your ass off, and suddenly it's like you're in a hot tub."

Fool's sober face and mocking eyes gave me no hint whether he was playing with me or offering serious advice. I tried to do what he told me, but the water felt like it was burning my abdomen. Nevertheless, I entered in stoically, and he gave me an approving nod.

"It's not really so hard, is it?"

"No," I lied.

"Now let me duck you under the water, and then take a look at you. You have to go completely under; otherwise it won't work."

"*What* won't work?"

"The baptism."

That stopped my mind long enough for him to lay me back. I let him pull my head under the water. Fortunately, I had a decent gulp of air in my lungs, because he didn't bring me back up immediately. I had the odd sense that he was waiting for something, and then suddenly I was released and my head was in the air again. The sun felt warm against my hair; the rest of me was freezing.

"Do you feel any different?"

My immediate instinct was to answer "no," but in fact something *did* feel different. Karen, at first I couldn't figure out what it was. Finally, after a lot of mental probing and exploration, I realized that the dull ache that I always feel over that last night with your mother in the hospital was less intense somehow. After a minute, I realized that my knee didn't feel quite as sore as it usually did.

"Yes," I said. "What did you do to me?"

Fool focused his attention on my knee. "They don't like water," he said after a minute. "Natural water, especially moving water, is the best way to sever the connection."

"The connection with what?"

"Demons," he said.

"What!?"

For the first time, he looked into my face, and then smiled. "I keep forgetting that everything has to be explained to you. Can't you see them yet?"

"I don't know what you're talking about."

"I can see that. When you look at my spirit, what do you see right now?"

I looked at him obliquely, and was pleased to see a reddish gold halo around his body. When I described this, he laughed.

"You can see the glow, like somebody who has just been healed of blindness can see light. But you can't make out the shapes very well yet."

"I can read a person's life story in his spirit—a little bit."

"That's still just seeing the light. Try focusing harder and I think you'll see something much more interesting than just weird colors."

"Like demons?"

"That's just what *we* call them. Over the years, people have had many names for them, as you'll realize when your vision gets better. They're actually more like parasites. They exist in the astral plane, which is actually the dimension that the glow from our spirit bodies radiates into, and they feed off of the electrical energy whenever your emotions take you to the darker end of the spectrum. Anything from the white spectrum is too hot for them to digest."

"And I had one attached to my spirit?"

"You had two, and one of them was quite annoying," he said, looking up in the air above my head, as if watching the progress of a fly. Then he made a mocking face at the blank air and looked back at me. "Once you've been properly ducked in water, they have to detach," he continued. "Apollo says it has something to do with the way water distorts the piezoelectricity from your brain patterns, but I think he made that up just so I'd stop asking him questions."

"So now my sins are forgiven me?" I asked, shaking the last of the water out of my eyes.

"Only the ones where you weren't molesting small children or feeding them drugs."

"I'm serious."

Fool smiled and shook his head. "You went to Sunday school, right?"

"Yes," I said warily.

"Didn't you ever wonder about how, in the accounts of the life of Jesus, he would heal people of demons and spirits? But now, today, they act as if these strange spiritual parasites and mischief-makers that vexed their Savior are somehow gone. Do the people who gather in churches think those things just went away between then and now? That they lost interest in the human race once Jesus had been crucified?"

"I've never thought about it," I said.

"You aren't alone. Isn't that interesting? Doesn't it make you wonder why? Doesn't it, in fact, make you wonder whether somebody or some*thing* has somehow managed to remove all interest in and discussion of the most important opponent that Jesus faced during his ministry?"

"So what did they know *then* that we don't know now?" I asked him.

"The Master says that when John the Baptist took people into the Jordan River, he was simply detaching these spiritual parasites. That's all. When he said their sins were cleansed, what he meant was that the consequences of their negative actions—which, of course, generated dark-spectrum emotions, which attracted the demons to begin with—had been removed. Somehow, the simple process of washing off the parasites every once in a while got gunked up with ritual, and the simple meaning became a complicated one-time ritual. Human progress is a wonderful thing, don't you think?"

"Is that why you called me down here? Because you saw parasites on my spirit?"

Fool smiled at me. "Actually, I thought you could use a few improvements in your personal hygiene. But if you can keep a positive attitude, the greater one might stay away for a few hours," he said, glancing back up into the air. "And if you can manage to believe that your knee will now heal completely, and ignore the pain instead of focusing on it, that lesser demon won't have a chance to come back either. It's up to you; if you keep giving off negative energy, if you pay attention to the pain and let it become suffering, you'll give them an opening to return and feed on you."

"What do they look like?"

Fool answered with another grin. "I'm going to let you find that out yourself," he said. "Don't worry," he said. "When you finally see one of them, you'll be in for an interesting shock."

Some of the others were beginning to wade to shore now, and I saw the woman I had almost met last night walking toward us out of the water in her full and unclothed glory, and I couldn't bring myself to look away. She approached me boldly.

"Well?" she said, twisting her hair with her hands in an apparent attempt to wring it dry.

"I think you're beautiful," I told her.

"That's not what I meant. I meant how are you today? Did we treat you too roughly? The Master asked about you."

"Where is he now?"

She looked up the embankment. "He's not part of the cult yet, Hag," Fool admonished her before she could say anything.

"Tell me your real name," I said.

"The Master calls me Venus, so that must be better than my real name," she said, drying her face with a towel. She slipped into a light cotton fabric that clung to her wherever she had been wet, which was everywhere, and then indicated the others who were splashing up onto the bank. "None of us go by names that we can be identified with any more."

"Why? Because of the police?"

"Who cares about *them*?" She tossed her head indifferently. "Hey, come here and meet the new guy," she called out.

I thought I recognized the spare, angular face of the first man who approached me. Was he a body builder? With his clothes off, his chiseled proportions looked as if his skin was stretched tight over bags full of large rocks. He approached me with exaggerated solemnity that could have been mocking, except for the intensely serious color of his spiritual emanation. Before I offered it, he took my hand with a slight bow that I associated somehow with the martial arts.

"I am called Mars," he told me in a deep sepulchral voice. "It is an honor to cross your path, my cousin."

"Challenge him to a fight," Fool suggested. "And then you can debate the dope over there," he said, indicating the man they had called Apollo the previous night, whose cropped golden-white hair and beard dripped with water. He nodded at me with casual disinterest.

"Hey," a voice came from behind me. I turned to see Cassandra, drying herself off on the same rock that I was standing on. "I knew you'd come back. You're in for a treat," she said.

"How so?"

"Not everybody gets to see Apollo in action," she said. "It takes a lot to get *him* started."

Fool looked at her and looked at me, and then shrugged his shoulders at the puzzled look on my face. "The best thing you can do with Cassie is ignore her," he said.

"It's all right," she said. "I'm kind of used to it now."

"Have you always lived here in this place?" I asked as we started up the bank.

"Oh no. We've been here, what? Six weeks? Eight?" Fool looked around for confirmation, but the others were all too busy putting their clothes on. "Hey," he called out, "did anybody here happen to bring a calendar?"

Cassandra climbed up beside us. "Hurry," she said. "We don't want to miss the show."

"Actually, we were single-handedly supporting the entire New York City economy for almost two years," Fool continued. "And San Diego before that. We were camping in the streets, playing hide and seek from the cops. The Master called it recruiting, but as you can see, we didn't exactly raise an army."

"You were on the streets because you have no place to live?"

"Oh, no; we all have houses or apartments or some place to go. But if the Master is going to live on the street, then *we* sort of have to. Where he goes, we go. When he came here to the palace, we came here."

"Why?"

Fool smiled. "When you meet the Master, you'll *know* why."

"But I still don't understand. Why here?"

"My theory is that the Master got lost on his way to Hollywood, where he was planning to become a leading man in shoot-em-up movies."

"You'd be wise to have a little more respect," Venus warned from behind us. "You're going to give Mr. Commuter the wrong idea about us."

"I think I was properly respectful. Isn't that the goal, to get Him into the mass media somehow?"

"Can you bring me to meet him?" I asked.

Cassandra and Fool looked at each other, and then both burst into simultaneous laughter. "Sure," said Fool. "Why don't we just walk over to him and say, here, this guy wants to hang out for a little while. And then we can catch a plane for a vacation in the Elysian Fields, or maybe a weekend in Valhalla."

"Are you saying—"

"I have an idea. Why don't we go instead to the White House for lunch?" Fool continued with a comically earnest look on his face. "And in the meantime, I think we should hire the Pope as our official gardener. *Somebody* has to pull out the weeds in the parking lot out back."

"It doesn't really work that way," Cassandra explained, trying to keep a straight face as Fool began an interesting pantomime of the elegant Pontiff bending over gravely to yank roots out of the ground. "He'll send for you soon enough," she assured me.

As we were climbing up the bank, I was watching with envy as Mars, a few steps ahead of us, strode up the steep, slippery slope with a brisk, unconcerned stride, talking in a low voice with Venus, who was, if anything, even lighter on her feet. Then, as they reached the top, I saw Mars turn his head slightly and stiffen in a pose of absolute stillness that reminded me of a hunting dog sniffing the wind.

The others must have picked up the odd gesture, because all but Cassandra and me stopped in their tracks. I slowed my steps, but Cassandra took my hand and pulled me forward. "Come on," she said. "You aren't going to want to miss this."

Gasping a little, I finally pulled myself up to level ground with the generous help of an exposed tree root, and looked off in the direction where Mars held his steady gaze.

"I do not think he has a gun, from the way he is walking," he said to us in a voice that sounded as if it had emerged from a crypt.

I still couldn't see anything except the wind stirring the tall bushes along the side of the property outside the fence. In the distance, perhaps two miles away from here, the skyline of Asheville shimmered in the warm sunlight like a mirage.

Minutes passed. Finally I was able to make out a movement along the narrow space between the tallest of the weeds and the metal mesh that surrounded my property. A preposterously dignified individual with a shock of white hair and a belly as prominent as a pregnant woman's tested the fence with his hands and began working his way in our direction.

After a few seconds, he noticed us standing there watching him. Immediately, his aura radiating confidence bordering on delight, he began clambering clumsily over weeds with more difficulty than seemed plausible.

By now the others had joined us at the top, and the fat one approached Mars and me with an air of superior authority.

Before he could speak, Fool called out from behind me: "George, I was *so* hoping never to see you again."

George favored him a glance and then, fishing deeply in his pockets, pulled out a large piece of paper. He looked at all of us, uncertain who to address, and finally, perhaps because of my clothes, decided to face me. "This," he said, "is a court order authorizing me to remove Arthur Bonnefield, III from your custody and control, and to return him to his rightful parents. It's signed by the county magistrate," he added, "and it gives me permission to use, on the property owned by your father's company, any force necessary."

"Custody?" Fool called out, stepping forward. "Do I look like they have me in chains or something?"

"Chains of the mind," George retorted, "are far stronger than chains of steel."

Fool laughed derisively. "You know," he told the group, "that's a real quote from his web site. He's a cult deprogrammer," he added, apparently for my benefit. "Another of my dad's henchmen."

I could actually feel Mars's muscles tense up next to me, and he seemed to grow physically larger in height and girth, though for the life of me I couldn't imagine how such a thing could be possible. But it was Apollo who stepped forward to block the path between George and his intended prey.

"Professor," George said in a genial voice. "I see that this cult is capable of ensnaring even the internationally famous."

"All I have is a voice to undo the folded lie. W. H. Auden," Apollo said softly. "You carry the stench of sanctimony into our pleasant afternoon. I advise you to leave while we can still forgive you."

"Well, you see," George drawled slowly, obviously enjoying the attention, "that was actually my plan. Arthur and I will take a nice drive back to my hotel room, and then we'll catch a flight out early tomorrow morning and both he and I will be out of your hair forever."

Apollo regarded him for a long second, and then raised his voice to address the ragged band of wet squatters on my property. "Bigger picture," he said, "this is yet one more symptom of the control of the overlords. Our society has complex rules which define our relationships as citizens and employees, but strangely few that define parenthood between adults. Over their children, parents first offer control, then influence, then hope. The chains of authority become ropes, then strings. But when and how do they change from one to the other? Why does the father of this foolish young man believe he has the right and perhaps even the duty to veto his son's choice of friends and his son's chosen belief system, simply because both have strayed uncomfortably far from his? Why has our society evolved no real guidance on how to claim independence from those who love us, and how to grant it? *What is irritating about love is that it is a crime that requires an accomplice.* Baudelaire."

"Isn't he incredible?" whispered Cassandra at my side.

I nodded slowly. The intonation of the words made you feel a kind of certainty that simply walked through skepticism the way a ghost walks through walls. I tried to imagine Apollo in a lecture hall. No students would long be able to defend their own opinions from such a delivery.

I was startled by the sound of George clapping his hands, breaking the spell.

"Bravo!" he called out. "A masterful speech, beautifully delivered by a man who left an endowed chair at Harvard in order to live in a warehouse. If you want to buy a few hours of my time, I think I might be able to give you your life back."

"*I am condemned to be free.* Jean-Paul Sartre, although even you should recognize the quote."

"Suit yourself," George shrugged. "But I think all of you should know," he said, raising his voice, "that this is a particularly dangerous cult you've joined."

"*What's a cult? It means not enough people to make a minority.*" Apollo answered back. "Robert Altman. I deny that you have any right to impose the way you think on any of us—or anybody else. Take your magistrate's order and leave this place. You have no idea what you're dealing with here."

"As long as you're on corporate property," George shot back with a note of finality in his voice, "I have every right to rescue this boy from you and himself."

There was a long silence, and then something strange happened. Apollo's eyes took on that oblique look that I now recognized to be the sight of the spirit, and he seemed to gesture toward the fat man's body.

"It must have been very hard when your daughter left you," he said.

George stiffened.

"Sleeping on the floor of a trailer with six other men, fornicating with any of them who cared to crook a finger at her."

"How dare you—!" George hissed.

"If you were so terrific at this deprogramming work, it seems like you would have been more effective with her," Apollo mused. "Of course, I imagine she blames you for your wife divorcing you for that ski instructor."

"I refuse to let you bring them into it!"

Cassandra pulled out her instrument and pointed it at the scene. "Apollo is attaching demons to his body," she whispered. "They're swirling around him like buzzards, feeding on the dark energy that he's releasing."

"You've had two bypasses, and yet I still see very clogged arteries," Apollo said in a weaving voice, as if he were speaking an incantation. "The discs of your lower spine are weak from years of carrying so much extra poundage, and you have frequent pain there."

George stopped, and I saw his face become noticeably whiter. Cassandra tugged at my arm. "You have to say what you're going to say now," she whispered. "Otherwise, Apollo is going to kill him."

My daughter, I had no idea what these words meant, but it was true that I had been waiting for a pause in the conversation, and for once, I didn't immediately try and talk myself out of doing what I knew was the right thing. As Cassandra shoved me forward, I spoke for the first time, feeling strangely bold, and George's pale face turned to mine.

"Your court order has it wrong," I said. "I'm the actual owner of this property now. And I want you to leave here immediately."

"What?" Fool demanded before George could even open his mouth. "Dad sold the warehouse?"

"Do you have any evidence of ownership?" George demanded before I could open my mouth.

"When?" Fool demanded from the other side of me.

"We closed day before yesterday," I said, trying to answer both of their questions at the same time.

"I don't believe it," George said.

"I don't believe it!" cried Fool.

I turned to Fool, astonished at his stunning ingratitude. "Who the hell's side are you on?" I asked him angrily.

"He would never sell this property!"

"Why the hell not?"

"I don't have to tell you!"

"You'd better damn well tell me, because I'm so confused right now that I just might have a breakdown."

"Perhaps I can help before it's too late," George insinuated smoothly from in front of me.

"*You*, I want to leave my property," I said. On impulse, I reached into my pocket and handed him a business card. "If you want to contact my office, I'm sure they can confirm everything I said."

George took a long look at the card, and then at me. "I want all of you to know I don't believe a word of this," he said finally, looking from me to Fool to Apollo and back again. "Make no mistake, professor of the alley," he shot back at Apollo, "I'll be back, sooner rather than later. And Arthur *will* come with me."

For a long second, he stood defiantly, and then abruptly he turned and began climbing laboriously over weeds that an ordinary person could have stepped through. After a few seconds, he was behind too many weeds and trees for us to see him any more.

VI

Is the human soul a part of your body or something entirely separate? If it is a part of your body, what role does it play in your health and your thoughts and your experience? If it plays an important role in your physical well-being, how can we use this knowledge to heal and improve our health? If the human soul is a source of our thoughts and understanding, how can we train ourselves to hear it more clearly?

These are nonsense questions in the old reality. In the New Age, they are arrows pointing toward knowledge that will change human life as much as— or more than—the modern advent of science and technology. It is worth remembering that modern science was born when a few Renaissance thinkers dared to ask their own nonsense questions, and the religious institutions of the day called them heretics.

—From *The Rutherfordton Spiritual Gazette*

Fool followed me inside the building, asking a million questions which were really all the same question, and of course I had no answers to give him.

"All I know is that I'm supposed to get all of you out of the building before they buy the place back from me," I said for at least the third time, trying to think of other words which would communicate exactly the same message in a different way that Fool might finally understand.

"Of course he wants us out of the palace. He wants *me* out of here, but he's too embarrassed or cowardly to do it himself. But why would he send somebody as ineffectual and clueless as you? That's what we need to figure out."

"You don't have to sugar coat it," I said.

"Compared to my father, you're Bambi," Fool assured me. "Compared to his *mailroom* guy, you're an incredible wimp. They're using you for some reason, and all I can think of is that it must be very important to have this place temporarily in the hands of somebody who is too deep in their bullshit to even *try* to figure it out."

"I think I know why they selected me," I said. "Heavy Hitter is starting to run out of people to do his arms-length transactions for him—"

"Maybe he thought we'd feel sorry for you," Fool mused to himself, ignoring me completely.

"I don't think it really matters what he thought, so long as all of you are out of here by Sunday afternoon. You don't want to stay here anyway, do you? George might come back, now that he knows you're here, and there might even be trouble with the police."

"There's always trouble with the police," Fool said absently, obviously putting 90% of his brain into some other subject. Then he cheered up. "Here, you want some more Soma?"

I gave him a long look, and he shrugged his shoulders and began stirring up something in a glass.

"Maybe everybody could go somewhere for a couple of days," I suggested. "I could spring for a hotel room, we could do the closing, you could move back in there as before, only this time I wouldn't have to worry about it."

"You have a totally one-track mind," Fool said to me sternly, taking a quick drink from the glass. "You only think about avoiding conflict. You should have let Apollo put George in a wheelchair."

"Cassandra said he was going to kill him."

"She's such an exaggerator. How can you kill somebody with words?"

"You tell me. He was talking to the parasites, wasn't he?"

"Yes," said Cassandra from behind me.

"You don't always have to be so truthful," Fool told her disapprovingly.

I looked across the floor at the neat rows of chairs and the podium, surrounded, on the floor, by various tools and many pieces of wood. Purple leaflets were attached at random along the wall. I walked over and read one of them, and felt my heart sink.

Learn the Secrets of Life and the Universe

A special seminar will be held at 75 River Road, Asheville, NC, 2:30 PM on October 22. Attendance is free. You will leave with an understanding of the world and the powers of the spirit and God and the universe, an understanding so profound that it will change your life forever.

The seminar will not be repeated in this location or any other. This is a one-time opportunity to understand the mysteries that were known to the human species only at the founding of every major religion.

If you have the courage to learn from those whose teachings the police want to suppress, from those who jails cannot hold, then you will be with us, and we embrace your courage and thirst for discovery.

"Oh my god," I said.

Fool frowned at the paper. "This isn't what it said last time I saw the finished copy," he said. "What does that mean about teachings the police want to suppress and jails cannot hold?"

"Have these gone out already?" I demanded.

"The Master told Apollo to put that in there," said Cassandra. She touched my shoulder sympathetically. "We spent most of last night stapling them to telephone poles and bulletin boards," she said to me. "They dropped about ten thousand more in the mail."

"Why?" said Fool.

"Why what?"

"Why did he put that in there?"

"Don't ask me. Ask Apollo."

"But we're closing this coming Monday. How am I going to—oh my god, what a mess!"

"Yes," Cassandra said, watching Fool walk away with his puzzled attention still on the leaflet. "But if I were you, I wouldn't waste a lot of energy worrying about it. Somehow, it's going to work out."

"How can you be so sure? And anyway," I said, swinging my attention back to her face, seeing behind the olive skin what I had seen last night, the interplay of spiritual colors more intriguing and beautiful than any jewel. "And anyway," I said, my voice softening involuntarily, "how did you know I was even *thinking* about telling George to get lost? Was it written on my spirit somewhere?"

"No," she assured me. "I'm sure your spirit was a bundle of contradictions and doubt, mixed with generous portions of fear and confusion. Just like everybody else on this godforsaken planet."

"Then how did you know?"

"If I tell you, it will scare you down to your bones," Cassandra said.

"Tell me. I like to be frightened. It tells me I'm alive."

"I can watch the future," she said. "Just like you can watch my spirit."

Karen, at that moment I felt as if I must have blacked out, or maybe misunderstood her. The words sat in my head, but they had no meaning, even though the meaning was clear. I looked around, saw the cripple being wheeled past in his wheelchair toward the front of the building and watched it for a long second, until the words finally bounced around enough times that they found a place in my brain where they could be interpreted and understood. Then I looked at Cassandra's eyes, and her words last night came back to me.

A sudden chill passed through my body, raising the hairs on my arms as if I had passed through a ghost.

"Tell me," I said.

"Imagine," she said, "that you're a character in a movie, and you can watch the movie, or any part of it, at any time. I can turn my eyes in another direction right now and see my mother pass away in the hospital bed decades in the future, and my father fall asleep one night in extreme old age, and never wake up. When I was a child, I watched my schoolmates blunder around as if they were completely blind to future accidents and unhappiness, and when I asked them why they didn't simply avoid things I could see in the future, they would stare at me in a way that left me frightened."

"Why don't you just do something different from the script?" I asked her.

"You think I haven't tried? Every time I did, there would be a kind of blackout, and when it was over, I'd realize that I'd said my lines exactly as I had foreseen them. As I'm doing now," she added.

"You couldn't change anything?"

"Nothing, not even the smallest word or gesture. Years ago, I realized that I was trapped, the mystery removed from my existence. I could have no illusions, no fantasies. I had only to look ahead and see the refutation of hope."

"You can see your own death," I said.

"I will die an elderly spinster who can no longer remember joy, in a nursing home in Portsmouth, New Hampshire," Cassandra answered readily. "My days, for years before my death, will be occupied reliving my earliest, happiest years, before I understood the truth about myself."

"No wonder you are invisible to them," I said.

"They know, all of them, that a few words from me would take the mystery out of their lives, and I doubt there is anything they fear more than that."

"Why do they let you stay here?"

Cassandra laughed, a beautiful laugh that stirred the colors of her spirit into a sparkling menagerie. "You still don't see it completely," she said with a smile. "If I am meant to be here, if that's how my movie is written, however could they prevent me? Only Fool treats me as if I'm one of them, I think because it annoys the others."

"Yes," I said. "That's it exactly."

"And you, who were slow to catch on," she said, "now you must learn to avoid me. And then, as the truth of what I've said sinks in, the aversion will be based on fear, and you will train your eyes not even to see me."

"Is that truly what you foresee?"

At this, Cassandra gave me a peculiar smile whose meaning I could not read.

"No," she said. "That is not what you'll do."

"Why not? Can you see that?"

"No," she said. "And right now, at this moment, that's the only mystery that is given to me. Thank you for that."

As we walked toward the kitchen area, I saw somebody in a light blue uniform talking with one of the disciples near the entrance, and she was pointing in my direction. The man walked up to me with a clipboard in his hand. He readjusted his hat so that it sat further back on his head, with the visor pointing toward the ceiling.

"You're the owner here?" he asked.

"For a little while," I said.

"Sign this."

"What is it?"

"Heating oil," the man said. "Twelve drums. I guess it takes a lot to heat this place in the winter."

"Who ordered this?" I asked Cassandra. She shrugged. "Maybe the Master?"

"Look, I just deliver it," the man said. "If you end up with some free heating oil, what's it to me, so long as I get a signature?"

"Doesn't matter to me," I said, taking the pen.

"It will come winter," he said.

I let my eyes roam over toward a place on the far side of the chairs, which seemed to have developed a magnetic attraction for the people who had, just a few moments ago, been seated in yoga postures or milling around the room in conversation.

"There's going to be a glimming this afternoon," Cassandra explained. "Everybody is excited about it. We're getting together to visit the Deva Community."

"Some kind of religious ritual?"

"It's only a 'religious ritual' if you don't understand why you're doing it and you have no certainty of the outcome."

As we walked past the kitchen, I noticed that Venus was hunched over a stack of papers, staring at what seemed to be an accounting ledger, with a pencil between her teeth.

"What are you doing?"

"The Master said I should keep track of our finances from now on—not that we actually *have* any finances," she said. "He said it would help me develop a better relationship with numbers."

"Let me see what you've done so far."

I looked at the neatly inscribed columns of figures, which had been written with no explanation of what they represented. Most of the numbers were in the millions; none were shorter than six digits.

"These are actual expenses?" I said.

"I was just practicing," she told me. "Every time I get going, I start wondering why the 8s are so angry all the time, not at all optimistic and forward-looking like the 5s. And the 9s have always seemed to me to be a little crazy." Look at them," she said, indicating a row of them. "Don't the 9s look crazy to you?"

"You know, I think they did, once, before I really understood numbers," I said, trying to catch a half-seen memory from long ago.

"I prefer writing the steady but unforgiving 2s or the quietly efficient 4s," Venus continued, frowning at the paper. "But the Master says if I'm going to do it right, I can't just leave out the numbers that I don't like."

"That *would* make it harder," I said with a smile.

"Are you going to glim with us?" Venus asked me suddenly.

"Actually," I said, checking my watch, "I have to go out to the office."

"But you'll be back?"

"I'm not sure. I have an important appointment."

Venus stood up and took my arm. "Sounds like fun," she said. "Maybe I could come along and learn about all those numbers you work with first-hand."

She was dressed in a long shift, made of some kind of shiny silky material that came down to her ankles and covered her body like a glove. My attention was so diverted by how she looked that it took a long second for me to process her words. When I did, I felt a jolt of something very like fear, and my spirit pulsed a deep yellowish color. The thought of her—really of any of these people, but especially her—walking around my offices, seeing what I lived with every day, was out of the question.

"I don't really think—I mean—" I took a deep breath and put my hand on the hand on my arm. "It wouldn't be a good idea," I said, taking on an air of adult finality. "People tell me their financial details, things they wouldn't want discussed outside of the office."

Venus threw a quick glance at my spirit. "Yes, I can see that," she said, a hint of mockery creeping into her voice. "This afternoon, you have an important financial appointment to explain how the quarterly performance of the Federmans' portfolio deviated from its customized benchmarks. No outsider should be allowed to witness *that*."

"I just don't think it would be a good idea," I said firmly.

"I think it would be wise if you just watched and didn't say anything," I said firmly twenty minutes later, as Venus followed me into the elevator of our building. "Giving out professional financial advice is kind of complicated, and the Federmans like an orderly, well-organized meeting."

"I understand," Venus told me.

"They've been married for 31 years, and he's been in the same job for the past 25. You could set your clocks by them."

"It wouldn't be a good idea to rock such a stable boat," Venus agreed.

I took a long look at her. "The more orderly, the better, as far as they're concerned," I said.

"I don't know anything about money," Venus admitted. "I'll just watch and learn."

I gave her a quick hug. "If you shake hands with any of the other brokers," I said, "be sure to wash as quickly as possible."

As I walked through the crowded reception area, Venus stopped at the drinking fountain, and suddenly, instantly, I felt invisible. There were at least a dozen people on the couches and chairs or standing by the magazine racks, and as I looked back, I saw that every single person was looking at her as she followed me back toward the offices. As we passed their doors, brokers stood up and followed us into the hallway. I felt a sense of relief when we finally reached the conference room.

The Federmans were already sitting on the far side of the long mahogany table, their backs to the window. Susan remained seated, but Joseph stood up and shook my hand, and gave Venus a long appraising look as I introduced her as an associate in training.

Everything about Joseph Federman, from the way his clothes fit to the way he dispensed with the small talk and opened up his performance statement, spoke of fastidious efficiency. He wore a suit and perfectly knotted tie, and the muscles in his face seemed to concentrate intensely around the eyes, from the clench of his narrow chin up the worry lines of his forehead. His claim to fame was that he had been Valedictorian of North Buncombe High School and had graduated with honors from the business school at Western Carolina University. He had been something of a phenom; within two years of graduation, he had worked his way up to a mid-level manager at the central office of a very large upholstery manufacturer, the largest in the state, although its manufacturing had mostly been outsourced to Thailand. But for some reason his career had stalled at that level, and he compensated for it by micromanaging everything he came in contact with—including me.

I saw now that his spirit radiated a contented orange hue; working through the numbers was, for him, an enjoyable activity. Susan's was a resigned greenish color as she divided her attention between us and a magazine she had brought in from the lobby.

"As you can see," I began, opening my copy of the report, "the portfolio as a whole is up just over 35 basis points more than the benchmark we created for the last fiscal quarter, almost 52 basis points year-to-date. Of course, the market is only up 2%, so we're not exactly jumping for joy at this point."

Joseph gave the summary a cursory glance and then turned to page seven. "I wanted to start off by asking you about this," he said, indicating with his finger a $14,000 investment in the Wasatch International Growth fund. "Did you notice that they've raised their allocation to Philippine stocks up to 1.3% this quarter? Is there something going on over there that I should know about?"

"Tell me you're not serious," Venus said. She turned to me. "Is he serious?"

"What?" Joseph asked, looking up sharply. His eyes narrowed even further.

"We're making sure the fund manager stays within the parameters outlined in the prospectus," I told Venus, touching her arm warningly. I pulled a laptop computer over from the far side of the table and called up the fund's latest profile off the online database. "Apparently that represents one new stock added to the portfolio," I said after skimming through a lot of irrelevant information. "The Philippine telephone company, PT&T, which just acquired an e-discovery vendor called—"

"How important is that to you?" Venus asked Susan.

Susan looked up from her magazine. "You mean which stocks are where?"

"Yes."

Susan shrugged her shoulders. "I'm sure it *is* important, but I've never been able to figure out why."

"Tell her why it's important whether or not this telephone company is in that mutual fund," Venus said to Joseph.

"I don't understand what you mean," Joseph said after a second.

"What I mean is, here you are, like a mosquito frozen in amber, repeatedly passed over for promotion for the past 25 years while you've expanded your responsibilities to the point that you handle all the office details that nobody else even understands any more. You spend all day every day quietly cleaning up the mistakes of people who pass through the department on their way up the corporate ladder, *hating* the weight and anxiety of trying to keep it all together and worrying about the constant random corporate layoffs, *hating* the extra hour and a half of work you have to do every evening—and for what?" Venus demanded. "Wake up and smell the perfume! Do you think there's a nice corner office that they've reserved in your name? Do you think that suddenly they're going to notice you when you've been invisible since the Reagan Administration?"

"It's 'Wake up and smell the *roses*,'" Joseph corrected her, his eyes blinking rapidly.

"Every year that goes by, you put more and more control into smaller and smaller things, until, God help you, you start taking pleasure out of this sort of nitpicky portfolio thing," Venus continued, leaning across the table and taking the quarterly performance report away. She closed it firmly and folded both her arms over it as Joseph reached for it back again. "You're coping in a particularly uninteresting way with the fact that your life is a disaster right now, and Susan here has basically opted out because she doesn't know how to help the man she loves if he doesn't even recognize that he has a problem."

"I'm not exactly sure—" I said, feeling like I should reassert myself into this conversation.

Joseph ignored me. "What problem are you talking about?" he asked, glancing at Susan and then back at Venus.

"Maybe it would be better if—"

"You don't think you have a problem?" Venus said, interrupting me. "Okay, then answer me this: what do you *want*?" Venus asked in a quiet voice. "If you dared summon the audacity to dream totally on your own behalf, what would that dream look like?"

Suddenly, the room was startlingly quiet. The question was such an interesting one that I decided not to interrupt. At least four different times, Joseph opened his mouth to say something, and each time he stopped, thought a second, and then shut it abruptly.

"I don't know," he said at last.

"*Abso-damn-lutely* you don't know!" Venus cried out triumphantly. "Like everybody else in this world, you think that every day should be like the last, which means if life is a journey, then you've decided that the best thing you can do is stop walking and squat where you are until something pushes you to some other random place. And even if that other place is better than the one you left, you probably resent whatever it was that forced you to move. Have you ever tried to shoo a fly out an open window in your house?" she asked.

"*I* have," said Susan unexpectedly.

"It's not easy, is it?"

"No."

"You've got a fly that is just banging and banging and banging away at the window because it can see the wide open outside and can't figure out how to get there. So you take pity on it, and you take a magazine and you try to nudge the fly up toward the opening. And you know what it does? It buzzes and fights and struggles to stay right where it is, even though you're trying to give it freedom, and it throws every curse it knows in fly-language in your direction for trying to push it somewhere that will take it exactly where it wants to go."

"That," said Venus, "is how we appear to the eyes of God. We fight against change, even though if we looked back, we would rather die than stay the rest of our lives in the place we came from. And it's not just you or you or you," she finished, pointing to each of us in turn. "It's everybody on the whole planet, fighting against the Hand that is trying to usher us gently to freedom."

Joseph gave her a long look. "What else should I do?" he asked finally.

"Try this on for size," Venus proposed, leaning forward. "Imagine that instead of working as an underpaid wage slave for the 181st largest company in the Fortune 500 listings, you get a chance to see the results of your own work, supervising people who are doing something more tangible and satisfying than moving papers around. You grew up in the country, and you would do anything to get back. Am I right?"

"Is that true?" Susan demanded with a look of shock on her face.

Joseph looked down at the table as if this were a shameful thing. "I always thought that if we ever got together enough money—"

"And how, exactly, are you going to do that when last year and every three years before that you bought your girlfriend here a Lexus," Venus continued relentlessly. "As a reward, though you would never tell her that, for sticking with a loser like you for all these years. Every week, the company takes a little piece out of your soul, while you use the little bit of money they throw contemptuously in your direction to buy the affections of your girlfriend, when all she would ever wish for is you to be happy. Hello??!" Venus called out. "It's called a budget. You decide what you want, and *that's* where your money goes."

"You never told me *any* of this!" Susan cried out, standing up and smacking her magazine in frustration on the top of the table. "You mean the car I drive takes you farther away from retirement?"

"What else could it *possibly* do?" Venus asked her. "You think he's the only one responsible here? How many times have you reminded your boyfriend here that whatever he is, whatever he does, you would still love him the way you loved him the day you were married? Have you *ever* told him that?"

"What business is this of yours?!" Susan shouted at Venus. "Maybe I don't say these things that I feel, but does that make me a bad person?"

"It makes you a co-conspirator!"

"You will not talk to my wife like that!"

"How many more years are you going to come into this office and niggle over whatever insignificant thing a basis point must be, when the world outside is calling you to escape through the window?" Venus demanded. "The way I see it, your best option is to take a couple of sick days and go to a hotel somewhere with your bank statements, and spend half the time purely on romance and the other half trying to figure out how to live on two-thirds of what you're spending now. Sell the house and take the company up on its never-ending offer to pay you big bucks to get off of its payroll because God knows the more people they cut the better off the company is, and drive north until you find a hundred acres out in some scenic location and a house to fix up, and create a business where you supervise the worst business people in the world, the carpenters and craftspeople who do home repairs and fix houses, who never understood how to stay on a schedule or handle their money."

"You think I can just take days off like that?" Joseph fairly shouted at her, his face and spirit both moving from deep red to a dangerous purple color.

"Of course you can!" his wife shouted back. "After all you've given that company, they would begrudge you a sick day or two, which will be a day or two more than you have ever taken even when you were practically dying on your way out of the house—"

"How can we live on less than what we make now?"

"Do you think I can't manage a budget for the two of us?"

"Oh, so you're telling me this is easy?"

"Just watch me!"

As Joseph and Susan continued shouting at each other, Venus settled back with a happy smile. She gave me a pleased look, saw that I was staring at my shouting-at-each-other customers with my mouth open, and patted my arm reassuringly.

"Once the home repair company gets going, you could probably spend what you're spending now," she said in a voice which somehow carried over the back-and-forth voices on the other side of the table. "Maybe right now, depending on the severance package. Right?"

It took me a few long seconds to realize that this last was directed at me. My mouth was dry, and it was hard to speak.

"Yes," I managed to say. "Yes, he—they could."

"Joseph, I feel like I'm talking to a stranger," Susan complained, but there was something gentle in her voice now. "Why didn't you *tell* me these things?"

"Maybe I didn't know it myself," Joseph admitted. "Or maybe it would have been too much to say." He took her hands in his, and his voice was tender. "Could you live away from here in a small house in the country?"

"So much less to have to clean. And it would take you away from that terrible company that I always hated."

"I think I can get you some numbers in a couple of days," I suggested timidly. "Can you work out the severance package?"

Joseph looked at me with those eyes that missed nothing, and for a second I actually felt sorry for his company, that a man who knew as much as he did would be dangling his own retirement before just the right person at just the right time, like a prize to be bid on, and then handle the negotiations with somebody 20 years younger and infinitely less savvy.

Venus stood up and the Federmans stood up and she grabbed their hands and put them together until they squeezed each others' hand, and then she pushed them toward the door. I walked out with them and saw, to my horror and consternation, that the entire staff of the brokerage office was gathered in the hallway, staring at us through the glass that separated the conference room like we were exotic fish in a fishbowl.

"You lovebirds work out the details without us around," Venus told them, adding an extra shove that took my clients around the corner out of my sight. She turned around at the audience. "Well?" she demanded.

After a second, everybody suddenly realized they had something important to do in their offices. "That was *so* much fun," Venus said happily, leading me back to my office. "I love your work. Do you realize that he's about to get his sex drive back?"

"Speaking of which—" said a familiar voice behind me. "I don't believe we've met."

I turned, and with a sinking heart realized that Heavy Hitter was standing at the entrance of his spacious office near the lobby. He looked long and hard at the silk dress.

Venus turned her eyes obliquely for a second, and then walked over to him slowly. "You're right," she said, her voice dropping to a low purr. "Please excuse me for not coming into your office and introducing myself. This is my first time here, and I didn't realize until now that you were the head broker around here."

"It's that obvious, is it?" Heavy Hitter grinned and spread his arms wide, as if he were waiting for the applause of angels.

Behind me, people timidly put their heads out of their office doors again.

"You have that certain air of confidence about you," Venus said in a meek voice. "I'll bet you could take all my money and I'd never have any idea what happened."

"I'll bet I could do better than that."

"What do you have in mind?"

"We could start with dinner."

"You work fast."

Venus began walking into the lobby, and Heavy Hitter followed. For some reason, I followed too, thinking I should interrupt but not knowing exactly where to begin. After a second, I realized that everybody else was crowding in behind me.

"I see what I want, and I reach for it," Heavy Hitter was saying.

"In some places, that's considered stealing."

"Not when you're with a consenting adult."

"So you already have me in bed," said Venus. "What then?"

"I'm thinking we could take it as far as it goes."

"Marriage?"

"Why not?"

"Haven't you been married four times already?"

Heavy Hitter stopped walking. By now, they were in the center of the lobby, and the two of them were the unrivaled focus of attention, not only of the customers who sat there, but of the other brokers who were standing at the entrance to the hallway. Heavy Hitter looked around, noticing for the first time that he had an audience. It seemed to give him confidence.

"I've been looking hard for the right woman," he said. "I'm not afraid to make a mistake once in a while, if the goal is worthwhile."

"Maybe the problem was that you didn't have what they needed after the lights went out," Venus suggested.

"I'm ready to provide a demonstration," Heavy Hitter grinned, spreading his arms again. He turned to the brokers, and some of them made the kind of cheering noises and whistles you hear at basketball games. "I'll lay my cards right there on the sheets, and you can decide for yourself."

"And it will be *such* a difficult decision, I might have to try more than once before I make up my mind."

"It could take all night," Heavy Hitter grinned.

"I can't believe my luck," Venus told him, when the next round of whistles died down. "Coming here and finally meeting a real man, that one special man in a million who has gone the extra half-inch and given his brain over totally to that little divining rod between your legs, following it like an infallible compass leading you always in the direction of trouble."

"Hey; tell me we don't have some chemistry going here."

"I'm imagining our future together. In the best of circumstances," said Venus, "you give your heart to a man, and within three months, four if you're lucky, his fantasy of an exciting good time is to watch any-other-woman-but-you take her clothes off. Having his baby makes you unattractive in his eyes, and when you finally give birth, his best attention goes to the baby and not to the woman who produced it, because a man loves himself first, and then anything that contains his precious genes second. Over the years, you watch your place in his priorities drop to somewhere behind beer and the wide-screen television set which he leans forward into by blind instinct every time the camera pans away from the stupid violence to a young cheerleader who has, in his eyes, the three great sexual attractors to every married man: that she is young enough to be his daughter, that he doesn't know anything about her including her name, and that she never messed up her body by having his baby."

Two of the female support staff let out a cheer, and it was this, not the words from Venus's mouth, which caused Heavy Hitter's face to darken into anger.

"I didn't realize I was talking to a lesbian," he snarled.

"What you don't realize," Venus answered calmly, "is that you are a woman's worst nightmare, all form and no substance, a shell of confidence wrapped around a coward, filled with zero loyalty to anything and anybody but yourself. Your only saving grace is that your smoothness, polished to a bright unpleasant shine like a cheap rhinestone, instantly gives you away as a dwarf pretending to be man. I'm grateful that I don't have to associate with you for one more second."

"You're a fucking bitch!" Heavy Hitter shouted as she walked into the elevator.

Venus turned to face him from inside the elevator, and gave him the full force of her fierce eyes. "Bitch," she said with careful enunciation of every word, "is the male term for a woman who has the bad manners to stand up for what she wants and needs, and who openly defies all the unfair unwritten cultural assumptions that scream at her, every day of her life, that she should always be sacrificing who and what she is for somebody else's agenda. And you," Venus continued, looking Heavy Hitter up and down once more, "are the most unattractive, disgusting human male I've ever allowed myself to get this close to. If we did have dinner together, I doubt I could have made it through the appetizer without vomiting."

She smiled at the rest of us, and the elevator doors closed on that beautiful smile, the smile an angel would be proud to wear.

For a second, the room was deadly silent. Then Heavy Hitter suddenly ran to the elevator doors and kicked them repeatedly, alternately with one foot and then the other, shouting every obscenity I had ever heard and a few that might have been in a foreign language.

Karen, this moment was the most fun I had ever had at the office. It was, at least, until suddenly I wondered what I would do when Heavy Hitter turned around and remembered that I was the one who had been walking with Venus down the hallway.

I decided to take the rest of the afternoon off, and—purely for the exercise—to take the back stairs down to the parking lot.

"Hey!"

"What?" I jumped half a foot in the air at the unexpected greeting so close to my car. I turned to see Venus sitting on the concrete wall.

"Aren't you going to drive me back like a gentleman?"

"How did you know I was going to come down here?"

Venus shrugged. "I figured you wanted to be back in time for the glimming. I thought maybe if I created enough of a distraction, you'd get uncomfortable and leave, and nobody would care."

"Nobody would care anyway," I said gloomily, unlocking the car and opening the passenger door.

"I don't think that's true. I'll bet they're looking all over for you right now."

At this, I had to smile. "Just promise me you won't come visiting again."

"After what I saw in there, I ought to make *you* give me the same promise."

I pulled the car into the alley between two fences and parked near the back of the warehouse, by the edge of the bank. Looking up, I could see a silhouette in the window of the building next door, which I assumed was Ellen Moore. This time I *did* wave.

"Friend of yours?"

"Neighbor," I said. "She doesn't think I should sell the place either. What nobody seems to understand is that I don't have a choice."

"Everybody has a choice with everything they do at all times of their lives," Venus told me, shimmying under the fence with practiced ease.

"Yeah? Tell that to Cassandra."

Venus was suddenly quiet.

"What do you think of Cassandra?" I asked her after a moment.

"She creeps me out. And I'm not the only one."

"Why? Because she can see into the future?"

"If it was just that, it wouldn't bother me," said Venus. "I know I shouldn't feel this way, but it's her handicap that gets to me."

"What handicap?"

"Are you telling me you haven't noticed?"

"I didn't know there was anything *to* notice. I mean, *all* of you are pretty weird."

"She's blind," Venus told me, and I could read surprise in her voice and her spirit. They were both saying: how could I not know that?

"Now I'm confused," I said. "Her eyes seem perfectly normal to me."

"Her spirit eyes," Venus said impatiently. "When she was very young, a demon must have attached itself persistently to the part of her spirit where the eyes were forming, and it did too much damage for them to heal themselves. Didn't you ever wonder why she carries that resonance field imaging device around with her? It helps her to know what colors you're vibrating on, but even *she* will tell you that it's a very pale imitation of the real thing."

"Does that have anything to do with her seeing the future?"

"Who knows?" Venus shrugged. "All I know is that I can't look at her without feeling a little weird."

I walked alongside her for a long time in silence, until we reached the side door. I stopped at the threshold.

"I think I'm going home," I said.

"You look depressed. Maybe you should glim with us."

"I don't think I totally understand what this glimming thing is," I said. "The last time I did it, I think I entered the body of a cricket."

"It's just sharing your vibrations. When you look at the spirits of people while they're glimming, you can see everybody's brightness go up a notch or two. They glimmer a little more. Get it?"

"But how does it work?" I persisted.

"I don't think anybody knows for sure. Apollo once told me that three spirits is a quorum, but who knows what *that* means? I think the truth is, your spirit, and mine and somebody else's, all vibrating together, makes up enough of the mind of the Almighty Awareness that it's possible to get a faint glimpse—there's that root word again, isn't it interesting?—of the Total Awareness. Of course, it can also take you clear out to the deva community, where *everybody* is in group therapy. See?" she said happily. "It's not so complicated."

"I *am* feeling a little depressed," I admitted.

"If you're glum, you glim," said Venus. "It might help you recognize that all your so-called troubles are nothing more than meaningless external stimuli."

Inside, the others were seated on the floor in a loose circle, their eyes closed. I noticed a curious buzzing noise coming from the air around me.

Looking around, I noticed the man in a wheelchair against the far wall, his head lolling back. He seemed so alone and helpless that I thought maybe I should give him somebody to talk to, but from the look on his face, I doubt he had the ability to notice me. Watching this unfortunate person, it occurred to me that I wasn't the only one in the world with problems.

"How do we start?" I said.

I allowed Venus to lead me to an open place in the circle, and sat down heavily next to Fool. "You know the drill," he said without opening his eyes. "Look at the wall, and at the space between you and the wall, and find the bits of holy spirit. Get your mind clear. The universe beckons, probably because it doesn't know you very well yet."

After a few moments of mental turmoil and self-doubt, I discovered that the second time you turn your awareness inward and then beyond yourself, it is much easier than the first time. I felt myself become the glow in my body, the glow that animated my body, the real me. I expanded its awareness in a direction that was previously unknown to me.

Once again, time ceased, and in that place, I realized that Fool was entirely right, that the humble, often clueless body that I thought was *me* was a strangely implausible accomplice to whatever Heavy Hitter intended with this building and these people. My value to them was that I was under their control, and would do what they asked without really questioning it.

A comforting sound interrupted my feelings of shame and remorse, a deep hum, synchronized among the group. After a moment, I realized that it must be the Hindu mantra, OM, only it sounded different than I had expected.

AUMMMmmmmm.

The low vibration penetrated my awareness, relaxing my thoughts. I lent my own voice to the chorus, humming clumsily at first, gradually matching the tone and pitch of the others.

After a minute, I suddenly knew I had it right, when the hum resonated deep into my body. As the harmony reached my bones, I experienced what it must feel like to be a violin.

AUMmmmmmmmn.

I realize that this chant is the opposite of speech. Speech is intended to leave the body, but this sound is intended to enter the body and take you deeper into its myriad energy and secret doorways.

AUMmmmmm.

The deep hum changes pitch, so subtly that I almost cannot hear the difference, but I feel the difference in my bone structure, and adjust to bring my note into harmony with the note around me. As soon as I regain synchronicity, there is another, bigger shift, another adjustment, higher this time. What had been a deeply contented hum now evokes a hint of concern, and then, as it shifts higher, the tone of the humming conveys fear. We move up the scale until the hum reaches a whine of melancholy and sadness, then back down past vexation and scorn, to affirmation, trust, optimism, forgiveness, reverence, serenity and finally the comfortable basso of powerful contentment—and I realize at some point on this journey that every human emotion represents a correspondent place on this strange musical scale, that all feelings that are and ever were and ever will be have a note, and I have quickly toured them all with the group.

AUMmmmmm.

It is a song, communicating all experience in the slight variation of modulation, the song of what it is to be human and alive.

AUMmmmm.

I realize, with a part of me which hears and appreciates this vibratory song, that the goal is to merge our voices into one.

To merge our voices is to acquire force and power. Why?

AUMmm.

With my eyes closed, I "see" the circle in spirit rather than in flesh, the bodies seated around me, and I see in each of us the vibration extend into our spirit bodies, harmonizing physical and spiritual, and then reaching out somehow to harmonize with the sparks of awareness that extend forever from where we sit.

AUMmm.

I have become the vibrations. And as I give up my awareness to the note, I follow the harmony through incredibly subtle variations in the extreme basso tone of contentment, and the variations are expressive of thoughts so intricate and finely grained that they are utterly alien within the overall background of familiarity. It is as if I had been looking at a rock, and now the scale has shifted and I am suddenly looking at the rock's myriad constituent atoms, and their unfamiliarity is unsettling and fascinating at the same time.

AUMmmmmmmmm.

I appreciate the group's patience with me, the primary straggler, as I learn to adjust second by second, then instant by instant, then more finely-grained than my imagination will allow me to comprehend, but in my bones I am harmonized and complete, and we are vibrating in a togetherness that is beyond intimacy.

AUMmmmmmmm.

Our awareness, and the levels beyond consciousness, and then things undescribed beyond, are merged. We are one.

AUMmmmmmmm.

I am somehow not surprised to find that I am aware of their awareness, and that there are more of them than I expected, that we are joined by others in distant corners of our planet.

And then we begin, together as one, to sing to the sky, and the earth, to the spaces between the stars and the spaces between the bits of tiny commotion that are pieces of the pieces of pieces of the atoms, and it is a song of joy.

AUMmmmmmm.

Our vibrations dance the harmonies of contentment and acceptance, and the larger awareness that is partly *me* is joyful, for this is the opening chorus of the Song of the Universe.

Karen, already I have talked of things for which there are no words, and in the telling I have felt inadequate, because the reality is so much richer and more interesting than the words. But here, as I think of this song, I reach a wall beyond which words will not go. As the song enters my body, I experience feelings that are even at first beyond all my previous definitions of joy, and the journey goes on at an accelerating pace from there.

The awareness of my terrestrial chorus expands, and in that state a million million miles beyond joy, I experience the intricate dance of the Sun and its collection of tiny irrelevant refuse and dust in a kaleidoscope of orbits.

The choral awareness carries my awareness beyond this, and I experience stars like brightly illumined dust in a strong wind, and then the galaxy itself is within our field of sight, and then a scattering of smaller aggregations of these bits of sparkling dust, and then the galaxies themselves are grains of sand, and still the expansion does not stop.

AUMmmmmm.

In a shock of recognition, I know that the beginning and end of our journey, the *all* that I see now, all of it, the macro and the micro, vibrate in exactly the same harmonic dance, and there is now an even bigger shock, for I see that the accumulation of galaxies and the tiny things that are constituents of subatomic particles are identical, that the universe that glows mistily in my vision extends in another dimension of space and folds back on itself—that the entire cosmos is, at the same time, not just one of its own tiny basic fuzzy mists of light that is the smallest piece of a piece of an atom, but that it is folded and refolded again and again, so that the universe is *all* of its constituent pieces, and the music of its vibrations is the very song we are singing now...

AUMmmmmmmm.

Now the group awareness turns from the ever-encompassing universal loop to the expanding roster of the choir itself.

Karen, as a small part of this growing awareness, I too turned my attention this way, and I can tell you now that if anything less than the Song of the Universe had filled my body at that moment, my body would have instantly died of a heart attack at what I saw next.

We of the dust mote called Earth have now been joined by a fantastic menagerie of creatures from everywhere else. There are squids in rainbow colors, lizards as delicate as butterflies, something that might have been either a tube of jelly or a living question mark covered by what looks like radiant hair. Creatures of living fire, and others of so many shapes and textures extending out to the spiritual horizon and beyond, all participating with us in the Song of the Universe, all joining their minds as one, as one with the ancient consciousness, nothing more or less than sparks from the flame...

The awareness that I am a part of is also theirs, and we share the Song of the Universe, and as nearly as I can see, this beyond-description beautiful song is the only thing we could ever share in common, and I know from the greater awareness that this is its most special magic, and this is why a few of the most spiritually-aware creatures of a million million planets can gather on their own worlds and sing it into their bodies.

It is the common language of all intelligent entities everywhere that *is* a where, and we are together now, looking a bit self-consciously at each other in what must, I think, always be the spirit of group encounter among such a diversity of forms.

AUMmm.

Out of the menagerie, I am approached by a creature who seems to be composed entirely of light.

Within the context of the song that we share, a kind of communication is possible. The living flame modulates its version of the deep universal vibration to harmonize with mine, and I sense a bit of impatience.

"Trade with me your experiences." Somehow, the creature vibrates this message into my spirit.

"I—do not understand."

AUMmm.

"Agree, and you will understand my meaning. I do not intend to harm you."

Some part of me must have given permission, because at that moment, I am roaring into the life of the creature of light, and the living flame is, I see somewhere behind me, experiencing my own life…

I swirl out into a chaos of travel, roar past galaxies and finally plunge into the spiral arm of a large one, down, down past stars of every size and color until I am hovering tight over the maelstrom surface of a yellow class G star, squinting into the endless cascade of light whose individual photons had been manufactured deep at the fusion-powered core 300,000 years ago, fighting their way up through the convection layers of the star's interior ever since. Directly below me, my attention is directed to a tiny pinpoint on the surface, a minuscule vortex of charged plasma no larger than the continent of Asia where—happy accident! I see a coming-together-in-playful-joy of a dozen creatures of light, the group holding itself together in exquisite pleasure for nearly a full millisecond before all scatter again like leaves in the solar wind.

Life in the Universe:
Prelude to an Aurora

I am the product of the joy of mingled essences, born an electrical dust-devil gestated now into the solar maelstrom and—Joy! It is joy to be alive, to feel the surge of gentle warmth caressing our bodies in the 11,000-degree perpetual storm that is our ecology and our home.

Fly, my cousins! Fly along the energy well! We who were born together in that instant ride the bundled magnetic fields millions of times smoother than ice, harder than steel to our gossamer bodies—a playground slide twelve times the size of the Earth. Slide and soar! Swirl and coalesce and reform in a journey that lasts nearly a ten thousandth of an instant, and carries my body more than a thousand miles to where I and another behold a fantastical sight, an infall of plasma, like an enormous waterfall into a thousand-mile-deep hole in the surface of the star, circular and broad enough to swallow all four inner planets of the solar system. The hole rotates at glacial speed, which contrasts with the roar of the surface plasma falling over the edge, plunging inward at speeds of a mile a second.

I join the other, whose appearance is strangely attractive to me. Eagerly, we swirl around the edges.

-*What is it?* The shape and color and kinetic movement of my body forms the question.

-*A sunspot!* The word is different from the human word; it is closer in meaning to "healing wound of the star."

-*I am wondering why it is here.*

-*What is "Why?"* My companion catches my odd thought, turns the concept over in her body, which is also her mind.

-*It is a perplexing word that comes into my thoughts whenever I see something. It has been doing that for nearly a second now.* Then, suddenly, I look at myself and my companion, still swirling around the infall below, joined now by others who have seen this interesting thing and have decided to help us explore it.

New questions form.

-*Why are WE here?*

-*Why do we play?*

An emerging leader among my cousins, a great one whose name is Fire in the Wind, surrounds us with his electric presence and admonishes me before my companion can answer.

-*We play to grow strong before the migration. It is unwise to question the way of things when we were made to act and experience.*

Dive, my cousins! Catch the eruption of an electromagnetic storm that arches outward between this and another sunspot, soar with the plasma archway across a hundred thousand miles and then fall into the spongy softness at the base of the electromagnetic loop.

In five seconds, I am an adolescent, and now some deeply rooted instinct tells me that it is time to begin our migration, and I wonder how the leader of my cousins could have known that there would *be* a migration so many instants before its urgency began to well up in our bodies. I follow many millions of my peers, a bright tide of gossamer vortices passing together like electric lemmings across this maelstronic landscape of light.

We call out encouragement to each other as we travel.

-*This way!*

-*Yes!*

Together, we plunge downward beneath the surface, sensing like a pleasurable explosion the rightness of the message. Deeper! We are battered by the urgency of photons too long denied their freedom, and by the blind creatures of the interior who graze passively on plasmoid crystals, and deeper, through the convection zone to the edge of the violent tachocline, the jagged boundary that separates the cool upper atmosphere of the star from the magnificent heat of its core.

This is the end of adolescence, the time for our metamorphosis. Borrowing from the swirling energy of the tachocline, each of us duplicates our bodies and we merge the two into one mind, and then the two duplicate, and then the four, the eight, the 16, 32, 64! Every millisecond we double, every instant we become more than what we were, until the child that I was is now no more than a tiny cell of the adult.

I am a living electrical storm.

-We are magnificent!

-See us!

Flexing the strength of my new body, I clasp the spinning vortices of magnetic fields bundled like spaghetti, and reach out in invitation to the interesting other, who shines with a powerful and subtle radiance that dazzles my awareness.

With a casual gesture, a flex of the torso, we explode once more toward the surface.

Here—Joy!—a civilization is in full flower and—Joy! We race through and between elaborate constructions, a fairyland kingdom of fused magnetic field that will last an eternity, perhaps some of it an entire hour. It will be seen by multiple generations of our species!

-Come! We are already at work! cries Fire in the Wind.

The labor is interesting and difficult and we are like gods playing with the fundamental forces of the universe. A city rises out of the maelstrom, order out of chaos, a miracle to match the miracle of our existence.

-What is the point? I wonder, looking at its beauty.

-It is its own point! cries out Fire in the Wind impatiently, urging us to work more quickly so that more and more will be built before we are gone.

-Why?

-Yes, why? whispers my interesting companion.

-These foolish questions distract from our magnificent project.

-Yet I feel they must be asked.

-We live our threescore and ten seconds in joy and achievement, and then surrender to oblivion, the philosophers cry. *Plasma to plasma, dust to dust. What more is there?*

-There is more, says my companion softly. *I feel it.*

The city rises. Then there is a solar earthquake, and we are scattered. A massive shear, a sunspot erupting into another infall from the plasma below, sends our construction into a glorious, terrifying spiral of destruction and photonic dust. The gossamer towers fall, the thoroughfares of magnetism and crushed plasma crumble and swirl away.

Silence. Then: a wailing echoes across the landscape. For almost an entire instant, we mourn the death of our life's work. Then, immediately, the project begins anew.

-*You must join us!* Fire in the Wind calls out, and there is a hint of threat in the words.

-*It was all vanity. It was destined to be a vexation, either for us or for others to come later.*

-*And you?* Fire in the Wind calls to my interesting companion, and the dust trembles ominously at his words.

-*I prefer to watch.*

-*There is no watch. There is only do.*

-*There is something more,* she whispers, the words barely visible in the trembling of her body.

The rage of Fire in the Wind is a terrible, humbling sight, and the construction ceases as a million other creatures witness it. They will speak of nothing else for more than half a second.

-*See?!? See how you have interrupted our labors?*

-*The labors will become as nothing. The work forgotten.*

-*You and this other are paired together in a way that is unnatural and revolting. YOU will be forgotten.*

-*When others can see us at every moment?*

-*I say both of you must leave us. The catastrophe was punishment for your questions. Who agrees?*

The agreement is slower than the leader would have wished, but it is unanimous. The plasma trembles with the reflective assent of many voices.

I turn to my interesting companion.

-*Perhaps others, somewhere else, can give us the answer.*

-*I will come with you.*

We race across the solar landscape, enter fantastic cities where our distant cousins are working too diligently to notice us.

-*Why?*

The answer is always the same:-*We are what we are. We do what we do.*

My companion and I pass through abandoned relics of haunting beauty and the faint smell of regret. I imagine the labors, the lives, spent there so that we would see this monument to their dreams. But what does it tell us of them?

-*Why?* I ask the dead remnants, which are all that are left to speak on behalf of the vanished builders.

-Perhaps the answer is ahead.
-Perhaps...
In 20 seconds we have circumnavigated the star twice.
-Where else can we go?
-There are two more directions, my companion replies. *Up. Or down.*

Then she does a strange thing. She stops, and there is no motion at all in her as the waves of light plasma break over her body and swirl in eddies that stretch beyond my vision.

-What are you doing?
-Listening. Can you hear it?

I still the incessant motion of my body, an unnatural act in violation of all physical logic.

And in the stillness, there is a distant buzz. It vibrates into my unmotion like a beacon.

-Down?
-Down!

We plunge once more beneath the surface, down to the twisted magnetic roots of a plasma infall, riding it down to the end and then plunging further through the jagged tachocline, from gas into liquid, and it seems that as we move deeper into the gravity well, time itself has slowed down. The density holds us in its grip, we push past the photons that are moving in the opposite direction, constantly bumped off course. But the strange buzzing is still below us, and gradually we become aware of the presence of another one like us, yet not like us, deep, deep within the heart of the star.

-This way, my children, it calls to us.

-I am—I call out my own name, a name that is color and light and joyful turbulence.

-And I—the name of my companion, a gentle name of swirling plasma and reflection.

-You are unusual to visit here.
-We sensed you. Who—what are you?
-Once I was as you are. That was many years ago.
-Years?
-Combinations of seconds. Perhaps 450,000 generations of our species.
-You must be the first of our kind!
-No. We are an old race. But we build our monuments out of sand. Our records are written on the water.
-Sand? Water?

-Look inward, my children. See beyond the glow of your bodies. It is a glow even more dazzling, if you have eyes to find it.

-I see it! My companion cries, and in her exultation she leaps upward and around us, and I marvel at her ability to push between the crushed photons of this cramped place. The other's body closes against mine, and at first I believe that it is time to mate, and then the vibrations from the body of my companion become the vibrations of my body, and we resonate with peals of wonderful sound that ricochet through the solar mass, a mosaic of energy, of harmonic beauty that is so overpowering that I shiver as if cold, even though I am bathed in five million degrees of heat, so strong that it threatens to tear apart the fabric of my gossamer essence.

-It is joy!

-Look beyond it. Look at the vibration itself, the steady voice suggests to me.

The majestic melody of light and vibration parts like a curtain before my attention, and beyond it I see a shadow of myself, somehow brighter than the beautiful photonic maelstrom that is me.

-Yes.

-It is—us?

-A part of you, yes. It is your connection with everything, the scattered bits of stars like ours, far from this small place that is our home.

The ancient one reaches out to scatter the plasma dust in a beautiful pattern that illustrates the tiny, glowing hearts of atoms, individually spaced, so many that they are limitless in this one bright swirl, and we marvel at the strength in this old one's body.

-There are as many of these, scattered across space, as there are bits of light on this thing that others call a star, that we call our home.

-We have no time. We must mate, and then, in a few minutes, our bodies will scatter across the landscape.

-There is no hurry. See what I have learned.

The old one extends itself in a gesture, and we see that its bright shadow is brighter somehow, and we see streaming into it a parade of glow.

-I have seen creatures who replace the tiny components of their body as a matter of automatic routine. See? I replicate my vortices, and my body is fresh and new. Death, unhealth, if the spirit-that-is-your-bright-shadow-inside is strong, then it exists in equilibrium with the body, and neither will cease to exist. There is a ritual, see!

Too quickly for us to respond, the old one, with a strength we cannot imagine, roils the fabric of light, creating a fantastic lightning of electromagnetic ribbons that extend through us, shattering the coalition of plasma and light that is our bodies. At the same moment, my physical sight is extinguished, and yet, somehow, I am seeing the scene through my spirit. By a joyful instinct, that other "me" joins the other "companion," and the bright shadows extend into the crumbling physical bodies that are us, replicate the dust devils that are the cells of our bodies, and heal the ruptures.

It is easy to replicate, once we have done it, and we look at each other in amazed happiness.

-You are rejuvenated. And now your bright-shadow-bodies are alive, for you have experienced what would have been certain death, and forced them to come alive to rescue you. On a million times a million stars, on a million times a million rocks orbiting those stars, creatures have learned every variation of this ritual, a simulated journey to the edge of death and back which is the only way to bring their own bright-shadow-bodies fully to life.

-I sense that I will not return to dust until or unless I wish it.

My companion has spoken my own thoughts.

-Leave me now. I will not see another like you for a thousand or a million generations, and there is much to think about between these distractions.

Up! We dive through the currents of the star, catching updrafts, swirling joyfully among the twisted shear of magnetic fields that carry us faster than the muddled photons which struggle mindlessly against every obstacle when there are so many paths of least resistance, and above the surface once more we unite in joyful reunion with distant cousins and their magnificent structure.

How long have we been gone?

-We have news! Joyful information!

Work ceases at our return. The others scatter playfully, and for whole instants we chase them, losing ourselves all over again in the feeling of touching the smooth, elongated surface of magnetic tubes for five, ten thousand miles, and at the end—

Fire in the Wind emerges from the towering structures, his body feeble and slow, but his voice stronger and angrier than ever it was before.

-You have no right to return!

-We have learned new wisdoms!

-Distraction! he shouts, furious that so many milliseconds of work have been wasted. He totters to the front of the crowd, an ancient vision of mottled darkness too feeble now to shape the fields himself.

-We have no time for distractions. See? A new structure arises!

-It is beautiful, I tell him.

-We have seen many like it, my companion adds. *It makes you wonder where the builders are; nothing more.*

-Lies and distractions. Leave us!
-Another second—
-Another addition to the structure!
-It is important!
-It is frivolous.
-Who will learn what we know? I call out to the others. *See how we have not aged! We offer you immortality in return for a quick rest from your construction labors!*

-Blasphemers! My invitation has driven Fire in the Wind into a frenzy of anger. He leaps forward, beating his vortices against mine in an effort to return me to dust, and I can feel the blind fury in his spirit. The force of his grasp nearly shatters my physical integrity, and then, slowly, his body begins to crumble, the center fails to hold, and his vortices scatter into bits of plasma in the solar wind, and there are swirls in the air and then there is nothing to hint that he ever existed except the uncompleted city behind the place where he is no longer.

I turn to the others.

-Who will learn?

But the words echo on emptiness. Everywhere, there is nothing. Our cousins are dissipating in this last burst of joyful energy, giving themselves back to the churning plasma with gratitude and homage to the leader who was born in the same instant that they were.

A powerful solar wind blows through the empty fairyland of structures and half-structures, their legacy to the sun.

My companion shivers.

-They were right not to listen. The answer to "Why?" is not immortality. It is something else.

-What else?

The city trembles on its foundations. For a very long time my companion doesn't answer. We see beyond this construction that another one is rising. Then, after a while, the builders die, and it stands magnificent, unfinished, as the one before us wavers and melts and waits for the next solar earthquake.

After a while, we travel toward the place of our birth. Below us, a generation is born in a glorious coming-together. Another generation dies, another city lies half-born.

-I am lonely, says my companion presently.
-We should mate.
-With who?
-Each other.

-Just two?
-There are many others everywhere. But perhaps just the two of us—
-No. I couldn't bear it if one who came from us refused to listen to our new wisdom.
-What will we do?

Without answering, the companion rises into the sky, and I see in her spirit an invitation to follow. We move higher than I have ever been. For a brief time, it is very cold, and then, suddenly, it is much hotter than near the surface, nearly as hot as it had been below the tachocline. There, at the outer fringes of this hot atmosphere around the star, we stand at the threshold of something new. Something so alien that it twists my mind.

It is Darkness, although there is no word for such a thing. In some curious way this new experience, so mind-twistingly alien to creatures of the light, matches my mood. I turn to my companion, and speak truth.

-I do not sense joy in you.
-It is a different feeling, learned from I do not know where. Look out at this new thing. What do you see?

From around the bend in the star that is our home, arrives a mote of scattered rubble that appears to be plasma frozen into something solid.

-There is emptiness. And others not like us. See there.

I turn my attention where my companion has indicated, and upon the surface of this tiny pebble, I sense what looks revoltingly as if small pieces of this frozen bit of stone have been granted a sluggish kind of life. These creatures crawl about with agonizing slowness—and they are covered, it appears, with complicated bubbles to protect them from the emptiness and (Can this be possible?) the heat on that frozen bit of dust.

-They are visitors to the nearest pebble. I think they come from that place.

My companion indicates a larger bit of frozen plasma, further away. She has seen what I did not, small containers moving about between these bits of flotsam at impossibly slow fractions of the natural, honest speed of light.

My companion stares out at the tiny frozen world with an interest that I do not share.

-There is one there who has sensed us, as the Ancient One senses things. I think it was an accident. I can see her looking up at the evening sky of her frozen world, up toward us now on what they call a setting sun, and I feel a connection in both directions, a sharing of our hearts. She is wondering what this is that she feels from me, and does not know, as we do, that it is our joy of simply being alive.

-She is foolish.

-Yet I have learned of a new thing, through this creature. An important thing.

-What is it called?

-A word with no meaning, but I think it may be connected with the missing meaning in our existence. They call it Love.

I shiver, not at the cold, but at the thought of mental contact with such bizarre creatures.

-We should return. Perhaps another generation has passed and they will listen to us now. Perhaps we can help one generation or another finish a city, and then they will hear the things we must tell them.

-They will not hear the different message that I have to teach. I do not think our species was made for this feeling, but it connects us, you and I, uniquely among our kind. That is how we are different. And...And I believe that in a million generations, perhaps more, it will be more common. It may prove to be the answer to your many questions.

-I do not understand.

-Nor I.

-I feel that we should mate.

I make this tender communication without thinking, but it seems to have an unsettling effect on my companion.

She faces back toward the surface, where twin plasma inflows far, far below us have expanded many times the size of the small inhabited rock in the distance. A monumental eruption is beginning now, a great arch being formed, unfolding, expanding—and then, impossible! It is detaching majestically from the dark spinning sources and arching rapidly outward, away, already disconnected from the surface of the star.

This is what my companion is moving toward, and I too am curious to see such a thing.

At the last moment, as it passes into and through us, my companion leaps to the warm energetic surface of the arch, riding it into the emptiness as it roars past me and outward, out, farther, farther, making its slow way toward the orbiting bit of frozen plasma that my companion has indicated.

-Goodbye, my love.

With this odd combination of words that have no meaning, she is gone. For whole minutes, while generations of my species are born and live and die on the rotating maelstrom below, I watch the traveling flame carry my strangely interesting companion farther from our home. When it is difficult to see, I hold contact with her spirit, which, in turn, holds precious, incomprehensible contact with a creature from the tiny bit of dust in the distance.

Finally, I see the traveling flame collide with what appears to be gossamer and gas surrounding the frozen place, colder but similar in substance to the halo around our star. As my companion adds herself to the flame, there is a glow at the top of this world that expands downward across the sky, and the old woman in the chair looks out at the evening darkness, wishing all over again for the tender companionship of her dead husband, wishing he were here to see this comforting sight—a brilliant streak of liquid fire shimmering in the air, the Aurora of all auroras melting like liquid wax into the clear sky.

She feels, inexplicably, that this remarkably brilliant light is a signal from another world, but only I know that some of that light is the last dying flame of my beloved companion's sacrificial body, and now her spirit is nowhere to be seen, dust and wind scattered across the top of the atmosphere—

And I am alone, utterly alone, a burning candle at the edge of the void.

VII

If God were to put on human flesh and return to our world, what would He experience? His miracles would be tested, debated, explained and watched on reality TV. His message would have to fight with the entrenched religious dogma, and there would be those who claimed that the holy books were a more reliable source of truth than He was.

Others would resent Him as a disrupter of comfortable beliefs and an insufferable know-it-all.

The final test of a true member of the New Age is whether he or she would be capable of recognizing God when confronted with Him, and would be able and willing to put aside his/her life at a moment's notice for the chance to walk alongside the Living Truth Itself.

—From *The Rutherfordton Spiritual Gazette*

Karen, do you remember when you and your mother and I would go camping in the mountains, and hike up to the foot of the waterfall to a deep pool that you loved to splash around in even before you knew how to swim? You made me wade out with you and hold you up while you went under the waterfall and back, over and over again, laughing as the water cascaded down through your hair while I felt like my legs were turning to ice. And in the late afternoons while we were cooking over the fire, you would gather flowers and twigs and leaves and moss and make elaborate little homes for the fairies that you knew must live in such a beautiful place.

You were so confident in your ability to know right from wrong, goodness from badness, and in those moments I was proud to the point of tears that you could have this clarity, because it seemed to me that in my adult working life I was forever trying to sort out ambiguities that to you, I think, would have been crystal clear.

I am about to make the most painful confession that I have ever made to anybody, and I hope you are in a forgiving mood as you read this. Because when you are finished, I'm afraid you will conclude that your father is an awful human being.

For 21 years now I have worked with The House, and for all but the first three days, I knew the damage its brokers were trained to do to the people who trusted their advice.

This is not unique to us. Other companies, some nearly as large as ours, are even better at this than we are.

Our most formidable competition in the marketplace is the many hundreds of small independent financial planning offices around the country, run by individual advisors who are not selling under the guise of giving advice, but who, for a fee, will readily lend their expertise and give their best advice about investments, life insurance, taxes, retirement and college planning.

None of these small companies have the money to buy Super Bowl advertisements, as The House does, and so they serve only the unusually discerning customers or those who have been financially abused by one of our brokers.

My goal, formulated in the first weeks of employment, was to work as those independent advisors do, to help people recognize what it is that they want in life, and to chart out for them a path through the financial wilderness which will allow them to travel safely from where they are now to wherever they want their lives to go.

And now for my painful confession. I had been developing, in secret, a plan to make an exception to this goal. This month, I had something up my sleeve that would send shock waves rippling through my little corner of The House.

I had finally thrown in the towel. I was going to play it their way. I was working on a case that would generate as much in commissions in one day as any of my office mates would make in months of hard, aggressive selling.

I had a Big Score, as the brokers liked to call it, and this man was going to make me, in one transaction, wealthy enough to retire.

That morning, sitting on the floor of the warehouse, I called to set up a lunch appointment with two colleagues of mine. Both of them were in my CFP study group, where we crammed enough information about investments and life insurance and trusts and charitable strategies and the tax code into our heads to pass the examination that made us Certified Financial Planners—a designation which is like the M.D. of the financial services world.

We were perfectly suited for each other. One of us had a strange affinity for all the complicated things you could do with the life insurance contract, the other was an accountant with a great feel for the tax issues, and I was the generalist who kept them focused on the subjects that they weren't drawn to.

When I arrived at the restaurant, Mort Freedman was already waiting for me, dressed, as always, in a rumpled polo shirt and slacks, with the sun gleaming on the bright, glossy spaces between the sparse hairs on his forehead. He wore dark-framed glasses on his nose and mostly looked over them at me, at the waitress, at the street, and there was something soft about his face which suggested that he'd reached puberty late in life and the process had never been fully completed. But he was a whiz with numbers, and was the first person I knew in the financial services business to renounce commissions in favor of simply charging a fee for his advice.

After we all passed the CFP test, Mort left what was then a Big Six accounting firm and started his own small planning shop, and now he employed two casewriters, a receptionist and a paraplanner.

I envied Mort the freedom to offer unbiased advice without anybody making him feel like he was a traitor to the organization. And yet every time he asked me to come work with him in his little planning shop, I found that I was unable to take the leap. I knew The House would reassign my clients to other brokers in the office, and I would have to start over, and those other brokers would do everything they could to pick my clients clean. My fears always seemed to trump my hope.

"You look good," I said as the waitress set our beers and glasses down on the table.

"You look like hell," Mort answered good-naturedly. "You might consider getting some sleep once in a while."

"I had a really tough night last night."

"Romantically?"

"It's way too complicated to explain." I said, changing the subject. "Look, I need you to look over a case I'm working on."

"Really."

"Yes."

"You have the resources of an in-house team of hundreds of attorneys and accountants and rocket scientists," he needled me, "and you have to come to me to get expertise."

"I just want to know if I'm totally crazy."

Mort laughed, and took a long, reflective drink from his glass. "You *are* totally crazy. There. Is that what you needed to know?"

"About this particular thing. The rest of it I know all too well."

"Well isn't *this* a distinguished group." My other colleague, Hal Weathersby, lumbered up to the table. Hal had played somewhere on the offensive line for Duke in his college days, and what had once been muscle had long since multiplied and morphed into a dense kind of jiggly obesity. The most impressive part of his body was his neck, which looked wider than his head and appeared to be squeezed between his collar and his chin. He wore an impeccably-tailored suit, and his broad, open face was always a bright red color.

"I don't want to butt in on your conversation," said Hal with a twinkle in his eye, "but I'd really, really like to get your autographs so I can show my kids that I'm a big shot who hangs around celebrities."

"Maybe you could buy us a beer," Mort suggested casually. He didn't have quite the same level of respect for Hal as I did; Hal, in his view, had gone over to the Dark Side, becoming the top life insurance agent in town. If you ever asked Hal how much life insurance coverage you should have, his answer would be a paraphrase of that line out of the Creedence Clearwater Revival song "Fortunate Son:" *When people ask how much they should give, their answer is always: More! More! More!*

But I admired Hal's grasp of the really complicated estate planning strategies that insurance agents used to justify their biggest sales. And this was a *very* big case that I was working on now.

"I've always wondered why insurance salesmen never have young groupies hanging around begging for sex, the way rock stars do," Hal told us with a wink. He sat down carefully with the air of a man who was never quite sure the chair would hold his weight. "What do they have that I haven't got?"

"Compiling a complete list might take at least a week," Mort told him. "And anyway, we have a mission. We have to decide if Adam here is or is not totally crazy."

"About what?"

"He hasn't told me yet."

The waitress brought Hal some kind of a clear fluid in a tall cocktail glass, and I wondered briefly how she knew what Hal wanted without any visible sign of a message between them. But Hal was known around town as an enthusiastic partier; he always had tickets to the Panther and Bobcat games in Charlotte, and spent more time outside the office than in it, playing golf or hanging around this or that upscale club. It was how he marketed himself. He told me once that in his business, whoever spends the most time in the office is most likely to have the worst sales numbers. The last time he invited me to one of his customer appreciation parties, there had been a high school marching band in the parking lot, and everybody was looking forward to the private fireworks display.

"You're not going to believe this story," I said.

"Try me."

"Ten or so years ago now, an Asian gentleman walks into our offices," I said. "He looks like he slept on the sidewalk. Because of the frumpy way he dresses and the old beat up car he parks in our lot out back, and the $20,000 that he wants to invest, none of the other brokers are willing to let him within ten feet of their offices. So of course the receptionist brings him in to me, because I'm known around the office as the garbage man, no customer too small for me to offer my services."

"$20,000 in cash?" Mort asked.

"It was in a checking account, and yes, I thought that was a little funny. But he tells me in a thick Chinese accent that he has saved nearly all of his income all of his life and he would like me to give him some advice on how to invest this money. And for some reason, he also wanted to know how to transfer ownership of property at his death to his two daughters and his son—which I assumed was a house somewhere. He asked about the estate tax, and I assured him that this wouldn't be a problem with *his* estate, but he wanted to know, he told me, in case he suddenly were to become wealthy. So I spent some time explaining the estate tax system. I told him about a will, but he seemed unwilling to go through the probate process. So I told him about living trusts, and how he could put whatever he owned into a trust where he was the trustee, and he could make his heirs the successor trustees, and when he died they would take over managing the assets in trust, which was, I said, functionally the same as owning them. No public documents, no probate, no muss, no fuss, have a good life because I'll probably never hear from you again.

"And I didn't," I said, "for ten years."

"About a month ago, I got a call from this man's personal assistant. Turns out that he has a few more dollars than he was letting on. In fact, he happens to be the sole shareholder of a private holding company that owns or controls real estate all over Western North Carolina and on up into Tennessee and down into South Carolina and all the way over to Atlanta. He specializes in distressed commercial properties purchased at fire sale prices, carefully nurtured back to health. Now he's in his 80s, and thinking about what would happen if he died and left what we estimate to be $685 million of low-basis real estate to his children."

Hal whistled appreciatively. "So what did you tell him?"

"That if he died the day after he called me, he would have had to sell more than half of everything he'd built up, just to pay the estate tax bill."

Mort, who had been following the story carefully, shook his head. "He's screwed. Dumping that much property on the market all at once would almost certainly have a nasty effect on local real estate prices. He might have to sell a lot more than half, and the IRS isn't known for accepting valuations that come from distressed sales."

"We've had two meetings," I continued. "In one, we went over everything he owned. In the second one, I showed him the possible cascading effect of the estate tax on his heirs, and he asked me to draft up a solution."

"And that's where you are now," said Mort.

"Sometime during the first meeting, as we were looking through all the property values and cash flow statements and everything, it suddenly dawned on me that this was my big score, my ticket out of the brokerage business," I told my two colleagues, leaning across the table. "Then, as I walked out, his assistant took me aside. "You are the only financial person he has ever talked to that he feels he can trust," he told me.

"I'm flattered," I said.

"He has an instinct about you. He told me so himself."

"And *that's* where I am now," I told the others.

"So when do you present your recommendations?" Hal wanted to know.

"It's supposed to be next Friday at nine. And now I'm having second thoughts about what I'm going to say."

My table partners exchanged a long meaningful look, and then turned back to me. "Is that your plan?" Mort asked, nodding his small chin toward the black folder on the table.

"Yes," I said.

"Let me take a wild guess here," he said. "You're going to recommend a single-pay whole life insurance policy with a face amount of $300 million."

"$330 million actually," I said. "The money goes into an irrevocable life insurance trust, and it comes out tax-free to the heirs, who can pay off the estate taxes in cash."

"That's a pretty big policy. Can you place that much?"

"The House has reinsurance lined up at Lloyds if they need to go outside. I think they'd jump at this and take it all in-house."

"So your commission would be—what? $15 million?"

"Closer to twenty," Hal said quietly. "Remember who he works for."

"And out of that, your piece of it would be, what, 40%? I assume that's enough to move you up to a 40% payout on all your gross dealer concessions."

"Yes," I said. "I go right through the schedule, from bottom to top, in one transaction."

"And what would you recommend if you were working on this account strictly on a fee basis?" Mort asked me.

"If there were no commissions involved, I'd have him transfer the properties into a family limited partnership. No tax consequences because there's no change of ownership," I added for Hal's benefit. "He'd set aside 1% of the value as the general partnership share, so he could continue to control the businesses as long as he held that piece of the pie, and we'd gift as many of the limited partnership shares as we could under the estate tax unified credit and the yearly exemptions, taking a valuation discount because the partnership shares have zero liquidity. I figure we can get a dollar forty in value transferred for every dollar's worth of shares. That's just nickels and dimes compared to the liability, but I might be able to save him a million, maybe two in estate taxes, depending on when he dies."

Mort nodded impatiently. "So how would you solve his real problem?" he asked.

"From there on, I'd watch his health," I said. "If he dies in 2010, there's no estate tax and no problem, and passing the whole thing on to the heirs doesn't cost him a dime. If he died in any year before or after that, we'd at least get the step-up in basis so there wouldn't be any capital gains taxes, and I'd roll over the remaining FLP shares out of the estate into a series of charitable lead trusts, where the charity would receive income from the trust for 10 years on some properties, 15 years on others, 20 years on the rest. After the terms are up, the assets in the trust would pass to the children and grandchildren. In effect, the businesses would be paying the estate taxes to a charity, and there would never be any discontinuation of ownership or control."

"Did you actually run these numbers?" Mort asked me.

"Six different ways. Not in there," I added, nudging the folder.

"And if you elected to show him Plan B, how much would you charge him?"

"In fees? Maybe I could justify $50,000 to organize everything. $50,000 compared with a little over $7 million in commission payout. Can you see why I'm sweating?"

"I'm wondering why you're even *thinking* of presenting Plan B," Hal said, munching reflectively on his sandwich. "If he buys the life insurance policy, there's no uncertainty about the outcome. The choice is between a lot of fiddling and maybes, or else locking down the inheritance for his heirs right here, right now."

Mort scribbled on his napkin. "I'd have to get back to the office and boot up the spreadsheet to be sure of this," he said. "But it looks to me like if he dies anywhere within the next four years, then the numbers just might come out ahead for him—or his heirs. But if he lives any longer than that, The House makes a huge windfall that very quickly becomes enormous. Heads, he wins a little, tails they win a lot, and they pay you a bunch of money to get people to make this kind of bet."

"Nobody but you and I and Hal know that," I said.

"And if the estate tax is repealed permanently, or if he dies in 2010, then I think the heirs have actual grounds for a lawsuit against you. They'd be out at least $100 million in totally unnecessary premiums."

Hal snorted. "You show me heirs who are going to sue you after receiving a $330 million life insurance settlement," he said.

"That's only because they don't understand the alternatives."

"Do you think they'd *care*? How much can they spend in one lifetime?"

"He has a point," I said.

"That's no point at all. Just because they have more than they can spend is no reason or excuse to confiscate some of it."

"What I want to know is, are the technical details right?" I persisted.

"On the life insurance side, I'm impressed with it," Hal said, tipping an imaginary hat to me. "It's pretty much exactly how I'd recommend he do things."

"Look," Mort said, laying his napkin aside and leaning across to me. "This is so unlike you that it scares me a little. What's going on? Why are you even thinking about this?"

"I'm leaving The House," I said. "I just wanted to make a little money before I left."

"You have more than a million in deferred compensation."

"They keep moving the vesting date on me. I'm beginning to think that the money doesn't really exist except as a piece of paper to keep us working at The House."

"He may be right," Hal conceded. "I've known people who've worked in the Charlotte office for a lot longer than he has, and they haven't seen a dime of actual money."

"So you just have to screw one person, and you'll be free of their clutches," Mort said, bearing down on me.

"I want to get out of the business and retire," I said. "If I'm retired, I can call my customers and tell them anything I want to, and The House doesn't have any recourse. I can send them all in your direction."

"Can't you just change careers? I don't understand what you want the money for. You've never been motivated by money."

"It's not for me," I said.

"Who then?"

Hal and Mort leaned forward a little to hear my answer.

"I've always felt like I gave up my relationship with my daughter Karen to work for The House," I said finally, "and I always told myself that I'd make it up to her, that it was worth doing because of the money I was going to make eventually. But I never made it. So I just want to give her something so that when she gets out of college, she has some options."

"If you give her a certain amount of money, then you'll feel like you're even?" Surprisingly, it was Hal who said this. He watched me closely.

"Yes."

"That's pretty damn ridiculous," Hal snorted indulgently. "But I think I understand exactly what you mean."

"I think it's *completely* ridiculous," said Mort. "Just spend a little more time with her and catch up with all the things that you missed."

"It's too late. She won't talk to me."

"What?"

"Whenever I call her at school, her friends say they're not even supposed to tell her that I called. She doesn't answer my letters."

"Don't you pay her tuition?"

"Yes. But it's only one more semester."

"So what, exactly, is she so pissed off at you about?" Mort asked me. "What did you *do* to each other?"

For a long second I didn't say anything. "It's not important," I said finally.

"Sounds like it's important to her," Mort said quietly.

"I didn't say it wasn't important to us. It's just not important that I tell you what happened. Let's just say that I screwed up at the wrong time in a very big way. I'm not even sure it can be repaired."

Mort looked at me for a long moment, while the waitress brought the check, without any visible signal, to Hal. Finally Mort pushed the folder back over to my side of the table with an expression of profound distaste.

"You want to know what I think?" he said finally. "I think until today, you were the only ethical, responsible person at that humongous evil company you work for. Now I think you're one of them, and I hope to hell you *do* retire before you do any more damage."

Hal just winked at me. "Welcome to the club," he said.

As I stood up from the table, my cell phone buzzed in my pocket. I groped for it clumsily. I've never learned how to pull one of those contraptions gracefully from my pocket, without either hanging up or taking so long that the answering message kicks in.

"Yes?"

"Where the hell are you?" Heavy Hitter's voice growled.

"I'm eating lunch."

"Like hell you are."

"Really. Why? What do you need?"

"Get your ass over to the office as fast as you can. We need to talk."

I was about to utter a meek "Okay," but the connection was broken before I had the chance.

As I parked my car in the lower lot, Heavy Hitter stepped out of a car, followed by two other men who were strangers to me. I had the odd impression that I had seen one of those other men before, but before I could speculate further, Heavy Hitter blocked my path, his face churning with anger, and I tried to control the trembling in my arms and legs.

"What the hell is this?" he demanded angrily, thrusting a purple leaflet so close to my face that it was impossible to make out anything more than the color.

"It's an invitation to—"

"I know that. Does he think I can't read?" Heavy Hitter demanded sarcastically of the other men, whose facial expressions did not change. "What I want to know is what you're going to do about it."

"I've actually been thinking about that. I thought maybe if we could delay the closing—"

Heavy Hitter turned with elaborate incredulity back to the other men, holding the leaflet above his head in a gesture of surrender.

"He wants to delay the closing," Heavy Hitter repeated. The two laughed heartily at this very funny idea, but the colors of their auras never deviated from a menacing red.

"It's just a week," I protested.

"I wonder," Heavy Hitter pondered aloud, "whether anybody, ever, in the entire history of the world, screwed up as completely and totally as you have here."

For some time now, the voice inside me had been pointing out the obvious, that I was powerless, helpless, once again incompetent to control the details of my own life. A flood of unpleasant memories hovered at the edge of my awareness, and at the sight of them, I capitulated, and looked up at one of the nation's greatest stockbrokers with genuine contrition and shame.

"I'm sorry," I said. I felt all the strength leaving my body.

Heavy Hitter nodded sympathetically. "There's nothing in your history with The House that suggests that you would have been capable of handling even a small role in one of my deals," he said.

"So what are we going to do?" one of the other men spoke up.

Heavy Hitter put his arm around my shoulders. "We overestimated him," he said. "And that's *my* fault, not his. Now we need to help him, and give him a chance to fix the mess he's made of things."

"What if he doesn't want to help us?" the vaguely familiar stranger asked.

"You want that chance, don't you?" Heavy Hitter said to me, squeezing my shoulders in a gesture of companionship.

I winced in pain. "Can you tell me why we can't wait a week?" I asked timidly.

"No," Heavy Hitter assured me cheerfully. "Now tell me, did you know that this—" he consulted the leaflet that was still in his hand—"spiritual master is in trouble with the law?"

"No," I said. "Is that really true? I mean—"

"To be specific," said the vaguely familiar face, "he's been accused of eleven counts of vagrancy, at least one count of destruction of property, plus solicitation of minors."

"I had no idea," I said. "Why don't they arrest him?"

"Yes." Heavy Hitter turned to the man who had spoken. "Why *don't* you arrest him?"

"We don't know what he looks like," the man grunted, and I realized suddenly where I had seen him before. He was the city police commissioner, and I had seen him from time to time on local TV news.

"So now you see how you can help us to help you," Heavy Hitter continued.

"I do?"

"There are a bunch of kids in there under the spell of a criminal, and all we need to do is find the criminal, get him out of circulation, and release the others back to their lives. That, by the way, is all George was trying to do. He told me you were an enormous help."

"George was working for *you*?"

"We're all working for each other," Heavy Hitter assured me with another painful squeeze of the shoulders. "Some of us just can't seem to get out of the way."

I thought about Fool and Cassandra and the others. The idea that they were under the spell of anyone with untrustworthy motives raised a powerful protective instinct in me. I wanted to help them. But I had seen so many remarkable things that a part of my mind refused to accept the version of reality that Heavy Hitter offered. I felt that I should disobey his wishes, and the feeling filled me with fear and exhilaration. I saw the change come over my spirit, and imagined with a pang of nervousness that they could see it too.

I steadied myself and looked at the ground.

"What can I do to help?" I asked.

"*That's* the right attitude," Heavy Hitter said encouragingly, giving me a sharp slap on the back.

The police commissioner touched my hand in an oddly tender gesture. "Have you met this spiritual master?" he asked.

"No," I said.

"He's too smart for that," said the other stranger. "I've been on his tail ever since he captured my son. He never leaves a footprint."

"Do you think you could *get* a chance to meet him?" the police commissioner persisted. "After all, he's living in your building."

"I might be able to," I said.

"Good. That's all we need. Sometime before Sunday evening, see if you can get close enough to touch his shoulder."

"What?"

The police commissioner reached into his pocket and pulled out a small bag of what looked like yellow powder.

"Sunday night, we're going to surround the place with a team of professionals," he said. "They'll be shining ultraviolet flashlights into the warehouse, looking for whoever has this powder on his shoulder. It will set off a glow, so they'll instantly know which of the people in the dark room is this spiritual leader, and get a fix on him before he can slip through our fingers again."

"That's all you want me to do?" I said. "Identify who he is for you?"

Something about the police commissioner's face told me that this was not a small favor he was asking. "You do the job," he said finally, "and then my best advice to you is to stay the hell away from there."

"I understand," I said, and I did.

VIII

There will never be a New Age scripture, or New Age dogma—or, for that matter, a New Age manifesto, because the spirit that animates the New Age movement is a core humility about what we know and what we can know. One of the few things we can say with certainty is that we mortals will never be able to know the Real Truth; all we can do is explore the possibilities and get better at determining what helps us in the journey, and recognize that what helps one person may be irrelevant to the journey of another. There is no final destination in our learning or in our lives; only a journey which, if we are fortunate and diligent, will keep taking us to better places.

Even if some distant generation of our children's children were to finally reach the horizons of what we imagine now and become what some call God, there is a high probability that in that moment when they understand everything about this universe, they will raise their eyes and see an infinite multiverse, each with infinite mysteries. And they will realize that they have reached a milestone on a road that truly goes on forever.
—From The Rutherfordton Spiritual Gazette

Karen, before I leave on my journey, I hope I'll get the chance to tell you something very important: the way I felt about the world when I was your age. I know that when you look at our society, you see a million problems, injustices, dysfunctional institutions, government officials and representatives who are indifferent and sometimes hostile to the will of the common person, police who defend the rich and bully the helpless, and everywhere people voluntarily living lives with diminished hope, promise, dignity or joy.

Do you remember when I volunteered to coach your soccer team, when you were 11 years old, and you helped me pick out the players who would be on our team, and I told you that my plan was to have *you* coach the team, because I thought you would be much better than any of the parents who had been screaming at you girls from the sidelines.

Do you remember what happened? Suddenly, all of you girls were playing for yourselves, for the fun of the game, and there were no coaches yelling at you, threatening to take you out of the game if you didn't follow their prescribed orders. You created a system where everybody played an equal amount of time no matter what the score was, everybody played the position they wanted to play, you created drills for the practices that you thought would help the team get better, and while the other teams were getting screamed at and controlled, your team went out and played your hearts out while I walked around on the sidelines making sure none of the other parents interfered with your decisions. You girls won every game that year, including two scrimmages over the boys, and I will always believe that was the best-coached team in the history of that little soccer league.

People will tell you that when you get older, you will see why things have to be the way they are. They will tell you that with more maturity, you will finally begin to understand why these unhappy things are inevitable and therefore right.

But today, with your young eyes, you can see what is possible, and what is very very wrong, more clearly than you ever will again. And you can see that so much of what people do is about control, even if having that control takes away motivation and takes away authority from the people who know best what should be done.

Karen, remember forever the way you see things today, and always try to see the world with fresh eyes, even as you get older and all the imperfections of our culture and society become more familiar.

When I was your age, I saw the world with the same clarity. Like many people of that age and time, I promised myself that we would do many things so that our children would live in a better, freer, cleaner, safer, happier world. And now, as I move into the shadow of retirement age, I realize that I have done nothing, personally, to fulfill those promises.

And I do not want you to wake up one morning and feel the same way that I do.

That morning, as I drove up into the lot, I saw an odd sight. A bulky man dressed in a black turtleneck, his hair in a long white ponytail, was peering into my windshield as I parked.

"Are you Adam Zakar?" he asked as I got out of the car. He had a square face with a strong jaw, and a large moustache that hung down at the sides and made him look vaguely like a walrus. The eyes were at once earnest and disturbingly cold.

In a moment, he was joined by two other men, both in business suits. One of them carried a briefcase. His face had settled into a years-old grimace, and I could see from his spirit that he suffered from ulcers. The other was younger, his hand fingering a narrow goatee, and I could see by his spirit that he was an architect of some sort.

"I'm sorry," the older man said again, gesturing with his hands in a way that would have communicated his apology even if he hadn't spoken. "This is most awkward. You must be Mr. Zakar. I am told that you are inevitably the first person in the office. My name is Armand DiStefano. These," he said, waving his arms grandly, "are my associates. Mr. Caves is an architect out of Charlotte, and Mr. Havender is my legal representative."

Caves and Havender nodded at me, and I nodded back warily.

"If it wouldn't be too much trouble," DiStefano said, "We'd like to take you to breakfast."

"I have to get to work," I said.

"It might be worth your while to listen to what we have to say."

"About what?"

"About 75 River Street," said DiStefano. "And a potential profit of more than a million dollars."

Five minutes later, we were settled into stuffed living room chairs at the back of the Bean Streets Cafe, which for my money serves the best coffee in the city. The two associates seemed uncomfortable with the bohemian atmosphere, but DiStefano leaned back appreciatively and looked around as if he owned the place.

"All we know is that you're now the owner of a property that we've been trying to buy from Zanto Industries for—what? Three years?" DiStefano looked at his attorney for confirmation, and the other nodded. "In fact," he continued, somehow pantomiming the words with his hands, "you managed to buy the place for about $700,000 less than our last offer. You're quite a negotiator, Mr. Zakar."

"I do my best," I said.

"Actually, we're pretty sure you're just a conduit," the lawyer spoke up.

"Conduit?" I said.

DiStefano gave the attorney a severe look and then leaned forward as the architect brought us our drinks from the front. He clasped his hands and then opened them in a gesture of trust that was not visible on his spirit.

"Please understand that my investment group represents some very important people, and we take our responsibilities very seriously," he said. "My attorney has a theory that the president of the company wants to buy that property for himself," DiStefano continued, a quick flip of his hands conveying his contempt for this behavior. "But of course if he purchased it directly from his own company, it would raise all sorts of questions. Like why the company would sell to a corporate officer for less than it could get from an outside buyer. That's a confusing way to look out for the interests of the shareholders, don't you think?"

"We told them we thought the SEC might be interested," the lawyer put in quickly. "Suddenly, next thing we know, they'd found you to take it off their hands."

I opened my mouth to tell them that the transaction was really a ploy to temporarily dress up the company's balance sheet, and then shut it again. That would be an even bigger problem with the SEC. And Heavy Hitter was perfectly capable of exactly what they were talking about. How did I know what the truth was?

In my confusion, it finally occurred to me to look closely at the spirits of these men, and when I did, the information was not reassuring. The outside investors were some kind of foreign cartel, which sent DiStefano around the country to find ways to recycle millions of dollars paid for cocaine and other illicit narcotics into legitimate investments. I saw that he was involved in a dozen projects like this in different cities. So far, this was the only one where he had run into serious obstacles.

I also saw that he carried a semiautomatic revolver.

I looked up into DiStefano's eyes. His spirit now radiated an ominous darkness, the color of danger.

"What do you want the place *for*?" I asked finally. "Why would anybody want it?"

The three men looked at each other, and DiStefano nodded. "Show him," he said, and his hands pulled an imaginary document in front of my eyes.

Slowly, the architect reached into a notebook and pulled out a thick piece of paper, which he carefully unfolded to four times its size. He spread it out over the magazines on the small table between us.

"This is a development plan along the east side of the river, DiStefano told me, his finger tracing what appeared to be a long avenue on the edge of the blue ribbon along the far side of the map, a river walk along the shore, with multistory buildings behind it. "This is going to be a hotel. And these, here, here and here are restaurants. And here," he said, touching my property, which at the moment was blank, "is to become a mixed-use development whose heart is luxury condominiums, four minutes by car from all the downtown amenities."

The river walk stopped abruptly at the blank space and resumed on the other side, which suggested the importance of my warehouse building. On the development plan, there were two contiguous holes between everything else. The other one was right next door.

"What about Ms. Moore?" I asked.

The three exchanged looks.

"You know her?" the lawyer asked me.

"Not really."

"She's a very stubborn lady," DiStefano observed. "It's a thing I admire, personally, although I have to confess that our investor group has become very impatient with her, and they think we are perhaps too...*unpersuasive* in our negotiations. But we think she'll come around. We haven't found her price yet. Which brings me to you," he added, leaning forward toward me. "My attorney here thinks you may be under contract to sell this property to a Mr. Bonnefield, president of Zanto Industries, for a price lower than what we're willing to pay. Me, I tell him that if such a contract ever came to light, as it surely would in an investigation by interested regulatory bodies, the whole arrangement would stink like a week-old fish. A flagrant example of—what do you call it?"

"Self-dealing," the attorney said. "By insiders. Looting company assets."

"But now that I've had a chance to sit down and talk with you," DiStefano continued, resting his hand lightly on my arm, "I can see that you are not the sort of person who would be involved in such a thing. I am reassured that you will listen to us with an open mind, and I will communicate that to our impatient investors."

"Thank you," I said.

"The offer we want to make to you is $3.65 million, for the property, the building, everything. I believe that's a little over $1 million more than you paid for it."

"Actually we think it's $1.15 million more, which is why we propose splitting the closing costs," said Havender the attorney.

"That's very generous," I said.

"Think nothing of it," said DiStefano with a careless wave of his hand. "Do we have a deal?"

"I'd like to think about it," I said, standing up.

"We understand you have friends presently living in the building," Havender the attorney said.

"Yes," I said.

"Have they signed any kind of a lease with you? How long before you can move them out?"

"That's one thing I need to find out," I said.

"As far as we're concerned, there is no hurry about evicting these people," said DiStefano. The attorney opened his mouth, but DiStefano waved him off. "I understand that they are planning some kind of rally down there," he added. "If you don't mind, I would like to attend, and see for myself what these people are like."

"I have no objection," I said, after trying hard to think of one.

The attorney stood up and handed me a business card. "Call me. The sooner the better," he said.

Karen, I thought that my day could not possibly get any worse. But when I walked into the office and turned on my computer, I discovered that a basket of 30 stocks called the Dow Jones Industrial Averages had lost 4% so far on the trading day. That means that if you had invested $1,000 in these stocks, you would have $960 of your money remaining, which to me is not quite as terrible as, say, a global nuclear disaster or an outbreak of civil war in China. But if you had listened to CNBC or CNNfn that day, you would have thought the entire world was about to collapse.

So, because of the vexing influence of newspeople who report white noise as if it was an omen of catastrophe, a few of my friends and customers had panicked and telephoned our offices, and now I had to call them back and reassure them all over again that a one-day drop was not something they should worry about.

Meanwhile, the dip had caused a more serious kind of panic internally at The House. The house account—the investments in the market that The House makes directly for its own profit—had lost value much more dramatically than the market as a whole. Part of the problem was that The House had been required to unwind its positions in several complicated derivatives transactions with two large pension plans, while neither admitting nor denying that the sales had been fraudulent from the start.

This, alone, would not have been such a big deal, but as a result of this and other scandals of the past, reporters began asking whether the company was actually holding shares of the companies that its analysts were recommending. To avoid any more bad publicity, The House's traders apparently *had* loaded up on the stocks its analysts were telling the world to buy, with disastrous results that were not totally unpredictable.

The shocking losses in the house account represented a doubly nasty black eye for The House, first because it meant that the company would have to report negative earnings on its balance sheet, and also (more importantly) because our brokers always point to the high returns The House makes on its own investments as evidence that The House really is smarter than the market. I used to believe this myself, until I noticed that whenever The House's analysts found evidence of trouble in one of the stocks the company had invested in, immediately a message would go out for all of us brokers to recommend this troubled stock to our customers before they, too, were informed of these troubles. This gave The House a wonderful chance to dump its losers at a premium on investors who thought they were getting a hot tip.

A joke that is told often in the hallways of The House's offices all over the world is that the ideal investment is one that would benefit the customer, The House and the broker, all at the same time.

Here is the punchline: Well, two out of three ain't bad.

I was on the phone with yet another customer when Jill appeared at my door. I took a long look at her spirit, but the baby wasn't anywhere to be found.

"How did you know?" she asked.

"Know what?"

"That I needed an abortion."

"I didn't say you needed an abortion. If I had known that was the way you felt, I wouldn't have said anything."

"As it happens, you saved me some money. You can do it with pills if you catch it soon enough. But that wasn't my question."

"You just had that glow about you," I said.

"Like hell."

"Call it male intuition."

"Well did your male intuition tell you that you forgot you were supposed to meet with the Branch Manager today?"

The truth was, I *had* forgotten. Not that these meetings were unusual; chewing me out for my low production numbers had become a tired ritual between me and the Branch Manager over the years, and I wondered why he didn't just tell me how much of a slacker I am every morning and not waste any further time and energy on me.

I knocked on his door, and he waved me to a seat. A sign behind his desk said: "Happiness can't buy money." There was an impressive-looking array of framed diplomas hung along one side of the wall, but if you looked at them closely, you'd discover that they were all certificates of graduation from various in-house sales training programs at The House.

"You don't have any obligation to give him a break," the Branch Manager barked into the phone. I surmised that he was talking with a counselor at the business that he maintained on the side. In form and filings with the state, the side business was a nonprofit consumer credit counseling service, and the Branch Manager had been lauded more than once in the local newspapers for his charitable activities there.

What they didn't know was that the service had been founded as a joint venture with the credit card organizations, and was really a collection agency in disguise. Its ubiquitous radio advertisements brought in people who were in severe debt, its counselors always strongly advised them to avoid declaring bankruptcy, and the company always charged a hefty fee to create a workout plan with the credit card issuer. On the other side, the counseling service would receive as much as 40% of what was collected from the debtor from— you guessed it—the grateful credit card companies, who would stand to collect much less if the debtor couldn't be talked out of filing for bankruptcy protection.

It was an incredible money machine, and of course, the bounty from the credit card issuers was never disclosed to the people who were teetering on the edge of financial ruin.

Although the organization was structured as a nonprofit, it paid millions of dollars a year in "salaries" to the Branch Manager and the partner who actually ran the operation, and the "salaries" always happened to equal the net revenues collected by the nonprofit that year. I often wondered why the federal or state organizations that regulate charities never caught onto this scheme, but had finally concluded that this was not a high priority for them.

"It seems to me, all you have to do is stretch out the payments a little bit and they'll back off of the advice this attorney is giving them," the Branch Manager concluded. "Don't let them out of the office until they've signed something. Lock the doors if you have to. Okay?"

He hung up the phone and offered me a resigned smile. "Some arms you have to twist a little harder than others," he said.

"You've been practicing on me for 21 years," I said.

"Has it really been that long? You're like some kind of fixture around here now, you realize that?"

I was surprised and wary at his cheerful tone. The normal routine was for the Branch Manager to get out my monthly production numbers and yell at me that they were unacceptable, and that he would have long ago fired me if I hadn't been such an effective garbage man. Then he would threaten to fire me, and brimstone would drip off of his tongue, and I would go back to work thinking that maybe variable annuities are not such a terrible thing to recommend after all.

But now he was polite, friendly even. "We just got new guidelines from the home office on production levels," he said. "They're really targeting people who refused to do their share for the house account, and the market thing this morning didn't sweeten their mood."

"I saw the numbers," I said.

"You know that we've bent over backwards to help you meet your quotas."

I did not say that they have offered me every opportunity to screw my customers for the benefit of The House. I simply nodded my head.

"I could never understand how you could live on the money you make here."

"I do all right."

"Nevertheless, I can't ignore the fact that you're no longer meeting our numbers. Even if I was inclined to do it, the home office has made it clear that I can make no more exceptions."

"Is there anything in their formula about benefiting the customer?" I asked him. "Is that something that anybody around here even tracks?"

"I think you know the answer to that as well as I do." The branch manager sat back in his chair and smiled at me, a warm, friendly smile that was ghastly in its manipulative power and insincerity. "Somehow, I haven't ever been able to make you see that there has to be a balance in every customer relationship," he added. "Yes, of course we want them to benefit; anybody who looks at our TV advertisements can see that. But we also need to earn something for our trouble."

"So far this year, I've generated $150,000 worth of aggregate revenues to the company," I said defensively. "That more than pays for the office space that I occupy."

"Yes," the Branch Manager said. "This has been your best year ever. But I'm prepared to make it even better."

"Better how," I said warily.

"As a reward for all the hard work you put in for all these years, The House is prepared to offer you a new position here, one which I think you'll find is much better suited to your talents."

I stared at him. "What position."

"We're going to do what we should have done a long time ago," the Branch Manager said with a smile. "We're going to take you out of sales and production altogether, and make you our office customer service representative. Your job will be to periodically call our customers, see to it that they're happy with the service they're getting, that we know and document their risk tolerance, that they know that their business is important to us, sniff out whether there are angry customers who might be about to file against one of the brokers here—that sort of thing. It will give us a chance to leverage the skills of the other brokers here in the office. I think you'll agree that it's a waste of talent for Heavy Hitter to be tending to all these details."

The cruel irony of the situation sank in on me. Just as I was about to close the biggest deal of my career, and generate enough money to finally leave this place, they were going to pull me out of production. Why now?

Then, suddenly, I realized why.

"This is about what Venus did to Heavy Hitter, isn't it?" I said, already reading it on his spirit. "He's got to take it out on somebody, and since I brought her into the office—"

"This was purely a business decision," the Branch Manager said, his smile going away.

"Then why not just fire me?" I demanded. "Why give me the job I would have killed for twenty years ago—"

And then I saw it. I saw the nature of the punishment in all its cruel glory.

"What about my book of customers?" I said quietly. "Who's going to be giving *them* investment recommendations?"

"The other brokers, of course." Here, the Branch Manager's face broke into a broad grin, and his aura fairly glowed with a brilliant darkness as he saw that I had finally recognized the odious thing that he was doing. "I've looked at your book very carefully last night and this morning," he said. "Really the first time I've looked for years, and it made interesting reading. Do you realize that you now have 23 customers with portfolios of more than a million dollars? And not a one of them, when they first walked in the door, would I have recommended we take on as a customer. Some of them didn't have a dime to their name."

"Yes," I said. "I know this. I didn't realize that you did."

"Each of these people became wealthy," said the Branch Manager. "And The House never got its share of it. If I didn't know better, I'd think you were hoping to hide these people from me."

Karen, I can't explain how much, at that moment, I hated the man in front of me. I actually thought of standing up and shouting at him, and walking out, but the wiser voice inside told me that I couldn't fight these people. The feelings were utterly familiar, a theme of my life: I felt angry and violated and told myself that I was completely impotent to do anything about it. I had nowhere to go and no hope of fighting, and so I swallowed it as best I could and tried to argue with a person who had no interest in me or my arguments.

"Are you saying that I cheated the company by helping these people reach financial independence?"

"I'm saying that too much of their money went back into their own pockets, and I need to do something about it," the Branch Manager said evenly.

"I don't see how I could do that," I said.

"Of course you don't," the Branch Manager said. He leaned back in his chair, and his glow was darkly triumphant, which my mind translated as an impossible combination of dark red and dark green. "I wasn't sure if you realized that you were the problem," he continued, drawing his words out for effect. "But you shouldn't worry. There are plenty of other people around here who know *exactly* what needs to be done."

"I'll keep them happy while the other brokers in the office fill their portfolios with expensive worthless junk, and undo everything I've done for them," I said bitterly. I stood up. "No deal. Not for a million dollars."

There was a long silence in the room, and the longer it went on, the more my fear of the Branch Manager swallowed my anger. By the time the Branch Manager deigned to speak again, I felt hopeless and weak.

"I think it would be wise for you to recognize that this is an opportunity for you to earn a salary equal to what you were making on the sales side, without having to scratch for commissions," the Branch Manager finally said. "The House is offering you a guaranteed income and relatively simple duties."

"I'll have to think it over," I said, wondering how long I could stall for time. If I could just close the one life insurance sale, then this smelly deal would be irrelevant. They'd *have* to credit me with the sale, perhaps in my last commission check.

"Can you give me a week to think it over?"

"I'll give you the weekend, and if you agree, we'll make the transition first thing Tuesday morning," the Branch Manager said with a note of finality in his voice, which told me that I was dismissed for now. "But I have to warn you, no matter what you decide, I'm already deep in the paperwork of reassigning your accounts."

I walked back down the hall in a daze. What was I going to do? I knew the drill; whenever a broker had the audacity to leave The House, The House would take out a temporary restraining order forbidding that broker from contacting any of his or her customers—who were, The House's army of lawyers would argue, property of The House. They seldom won these cases (how can customers be property?), but the restraining order kept the representative away from the customers long enough for the Branch Manager to assign them to one of the other guys in the office.

Meanwhile, the new broker would call the customer and ask questions which would strongly imply that the disloyal representative had been embezzling money from his or her accounts, and would ask about what was in the accounts and if they had noticed anything suspicious.

Long before the end of the conversation, the customer would be relieved that the new broker had saved him or her from the scandalous clutches of the old broker. The new broker would close with an apology about the sloppy service, promising that he, personally, would make sure no such shenanigans ever happened again.

By the time the restraining order had been lifted and the judge had ruled that the customers were not the property of anybody, the relationship between the old representative and his customers would have been fatally poisoned, and The House would have them back in its fold. It was an ugly process, and I had no desire to see my clients suddenly in the hands of Heavy Hitter and his crowd.

I fought the emotional tide going on in my body, trying to think, discarding one improbable idea after another, finally settling on one if only because it kept my hopes alive.

There was a lot to do.

My first call, on the office phones, was to The Big Score. Suddenly I needed to close his deal in a hurry. Over the weekend, if possible.

I reached his secretary on the first call, and discovered that it was *not* possible. "He's not going to be back in town until Sunday night," he said. "And his schedule is somewhat crowded on Monday. No, nothing in the morning. One o'clock at the earliest. If you'll come here to the office, I think I can squeeze you in."

With a sinking feeling in the pit of my stomach, I suddenly realized that Monday was the same day I was supposed to do the closing on selling the warehouse. There was no way I could get through the presentation, get the paperwork started and then make it back to the office by 2:00. I felt trapped, like a claustrophobic person squeezed into a tight place deep underground.

"Can't we do it any earlier?" I asked forlornly. "Say, at noon?"

"I wish I could accommodate you. If you cannot meet him at one, then it will have to be on Friday."

I stared without seeing at the walls of the building. I was looking at $150,000 versus more than $7 million. Heavy hitter's priority or mine.

The wiser voice inside told me that I was being selfish, and risking my career for nothing. For a long second, I fought the almost-overpowering urge to subordinate my own wishes for the needs of my stronger co-workers.

I took a long breath, and remembered the sign in the branch manager's office.

They almost had me, but not quite.

"I'll be there at one," I said.

I hung up the phone. Then, trying to ignore the loud voice of my own misgivings echoing around in the background of my mind, I connected my Palm into the computer and downloaded every active client's name and telephone number. I was surprised to see that there were 119 names in there. For a moment, I considered adding their e-mail addresses, but finally decided against it. I didn't want to leave an electronic paper trail.

Then I gathered up the Big Score's estate planning documents and other assorted papers and walked down to the lobby and through the glass doors and out into the sunlight. I called the first name on my list.

"Hi, Cindy?" I told her who I was and asked her about her son. We talked about the restaurant I had helped her start up five years ago, which was starting to become popular after years of red ink and empty tables. Finally I got to the point.

"Cindy, I need you to listen to me very carefully. You're going to get a call from one of the other brokers in The House, maybe Tuesday, no later than the end of next week, and they're going to say that I've been reassigned. I could get fired for saying this to you, but I want you to do yourself a big favor. Do not trust this person. Do not follow his advice or recommendations, no matter how plausible they sound, until you have called me that evening, on this number, and asked me what I think about it. Do you understand what I'm saying?"

"I think so, yes. Do you mind telling me what this is all about?"

"They think I—or The House—is not making enough money on you. And they're planning to fix that in a hurry."

"My God—I see why this could get you fired. And…I'm grateful that you're willing to keep giving me advice like this."

"Just promise me."

"I promise," she said. "But I do have a question."

"What."

"You don't trust these people, and yet you still work there. Why?"

"I'm wondering the same thing myself," I said, and hung up before she could ask me any more questions.

I took a deep breath.

Only 118 more to go.

IX

In this early stage, a small number of people are just beginning to explore the energy body and nontraditional healing, and the progress has come mostly from trial-and-error. In the scientific world, it is taken for granted that for every discovery, there are countless failures that eliminate blind alleys and expose false ideas. Yet those who want to protect the status quo have made it seem as if all the failed ideas and proposals and experiments are the true picture of the so-called New Age.

But if the New Age has to answer for the many ideas that ultimately had to be abandoned, then let us give it full credit for those that are powerfully alive: meditation, acupuncture, healing massage, kya therapy and diffusion work, muscle testing, maintaining a positive mental outlook in healing, regular nutritional supplements for body maintenance and the idea of holistic health itself—all ideas which have emerged out of the New Age culture to be either embraced or seriously examined by the medical community.

The real truth is that science is slowly catching up to the facts on the ground, and history has shown that you don't always have to understand how something works in order to have it work for you.

—From *The Rutherfordton Spiritual Gazette*

I called people all that afternoon, one after another, but nobody was there. I reached answering machine after answering machine, left message after message, until my voice felt hoarse and my throat rasped. By dusk, when I normally would have been leaving the office, I realized that I still had 25 more to go, and none of the people I called so far had returned my urgent messages.

My policy is to never call my clients at dinner time, so I sat on my back porch with an untouched scotch and soda in front of me, staring at the silhouette of mountains against the orange glory of the setting sun. I willed the phone to ring. I asked God, and then demanded of God for just one person to call me back so I could give the warning, so I would have some hope that my brave feelings of just a few hours ago had some, however tiny, basis in reality. And then I confronted the silliness of me trying to order around the Awareness of the Universe. What did my problems matter, compared with the vastness of the cosmos?

The phone sat inert on the table in front of me.

Gradually, as the darkness closed over the forest behind the house, I faced the full reality of my situation for the first time. I was trapped. I couldn't sell the building back to Heavy Hitter because if I did, DiStefano's lawyer would send damning information to the various regulatory authorities, I would be charged with participating in a sham transaction, and The House would protect Heavy Hitter and use the full force of its global power to make me the scapegoat—and everybody would be glad to be rid of me.

If I sold the property to DiStefano, then Heavy Hitter would produce the contract I had signed, promising to sell the property to his customer at the agreed-upon price. I would be the subject of a lawsuit and investigations, and my brokerage career would end in disgrace.

Meanwhile, apart from everything else, The House intended to screw every one of my customers, and only a miracle would allow me to close my transaction with The Big Score before I was taken off of production. Even if I did manage to close the deal, The House would be in such an uproar over whatever happened with the property that they would probably reassign the account and put my commissions aside. In order to claim them, I would have to spend years in court and hundreds of thousands of dollars in legal fees.

And if I didn't cooperate and mark the Master, if I went completely crazy and warned Fool and Venus and Cassandra about the raid, I would be in even more trouble—as if such a thing was possible.

They had me. I turned the situation around and around in my mind as I waited for the damned phone to ring, and with each turn, my mood became more and more depressed. I knew I should go inside and go to bed, but I didn't have the energy to stand up and walk into the house.

So many times in my life I had felt hopeless, powerless, victimized by others who were stronger than me. Strip away all the details, and this was the clear pattern of my existence. Always before, I had found the willpower to get up and get on with my life. But now, I had swallowed so much humiliation that it had become an anchor in my stomach.

How could I fight Heavy Hitter, and DiStefano, and the Branch Manager, and the regulators, and the chief of police, and The House, all at once?

How could I have been so weak when Heavy Hitter put the contracts in front of me?

Why did I let Venus come with me to the office? What was I thinking?

For a long few minutes, I stared at the darkness of the trees behind the house. Then I stood up and walked to the car, and finally started the engine and drove up toward Hot Springs and just past it, to that beautiful place where, Karen, you and I used to walk when you were young, where the Appalachian Trail moves alongside the French Broad River for a couple of miles.

I parked in the dark woods, locked the car and threw the keys off into the bushes, far enough away that I couldn't hear them strike the ground. Then I walked down into the undergrowth, groping around until I found the path, following it along the side of the water until I reached the side of a tall cliff. There is a path around behind it which takes you to the top, but I never showed it to you, because I knew you would want to climb up and see out across the landscape, all the houses and farms and the course of the river for miles in either direction, and I knew that I would be frightened that you would fall off of the steep edge.

I climbed purposefully, sure-footed in the darkness, until at last, gasping a bit, I stood on a flat rocky space more than a hundred feet above the trail, looking at the distant lights of human habitation and the wavering reflection of the moon on the water.

Finally I sat down on the very edge, and at long last, I was able to experience a sense of freedom, a sense of control, a sense that there is nothing more to lose, except for one simple thing.

I looked up at the stars, dim now because of the bright moonlight, yet there were still too many to count. Would I ever look at the sky in quite the same way again? I tried to imagine the distances from where I sat to the surfaces of these scattered dots of light. The closest were trillions of miles away. On many of them, the light I was looking at had left the surface of the star long before my species existed on this planet. Beyond those, stretching out to forever, endless space, galaxies scattered like dust, more numerous than the grains of sand on a beach.

Hadn't I seen them? Or was that just a dream?

In that moment, I faced, in all its many implications, the smallness of Adam Zakar. The difference between me, sitting on the small patch of high rock, and the empty space beside me was too inconsequential to measure, too small to consider, too unimportant. And yet, somehow, this unimportant wisp of slightly-more-than-nothingness had made the mistake of attracting the attention of giants.

An hour passed, and then another. The misty air deposited a thin film of dew on my hair and clothing as I watched the moon cross the sky and disappear in the western mountains. And then, after a while, the darkness was tentatively interrupted by a faint glow on the opposite horizon. A tear ran down my face, and then another.

Soon there would simply be two empty spaces on the rock, and the universe would go on as it always had, and the giants would turn their attention elsewhere. My customers would have to learn to take care of themselves, and if they didn't manage this simple thing, I doubt the universe would notice anyway.

I stood up, feeling stiff and awkward, took a step toward the edge of the cliff, trying to see the ground in the semi-darkness below.

As soon as I leaned forward, the phone in my pocket rang. For a moment I considered leaving it in my pocket, but then it occurred to me that I could give one last bit of advice.

"Hello?" I said.

"Hi," the voice on the other end said cheerfully. "You sound like hell. Didn't you sleep tonight?"

"Who is this?" I asked, trying to keep the annoyance out of my voice. "Are you trying to sell me something?"

"You wouldn't have enough money to buy it if I was."

"Fool?"

"Mr. Commuter?"

"How the hell did you get this number?" I demanded.

"We know everything," Fool assured me. "Actually, the Master gave it to me."

"How did *he* get my number?" I demanded with exaggerated patience.

"He walks with God," Fool explained with exaggerated patience. "God lives, in addition to a lot more exciting places, in your phone."

I actually took the phone off my ear and stared at it suspiciously.

"So?" I said when it was back on the side of my head again.

"So what?"

"Is there a point to this call?"

"I think so. Yes, I'm pretty sure there is."

There was a long silence.

"Well?"

"I said yes, there is."

"What *is* the point?" I demanded.

"Don't get so riled up. I thought you'd be glad to hear from me. It's not like we talk on the phone all the time."

"Fool—"

"You could at least *pretend* you're happy I called."

"Fool—"

"After all the time we've spent together in the most intimate activities, sharing psychotropic drugs and bathing nude in the river and exorcising demons, and now you're getting riled up over nothing more than the usual pleasantries that close personal friends—"

"I'm not riled up!" I shouted into the receiver. "I just spent nine hours calling hundreds of people and none of them are calling me back, and I got chewed out by law enforcement officials, and what happened to me yesterday ranks with the worst things that have *ever* happened to anybody anywhere, and then you call and play games with a telephone number that I would never, in my right mind, have given you. And you're expecting me to be *calm* about it!??"

I snapped the phone closed and jammed it angrily back in my pocket.

"It's when things get the darkest that you always get the best news," Fool replied cheerfully. "Instead of feeling sorry for yourself, you should have realized that all this gloomy stuff was leading to something pretty damn wonderful."

Slowly, my mind numb with disbelief, I turned around. There, not ten feet behind me, sat Fool, his bland innocent face turned up at mine, a phone still on his ear. I simply looked at him, unable to make my mind work in any coherent way.

"What are you doing here?" I finally asked him through gritted teeth.

"I've been trying to tell you that the Master wants to see you. He says you should come over to the palace immediately."

I stared at Fool for a long second.

"What if I don't want to meet him?" I asked cautiously. "What if I'm too busy?"

Fool laughed. It was a long laugh, and I had the feeling that he was embellishing it a little when he started uttering deep wheezes that sounded as if he was choking to death on his own mirth.

"You know," he said finally, gasping for air, "you are the only person I ever met who can be funnier than I am."

He stood up, looked me over, and then held out his hand.

He was holding my keys. When I reached for them, he shook his head.

"You look like hell," he said. "You'd better let me drive."

The sun was not yet fully above the rim of the horizon when I squeezed under the fence and walked across the weed-strewn parking lot to the warehouse, trying to ignore Fool's constant banter.

Inside the building, the darkness was absolute. I stumbled over the threshold and stopped, afraid that I would bump into something and hurt myself.

"Anybody here?"

Silence.

"Hellooo…"

Silence.

I noticed a spiritual glow off toward the kitchen area, and after a minute there was a pale physical glow as well. I walked carefully toward the front wall, feeling my way with my feet.

Fool walked past me impatiently and poured himself a glass of Soma. He sat down and stared sourly into the screen of a laptop computer, his finger on the delete button.

"If I ever catch the person who told these e-marketers how small my breasts and penis are…" he muttered.

"So what do I do now?" I said after a minute.

"They'll be with you in a minute. They're setting up the ceremony now."

As he said that, I could hear the familiar low humming of insects, which my body recognized as the Song of the Universe. Looking back across the room, I could make out the glow of mingled spirits in a rough circle behind the nearly-completed podium, looking like the embers of a campfire. At the same time, I realized that somebody was standing alongside me, and it seemed like she had been at my side ever since I had walked through the door, although another part of my mind rejected this as impossible. The light of her aura was a strong white-golden color, so bright that it actually illuminated the room. She was examining me curiously, and I turned to face her.

"I came here to see the Master," I explained. "But of course if he's busy…"

"I am Medetrina, or so they call me here," the woman said, turning her eyes briefly from my spirit to my eyes. "We've been waiting for you. Are you prepared for the healing?"

"I think you may have a mixup here," I said cautiously. "Nobody said anything about a healing."

For a moment, the whiteness of the woman's spirit dimmed to an uncertain shade of yellow-green, and once again she scanned my spirit, from foot to head. "You do not wish the healing? Have I been misinformed?"

"It's just that I don't know what you're talking about."

"He *never* knows what anybody is talking about," said Fool. "That's his special gift."

I turned to Fool in exasperation. "Can you tell me what's going on here," I said. "Was this just a trick to lure me down here?"

"Med, here, is going to do her normal thing, which is to lead a ceremony that will cure you of The Curse—or, at least, your particular version of it. Your job is to try not to screw it up too badly, although I can tell you that most of the rest of us have more or less painful stories to tell about how *we* handled the process."

"It is necessary, if you are to meet the Master," Medetrina said in a soft anxious voice. "He, of course, will finish the ceremony."

"It's not nearly as painful as some of the more creative forms of torture, and there's hardly ever much blood," Fool added with a sly smile. "The survival rate is way up over 20%."

"I'm not sure you're helping matters," Medetrina observed mildly, taking my arm. "Please trust me," she added, looking me full in the eyes as she said it. "For our small community, there is nothing more joyful than a healing. And there is no person here who has ever regretted receiving this blessing. Or, I think, ever will."

Something in my spirit must have given assent, because her aura became a serene white again, and she drew me unresisting toward and finally into the group of seated gods and near-gods. I sat down on the floor, and almost immediately my attention was lost in the mingled interplay of holy spirit, the ghostly beauty of its aura light. It was possible to recognize people now; the brilliant purple of Apollo, the smoldering red flame of Mars, the golden light green glow of Venus, and the strange, exotic mixture, unlike any of the other spirits in its complexity, of Cassandra seated in the darkness at the back.

"Another healing," Medetrina said to the group, and there were murmurs which might have been agreement. "Another chance to help one of our own recover the potential of his human birthright. For each of us—" she was speaking to me now—"and for each person now living and for many generations in the past, there is a time in our early years when chains are forged on the spirit by an event or a series of incidents, carried out by people, orchestrated by things unseen, for the purpose of making us doubt our talents and abilities and our worth. Thus are we cursed. Thus are we denied the full power of our human potential, so that we will live unquestioningly in the servitude of parasites, and become citizens of a culture whose purpose is not to serve our species, but to feed the demons who govern our world."

"I still don't understand," I said.

"You are not alone," Medetrina observed dryly. "The question is whether you trust me, and whether I have your permission to take the chains from your spirit and cure you of The Curse. You actually do the healing yourself; all I do is show you how."

Karen, I wish you could have been standing at my side during the silence that followed, when Medetrina and everyone else looked at me. It was and always will be the most confusing, conflicted moment of my life.

I stared at this woman for a long second, and then I was no longer looking at her. I saw, in that moment, my life as it truly was.

Karen, our lives are a journey which, in the beginning, stretches ahead of you with all the unseen spiritual wealth of promise and optimism, dreams and goals and ambitions and hope, and the road from there to old age is littered with cast-off treasures that all of us have reluctantly, painfully, sometimes unknowingly left behind. There, in front of the gods and near-gods, I saw among the scattered, random debris so many things that I had confidently expected to do, so many things I had hoped to become, so many dreams and forgotten promises to so many others, to you, Karen, to your mother, most of all to myself.

I looked at my future, and saw the few tattered hopes I still harbored, set aside, one by one, by the side of that road. I saw myself silhouetted in the distance, aged, walking alone, unburdened and without illusions, and then I saw that lonely traveler fade away, and it no longer mattered, for he had nothing to offer and nothing left to give up.

Somewhere, a cricket was chirping, the last cricket of the year, because in a matter of days the frost would come. I shivered at the thought of it, and my eyes cleared and met the soft, sympathetic eyes of Medetrina, who had seen in my spirit the same things I had seen in my memories. And I saw, in her spirit, that everyone else who had stood where I was standing now had felt essentially the same way and had seen the same things about themselves, about us, about the road and the debris. Somehow, this made me feel at once a little better, and a little sadder.

Just a few hours ago, I was going to end my journey. Could this be any worse?

These people had taught me to see the glow of holy spirit. Was it really possible that they could help me go back and collect the only belongings that matter in a person's life?

I remembered the question. And now I knew that there was only one answer.

"Yes," I said.

"Tell me a story," Medetrina invited me.

Karen, to this day I do not remember the story that I told the group, because the roaring in my ears and in my mind swept away all thought except the telling itself. Even so, I know what the story was about, because it was the one that still cast its deep shadows across everything that I was. I told the story of your mother and I, of me taking her into the hospital, of me in her room trying to defend her from the last medical intrusions against her death. How she had looked into my eyes with an expression that tried and failed conceal the pain that she did not want us to see, how ready she was to die. I told them how I had failed to stop the doctors and nurses from keeping her pain alive with machinery and tubes, and most importantly how it felt, the sickness of anger that is smothered with hopelessness, the all-too-familiar feeling of knowing that I was powerless to change the many cruelties and insensitivities of the world, and now yet another injustice was taking place, so close to my heart, knowing with that sick feeling inside that struggling against it would have no effect, because I was not strong enough to prevent the doctors and the hospital and its staff and the world from imposing their will on me and my loved ones.

In my story, I had participated in an unwilling betrayal of all the tender and ambitious hopes that we shared, your mother and I.

How I told the story, I cannot tell you, because the words came not from me, but from the deepest places in my spirit. As I talked, the audience of gods and near-gods sat as if in a deep, stunned trance, and when it was over I did something that I had not done in 40 years, not even when they came and told me that your mother was gone from my life forever. I cried, and the tears and the sobbing were good, and even so, another part of me was mortally embarrassed to be doing this shameful thing where so many others could see it.

"Why do you feel like this is a weakness?" Medetrina asked me gently.

"I don't know. I should have been able to make them do what she wanted. You're weak when you have no effect on the world."

"What does it mean to *feel* weak?"

"It means that I'm not strong."

"Is that a problem?"

"Of course."

"Why? Many people are not strong. Perhaps most."

The question stumped me. "It means I cannot protect those I love," I said finally.

"Can they not protect themselves?"

"I don't know."

"Would they prefer you to defend them if there is danger, or would they want to participate?"

"I think they'd want to help."

"Then what does it mean not to be strong? What does it mean to you?"

"It means I cannot defend myself effectively," I said after a moment.

"Is that true? Are you always defenseless?"

"There are people who are stronger than I am."
"Is that not always true?"
"Yes."
"What does it mean to be defenseless?"
In that moment, I suddenly recognized something astonishing.
"It means," I said slowly, "that I feel, somewhere inside, as if everyone I meet is a potential threat. It means," I said, experiencing the wonder of self-revelation, "that I am secretly afraid of people, of what they might do."
"Why?"
"Because they could hurt me."
"Of course. Everyone could hurt you. But does being afraid of people make you any more safe?"
"No," I said.
"In fact, it could mean that they would be *more* likely to attack you, since they might sense your fear."
"Yes."
"When did you first feel defenseless?"
As we talked, I could feel the eyes of the gods and near-gods on my face, and also, of course, on my spirit, and I knew that I could not voice anything but truthful answers. Any hint of falsehood would be instantly detected.
As I tried to find the right words, something strange and frightening happened. I began to experience a sequence of memories from my childhood. I would call them buried memories, except that they were always there for me to view; had I chosen to look in this particular archive of my history.
"My family moved to Hendersonville, North Carolina when I was in the second grade," I said. "And in the neighborhood, there were many boys who were years older than I was," I said.
"Let me see," said Medetrina, and she touched my forehead.
In the breadth of an instant, I am somewhere else, roaring into the film library of my memory. The room is gone and there is the coolness of an autumn breeze in my face and the smell of moist dirt and newly-cut grass and the brilliance of a cloudless sky, and I am nine years old in the vacant lot up the street in my old neighborhood. As I look down on the scene, there is a baseball glove on my hand and I am standing in the outfield looking intently toward a weedy, makeshift baseball diamond whose bases are pieces of cardboard with rocks on them to hold them still in the wind.
There is a feeling of dread in this boy's stomach and in mine as I watch the scene, not quite fear, more a sense of impending, inevitable disaster which is so familiar to my emotional makeup that I-now and I-then am not even yet

consciously aware of it, any more than I am aware of the fact that the sky is blue or the ground is solid under my feet.

How is this possible?

I recognize the pitcher, Jack, two and a half years older than me, a sixth grader who throws the ball toward the plate, and my floating perception is able to zoom in and travel an inch above the ball as it strikes the bat, and then I suspend the moment, the better to see the compression of the white, mud-stained, stitched surface the instant before it leaps upward past the cardboard first base, rising into the perfect sky above the boy who is/was me.

The boy, recognizing that this is his play to make, freezes for a moment, fighting a sense of panic as he tries to judge the flight of the ball. The ball goes up and up and up, and as it descends, there is a rare sense of certainty. He is embarrassingly clumsy as he backs up through the moist grass, but now he is under it, has it in his sight, has the glove ready.

But his right foot steps unexpectedly into a shallow hole, twisting his ankle, spoiling his balance, and the ball and the boy fall down together in approximately the same place.

While the ball lies on the ground inches from his glove, a gleeful seventh grader rounds third base and scores behind two others.

And then it starts.

Shit! Goddam shit!

I told you we shouldn't've let him play. He's useless.

The game is not yet over, but a new, more interesting one has started. A dozen boys, all of them older than he is, from both teams, now surround him.

Jack, the pitcher, takes the lead; the others watch.

You hear that, you piece of shit?

I called you a piece of shit? You hear that, asshead?

The older boy's round face gets right up in mine, where there is no avoiding it.

I said, you hear that? Are you too good to talk to me?

No, the boy who is me mumbles, pulling his head back.

You're damn shit-fucking right about that. You know what I think? I think your mother's a damn slut.

Inexplicably, the boy smiles awkwardly.

Well? You gonna say something to me? Didn't you hear me call your momma a slut?

Awkwardly, the boy tries to pull himself up to a stand, thinking to punch his tormentor in the mouth and rescue his mother's honor. But Jack reaches out a long arm and pushes him back to the ground before he can gain his feet. He tries to stand up again, but this time he is pushed forward from behind, and his face collides with the ground.

It's a free country, he says finally, and fights back the tears.

I, floating above, suddenly realize that everybody in the room can see my shame, the thing I have hidden from the world for all my life. My mind is flooded with a searing emotion that is as much more than embarrassment as a solar nova is more than an earthquake.

I wish, at this moment, that I could die rather than have others see this part of my life.

I want to tell the boy on the ground to run, but there is really no escape. I want to tell him to fight, but there is no chance. I want to put my arms around him, but there are too many years between here and there.

The boy that was me is finally allowed to stand up, and I look around at the circle of boys around Jack and me. Wearily, feeling the familiar dread of helplessness, I raise my fists. This time the older boy leans the heaviness of his body into my face with a smile, punches me hard in the chest, and I tumble backwards on the ground again. My ankle buckles a second time.

Yeah? You feeling free right now?

I am afraid, but the fear of being hurt is nothing and less than nothing compared with the enormous, overwhelming fear of humiliation in front of these boys who, despite all evidence, I still consider to be my friends. I know I am powerless to stop what I know is coming, and to my adult awareness, watching the scene with a searing hatred of myself then and now, I recognize that this same feeling of helplessness against forces which are too strong for me to fight has become the background of my life, the context of my thoughts, in the same way that the sky is the context of the clouds that pass across it.

This feeling is so omnipresent that I have stopped noticing it.

This is the Curse.

Now I can see where it came from.

It has been, all my life, an open wound leaking dark energy like blood.

No, the boy says, desperate to keep the fear out of his voice. It comes out a mumble.

What?

I said no.

You hear that? He says he ain't free around us. Like he's saying we're dirty Russians. You calling me a dirty Russian, huh?

Jack hits me with a closed fist in the back of my head, and for an instant it feels as if the world is inside out, and then it is like I am swimming out of the deep and dark through a surge of anger. But when my eyes are working properly again, there is no place to direct the anger except at myself, at my own fear and weakness, at my own inability to defend my mother from the things they're saying about her. As angry and frightened as I am, I still want to tell them that I tried to make the catch, to say that if one of *them* had been the youngest kid in the neighborhood, and fell down trying to catch a baseball, I wouldn't do anything except keep playing.

At that moment, the most important thing in the world to me is that they not see that I'm afraid.

Why can't they leave me alone? I wonder. Why is it always me they do this to?

The next punch catches me full in the stomach, and I fall on my knees and elbows, my forehead on the wet grass, gasping in panic because my lungs suddenly won't fill up with air. Another punch collides with the back of my head.

Two or three boys are kicking my back, and I roll over and curl up tighter, feeling a searing fury at myself for not fighting back, for letting myself be so helpless. Then, for a long moment, there is a stillness, and I hope if I don't move, perhaps they'll think I'm dead and leave me alone.

After a minute, I am almost certain that they have left, and I uncurl cautiously. Then my hair is nearly yanked out by the roots. My head snaps up as the older boy lifts me off the ground by my hair, holding our faces an inch apart, and all I want, the older me looking down on the scene and the younger me looking into the satisfied mocking face of my attacker, all I/we want right now is not to cry in front of the audience of boys then, and the audience of gods and near gods now.

But it is too late, and the face is twisted in a vain effort to hold it back, instead making it more visible. And I, the adult facing his weakness decades later, can do no better.

The baby is crying! Look at the baby! He's scared and he's crying!
Let's go. We don't play with babies.
Yeah.

They walk off up the hill. I sit up, trying to breathe, and the way my younger self rubs the soreness on the back of my head is touching and mortifying at the same time.

Yes, I was this helpless, my spirit says to the audience of gods and near-gods. *Are you satisfied? Is this the humiliation you were looking for?*

Finally the boy stands up gently on the sore ankle, wiping the tears off of my cheeks. All I want to do now is get cleaned up so my mother won't see what happened to me. Why? Because she must never know that they called her a slut and I did nothing to defend her. Because I feel that searing emotion a million miles beyond ashamed to have her or anyone else know that I'm not brave enough or strong enough to defend myself.

But the secret is out, and I know that the gods and near gods are able to see that I and these boys and (later) I and different surrogates of these boys have played this scene many times, until the pattern became the theme of the story of my life.

Finally the show is over, and my awareness is back in the room, and I am standing in front of the gods and near gods with tears running down my face.

I hate myself far more than I hate the boys who hurt me.

I will always hate myself.

The only secret I have ever wanted to keep has been held up for their inspection.

I want to die.

Medetrina was standing beside me, and the compassionate glow in her spirit made that moment somehow bearable.

"They routinely hurt you, and yet they were your only friends?" she asked.

"Yes," I said. "And most of all, I was afraid of them."

"And you are still afraid?"

"Yes. And I am ashamed of it."

"Why?"

"They made me feel helpless."

"Why are you ashamed of that?"

There was a long pause, nothing but the cricket filling the silence, and I shivered again.

"I don't know," I said.

"What does it mean to be helpless?"

"It means I cannot defend myself as a man should be able to do."

"Was there any child, your age and size, who could have defended himself against all those boys at once?"

"No. Of course not."

"And yet you are ashamed because *you* could not."

"It doesn't make any sense," I said. "Why couldn't they have left me alone?"

"You said yourself that you couldn't have prevented them. So how is any of this your fault?"

"I don't know."

The room was intensely silent. I had desperately wanted to avoid giving her that conclusion, but I knew that I had to, for they could see it already on my spirit.

"What does that mean?"

"It wasn't my fault," I said, and it felt as if the world was suddenly spinning on its axis around me.

Karen, this was the pivotal moment of my life, the center of my life's story, the moment when I would no longer throw the gifts of my spirit, with tired resignation, along the side of the road.

"It wasn't my fault," I repeated, shaking my head in wonder.

"It really wasn't my fault," I said again, and this time it felt like I was hearing those words for the first time. "There really wasn't anything I could have done," I said, and the truth of what I said came crashing into my awareness. I felt my mind rearranging itself around this insight, and some of the tension that always lived inside of me began to ebb, as if the conversation was lancing a boil in the center of my heart.

What *did* it mean?

"For the rest of my life," I said to her, my eyes pleading for understanding now, because the conclusion made no sense and yet I had built my life on this foundation—"For all the years afterwards, I've felt as if everybody could see how helpless I had been, that I had not managed to defend myself, that I couldn't do the things a man should be able to do. I can see now that I have ever since, wherever I went, whatever I did, carried a ball of anxiety and anger and frustration around in my stomach, and lived with the self-image of a failure. It became a self-fulfilling prophecy. I cannot defend myself against bullies, and they have done whatever they wanted with me. Therefore I am worthless."

"And what does that mean?" Medetrina persisted.

This time the answer was easy.

"It means I am not a man," I said, and there was a sudden rush of relief in admitting this painful thing that I had covered over with so many layers of denial for so many years of my life. "I have never, ever felt like I was a real man," I said, wiping the tears off of my face, where they itched and distracted me.

I took a deep recovery breath that ended the shaking in my chest.

"Did you not act more nobly than your bullies and tormenters?"

"Yes. I never told on them, and I never bullied anyone smaller than me."

Karen, as I was saying these words, it felt as I imagine a person feels when he finally stops hitting himself on the head with a hammer.

"You *could* be proud of your more noble behavior. But you have chosen to feel shame and embarrassment instead."

There was no answer to this.

"The boys in your neighborhood gave you beatings, and they made you fear the beatings, and then they left you with a souvenir to carry with you afterwards, a souvenir of shame and a sense of un-self-worthiness."

"Yes."

"What you experienced cannot be changed," said Medetrina gently. "How you feel about these things after the fact, however, is voluntary and completely under your control. The way you interpret it, the way you assign feelings, can be changed now that your adult mind has looked at the scene impartially, with adult judgment. Do you understand that?" Medetrina persisted, and it felt as if the words were boring into my mind. "You did not have the physical strength to defeat the bullies, but in the privacy of your mind, you have the right and the freedom and power to assign to these unhappy incidents whatever feelings you want. The feelings you chose were not illogical. But can you see that they have not served you well?"

"Yes."

"You are voluntarily carrying this feeling of shame, which is their gift to you for the rest of your life."

"Yes," I said again.

"Do you want this gift? Or do you want to drop it now by the side of your life, the way you have so many of your dreams?"

"I don't know," I said, and there was a moment of profound wonder as I looked at those years of random terror with logical eyes, with the eyes of an adult.

"I don't know," I said again. "I'll be damned. It makes no sense at all."

"Does it make sense to be secretly anxious whenever you are around people, because of what these boys did to you?"

"No."

"Do you still feel the pain?"

The question was abrupt and unexpected. I turned my attention to where the ball of anxiety and frustration and hopelessness had been buried, deep within my body, deeper within my soul, radiating unhappiness and insecurity from my core into all of my thoughts and actions. Somehow, during our conversation, whatever had been inside that ball was now gone, lanced and dissipated, and I felt that a healing had started which would cause me to readjust the way I interacted with everything and everybody.

I took a deep breath, and the air was strong in my lungs.

"No," I said, and there was a strength in the modulation of my voice that made the words it spoke somehow important.

For a long time, I don't know how long, the room was absolutely silent, and it felt as if my mind was rearranging all of its circuitry, reassigning new meanings to all of my memories. I closed my eyes and images passed one after another across the backs of my eyelids, as if I was seeing my life in a series of still pictures, too fast to interpret.

"Damn," I said, and this time my voice carried across the room, and it demanded attention. Later, many different gods and near-gods would come up to me and tell me that this single word, spoken at that moment and in that exact way, communicated everything. It gave the demons their due, for their remarkable efficiency in getting us to enslave ourselves; and it also conveyed the wonder of awakening, the realization of our potential once the chains were lifted from our souls, the potential that exceeded anything we would have expected just a few moments before the lifting of the Curse.

"You have broken the chains on your soul," Medetrina told me.

"The Curse is lifted," I said gravely, feeling it inside me.

Medetrina turned her face to the seated audience. "He is one of us now," she said. "The god Plautus, whom the world calls Adam Zakar, is now known in our community as..." Medetrina paused, obviously searching my spirit for an answer.

She continued looking, and with an expression of happy surprise, she turned back to the group. "As Proteus," she said, although it sounded more like a question than a statement.

At these confusing words, the audience of gods and near-gods stood up and embraced me and took my hand, and there were many tears on many faces.

Venus walked up and wrapped her arms around my neck and her body molded to mine like gentle putty for a long second. "You did it," she said, talking into my ear softly. "In the hierarchy, there are men, then women above them, then gods, then goddesses," she added, stepping back and looking at me, her hands still lightly holding my elbows. "Never imagine you can get to the top rung."

"In your eyes, I'll always be Mister Commuter."

She smiled at that. "The man who was not quite clueless enough."

Mars elbowed past her and clapped me on the shoulder gently, and it felt as if my spine would break. Then he took my hand with a surprisingly tender gesture. "Damn," he said, repeating my own word back at me in his remarkable subbasso voice, shaking his head in appreciation. His spirit said: "I wish I'd thought of that when *my* curse was lifted."

I shook hands with Briarius and Mercury and Rhea and a wild dark-haired woman who called herself Alecto, whose hand was so cold that I shivered, and at the back of the crowd I saw Cassandra smiling at me and I smiled back and waved, feeling confused and strong and self-satisfied in a way that would not, I think, have been possible just ten minutes ago.

After a minute, Cassandra worked her way to the front and embraced me and left a tingle in my spirit where hers and mine touched.

"Look at me," I said. "I'm almost functional."

Cassandra shook her head with a smile. "It will take hours, perhaps days for your mind and your spirit to reintegrate themselves," she said. "You will feel a deep satisfaction where once you felt anxiety, and you will be constantly touching the place where you feel this difference. Eventually, the satisfaction will feel normal, and you'll hardly notice it."

"Is it the same for everybody?" I asked.

"The particular chains are different for all of us," she said. "The story is always different. But I think the feelings after it's over are pretty universal."

"Now comes the hard part. I have to live up to this."

"Yes. Your behavior may not change immediately, but it *will* change. Habits are born out of the soul's necessities. You must start to develop new, more constructive habits, so the old ones, so strong now, can wither away and die."

I shook my head. "It seems too impossible that such a brief thing could make so much difference."

"Nobody believes it. Nobody is *allowed* to believe it."

"By the demons?"

"Soon you will see them, and you'll know for yourself."

"And you can do this for everybody? Everybody in the world?"

"Yes," said Cassandra. "That's exactly why we're here. That's exactly what we want to do. That's why they want so badly to crush us. If enough of us were to escape their pen, they'd have to face the human race in its full power and fury. They'd be swept away like flies in a hurricane."

"I need to go home and think about this," I said. "I need to get used to this feeling."

"Not yet. You haven't met the Master yet."

Somehow I had managed to forget that this was why I was here. "Now?"

"Now. He will complete the process that Medetrina started."

I looked away for a long second.

"He's waiting for you."

"I'm not sure I'm ready to see him."

"I can assure you that *that* doesn't matter," Cassandra said, tugging my arm in the direction of the far wall, toward the front of the building.

"Will you be there with me?"

"No."

"Suppose I want you there."

"You'll be fine. Come on!"

"She gave me the new name," I said. "What did that mean?"

"I don't know. Ask the Master that, if you get a chance. A lot of us were really surprised."

"Can't *you* tell me? Don't you see it in my future?"

"I see something," Cassandra admitted. "But I really, truly don't understand it."

The desire to get an answer to these questions, which were still blurring in my head with the implications of the lifting of The Curse, gave me an incentive to keep walking. From habit, I expected to feel a kind of dread in my stomach, but instead I felt contented and curious, as if the pain inside had turned into a kind of tickling sensation. Cassandra led me to a door, and stopped, and after a long hesitation with my hand on the knob, I opened it slowly, and walked into the presence of the Master.

Behind me was darkness punctuated by the gaily multicolored glows of satisfied, completed spirits. Inside was a brightness that at first I thought must be a colossal spiritual flame, but which turned out to be the orange ascending sun through a window in this side office of the warehouse. The light shone directly into my eyes, so that it was hard to make out the person sitting in front of it

For some reason, the intensity of the brightness made me sneeze. I reached in my pocket for a tissue, and my fingers closed instead around the plastic bag I had been given two days ago.

The person in the chair didn't speak. Slowly, I walked forward, shielding my eyes with my hand.

It was the cripple in the wheelchair. He was a younger man than I had realized, with long brown hair cascading over his shoulders and a thin, ropy physique that suggested malnourishment or neglect. He was dressed in a casual pair of jeans and a vest that partially covered his chest, which was so thin that I could see more bone than muscle. The cripple's face was slack, and his mouth hung open in a broad vacant smile that I had seen a few times on the faces of people who were extremely old and in the last stages of senility. In his hand, he clutched what appeared to be an elaborate wooden flute.

I was moved to sympathy, and touched his hand gently. The eyes revolved slowly in my direction, but there was no spark of attention in them, and I couldn't tell if he saw me or not. For some reason, the vacant smile intensified, and I shivered and tried to figure out what to do with my suddenly-awkward hands. I rubbed his shoulder, hoping he had enough feeling in his body to recognize the gentleness of my touch.

Then, suddenly, looking at him, I realized that at my core, I, too, was a cripple, that I was really no better off, even though my wounds (so newly exposed) were easier to hide. That was the message of this person in front of me, written out not in words but in the example of his manifest, cruel disability. The strange words formed themselves in my mind, and I nodded at the rightness of them. *Every person's life is ultimately tragic. The only truly important mission in life is to change that.*

I looked around for the Master. Had he stepped outside? I walked across the room to the window and looked out at the street on the far side of the property, where high bushes encroached on the edges of the asphalt. I looked as far as the window allowed in both directions, but there seemed to be nobody out there.

There was a long, uncomfortable silence. I turned back to the cripple, and was startled down to my core to see that he had managed to swivel his head around, pointing his unseeing eye in my direction again. I looked at the glow of his spirit, and the radiance was surprisingly strong, a yellow-gold color almost too intense for my spirit eyes to look at directly.

I wanted to know where the Master had gone, and perhaps also to see how this young man had become so badly disabled, so I read the text written on the spirit of this crippled person, and after a second I stopped reading and stared at him in a kind of numb shock bordering on horror.

"You're the Master," I said to the uncomprehending face. "You're the one I've been waiting to meet ever since I came here."

The Master didn't answer, although I thought maybe the vacant smile grew a hint broader.

"I'm Adam Zakar," I said finally. "They call me Proteus now," I added, "but I suppose you know that already. I'd still like to know how you got my cell phone number."

The cripple in the chair made no sign that he had heard me. I stared into his eyes and then at the glow of his spirit, waiting for—what?

What could I do?

Then, abruptly, I put my hand in my pocket. It closed once again on the plastic bag, and a kind of certainty came over me. For the first time since my encounter with Heavy Hitter in the parking lot, I knew, as clearly as if it were written down by the hand of God, what I should do.

I sighed with relief. And then I approached the man that my new friends called the Master, who still seemed completely unaware of my presence, and tenderly put my hand on his shoulder again. "You have my undying gratitude," I whispered. "For what, I am not yet sure."

He also had my sympathy. Perhaps he walked with God, as they said, but it seemed to me that I, who held his life in my trembling fingers, was the more powerful of the two.

The process took only a few seconds. I dropped the empty bag at my feet. Then, not wishing to prolong the moment, I turned to the door, fumbled for a long minute to get the handle turned, and then walked back into the darkness, which seemed absolute when I shut the door behind me.

In front of me, an audience of ghosts glowed faintly, their auras merging and blending in an interesting array. I felt intensely sorry for them all.

"Well?" Fool finally demanded. "How did it go?"

My daughter, I did not have words to answer him. I simply walked through a parting cluster of ghosts like Moses through the Red Sea, and then sat down on the ground to take stock of what I had seen, and the enormity of the decision I had made, for the Master, for all of us.

"He's in total shock," somebody said.

"What did you expect? The Master always has that effect."

"Give him space. He'll come around eventually."

They gave me space, and I took full advantage of it. It felt as if the world was upside down, turned inside out, and then I felt an enormous sympathy for these people who were so trusting and wonderful and naive.

Their Master was an imbecile.

My new friends, the people who were living in my warehouse, were followers of an idiot.

I was in the middle of the biggest mess of my life, and I alone, of all of them, knew that it was about to get very much worse.

X

The biggest danger with the New Age movement is that people will open their minds too far and forget to be discerning. When we open ourselves to the light, many dark spirits will also accept the invitation. Let us agree that we are open only to the Almighty and goodness and joy and the healing energies. If we cannot distinguish between these and the many charlatans and opportunists and the spirits of darkness, then it is better to close our hearts altogether and wait for our discernment to catch up with our hope.
—From *The Rutherfordton Spiritual Gazette*

Before I was out of bed Friday morning, my cell phone was ringing with the first of my customers calling back. As soon as I hung up, there was another ring, and when I hung up this time, I discovered that there were four returned calls waiting for me. The calls kept piling up until finally, at eleven o'clock, I called in sick, leaving a voice message for the Branch Manager that I would use the time at home to think things over. He was used to my automatic subservience over the last two decades. I was certain that he wouldn't be able to guess that I would fight back.

I sat on the back deck and gave different variations of the same advice: be careful, don't follow the advice of the new broker until you've talked with me, pass the word on. It was another warm day but the wind was up, pushing the brilliant white clouds along the sky. I watched their shadows travel across the valley as I talked.

Karen, the more people I talked with, the less futile my plan seemed to be. I found in myself a confidence and courage that I would not have imagined just a few hours ago. In a couple of days, I would sit down with the wealthiest man in four states and write myself a generous ticket to freedom from The House, and later that afternoon, I would sell the warehouse back to its rightful owner. Then, perhaps, I would sell the house and move deeper into the mountains, to a place where people buy their groceries from a country store, and sit on the swing rocker on the porch and watch the way the wind stirs the leaves. Sometimes the phone would ring, and I would give honest financial advice without any expectation of payment and without anybody else's agenda intruding on the conversation. If there happened to be a course around somewhere, I would learn to play golf.

After a long time, I hung up on a call and the phone did not ring. I gave it a few seconds, and then shrugged my shoulders. My stomach began to talk to me, so I went inside and found nothing acceptable in the refrigerator. I decided to drive downtown for lunch, maybe watch a movie, maybe not. It was a joy not to feel the ball of anxiety in my chest and stomach, to feel as if I was thinking clearly. I simply felt like enjoying the miracle that was my life. Soon enough, I'd get back on the phone and finish my calls and take one last look at the Big Score's proposal.

Still not sure where I wanted to eat, I parked next to a meter across from the large flatiron at the start of Wall Street, and walked out into the cultural heart of the city: the civic center, the city library and Malaprops Bookstore all virtually next door to each other, one block above the bohemian district, up the street from a variety of restaurants and art galleries and Pack Square.

I passed a restaurant with outdoor tables and the first scatterings of a luncheon crowd, sat down at the first unoccupied outdoor table, crowded in between two others, and stared for a long second at the menu before I realized that my mind was otherwise occupied. By habit, I opened the eyes of my spirit and looked up, and then stared straight ahead with a sense of alarm.

Slowly, I turned my face to the left, and brought myself nose to nose with a squat, ugly yellow-eyed creature, a miniature human caricature who looked exactly like children's book pictures of a troll.

The creature was attached, by the claws of its feet, to the heart of a young woman, who, to mortal eyes, was mostly noticeable for her bright blue hair, tattoos and the piercings on her cheek and nose. The troll's fierce yellow eyes surveyed me coldly for long seconds, while the panic built inside me like a volcano.

I turned away slowly, and discovered that in this direction, my face was just inches away from a bizarre hag who stared at me with unconcealed hatred, attached to the neck of a young man with dark hair braided down his back.

With a yelp of alarm, I jumped up to my feet and lunged for the safety of the open sidewalk, backing away from the restaurant while everybody at the tables and an assortment of demons and creatures watched me in astonishment and alarm. In blind fear, I turned and ran a step, and immediately collided with a middle-aged man in a dark business suit who, I saw from his harried yellow glow, was returning to his office from an early lunch. From a place near his bowels, two fat elves with nasty eyes glared at me malevolently.

I screamed again, and turned and ran up the street, in the direction of a small crowd of people who carried, like barnacles, a menagerie of human caricatures. I stopped in my tracks and turned, but up the street another group of people carried more nightmares.

Karen, by this point, I was no longer thinking at all; the panic had turned my mind into a gridlock of conflicting impulses, none of which seemed to be safe. What was happening to me? Were these illusions? I knew they weren't. Were they demons? A part of me knew the answer, but my mind didn't want to acknowledge it. Shaking, I backed across the street toward the nearest building and stumbled through the first door I came to, which brought me inside a little Christian bookstore. I turned around with a sigh of relief.

My entrance had been so clumsy that a dozen pairs of eyes glanced up from various aisles, and perhaps three dozen more creatures attached to them gave me a long measuring stare. Elves with faces so thin they looked as if they could cut your finger, stocky dwarves with shaggy arms and feet, here a vampire sucking greedily on the base of the neck, there a fairy, beautiful, delicate, yet with a terrifying expression on its dainty visage, creatures of mythology clasping to the men and women browsing the aisles, the cashiers, even the children. I saw one float through the walls of the store and land on a pensive woman with a book in her hand, and I saw that her aura was a deep melancholy blue-green, and as the creature attached itself to the base of her skull, the unhappy aura glowed more strongly, as if the creature were somehow reinforcing the sadness and despair.

For long seconds, I simply stared into the store, until an elderly woman pushed past me, and I recoiled in horror at the dark, hooded creature who turned to hiss at me as it rode its human host out the door.

Carefully, tremblingly, I backed back out the entranceway, and leaped aside as people walked past, their demons swiveling their heads to watch me. I walked backwards, turning frequently, darting out of the way of anybody who happened to share the sidewalk, trying to stay at least ten feet away from physical contact.

And then I looked up.

High above me, a flock of these creatures swirled around in the air like buzzards, centering on a place directly above where I stood. By now, my mind was edging closer to the truth, and I remembered that these parasites were attracted by fear, by the dark energy that I was now radiating in generous measure from my spirit.

The flock swirled closer. A hag with a frightening smile and a troll whose face was set in grim contentment hovering like hummingbirds close to my face. Instinctively, I thrashed my hands to knock them away, but my hand passed through their bodies, and the faces turned to each other and laughed.

In a blind panic, I bolted and ran down the street, knocking aside anyone who happened to be in my path, pursued by a cloud of dreams and nightmares, a terrifying cross-section of mythology, trailing behind me the overpowering panic-stricken smell of an emotional feast.

There was no chance to outrun them. I turned and leaped to my car and managed to get the door unlocked before the swarm had caught up with me. I slammed the door shut, and then saw with wild despair that the creatures simply melted through the windows and roof as easily as they had passed through my hand.

And now they had me trapped.

I shut my eyes and the eyes of my spirit and tried to will them away. At first I deceived myself into thinking that it was working.

Then suddenly, chillingly, I began to feel them.

Karen, when a demon attaches itself to the energy centers of your body, you feel an unpleasant momentary sensation on, in this case, my arm, as if a nerve had been touched for just a second by a sharp object. A place on my back suddenly itched. A nerve twitched in my leg. With my physical eyes still shut, my body trembling, I opened the eyes of my spirit, and saw creatures everywhere around me, taking their deliberate time about slowly inserting their talons into different parts of my anatomy.

The skin crawled on the back of my head as a hag—her leering face inches from mine—slowly pushed her nails into and through the back of my skull, reaching all the way into the nerves of my brain. Instantly, the beginnings of a dull headache pounded in my skull.

My left ear twitched slightly, and I watched an elf, its face full of malicious glee, lay back across my body and idly dig one of its clawed fingers into my ear lobe.

There was an itch on the back of my leg and another on the bottom of my foot, and below my knee and along the back of my leg. It felt as if ants were crawling everywhere over my body.

I sobbed in fear, and instantly the fear took on its own momentum, cascading through my mind with an irresistible acceleration as if my mind itself were falling down a steep hill. I trembled with revulsion and panic, trying to maintain control, but there was no control. The faces of the creatures attached to me in a dozen places took on a serene, faraway look, and they had thousands of years of practice, reaching into my thoughts and magnifying the dark emotional fear and panic and despair and revulsion that I was feeling, until my mind fogged and I was nothing more than a conduit of energy all across the dark end of the spectrum.

My brain had become a closed loop of increasing panic growing to hysteria. I screamed and began pounding on the window with my fist. The pain in my hand added to my torment and I was suddenly filled with an urge to throw myself through the glass.

I screamed again and clawed at the door and somehow tumbled heavily out of the seat down to the hard pavement, and realized through the thickening fog of my distress that I was free to run.

But where?

Karen, I do not believe it was my physical mind which gave me this thought, for as soon as my panicked mind recognized the idea and brought it to my attention, there was a roaring sensation in my brain that felt like a thousand screaming voices, as if the universe itself was trying to tear the idea away from my awareness and bury me in blind fear again. But I held the thought and stumbled to my feet and ran up the street, feeling all the more urgency because another idea had been provided to me from the mind of my spirit.

These creatures had noticed that I could see them. They intended—with every expectation of success—to kill me before I could give away the secret of their existence to their hosts.

I sprinted around the corner and ran straight across the next street and into traffic, dodging cars that whizzed past with a blare of horns and the much too late sound of brakes after I was already on the other side. I sprinted past the Vance Memorial, which looks a bit like a very small version of the Washington Monument, and in another few steps I was able to leap into the chilly waters of the ornamental pool which covered half a block behind the obelisk.

The water was just deep enough for me to submerge myself completely, soaking my clothes. I gasped for a breath and held it, lay on my back and gave myself over to the water and the coldness of it, forcing myself to stay below the surface even though my lungs craved oxygen. I felt an itch in the back of my neck, and then it was gone, and my leg and ear and foot and shoulder experienced the pinprick sensation of spirits leaving with a backwards glare of annoyance and regret.

Finally, my lungs could stand it no longer. I sat up and gasped for air.

The parasites had not retreated far. The air overhead was thick with them, and as soon as they felt the glow of my anger, they plunged down once again.

"You bastards!" I shouted, and ducked back in the water.

I came up again almost immediately, drew in more air, went back down, and repeated this until I had paid off enough of my oxygen debt that I could lie back for the better part of a minute without feeling as if my lungs were in danger of exploding. I stared up through the water at the sky, trying to put myself into a meditative state, trying to give myself time to think. What would I say if the police came and dragged me out of the water? I raised my head and gulped in more air, watching the parasites warily, checking up and down the street. The demons swirled around too quickly for me to be able to track all of them, so after a moment, I dropped back into the water again, half floating an inch below the surface.

Why hadn't they attacked me this last time?

As my thoughts grew clearer, I realized that my spirit had settled into the oddly contented feeling that I had experienced last night—a default sensation that was amazingly different from what I normally carried around.

Could that be why? Hadn't Fool told me that the demons could only feed on the darker emotions?

Once more, I raised my head out of the water, but this time I faced the creatures of myth and fantasy with an inner confidence and self-imposed serenity. I watched them closely as they descended, but now it seemed like I was giving off a repulsive effect, as if I had become the other end of the magnet, pushing them away instead of drawing them into me.

The parasites of the spirit, like a cloud of images ripped from children's story books, milled about in the air. Slowly, still watching them, I pulled myself to my feet, shook some of the water off my face and clothes, and marched defiantly through calf-deep water out of the pool and onto the sidewalk and down the street in the general direction of the river. The parasites continued to follow me, but my energy pattern didn't waver, and I sloshed and squished and shivered in the breeze, my steps guided by dead reckoning for more than an hour before I ran across the highway and climbed down a steep grassy slope to River Road, my warehouse already in view half a mile ahead.

I walked around behind the back of the fence, and there was Apollo, sitting quietly on a rock at the top of the bank, nearly hidden in the weeds.

He looked me up and down as I approached, and then up at the frustrated cloud of demons who stalked me.

"Well," he said with a faint ironic smile. "Don't *you* have interesting friends."

"They look so familiar!" I said, shaking my head, aware that I had said this before just a few minutes ago. "Trolls, fairies, hags, dwarves, vampires and elves; how is it that we know what they look like? Somebody, somewhere, must have seen them pretty clearly."

"Oh yes." Apollo squinted into the sky. "We've traced the best descriptions at least back to a peculiar period in the Middle Ages," he said, "though the church did what it could to suppress these folk tales and occasionally burned people who insisted too much. *All great truths begin as blasphemies.* George Bernard Shaw."

"How could *they* see these things when we can't?"

"They had interesting help. Sometime around the year 1,000 AD, and for some centuries before and afterwards, the month of July was the most common time of starvation. It was the month before the first harvests of grains made bread plentiful again."

"So?"

"During that mid-summer period, the farmers and their families all over Europe would try to survive on the remnants at the bottom of their granaries—moldy rye and cakes made of it. We know today that the ergot mold that lives on rye plants was a plentiful source of lysergic acid—better known today in the form of the cult recreation drug LSD. The desperate July diet also included hemp—marihuana—baked into what the people of the time called, with perhaps too much accuracy, *crazy bread*."

"I still don't understand," I said.

"Use your imagination," Fool interrupted. "I've eaten dinner, and now I'm full of LSD, and I decide to eat baked crazy bread for dessert. Imagine the visions I see! Look; is that a tree or a giant toadstool? Did my arm just turn into a banana? And maybe it loosens me up just enough that my spirit eyes open up and I catch a glimpse of an elf winking at me as it rides past me in the fields on my wife's shawl. Somebody else catches sight of a troll perched on the back of her neighbor, and that night, after they come down a little, they sketch out what they saw and imagine that these are physical creatures like us, only *very* good at hiding."

"I also believe," Apollo added, "that children are able to catch a glimpse here and there, enough to confirm the myth in their minds and lend accuracy to the children's book drawings that they create from memory in adulthood."

We were walking along the side of the highway in the general direction of downtown and the baseball stadium that lay behind it—to, as Fool put it, "check out the competition." Justin Macaulay, a renown evangelist, had included Asheville on his national revival tour, two nights only, the last stop on a tour that included Charlotte, Winston-Salem, Roanoake, Lexington, Richmond. The itinerary was laid out in the flyers with a little map, apparently on the theory that if you missed one, you could drive up the road to catch another.

The first Asheville show, which promised "a return to First Century Christianity" and "a rekindling of the fires of faith in Christ Jesus" was to begin tonight at seven. As we walked toward the baseball stadium, the crowd grew thicker and moved in generally the same direction. I found myself staring at them and their parasites. The one consistency was a kind of dullness about their eyes, something I had never noticed before. It looked, to my eyes now, like many of the people we walked with were sleepwalking, while the eyes of the demons were bright, alert and confident. In a kind of panic, I stared around at others, and everywhere the eyes had the same curious absence of life.

Is *this* how I had been, just…days ago?

"I *love* these fundamentalist gospel extravaganzas," Fool called out happily. "It's an incredible spectator sport. Let me tell you what to watch for. Watch for how the evangelist plays the audience like an organ, drawing out this emotion and then that one, one at a time, and then sometimes a fugue, where the same words bring out different emotions in different groups of people in the audience. And watch the parasites flock to the feast he's delivering for them. If you do nothing but watch the audience with the eyes of your spirit, you'll see an incredible light show delivered by an accomplished master."

"I'm not sure I want to be around a feeding frenzy of demons," I said.

"Fear not," Fool assured me. "They'll be focused on the feast, not on the meager pickings that *we* represent. Besides, all you have to do is feel mellow and happy and tranquil and they jump off of you with scorched talons like a cat on a hot tin roof."

"But *what* are they? I mean, I know they're parasites, but what are they made of? I don't see any holy spirit in them."

"They are energetic attractor patterns in the human mind," said Apollo. "They are living astral byproducts of certain closed loops of thought and emotion, who caricature our form because they are our shadows, and feed off of our energy. They tend us like cattle in a feedlot, harvesting our spiritual suffering."

"Now let me translate," Fool cut in. "Have you ever had a conversation with yourself?"

I thought a moment. "Yes."

"Knowing you, I'll bet it was unbelievably boring."

"What does *that* have to do with it?"

"Now suppose that one of those participants in the conversation takes on a life of its own. Suppose there's a part of your mind that begins to have its own personality, to have its own thoughts."

"Like we have *our* own thoughts, separated from the universal awareness?"

"*Now* you have the idea. It is exactly the same problem, but on our scale, rather than God's."

"Isn't that what I said?" Apollo grumbled. "In the astral realm," he continued; "in a dimension that lies immediately adjacent to ours, those thoughts represent real energy. In fact, they're *most* of the energy in that place. And when our energy extends into that cold, empty place, and it has thoughts already attached to it, is it such a giant stretch to imagine that some parasite ecology would be born, to live on our warmth?"

"It's a stretch for me," I said.

"The Master says that the demons are vexed by rogue thoughts of *theirs* that extend into yet another dimension and feed off of *them*," Fool added.

"And we're their food source," I said. "And they milk us, like cattle, to feed themselves."

"The analogy goes beyond that," Apollo corrected me. "They have us herded into an elaborate feedlot that we call our society and culture. Over the course of many centuries, they've convinced us that we, ourselves, created this economic system, this array of cities and highways and consumerism and 9 to 5 jobs and lives of quiet desperation that is the food for their insubstantial bodies. In fact, it is all, every bit of it, completely *their* creation."

"That's the part I don't understand," I said. "How can they be responsible for what we create?"

"When they attach to the brain, they can nudge our thoughts in certain directions, plant ideas, make suggestions, sometimes even exert direct control for a time," said Apollo. "Didn't you feel it when they attacked you?"

"Yes," I said, shivering involuntarily.

"Now imagine that the control extends to nudging people to create certain social structures, to build or work for certain institutions, more and more elaborate as time goes on."

"You mean, the way we live is for *their* convenience, rather than ours?"

"Look around you—" Apollo invited, gesturing at the highway, the strip shopping center we were walking past, the taller buildings in the distance. "Everything—our culture, our inventions, our way of life, our politics, our business environment, our money, our art and literature and movies were all created with a nudge here and there from our invisible guests. The concept of status and greed and the invention of unnecessary expensive physical luxuries, and the advertising which promises that they will fulfill your soul—these are wonderful generators of dark energy, disappointment, frustration, anger and despair.

"Career paths and office politics are their daily feast. Wars are their banquet, and they see to it that we are never without them. Why have we never fixed the endless and painful misunderstandings and dysfunctions of human mating? Because it sustains parasites by the billions. Every sports stadium is a banquet of dark elation and despair, of rage and primal excitement. Our movie industry sends gourmet delicacies of emotion and lust streaming from our souls. Music and television and schools and politics, memos from the CEO and messages from the pulpit were all whispered into the human mind by creatures who know much better than we do how to organize the world to draw out endless harvests of hopelessness, anger, jealousy, envy, shame, bitterness, despair, sadness, pain, regret, anxiety, depression, disgust, fear, famine and illness from the garden of humanity."

I saw what he was talking about. Suddenly, many inexplicable things made perfect sense. I wanted to do something about it, but my mind stopped there. Where would I start? How would I go about tearing down what was ten thousand years in the construction?

"What do you think?" said Fool, reading my spirit. "Should we try to warn people about them?"

"Yes," I said.

"And how would you do that?"

"I'd go on television."

"Great idea! With what evidence? Of course, the producer of whatever program you want to appear on has a demon or two attached to her brain. Do you think it's telling her to give us access to an audience of millions?"

"I'd write articles. Books."

"A sound suggestion! Who would you approach first, knowing that every reader of manuscripts has a demon perched on his shoulder?"

"If I had to, I'd tell everybody personally."

"Very practical," said Fool. "Billions of them, a handful of us. But I'm willing to give it a try. Excuse me," he said, turning without warning to the random man and woman who happened to be passing us, heading in the same general direction as we were. "I wanted to let you know that you," he said, indicating the woman, "have a demon spiritual parasite type creature which seems to be attached to your abdomen, and it looks a lot like pictures of fairies that you've seen, except for the scary facial expression. You," he said to the man, "have what looks a lot like a small gnome attached to the back of your neck, which I imagine is pretty sore at the moment."

Karen, I wish you could have seen the expression on these peoples' faces as they backed away from Fool in alarm. He described the hag attached to the man's chest in the most sincere possible voice, and my companions were laughing both at him and at my stupid idea, which was being played out for the world to see. After a minute of this, the man threatened Fool with physical violence if he didn't back off and take his crazy rantings somewhere else, and they stalked off with their hag and their fairy and their gnome looking back at us with expressions of smug triumph.

"Grouches! Maybe those people over there would be more receptive," Fool suggested.

"No," I said.

"I'll bet that older man would listen to me."

"Leave it alone," I said. "I get it, okay? But surely there are others like you? Or does everybody have parasites attached to them?"

"Not everybody," said Apollo. "We find isolated free-range humans, here and there, who seem not to be susceptible to them, who have naturally positive and optimistic and energetic dispositions that make it hard for the demons to get a foothold. And if you look at the lives of these unusual people, they tend to be the ones who are always worrying about doing what's right rather than what's expedient, and they can never figure out why our society does everything it can to ostracize them. And of course there are the Buddhist priests. The Buddhist scriptures are almost completely focused on living a parasite-free life, by never giving them any emotional energy in the bandwidths that they can digest."

"So we do have allies," I said.

"Potentially, yes. But the enemies still outnumber us a million to one."

"This sermon tonight will be a perfect example of what we're fighting," said Fool. "Remember what George said about a cult? Now it's up to you to decide whether this particular person is a cult leader or not—by George's own definition."

"How would I decide that?"

"Listen to Macaulay's words," Apollo suggested. "Listen carefully, and see if he encourages the audience to think for themselves, to act on their own volition, to be tolerant and compassionate of others who may not think the way he does."

"It's been a while since I was in Church," I said. "When Karen was little, we went, but I always felt like I was being shouted at from the pulpit. And I could never quite buy into the idea that this person in front of me was a spokesperson for God."

"They're spokespeople all right," said Apollo. *"We know how to speak many falsehoods which resemble real things.* Hesiod. A handful of truly enlightened spiritual masters have, over the course of history, offered the same information that you have now, which we believe is the most important message in the world. Jesus of Nazareth was a speaker of truth who merged his spirit and his awareness with the God of the universe. Notice tonight how the demons have taken our memories and recordings of that message and used it for their own purposes. They turned it into a religion where you worship the messenger and conveniently ignore or garble the message. They create elaborate scriptures which take the words out of context or add volumes of commentary, and they turn even the words of truth into another mechanism for control."

I thought about that for a minute. "Aren't you afraid that's going to happen with the Master?" I said.

"Life is a gamble at terrible odds—if it was a bet, you wouldn't take it," said Apollo. "Tom Stoppard. Of course we worry about it. But, unlike the others who came before us, we have taken a few precautions."

"Like what?"

"Do you know the name of the Master?"

I stopped walking.

"No," I said.

"Do you know ANY of our names?"

"No. I don't."

"Did you think that was an accident?"

"I never thought about it."

"The perfect saint," said Apollo, "would deliver the important message and then vanish before anyone knew where it came from. In fact, that would send them a double message. It would show them that compared with the message, the messenger is of little consequence."

"So you do have a plan?" I said.

"Yes. The solution is pretty obvious."

"Not to him," said Fool.

"I can't imagine what it could be," I said after a few minutes of walking. "I honestly don't see anything you could do."

"Imagine a group baptism," Fool suggested.

"You mean dunking everybody with water, all at once? That's no more practical than trying to talk to them in the street."

"There are several kinds of baptism, several ways to change the energy streaming out of a person's spirit from dark to light, from nutritious to indigestible," observed Apollo. "Suppose you were to do your baptism, instead, with something that is a bit more accessible than water, that is everywhere where there are people."

"Air?" I said.

"Holy spirit," said Apollo.

By now, we could see the lights of the stadium against the sky, and the distant roar of what sounded like a considerable crowd. As we got closer, we merged with a flood of people who had parked their cars haphazardly around the sides of streets, and all together, we walked through the gates.

A group of women stood in the center of the field, swaying and singing a hymn.

> *Jesus is God! The glorious bands*
> *Of golden angels sing*
> *Songs of adoring praise to Him,*
> *Their Maker and their King.*
> *He was true God in Bethlehem's crib,*
> *On Calvary's cross true God,*
> *He Who in Heav'n eternal reigned,*
> *In time on earth abode.*

Apollo led us up and to the very back seats, and as we passed, I studied the people who attended. I was not encouraged. It was an older crowd. The faces of the men were every variety of grim rectitude and smug determination and a terrifying certainty. The silver-haired women were all the facial possibilities of obedience and uncomfortable, sometimes painful, toleration. When we reached the back, we were at least ten rows away from anyone else, but the seats filled up quickly as the hymn ended.

Finally, with a flourish, the evangelist strode up on the stage, and the music roared again, this time a different hymn:

> *The judgment has set, the books have been opened;*
> *How shall we stand in that great day,*
> *When every thought, and word, and action,*
> *God, the righteous Judge, shall weigh?*
>
> *How shall we stand in that great day?*
> *How shall we stand in that great day?*
> *Shall we be found before Him wanting?*
> *Or with our sins all washed away?*

The evangelist's voice could be heard above the rest as he sang into the microphone about the Day of Judgment, raising one hand over his head, palm open, swaying slightly as if to catch spiritual rays of sunlight from the sky. But it also looked, to my eyes, like he was signaling to a host of creatures who were descending from all directions on the audience. I shuddered.

"Does he know about them?"

"His demon does. Can't you see it?"

I had assumed I was too far away to see whatever elf or fairy or troll clung to the evangelist, but now that I fully opened the eyes of my spirit, I managed to make out what I thought was an enormous bat, almost perfectly camouflaged by the brilliant darkness that radiated from Justin Macaulay's soul. Then I realized that I was only looking at a small part of it, at the boots that rested on his shoulder, and I raised my eyes to see an astonishing sight. The spirit was the size of a building, with dark folded wings across its back, a powerfully muscular torso and teeth that emerged on either side of its mouth like a vampire. Its arms were folded and mouth set in a smile of grim satisfaction and triumph as it looked down over the gathering audience. Then, as they swept the crowd, the creature's red eyes settled on me, and a smile crossed its lips as it saw that I could detect its presence.

Suddenly, my heart and stomach felt as if they had turned to ice.

"Oh my god—"

"Shhh. Listen!"

The evangelist looked out over the crowd with an expression very much like the demon's, and the crowd grew very quiet.

"Just a few moments ago, I talked with a lady in your own community who told me that she is a Christian," he began, his voice low and conversational.

"I was going to congratulate her for her courage, to believe openly in this day and age, but before I could say a word, she told me some things that made me realize that there is not a true Christian spirit in her. She said," the evangelist said with a twisted mockery coming into his voice," that she does not *believe* that she should support things like getting prayer back in schools, or stopping abortions, or not recognizing sinful marriages between people of the same sex or gender. I asked this person why? And this was her response: 'Even though I am saved, everybody else does not *believe* in what I *believe* in. Why,' she asked me, 'should I force others to do things they do not believe in?'

"Brothers and sisters," the evangelist called out in a soft voice, "I can tell you that I was completely flabbergasted! *Wow!* I was absolutely stunned that a Christian could reason with herself like that. There was no Word of God in her statement whatsoever. Do you know how dangerous it is to live in the midst of others doing evil and you refuse to fight for their souls?

"And yet," Macaulay continued, his voice turning low again, "isn't this exactly the trouble with the world today? We say we are Christians, and that we want to serve God, but when we have the opportunity to do so, we say things like, "I am a man of faith but I do not wear my religion on my sleeve." How dare we cheapen Christ Jesus by saying and doing things as if He does not lead us?"

At these words, you could see a wave of yellow-blue dread come over the spirits of the audience, as they compared the behavior he expected from them with their own accommodations with a world that was not universally, fanatically Christian. And, as Fool had predicted, the evangelist continued to draw this dark unhappy energy from them like he was milking a cow, and a cloud of creatures out of mythology and dream descended to feed on it.

"Watch," said Fool. "See if he ever, even once, evokes a joyful, happy glow from the audience that would be out of the food bandwidth of the parasites."

"Brothers and sisters," Macaulay called out, "I came here today to tell you that it is time and long past time for us to cast out from our lives those who do not share our faith in Christ Jesus. Remember God's admonition in II Corinthians 6:14: *"Be ye not unequally yoked together with unbelievers."* Well, I can tell you right now, right here among us in this very audience, there are Christians who belong to clubs and lodges and associations right alongside unbelievers. You know who you are!"

I watched individuals all over the audience light up with an embarrassed red-yellow color, and swarms of creatures followed the glow.

"We have Christians who are in business with unbelievers," the evangelist continued. "Today, there are some of you who may not even know if your grocery store is run by Christians or not! The mechanic who works on your car may not be a Christian. The man who cuts your hair may not be a Christian. God said there is never to be a communion between a saved and an unsaved person. Yet here we are living in open defiance of His holy word."

By now, most of the audience was radiating this embarrassment and uncertainty, and I was no longer focusing on the words, but on the effect they were having on the souls of the audience. It was like watching rather than hearing a symphony; beautiful and frightening, and the beauty was spoiled and made terrifying by the presence of the parasites.

"But wait a minute, you say," cried out the evangelist. "Isn't my faith a private matter between me and God? Don't I have the right to decide for myself how and when to share the Word of God, and decide what's right for me? For you, I have one simple answer: there is nothing in the Bible which encourages that belief. In fact, it says exactly the opposite. Listen to God's voice in Proverbs 3:5: *Lean on, trust in, and be confident in the Lord with all your heart and mind, and*—these are the important words coming up—*do not rely on your own insight or understanding.*

"Now why would God say that?" Macaulay demanded. "Because the Bible teaches us that we all have a depraved nature. Romans 3:10 says, *"As it is written, There is none righteous, no, not one."* Then verse 19 says, *'that every mouth may be stopped, and all the world may become guilty before God.'* God," Macaulay continued, "wants you to admit that you are a sinner. Verse 22 says, *'for there is no difference...'* not a bit of difference in the world between the person who thinks he is righteous and the person behind bars. At their core, they are exactly the same. When you see the drunk man stagger down into the gutter, you say, "How pitiful." But the fashionable lady with her silks and satins and perfume and her riches and luxury who has never been born again is as lost as the drunkard in the gutter or the harlot in the red-light district. In the eyes of God, there *is no difference!"*

The colors in the audience were shifting again, to a dark, almost black radiance that I recognized as despair and self-loathing, mixed here and there with defiance, which seemed to be equally edible to the creatures who were now thick about the stadium.

"Brothers and sisters, if you are *thinking*"—and here the evangelist lingered on the word sarcastically "—about what is good and evil, then you are committing a grave moral error. It is not what you *feel* is right that matters; it is what God *says* is right. You already *have* the definitions of good and evil. Instead of exercising your mind, you should be exercising your faith. Your slogan should not be, "I will try to determine what is right and wrong;" it should be: "The Bible says it; I believe it; that settles it."

"Amen!" chorused the audience.

"And what *does* the Bible say? There are those who hear only the comfortable, loving passages, and dispense with the rest, and there are those who accept only those words from the Holy Scriptures that conform to the world they want to live in. But I tell you now that you cannot accept some parts of the Word of God and reject others. Because homosexuality is not legally forbidden in this nation, we conveniently ignore that the Bible condemns it. We go to the local restaurant and order crab legs, even though eating shellfish is specifically forbidden in Leviticus 10:10. Because slavery is no longer legal in this nation, we conveniently forget that it is specifically condoned in the Bible. I have not forgotten, as many have, that the Southern Baptist

Convention was founded on the idea that whites owning blacks in slavery was an acceptable behavior for Christians. This is an unpopular view today, but it must be accepted if we have the courage to believe in the literal truth of the Gospel. Leviticus, chapter 25, verse 44 says that I may buy slaves from nations that are around us. Exodus 21:7 even says that it is permissible to sell your daughter into slavery. The Bible says it; I believe it; that settles it."

From here, the waves and pulses of dark colors were coming too fast for me to follow. I turned and saw Apollo standing up behind me against the railing with his arms folded, a look not of disgust, as I had expected, but of pity on his face. He saw me looking at him and shook his head. "Once a parasite attaches itself to you, it is very difficult to shake it," he said quietly. "Particularly if you don't know it's there. They'll be going home encrusted from head to toe."

"God reveals through the Bible how He wants us to live!" the evangelist was shouting now. "He lays down absolutes. But then there are those who say," and here he adopted a theatrical whining voice, *"but there are children who don't want to pray. Or parents who don't believe in prayer.* Brothers and sisters," he said, bringing his voice back to full thunder, "whether or not they *believe* in prayer doesn't matter, any more than it would matter to the mountains or the clouds or the trees above my head if I tried to tell you that I didn't believe in them. The truth is the truth is the truth, and we make the gravest of mistakes if, in a weak moment, we allow others to deny that absolute, irrevocable higher truth in the name of so-called "freedom of expression." Youthful experiments with the sinful activities of sex, alcohol and drugs are the terrible consequences of a value-free education. Moral absolutes circumvented by "freedom of expression" degrade the morality of our youth by taking prayer out of the schools. It is nothing less than a crime against young people to allow them this freedom.

"And I see, here in front of me, many examples of immodest dress. God knows that you women—and you can see who you are—are helping to send this country to Hell. Women, we want to respect you, but for the sake of God, for the sake of Jesus, dress like a Christian. Paul wrote in I Timothy 2:9 and 10: *"In like manner also, that women adorn themselves in modest apparel, with shamefacedness and sobriety; not with braided hair, or gold, or pearls, or costly array."* God said it, I believe it, that settles it. Some of you don't like it. Some of you want to be attractive in the eyes of men. Well I say to you women, people are going to Hell because of you, and you too will answer for it on the Day of Judgment."

There were a few scattered "Amens," but with less enthusiasm as women paused to consider the time they had spent preparing for this revival. The audience was like a Christmas tree now, with many women flashing an embarrassed blue-yellow, the men an orange-green flash of uncertainty.

"Today in this nation we are harboring a sophisticated type of atheism," the voice echoed over the stadium, moving on to a new subject, "which started out as a national debate over whether evolution is a fact or a theory. Evolution has been taught in our schools for the last sixty years—from the early grades of elementary school right on through college.

"Brothers and sisters, you cannot be an evolutionist and a believer of the Word of God at the same time. Evolution is not just a theory; it is a wicked attack against the Bible! More than that, it is a wicked, personal attack against the very person of God Himself!" the evangelist shouted. "The Bible says, *'Let us make man in our own image.'* The Bible says that God made him out of the dust of the ground and breathed into his nostrils the breath of life, and he became a living soul. Evolution says that man came from a lower form of animal. God says, I made him, and I made him like I am. When a person teaches evolution and claims that evolution is a fact, he is making a personal attack on God Himself and against the Bible."

There must have been a lot of people in the audience whose children had been taught evolutionary theory, because the stadium fairly glowed with shame, remorse, concern and every spiritual glow from the blue-black to the black end of the spectrum. I could almost feel the heat of it rising from the audience, and the dream-like expression on the faces of the demons sent a shiver all the way down to the base of my spirit. And then the evangelist changed the subject, and the glow shifted on a dime to the colors of hatred and fear.

"And everywhere we go, there is an abnormal sexuality in America," the evangelist cried out. "You would not believe how many homosexuals there are in America. Some operate in high places, in politics. Some are millionaires. The whole human structure of society is shot through with an abnormal, godless, wicked sexuality that God abominates. It is widespread. It is everywhere. It is going on in high society, with well-to-do people, people with college degrees.

"Nonbelievers will tell you that the world is not black and white, but shades of gray. Absolutes are old-fashioned, or they are too extremist. But I tell you that without black and without white, *gray would not exist!*" the evangelist concluded triumphantly.

"Our country is filled today with what is called common law or live-in marriages, when a boy and girl start living together without a marriage ceremony," he continued. "There are people who have raised a family and have grandchildren, yet they have never been married. These people have called me and said, 'Preacher, can you marry us? We'd like to get our lives straightened out.' I tell you now, when people have no respect for the institution of marriage, it is only a matter of time until their nation disintegrates.

"There are four things about the American home today that are ruining it," Macaulay called out, evoking different color responses from the men and women in the audience. "First, we have a lack of male leadership. God ordained that the man be the head of the home. A man who is a man ought to be the head of his home.

"Second, we have women working outside the home. Now some of you, God bless you, are good women. But the Bible says, *'Let the women be keepers at home.'* You cannot pick and choose from the Word of God, take some of it and leave the rest behind, substituting your judgment for God's will.

"Third, we lack discipline. Our children today run wild. They have no rules, no strong guidance that forces them to obey the laws of God.

"Fourth, we have no strong influence toward Christ in the homes of this country! We need godliness from the mother and father. We need family altars."

This was the climax of the colors of remorse. If you knew how to interpret the colors of the spirit, you could see that virtually everybody in the place felt scolded and their lives second-guessed. I closed my eyes and looked away as the creatures of the air, some of them just a foot or less from my face, sucked emotional energy from the members of my species, their faces bloated with malicious contentment.

"Brothers and sisters, I am here to tell you that the rot comes even from within our own church. Everywhere you look today, you see liberalism corrupting Christianity. There is a passage in the Bible which predicted that this would happen to us. Matthew, chapter 13, verse 25 says: *'But while men slept, his enemy came and sowed tares among the wheat, and went his way.'* You hear from the pulpit today, not the uncompromising word of the Lord, the good wheat, but the words of compromise. The pastors are feeding weeds to their sheep! We find in America today blind leaders of the blind. You see men who profess to be called of God, men who profess to be prophets, teachers, leaders in the truth. But Jesus spoke of them in Matthew 15:14: *"Let them alone: they be blind leaders of the blind."*

"Brothers and sisters, go to some of the pastors of this city and ask them point blank: Have you been born again? Are you absolutely sure today that you are on your way to Heaven? People tell me: I don't hear the truth where I go. *Then why do you keep going?!* Why do you send these godless people your money?! Why do you help support a man of the cloth who denies the Bible?! You are as guilty as he is!"

Hoo, boy! Did *this* hit home! The audience radiated a dark anger now, alternating between self-anger and anger at the wimpy pastors who dared to reveal doubts about their own after-death destiny.

"Brothers and sisters," Macaulay cried out, "I can tell you that everything I am telling you was predicted and written down in the Bible for us to read today. This is the consequence of seeing the world in shades of gray. In the Book of Daniel, chapter 7, verse 25, it is written of the Antichrist that *'He will speak against the Most High and oppress his saints, and try to change the set times and the laws.'* We read in the Book of Isaiah, Chapter 5, verse 20: *'Woe to those who call evil good and good evil, who put darkness for light and light for darkness.'*

"And what can we say about the world, that cries out in darkness for us, here in America, to save their souls before it's too late? For some reason Christians try to wimp out and leave Christ out of world situations and political decisions. The Atheists of America are screaming for the separation of church and state, but they are the ones who are attacking our faith. I do not want to live in a country that has turned its back on Christ and His Holiness."

"Amen!"

By now, the spiritual fires were becoming less and less bright, the audience becoming numb to self-loathing and anger, less and less able to sustain the deepest black emotions. Somehow, the evangelist seemed to sense that—or, more likely, the vampire that stood on his shoulders could see it—because now the mood shifted to one of unreflective, self-righteous patriotism, which was a stunningly ugly shade of blue.

"In these days of national strife and international confusion, when the seeds of hatred are being cultivated in the richly manured soil of radicalism and Islamic Fundamentalism, let us throw back our shoulders, and raise our fists though they be rough with the calluses of honest toil, and stand up for true, fundamental, godly Americanism. The Bible teaches patriotism, and patriotism was the light that burned in the hearts of the faithful in the midnight gloom of the dark ages. It was the torch that lit the fires of revivalism. It was the rock upon which Western civilization survived the onslaught of the Red Scourge. Christian patriotism will fuel the lamps of truth and protect our society and provide morale in the fight for freedom in nations around the world. America has great responsibilities. Its responsibility is to God, and we are duty bound to bring the world into the light of Christ Jesus. The Bible says it, I believe it and that settles it!"

"Amen!"

The sermon began to take on a rhythm here, with people swaying to the words as I have seen them do at rock concerts. The jaws of the people around me took on a renewed hard clench of certainty and self-satisfaction and grim determination, which might have looked noble and strong if you couldn't also see the greedy faces of the creatures attached to their souls gorging themselves on the dark glow of rectitude and pride.

"The people of this planet are, in their ignorance, preparing organizations for the convenience of the Antichrist," Macaulay continued. "Groups like the United Nations and the Council on Foreign Relations and the European Union, all of them run by atheist elitists whose goal is to create a new order for the human race under the dominion of Satan and his followers. But where these so-called "world orders" are born in iniquity, we, the believers in Christ Jesus, have a world order of our own. Our pride is in the righteous birth of our native land. Other nations were born in the blood of plundering conquest, but not America. This glorious nation was conceived in the noble hearts of courageous, righteous men. She was born in the holy prayer at Plymouth Rock, cradled by the strong hand of stalwart faith, nourished at the bosom of living, vital, sincere religion, fed on the wholesome food of the highest ideals and developed to her towering stature under the smiling approval of Almighty God. America stands today a fortress of freedom, loved by all free men, respected by the liberty-loving peoples of the earth, feared by the enemies of God and human liberty.

"In Romans chapter 13, verse 1, there is an explanation that tells us why America has become the mightiest nation on Earth," the evangelist called out, bringing his mouth closer to the microphone so the voice seemed to come from the heavens themselves. "*Let every soul be subject unto the higher powers. For there is no power but of God: the powers that be are ordained of God.*'

"Brothers and sisters, only the approval of God makes a country great, not the genius of politicians or the form of government or the energy and creativity of its people. It is only, one hundred percent, the level of the national morals and the depth of national faith in God."

"*Amen!*"

"As we go out in the world armed with the literal, fundamental truth of the Bible, as we rebuke the weaklings and idolaters and compromisers who are hateful in God's eyes, we will be accused of intolerance. We will be told that it is wrong to base your value system on the fundamental word of the Lord. My answer is that the world is like a blazing fire of sin and compromise and liberalism burning through the spiritual backbone of our nation.

"See how far we've fallen when homosexuality is considered "an alternative lifestyle!"

"See how far we've fallen when we murder babies that are socially inconvenient!

"See how far we've fallen when we change marriage partners like a fashion statement!

"See how far we've fallen when we have abandoned the sanctity of commitment in all our relationships!

"Our politicians have condoned and covered up abominations and deviancy. Our entertainment industry celebrates fornication and adultery, violence and abhorrent sexual practices and every imaginable form of evil. Why else would God raise up righteous ministers with mouths of fire, to fight their fire with His fire? That's why they accuse us of intolerance; because our words burn in their consciences, Glory, Hallelujah, Amen!"

"Amen!"

There were many more Hallelujahs, but by now organ music had risen up from what must have been a recording, because there was no visible instrument on stage or behind it, and the evangelist led the congregation in a song while we, in the back, made our way out into the clean air beyond the trees.

> *Christ will gather in His own*
> *To the place where He is gone,*
> *Where their heart and treasure lie,*
> *Where our life is hid on high.*
>
> *Day by day the voice sayeth, "Come,*
> *Enter thine eternal home";*
> *Asking not if we can spare*
> *This dear soul it summons there.*

I discovered that I was shaking as I walked, not from the cold, although the air had turned chilly, not even from the sight of so many parasites in one place.

"Well, what did you think?" Fool asked me jovially, noticing my discomfort. "A hell of a show, wouldn't you say?"

"It was the scariest thing I've seen in my life," I said. "I felt like it was evil."

"We don't call it evil," Apollo corrected me. "It was more like a message to the cattle that really serves those who eat the cattle. The Master says it's a matter of understanding the agenda, and whose agenda is being served."

"Those *people* were being served, on a platter," I said, shivering all over again.

"Hell, that's nothing," Fool assured me. "Compared to the spiritual feast that is laid out at every professional football game, this guy is nothing more than a short-order cook." To Apollo's annoyance, Fool lined up behind him, pretending he was a quarterback with his hands inserted between the older man's legs. "Seventy and three-quarters!" he barked out. "Eleven point six eight four! The square root of negative thirteen! Let's knock those bastards around in the name of quality entertainment!"

"So is professional football evil?"

"A fine wind is blowing the new direction of time," Apollo said quietly. "D.H. Lawrence. You are facing, now, the magnitude of what has happened to us, and the sheer size of what will have to be done to fix it. What we saw today is no more—or less—evil than the anxiety produced by every corporate downsizing and the yearly performance evaluations, or political races that turn nasty and partisan, or chronic poverty and hunger in a nation that produces more than enough food, in aggregate, to nourish everybody. There are myriad ways that they use us, and our own rituals and institutions, to feed themselves. Everything we do sets their table."

"This feels different to me," I said. "From the pulpit, they're telling you how to think. They're feeding you actual disinformation about holy spirit and the nature of God and how the universe really works. You don't expect to get spiritual enlightenment from a sporting event."

"Every religion is made up of a large number of sincere, dedicated people, plus a lot of groups who operate what amounts to cults," said Apollo. "But because they're both quoting the same scriptures, people think that if you attack a mean-spirited preacher or suggest that people walk away from an evangelist with a fanatical gaze, that you're attacking the religion itself. The cults themselves have seen to that; they operate under an umbrella of safety. Even more remarkably, they launch harsh verbal attacks on those who do not share their faith, and at the same time act as if the world is persecuting *them*. It is permissible for them to fight, but for no-one to fight back. You have to admire the power and subtlety of what we have allowed them to construct."

I shivered. "Is there any hope at all?" I asked.

"We ask that question all the time," said Apollo. "How do you organize people to fight against ten thousand years of their own construction? When the rules of the battle are defined by the society that the invisible demons created? *"Politics, as a practice, whatever its professions, has always been the systematic organization of hatreds.* Henry Brooks Adams. Whatever we do has the chance to stir up passions and destruction beyond anything you've seen in recorded history."

"Then people are better off not knowing," I said.

"Now you're catching on," said Fool. "Wallowing in despair—why didn't *we* think of that strategy? How could they resist, if we're able to successfully harness the power of despair and defeatism on our side?"

"Can't you shut up for once?"

"Anger is good too. Feed them dinner while we fight against them."

"There is room for hope," said Apollo, "It is remarkable how much of the truth actually managed to make it into our scriptural texts, considering that every scribe who copied or translated the original texts probably had a demon attached to the base of his brain. In the accounts of the life of Jesus, the first thing you notice is that he spent a great part of his ministry detaching these demon parasites from people, with remarkable results—healing the lame, restoring sight to the blind, returning people to sanity and all the rest. Yet you never hear about *that* from the pulpit. He refers to the human race as "sheep," as domesticated animals, picking up a theme from the Jewish scriptures. Yet nobody asks what, exactly, that means."

"Why would the demons leave such clues?"

"Maybe the original words echoed too loudly for them to erase completely, and so they had to change the message from the pulpit, make baptism a once-in-a-lifetime event, cover the original teachings with dogma and ritual. The Master believes that as long as you can point to the core truth in the scriptures, there is hope that people will listen to it."

"And you believe it because he says so?" I asked.

"All I know for sure," said Apollo, "is that the demons are deathly afraid of him. My guess is that they know something that we don't, and that whatever it is they know, it works in our favor."

I dropped behind the others to walk with Venus. I was surprised to see that she was boiling with anger.

"What's wrong?" I said.

"You heard what he said just as well as I did," she retorted.

"Maybe I don't understand it like you did."

For a long moment she didn't say anything. I was acutely aware that every man we passed would fix his eyes on her in a kind of rapt absorption. She was the only person on the street who didn't seem to notice.

"I was raised to believe that Jesus was the son of God," she said finally. "I was raised to believe in His kindness, the beauty of him and his message. And then, in the library at Asgard, when I actually was able to watch him walking along the shores of the Galilee, comforting and consoling and giving courage and wisdom in that beautiful way, to hear that bastard twist the message for his own purposes…I wanted to go down there and kill him for what he did to the memory of that man who had one foot in this world and the other in infinity—"

"Wait a minute," I said. "Did you just say you watched Jesus?"

"Was I speaking some different language?"

"How? How was that possible?"

She looked at me for a second. "It doesn't matter," she said, her voice softening a little. "You'll find out soon enough, if the Master decides to keep you around."

Then, abruptly, she was crying.

I didn't know what to do, so I put my arm around her, and she pressed her head against my shoulder as we walked.

"It isn't even what that horrible man said today; I guess I should be used to that by now," she sniffed, wiping the tears off of her face. "But the thought that someday, somewhere, they're going to take his words and twist them up and around and destroy his message, and he's working so hard to give it to us straight—"

"You mean the Master?"

"I just want to protect him from them, and there's goddam nothing I can do except scream, and know that my voice won't carry down the years to where it's going to really matter. Oh, God, I just want to go and throw up somewhere."

"I'll help you," I said.

She stopped walking and looked at me. I think there was surprise on both of our faces.

"You mean that," she said. It was a statement, not a question.

"Yes," I said.

"But you don't have a fucking clue how," she said.

"No."

"You're one of us all right," she said, taking my arm with one hand and brushing the last of the tears off of her face with the other. "God help you."

We walked in silence, falling further and further behind the others. Finally Venus turned at the river and sat down on a bench in a grassy area under the branches of a large tree. We watched the others walk up the street and out of sight. I felt like sitting there and healing, letting the honest wind wash the sermon off my spirit before I talked about it again.

The multicolored leaves of the trees overhead trembled in the wind, and scattered around the ground in a little whirlwind. I felt the warmth of the sun falling down across my shoulders through my shirt, and the smell of the earth brought back still-healing memories of my childhood.

"I don't know what to say that will make any difference," I said finally. "I've always believed that the right words could change anything, but I've never been able to find them when I needed them."

"You were a fool," Venus replied in a soft voice, watching the water. "The Master says that every conversation is the eternal spirit calling out to itself for reconciliation. Our minds always mistranslate the message before it has a chance to come out of our mouths."

For some reason, I found the thought behind her words to be unbelievably frightening. In an instant, I felt defensive and angry. "Do you believe that?" I asked after a few seconds.

"Abso-damn-lutely. Everything the Master says is true, and maybe a little bit more than true."

I shook my head stubbornly, remembering my own encounter with this Master. "I can't believe you just let everything this man says to you go right into your belief system," I said. "He has all of you under some kind of spell, and I have to tell you, from where I stand, it looks pretty weird and scary."

For a long second, Venus said nothing. "You're like everybody else," she said finally in a voice that conveyed more sadness than accusation. "You've been fooled so many times by false alarms and false prophets that you've closed your heart to every religious possibility, even to the things that you've seen with your own eyes. That's not really very smart, is it?"

"At least I have the power to think for myself!" I retorted angrily.

"Were you thinking for yourself when you walked through the Deva Community?" she demanded. "Let me tell you something, Mr. Commuter," she said, her fierce eyes staring me down. "When you came in here, I didn't see any sign that your life was anything more than a big bundle of pain and humiliation and heartache and confusion, and all that means is that you were and are a dues-paying member of the giant dysfunctional club we call Humanity, where the normal social activity is to do mutual emotional damage and retreat back into a shell that hides your pain as best you can because it's embarrassing and even more because you're scared to show weakness to another member of your species, and given our history, you and everybody else have damn good reason to feel that way. So if I were you," she continued, her voice rising over my objections, "I'd be a little less proud of this power to think for yourself and all the things it has so far gotten you, and I'd be a little more open to hearing somebody who has no reason at all to share the Answers with us, and who may be the gentlest, most beautiful, most caring man who ever walked on this planet. And if you can't—" she said, suddenly choking. "If somebody like *you* can't hear him—"

Suddenly she was crying again, and after a long second where I was actually afraid to touch her, I found myself putting my arms around her shoulders, and felt her head and her body melt into me. She kept shaking her head and wiping tears all over my shirt, and I pulled her deeper against me, and for those few seconds it felt like she was a real person instead of a goddess.

"We've tried to make people listen; God knows we have," she said, the words almost indistinguishable against my chest. "The only reason I care any more is because *he* cares so much. That's what they always say, is we're too weird, too dependent on *him*, that we're incapable of thinking for ourselves, and you know the words are put in their heads and they're just mumbling what they're told to mumble, but it's so damn frustrating…"

"I'm sorry," I said. "I had no right to judge you."

"You have no right to judge *him*," she said, leaning back on the bench and using my shirt to dry her face.

"You love him," I said. I tried to imagine Venus and the cripple I had seen in the room, together as lovers, but the image was too strange for me to assimilate.

"I never know what to say to him; I never know how to act around him. I feel like I can't touch him; he's too far out there to even notice the little thing that is me, and it makes me feel small and alone whenever I think about him.

"I know—" she brushed back the tears, shook the hair out of her face and looked back down at her hands. "I know that I should feel happy that he's here with us. That's what everyone tells me when I get like this. I *am* happy," she said, looking up at me as if she wanted to see if I could believe her. "I know I'm happy. Just being on the same planet with…With *him* is an incredible privilege that someday people will look back and envy all of us for, and they'll say that we had an unfair advantage, because we are the only ones who don't have to take who and what he is on faith. But what they won't ever understand is how goddam hard it is to love him the way I can't help loving him and knowing that the way he loves me is and always will be forever different from what every goddamn molecule of my body screams out for every time I see him or think about him. Do you understand?" she asked me, her eyes locking mine in a desperate embrace. "Is this making any sense to you?"

"Have you told him any of this?" I asked, wondering at the same time whether the Master was any longer capable of hearing the spoken word.

"My spirit does cartwheels of joy every time he's nearby," she said. "I don't think he needs any words to know how I feel."

"When I finally have a talk with him, I'm going to find a way to tell him with actual words," I said.

Venus looked up at me for a long second, and I found myself swimming in the exotic beauty of her face, contorted though it was at that moment. Finally she stood up.

"You do that, and I'll kill you," she said, and walked away.

Interlude: The Big Questions
Who, or what, are the modern gods?

Karen, as I write this, Cassandra and I are sitting on the back of the loading docks, our feet dangling over the edge, while others are busy making the final arrangements inside—the arrangements that Cassandra has been uninterested in supporting because, she insists, it's wasted energy. Finally, my thoughts aching with curiosity, I look for some answers to questions that I think you, too, would have been curious about.

"I don't understand these people, Can you help me know what I've stumbled into here?"

Cassandra: "You are with the gods now."

"What?"

Cassandra (laughing at the look on my face): "The last people in history who lived without the curse, who used their full human capabilities, were worshipped as gods. We have taken their names to remind us of how much we have yet to recover."

"But what are their capabilities?"

Cassandra: "It's different for everybody. Look at Venus."

"I don't always dare to. Every time I do, a part of me flops around and my mind is confused."

Cassandra (giggling a little): "The men are all deathly afraid of her. What would you say if I told you that she looked quite ordinary before she met the Master?"

"I wouldn't believe it."

Cassandra: "It's true."

I shake my head. "What about Apollo?"

Cassandra: "Before he met the Master, he wrote scholarly papers about obscure and ancient texts. It was said that never once, in all his lectures, did he ever make eye-contact with any of his students. Now he is master of the secret, that the right words, spoken at the right moment, can change anything."

"What about Mars?"

Cassandra: "The Master found Mars sitting alone outside a bar. A few hours before, a group of young men who belonged to an Aryan cult had managed to lure a prostitute of color into the back offices, and they were in the early stages of raping and killing her—a process that was planned to take hours. Mars, sitting alone with his drink at a table near the back, could hear the commotion, and it was disturbing his thoughts. In his irritation, he put his fist through the wall, yanked off some of the broken sheet rock and, where you or another man might have jumped in with chivalrous intent, he simply told them to make less noise.

"Their answer to this interruption was not sufficiently polite. Forty minutes later, when the police finally arrived, they found the back room completely intact. Not a broken glass, not an overturned chair, no sign of a struggle. But they also found, laid out on the floor in the sign of a Jewish star, twelve unconscious skinheads, leaking blood and all badly in need of emergency room attention. Mars, meanwhile, was sitting on an overturned trash can across the street, watching the ambulance arrive with stirrings of sadness and remorse that brought tears to his eyes. The Master touched his shoulder and said that he could remove the pain. We've never actually seen what Mars could do without chains on *his* soul. He was a little bit scary before."

"Fool?"

Cassandra (with an exasperated snort, covering her mouth with her hand): "You're free of The Curse when you've banished self-doubt altogether. But all the magic is in the last little bit, in the transition from .00001 to zero, because if you have *any* self-doubt, if you are anything less than a superconductor, then the magic won't flow.

"Fool's secret is that it works just as well the other way. Instead of removing The Curse, you embrace the doubt that is its primal element, and if you can ever get all the way to total doubt, that, too, confers enormous power. His pestering keeps the others honest and as humble as possible, but I think it's a great deal harder to go in his direction than to fight The Curse directly. Some of us have a lot of respect for his discipline."

"What about you?"

Cassandra (in a strangely even voice): "What about me."

"I look at your spirit and I see every color except happiness."

Cassandra looks down at her hands. I think she is going to say something, but she simply takes one deep breath after another.

"I would very much like to see what happiness would look like in—in your amazing spirit. What would it take to make you happy?"

Cassandra: "Anything at all?"

"Yes."

Cassandra: "I want to die."

For a long second, I think I have somehow misinterpreted or misheard her. "What?"

Cassandra (without a hint of self-pity in her voice or her spiritual glow): "I want to escape the movie that I'm trapped in. And unless you know of a trap door I haven't heard of, that's the only way out."

XI

Today's most widely-accepted theories of matter and energy say that the universe is made up of our familiar three dimensions, plus time, plus at least seven additional dimensions that we cannot yet see, touch or find through our experimental instruments. The most widely-accepted New Age theories suggest that we touch two of these additional dimensions every day in the most routine and intimate way.

The spiritual dimension is the unseen direction that our bodies extend into, and the extension of US into THERE is called our spirit body—the part of us that is ultimately, in the most important sense, who and what we are.

The astral dimension contains extensions of our collective and individual thoughts, which take on a quasi life in the ghostly form of our collective agreements and cultural underpinnings. It is here that each generation stores its musical taste, where novelists obtain the literature of their times; here lives the oversoul, sometimes called the zeitgeist, and it is not a creature of god or the spirit, but entirely a cumulative, accidental invention out of the imperfections of the human mind.

—From *The Rutherfordton Spiritual Gazette*

I sat on the broad flat rock by the river and watched the gods and near-gods splashing in the current. Each day now, one or another of the group would bring a new person to be baptized, and there was talk of more ceremonies to remove more curses.

Behind us, Orpheus was bent over his guitar, experimenting with a new song. Finally he offered a grunt of satisfaction, and began pulling the chords, lending his beautiful voice, haunting now, to the sounds of the water.

*The world is woven in fantasy
and we believe our dreams.
Our myths define reality
and it's always less than what it seems...
Who dreams of the corner office?
Or the world a better place?
Our movies, books and magazines
Handicap our human race.*

*You take my hand
you take my heart
The world can't hold us now.
We've learned to walk where chaos lives,
Beyond their here and now.
Don't sweep their broken daydreams,
Or milk their sacred cow,
There's nothing there for you and me
In that dream they call reality.*

*We can't do more than we believe;
Our faith is on a chain.
You learn and practice to deceive,
so generously we share the pain.
Who sees the phantom spirits
in the ghost town by the street?
Their flesh is mist, the real world
is dust beneath their feet.*

*You take my hand
you take my heart
The world can't hold us now.
We've learned to walk where chaos lives,
Beyond their here and now.
Don't sweep their broken daydreams,
Or milk their sacred cow,
There's nothing there for you and me
In that dream they call reality...*

"I've been thinking," said Fool, taking a long drink from a canteen filled with soma. He looked at me and the woman sitting behind me, who called herself Hestia, who had been talking with a friend from college, a woman who had just had her demons removed.

"Yes?" Venus said after a long silence.

"Maybe we ought to start breeding," Fool said.

"With what?"

"With each other. Start a whole new community. Take you for example," he said, leaning back so his face was inches below her uncovered breasts. "Even though my normal preference is for physically-attractive dead barnyard animals, I think I could manage to get through a sperm-donation with you without vomiting."

"Why that's *so* sweet," said Venus with a dangerous-looking smile.

"You might even find it a welcome change from Mars."

"I hardly even talk to Mars."

"No, but you secretly crave his body."

"If I were in love with anybody, you'd know it," said Venus.

"And just exactly how would we know it?" asked Apollo from behind her, drying his back off with one of the towels as he stepped out of the water.

"You'd see him crawling behind me on his hands and knees begging for a little of what I gave him two days ago in a weak moment," she said. "You'd see him hiding like an injured dog in a hole somewhere because I was annoyed with him. And you would see it a lot, because I am usually annoyed with men."

"You make it sound so attractive," Apollo murmured. *"In olden times, sacrifices were made at the altar, a custom which is still continued.* Helen Rowland."

"What is *that* supposed to mean?" Venus demanded, standing up and pulling a towel around her hair.

"It means that romantic love and the institution of marriage are artifacts of the demons, created to generate feasts of dark emotions in the men who are ensnared by them."

"You think so?" Venus asked quietly. Her eyes acquired a flash that I remembered all too well.

"It's self-evident. You go to any singles scene, anywhere in the world, and the demons of the men are whispering of the possibilities of sex while the demons of the women are whispering about the possibilities of marriage."

"Abso-damn-lutely! And you, yourself, have done the field research on this subject?"

For the first time, a slightly uncomfortable look crossed Apollo's face. "I am not naturally attracted to the singles scene, personally," he said. "I prefer to avoid entanglements under rules that are a mystery to me. *It is assumed that the woman must wait, motionless, until she is wooed. That is how the spider waits for the fly.* George Bernard Shaw."

"When my Curse was lifted," said Venus, "I began to see marriage as one more coerced act of self-destruction created by the demons to provide them with an endless feast of women's misery. I realized that marriage is inevitably a union of the idealist and the clueless."

Hestia, from above and behind her, clapped her hands. "You got my vote," she called out.

"Shouldn't you be defending us?" Fool demanded of Apollo.

"Women never love the men they have," Apollo replied, staring into the air above Venus's head; "they fall in love with the improvements they can make to them."

"Men," Venus retorted, "never fall in love at all. They go into heat, and their idea of commitment is to stay awake long enough to have their own orgasm. Their idea of self-improvement is to reduce their handicap on the golf course, and the only positive changes any woman has ever made in a man in all of recorded history is to teach him how to work the toilet seat and sometimes avoid farting in public."

Apollo winced each time she listed another shortcoming. "And you know about these things from your own great experience with marriage?" he said finally.

"It so happens I've been married twice."

"Is that true?" Hestia's friend asked, her spirit radiating surprise bordering on astonishment. "And these things actually happened to somebody as beautiful as you?"

"Beauty has nothing to do with it," Venus told her. "Beauty, or lack of it, is how women try to explain the natural shortcomings and insensitivities of their men."

"*Marriage is the only war where you sleep with the enemy,*" Apollo answered her. "Duc de la Rochefort."

"I suppose it *would* look like war to a man, since everything else does. That's why the world has been so goddam peaceful these past ten thousand years." Venus flashed her magnificent hair and stalked off up the embankment.

Fool clapped Apollo on the shoulder. "Nice job, Dope," he said. "You really told the hag a thing or two."

It seemed like everybody was out in the water, or glimming in small groups on the rocks, perhaps sensing that this was the last warm day of the season, the last opportunity to baptize each other in comfort. I wondered if they would keep coming down to the water all winter.

By now, it was possible for me to see the difference between the gods and the near-gods in the way their spirit bodies were organized. Every spirit body glows especially brightly along a rough line from a place at the base of the spine to the tip of the head, with nodes of brightness that Apollo had told me were Chakras, but which looked to me like slightly denser clusters of holy spirit.

The difference between the gods and the near-gods was that the center of gravity of the brightness tended to be higher with the gods than the near-gods; they tended to be brighter toward the top. And with all the gods, but none of the near-gods, you could see a faint additional glow above the head, which made me wonder, sometimes when I would catch a glimpse of it in the darkness, whether somebody somewhere had seen this extra floating Chakra and called it a halo, and then as people lost the ability to see the energy body, the idea of a halo as a golden floating crown took its place among the rest of our myths and fantasies and distorted truths.

I lay back and let the sun warm my body, wondering why the cell phone didn't ring with the last of my customers who had not yet returned my calls. Saturday morning was not an ideal time to talk financial business, but the messages I had left should have been alarming enough to provoke a response. I rolled over and checked my Palm, and rechecked the list. Still 11 people I had not talked with personally. I checked my phone again, and discovered to my dismay that it was out of batteries. Dead.

"That explains it," I said.

"What?" Cassandra asked me, emerging from the water.

"You know what," I said, irritated.

"Yes, but in the movie you tell me," she said, smiling.

"People suddenly stopped calling because my phone is dead. I probably have a dozen messages piling up. Is there any place with electricity around here?"

"Gas stations. The college up the street." She shrugged and tossed her hair.

Fool looked up. "Didn't the Master tell you *anything* about how we're going to get an audience to hear him speak?"

"Learn to deal with the ambiguity," Apollo advised him.

"I'm all for ambiguity, so long as it's clearly laid out," Fool retorted.

"I wouldn't question the wisdom of his actions," Apollo said sternly. "The Master knows much more than you think."

"But I think he knows everything!"

"He knows a great deal more than that."

For some reason, at that moment, I was watching Mars, who had become as immobile as a statue, and who stared up the side of the embankment toward the warehouse, the muscles along his upper back and neck twitching inquisitively. Apollo looked at him with a questioning expression, but Mars held up his hand.

"It is better to meet them here, my cousin," he rumbled softly, so low that it passed under the voices of the others.

He stood up, and I did too, and Mercury climbed out of the water and stood on a rock to our right, trying to see over the trees. Presently we heard voices, and the beautiful face of Venus appeared at the top, looking more amused than angry. After a second, we could see that each of her arms was held by two muscular boys, not much older than high school age.

I was surprised to discover that I recognized them. Darius and Thaddeus were two of the most competent entrepreneurs in town, whose acute business skills had been a constant amazement to me ever since I had watched them drop out of Asheville High School six or seven years ago. They were quite distinctive in appearance; twins who were nearly as wide as they were tall, with their braided hair cascading down across their shoulders, no body ornament except the hottest cell phone on the market, which they would exchange as soon as something newer came along.

In just a few short years, they had become a significant presence in the local economy. Whenever a hot new pair of sneakers were introduced, they always had an arrangement with the employee who opened up the store in the mall, and got a few dozen pair for people who were willing to pay a premium to be the first to wear them. When people wanted to buy various recreational drugs, Darius and Thaddeus were a reliable and cheerful place to shop, and although you could argue about the price, nobody ever seemed to complain about the quality of the product. They had season tickets to the high school football and basketball games, and you could always put down a few dollars on either side and be sure that the money would be handled fairly even on the rare occasions when Asheville lost. They both carried revolvers in their pants pockets, but I had never heard of either of them using them as anything more than a threat to keep order in the untidy economy where they lived and worked.

Apparently they also lent themselves out as protection. I guessed that they had probably been responsible for rounding up this lumbering collection of ex-high school jocks that now surrounded George, probably for a considerable flat fee, considering that he was an out-of-towner unfamiliar with local business practices.

"We have company," Venus called out as they reached the place where the weeds ended abruptly. "Put on your clothes and your best manners, for we always want to be good hosts, even to the devil's friends. Even if they do bring us an updated magistrate's order."

"Tell him to come down here and we'll talk," Apollo called back.

"Oh, I don't intend to talk." George's face peered cautiously over the edge of the embankment, taking care not to get too much of his weight too close to the tipping point. George said something to Darius and Thaddeus in a low voice, and then called down to us again.

"I have great news for you, Arthur," he said, waving the new court order in the air. "Your father has tripled my fee on the proviso that I bring you back before tomorrow night," he called out, giving me a quick glance. "I think this is pretty solid evidence that he really does love you after all."

"Let's raise a cheer for Arthur's father!" Orpheus cried out from his perch near the top of the slope. "No, I mean it," he said, when it became comically clear that there was not going to be a cheer. "In the eyes of the world, this is a great man. I can hardly wait to sing at his funeral."

Orpheus put his hands on the guitar, and intoned the words slowly, allowing the melody behind them to provide the irony:

We are here to bury Arthur's dad.
He was a man of greatness, who embodied the American Dream.
While lesser men were home with their sons and daughters
He worked his way up the ranks to become president and chairman
Of a company which successfully fought air and water pollution controls
Wherever they threatened its bottom line.
While lesser men were eating dinner with their wives
And attending the soccer games of their children,
Arthur's dad was putting the details on corporate takeovers
That reduced competition in his industry
And laid off thousands of workers from their jobs.

We are here to bury Arthur's dad.
He was a man of strong and uncompromising faith.
Every Sunday morning, while other men scheduled picnics at the park
He served as elder and deacon of a church
Whose pastor preached hatred of the gay and lesbian lifestyle
And taught that God wanted women to submit to their men.
While lesser men read books to their children at bedtime,

He served on committees to ban the teaching of evolution
In public schools, and to have children of all faiths
Hear and repeat Christian prayers in the morning.

We are here to bury Arthur's Dad.
He was an important contributor to American politics.
Where lesser men gave what they could to the local food bank,
He donated more than ten million dollars of his own money,
Plus company profits that might have gone into bonuses for its workers,
To help elect men to Congress who voted to remove affirmative action laws,
Reduce taxes on the wealthiest Americans, build up the military,
and scale back
Government protections of workers and customers of corporations like his.

We are here to bury Arthur's Dad.
Whenever great men are listed, we will hear his name,
Spoken in reverence as the man who had everything and always
wanted more.
While thousands of children died, penniless, for lack of food or shelter,
He died with more money than it would have taken
To feed children all over the world through their formative years.
Here at his funeral, we offer our tears at the passing
of a great one among us,
For Arthur's Dad was an example of everything that we hope to be ourselves,
As people, as family members, as Americans.

Karen, I don't think you will believe this, but the words had an interesting effect on the men who surrounded George. I saw in their spirits that they had grown up hating men like Orpheus was describing, that each of them had spent their childhood years in a place of scarcity where the divide between rich and poor was well-defined and exploitive. I was reading the life of one of them, who had served two bitter years in the county jail for vandalizing the home of a woman who had once employed his mother as a maid and then refused to pay her, when Venus reached her hand out and touched one of her captors on the leg.

"I'll bet it's hard working for an asshole like George," she said softly. As she spoke, I saw something I had not noticed before; I saw Venus projecting an erotic charm from her spirit directly into the other's dark glow, actually manipulating the colors inside his holy spirit body with an interesting combination of desire and romance, one color on the dark end, the other from the white, both nearly identical. The sudden outflow of white energy took a large ogre perched on Darius's chest by surprise, as it leaped off of its host in pain and hovered angrily like a giant hairy hummingbird.

Darius released his grip on the lovely arm he was holding, and Venus turned to Thaddeus, who was holding the other one. "What about you?" she said, projecting again, her emanation causing a dark angry hag to detach its claws from the back of his head. He, too, released her, and she leaned up on her toes and kissed him gently on the side of his face. Then she skipped with remarkable grace down the rough pathway of stones to stand beside Mars.

"You can join us," she called back to the two. "In fact, why don't you all take off your clothes and try a clothing-optional swim? All except you," she said to George. "For you, the more clothes the better."

"Close your ears," George called out to the others. "Or they'll have you believing that up is down and down is sideways. Remember what this is worth to you."

Fool stepped forward. Apollo reached for his arm, but Fool yanked free. "Hey, you guys get to show off, but not me?" he said. "Am I not a god too?

"Why don't you tell them what this is worth to YOU?" Fool called back up the hill. "Knowing my father, the original bounty, before he tripled it, was at least $200,000 for a day's work. And George couldn't do it without you guys. He was here a few days ago and found that out for himself."

From this distance, I couldn't read how much Darius and Thaddeus and their friends were being paid, but from the sudden shift in the colors of their spirits, I was able to guess that they felt like they ought to renegotiate.

"You should also know that he's working with the police, and they were his first choice to enforce this court order he's waving around," Fool continued. "But you couldn't convince them that this was totally legal, this thing you're doing, could you? Did you tell them that? That someday I'll get free of you and your brainwashing, and I'll file charges for kidnapping and assault? How much of their legal fees were you planning to pay, Georgie?" Fool demanded.

The young men who had come with George were staring down at Fool with no discernible expression on their faces, but there was indecision in the color of their spirits, and Fool knew that he had gotten their attention. "We'll still be here tomorrow and for the next few days," he promised. "I've given you the information you need to get a better deal. At least get yourselves a fair price for this thing you're doing, and then you can come back and take me away from the people I've chosen to live with. Or," he suggested helpfully, "you can take the hag up on her offer and we'll show you what a group baptism looks like. Hag is really something without her clothes on," he added.

George said something in a low voice that I couldn't hear, and the heads turned in his direction. One of the others said something unintelligible, and for a second I thought they were going to throw George over the side. George apparently thought so too, because he backed away a step and said something else, and then the colors of his henchmen returned to a grim shade of brown tinged with dark green, and I knew the renegotiation was complete.

"This is your last chance to do this peacefully," George called out. "Send Arthur up here to us and we can leave without anybody getting hurt."

"Why don't you come down here?" Apollo called back.

"Have it your way."

They started down the hill, a process which took some time, because George was unbelievably clumsy on his feet and every step was a significant undertaking. The others moved solemnly, slowly, with a kind of stoic determination as they watched what must have looked like a small group of sunbathers for some indication that we planned to fight for Fool's freedom. I could feel Mars tense up, and took a prudent step back.

"So much for *your* powers of persuasion," Apollo muttered at Fool in mild vexation. "You are following a loathsome creature who lives at the pale edges of the law," he called out to the henchmen as they followed George down the hill. "Your employer is a worm of society who operates without any sanction except what is provided by those who are wealthy enough to confer their bullying power on his bloated body. His business is to snatch free spirits away from the influence of people who think, God forbid, differently from the norm."

They were nearly at the bottom now, but Apollo's words were having a strange effect. As he spoke, more dark energy emanated from the spirits of the men on the side of the hill, and this attracted a swarm of demons, who descended and attached to the men as hosts, feasting greedily on this indecision and reinforcing it. Apollo opened his mouth again, and I knew from his aura that he was about to address the demons directly, show them places where the pain could become intolerable, suggest blockages of arteries, closing of lungs, small changes to the fragile internal ecosystems of six men who threatened to snatch Fool from among us.

Before he could open his mouth, Mars put a hand on his arm and stepped forward.

"My cousin, there is a time for words," he said softly, "and a time for acting. Let us waste no more talk on them."

My daughter, what happened next is still difficult for me to sort out, because my eyes couldn't follow everything, and because even though I thought I knew what to expect, the actual events were completely unexpected. One second, George was indicating which of us was Fool, and the young men he had brought with him were moving forward to do the thing which they were now extremely well-paid to do.

The next second, the next frame of the movie, Mars was stepping forward in front of Fool, and his face became absorbed and expressionless and serene, like a person in deep meditation. He clasped his hands in front of his chest and tugged them apart, perhaps to loosen his wrists, perhaps simply to cause an earthquake of muscular activity across his shoulders, chest and back. His eyes were closed, and his glow had turned, inexplicably, to a joyful golden red color that radiated from his body with such intensity that it cast actual shadows behind the rest of us.

"My brothers," he said from the deep crypt of this throat, "perhaps it would be wise to stop where you are."

These words had no effect, and I could see from Mars's aura that this gave him a brief flicker of regret. Then the spiritual glow inside him intensified, and it seemed as if the world stopped to gather strength for the thing that would happen next.

For some inexplicable reason, I found that I, too, was holding my breath. Instead of moving in to protect their friend, the others in our group backed away with a kind of curious reverence, and I had the odd feeling that their movements were ceremonial.

By then, Darius, Thaddeus and the other muscular young men were pushing past Mars, reaching for Fool, and as the first of them touched him, the scene seemed to explode with the intensity of a bomb. To my eyes, the air in front of Fool became a blur of grunting sounds and other noises that might have been flesh colliding with bone or the other way around. Then, with shocking suddenness, the confusion was over and a tangle of young men lay awkwardly along the edge of the water, and Mars was standing ankles-deep in them with a strange look of bemused distaste on his face.

Then, looking up, he stepped carefully out of the pile of unconscious bodies at his feet and approached George with an apologetic expression of deep contrition.

"My friend, I could not allow you to threaten my brother in such a fashion," he said, as George, looking considerably less self-important and confident, took a step back and nearly fell off the rock he was standing on. He was about to take a second step, but Mars was already at his side. Mars took the court order from George's unsteady hand, carefully tore it into pieces and then put the pieces into his mouth, chewing them with a contented expression as he put his arm around George the cult deprogrammer's shoulder, and drew him into the water.

"My friend, I want you to promise me now that you will not return to us," Mars said, managing to put a surprising degree of gentleness into his voice. Then, without warning, he ducked George under water for what seemed like a long time, but was really only 15 seconds or so.

Two demons emerged from the churning place where we could no longer see George, buzzing angrily. Then Mars brought George's head back out of the water, and the smaller man gasped desperately for air.

"You must know that I treasure your perfect life," Mars continued. "But if you bring that perfect life here again, if I ever even find out that you are within sight of my beloved brother here, then I will set your soul free of your body, that it may joyfully return to the unimaginable glories from whence it came." He abruptly ducked George back under the water, and three smaller demons emerged out of the bubbling froth.

"Perhaps you should indicate that we understand each other," Mars said after giving George access to oxygen again. He offered an affectionate embrace around George's shoulders that seemed to leave permanent indentations, and then ducked him under again, even though there were no more demons to baptize away.

Finally, he raised George back up out of the water, and this time George gasped and nodded his head, trying to speak before he had anything in his lungs.

"Yes," he said breathlessly. "Yes, I understand."

With a casual gesture of dismissal, Mars propelled the smaller, rounder man toward the weeds and muck where there were no rocks. George floundered in the water, fell on his face and submerged again, which caused one of the demons to re-detach itself from him angrily. Then he sat up in the water, wiped the wetness out of a forelock of hair, rolled over and finally, gasping for breath, managed to drag himself on his hands and knees to the side of the river and seat himself on a cluster of weeds. I wondered how he was going to get back up the embankment, but that didn't seem to concern Mars, who glided easily back to the shore and lifted two of the unconscious young men by their belts, one in each hand, like large limp sacks of flour.

"What are you doing?" Fool asked.

"My cousin, we cannot let them leave here without removing the evil things that plague them," Mars rumbled.

George had finally found his voice. "Were you threatening me?" he called out from the shore, the words sounding a bit whiny because he hadn't fully recovered the air in his lungs. "Were you making a death threat?"

Mars stared at him for a long couple of seconds. Then he turned his attention to the men in his arms, and there was a soft sound of water against the shore as he ducked first Thaddeus, and then Darius into the water, shaking them a little to help them recover consciousness.

"Well?" George demanded.

Mars looked back up and smiled, and perhaps I will never see a ghastlier thing than this smile on this face, ever again.

"Yes," he said, "I was."

"I think I need to glim," Fool muttered as we walked back into the building. He grabbed my arm. "Come and glim with me. Who can we badger into joining us? Venus!" he called out. "Are you too busy to glim with Proteus and me?"

"I'm always up for it," she called back, and after a moment she sat down between us, looking at Fool's spirit with an expression of concern. "It wasn't necessary to stop them all by yourself," she said.

"Can't we just get on with it?" he demanded.

"You don't have to be grumpy. Proteus is kind of new at this. All we're going to do," she said to me, "is close our eyes and sing the Song of the Universe, wherever it takes us, and merge our spirits into one spirit. That one spirit will do our thinking for us, and it will know what each of us needs."

"Think of it as a healing ceremony," Fool muttered.

I closed my eyes, and then opened them a little, to see the others apparently totally immersed in their own humming, their eyes closed, their hands resting against their legs. I reclosed my eyes and began humming the Song of the Universe, feeling the notes, harmonizing with the others, trying to glim or at least not spoil it for the others.

Before long, I felt the vibration in my bones matching the vibrations of the sound, and once again I experienced that peculiar feeling of expanding my awareness beyond my body. My sensory apparatus blurred with momentary overload, and then it felt as if I were looking at myself with uncommon clarity, seeing myself sitting on the ground, a small person in a small place, and I experienced a sense of perspective that was different from anything I had ever known.

Suddenly, this scene in front of me, and this person that was me, had Context. It existed in a framework that was everything and more than everything, a framework that included stars scattered like sand across the galaxy and galaxies scattered like sand across the cosmos, and the light and the darkness, the order and the balance and the finely-poised chaos was so vast and powerful that what I saw in front of me was hopelessly fragile, a momentary agreement among a few scattered atoms that they would cooperate for a few instants of cosmic time in this temporary absurdity called intelligent life.

Karen, this profound awareness of my own physical insignificance did not depress me, as you might imagine. Because for the very first time, I saw that there was more to this picture. There was not only hope, but a kind of grandeur in the life that I saw written in my own spirit.

Somehow, by a miracle that transcended my imagination, this absurd accumulation of dust and wonder had managed to build a story out of its experiences, and the story was about hope and hope denied, about sacrifice and an unwillingness to live by the terms of the sacrifice, of survival in a hostile work environment, of missionary work to the financially uneducated and mercy to the unwealthy who knocked on the doors of one of the largest financial services institutions in the world.

I saw that I was the spirit and the conscience of this large institution, a mythic hero who battled against dark forces and often won against impossible odds, and that the challenges facing me now were worthy of the challenges that the gods themselves had once faced, equal in measure and danger, and that somehow I actually, somewhere in the back of my awareness, hoped to overcome them with nothing but my wit and resources and idealism.

Implausibly, the insignificant thing that was me had become an enormous entertainment to the Awareness of the Universe. I saw that I was a treasured part of Its existence, a story worth telling, a jewel of a life worth collecting. I saw these things without any words, without anything except the shift of context from my miserable eyes looking out, to the unbelievably powerful eyes watching me from within and without, loving me and my story and my journey and my struggle and waiting with interest to see how I would handle them.

My perception shifted, and I saw Venus, trembling in her seat on the floor, and I saw that she, too, was in this hall of mirrors, that she, too, was fighting a mythic struggle, and hers was the equal of mine or greater. She had dared to become the ideal that we humans had, for this period in our history, created for our physical forms; she was what we had agreed that we wanted, or wanted to be, and so she lived in a web of intense envy and desire that distracted and interfered with everything she did.

She pursued the goal that billions of other women pursued, knowing that the closer you get to its achievement, the more distraction and envy and complication will attach itself to your life, and that its achievement will be brief, and leave you afterwards with an aftertaste of anticlimax that will last for the rest of your years. And even now, as she lived in the close approximation of the ideal, she, like so many women, had to live with the knowledge that the ideal was shifting, that it required constant awareness to know what the ideal demanded this day and the next for those who dared live up to it.

And yet, as she balanced on this thin rope, as she aspired to an absurd construct of collective human agreement, this struggle became interesting, because it was the human pursuit of the ideal, the manifestly ridiculous idea that a brief collection of organized dust could aspire to anything like perfection for the entertainment of the thing which *was* perfection, and the thing which *was* perfection had never, Itself, struggled so heroically, and so it had to experience this struggle through this woman, here, and feel the momentary feeling of triumph always mingled with the fear that now was the time when it would finally end...

Her light, too, shined brighter than galaxies in the cosmic estimation of worth.

And I saw Fool, who defined his life in defiance of whatever he encountered, and found through this negation the back door to harmony, a close synchronicity with madness, aligning his awareness with the ultimately chaotic nature of the universe, embracing and even loving the impossible complexity that the rest of us spent our lives trying to tame.

This, too, was an amazing struggle, and as Venus and I turned our full attention on our companion, we found through the Universal Awareness a healing insight: that his cynicism was ultimately right and true, a completely self-consistent theology that recognized only one thing in the relationship between the finite and the infinite: an endless absurdity that could be bridged only by the Universal Awareness at its own whim and discretion, and only so long as we were courageous enough to be interesting.

And because we were so totally finite, the most interesting thing about us, necessarily, was how we handled our inevitable failures as we blundered and bumped against the rest of the universe, and it was a measure of Its generosity that It handed out the opportunity and experience of failure in quantity, so that we would have less trouble holding Its interest.

"So *that's* what it was," Fool blurted out suddenly, totally destroying our meditative contemplation. He looked up at the ceiling. "So all right; I feel humiliated," he said to Whatever might be listening on the other side of the corrugated metal. "You got me this time. But notice," he called out, "that I'm still free of those bastards. I don't think you're half as tough as you think you are, and if you're not too chickenshit to stop hiding behind George and his thugs and come down here and mess with me, mano a goddo, I'll be happy to designate Mars as my appointed stand-in, and he'll whup your ass six ways to Sunday."

"Did he actually say that? Cassandra asked me, as she turned her truck onto the I-240 on-ramp.

"It went on for a while. Venus and I couldn't stop laughing. He told the Universal Awareness that It had been living on Its reputation for the last eight billion years, and from where he stood, It was getting dangerously senile. The only thing funnier than watching him was knowing that the cosmic awareness was watching everything, and trying to imagine how funny It must have thought he was."

"So what are you going to do?" Cassandra asked me.

"What do you mean?"

"Sell the place? Keep it?"

"I don't know," I said. "I don't really have any good options any more. It feels like I'm the rope in a tug of war between giants."

"These people scare you that much?"

"Actually, I'm a lot more nervous about what the NASD and the SEC might turn up. If DiStefano and his lawyer are right, and I suspect they probably are, then all of a sudden I'm in two kinds of hot water. And you know that with my inconsequential production levels, the company would have no qualms about handing me over to the regulators and protecting Heavy Hitter. They probably have a story manufactured already."

"So what if you sell to these people?"

"Then I'm in breach of a contract with my signature on it."

"So? Would they dare to enforce something that would get them in trouble with these regulators you're so worried about?"

"I don't know," I said. "Why are you asking me these questions, anyway? Don't you *know* what's going to happen? Can't you tell me what I'm going to do?"

Cassandra sighed. "I can only see my own life. Where it doesn't intersect with yours, I'm as clueless as you are."

"That's pretty damn clueless," I said.

Cassandra drove in silence for several minutes.

"I don't think you ever told me where we're going," I said finally.

"You're right; I didn't."

"Where are we going?" I asked.

She giggled a little. "I *love* this moment," she said. "This is one of those times that I go back to over and over again, even though it seems like a stupid little incident. I watch you get in the car having no idea where I'm planning to take you, all preoccupied with your own problems and suddenly you're totally in my power. I could drive you anywhere."

"Is that what you're doing, kidnapping me?"

"No, actually we're driving to Rutherfordton."

"What? That's halfway to Charlotte!"

"*That's* the moment I really love," Cassandra said, turning more of her attention to my face than to the road in front of us. "This look you get when you realize there is no chance of escape, and you suddenly wish that you had asked before you got in the car with me. You trusted me, and I love that."

"I made a mistake," I said, smiling in spite of myself. "But I still don't understand. What's in Rutherfordton?"

"It's where I live when I'm not sleeping on the concrete floor. It's where I practice the Dark Arts."

"The what?"

"That's what the local pastor calls it, but I think he's teasing me. I do spiritual healing, and I publish a little pamphlet to try to raise the spiritual awareness of the community. There are a few copies in the back seat," she added.

Now that I looked, the back seat was full of boxes, each mostly empty except for some remnant newsletters printed on a paper stock and in a typeface that made them look like they might have been left over from the age of Ben Franklin. The title across the top, in the same typeface as you might print a Farmer's Almanac, was: "The Rutherfordton Spiritual Gazette."

I pulled a bunch of different ones out of various boxes. They were all eight pages long, and contained, in addition to lead stories about different aspects of New Age thinking and spirituality, some health food recipes, descriptions of different types of healing methods and advertisements for massage therapists and Reiki healers. Once I started reading, it was hard to put them down. There was something magic about the way the articles were worded.

"You wrote these?" I asked.

"It turns out that's a *very* interesting question," Cassandra answered. "At any time in my life, I've always been able to look ahead and see what I was going to write, right down to the last word. So all I had to do was copy my own advance memory, and there they were, without any real effort on my part."

I thought about that, but after a few seconds it was starting to make my head spin. "Then who wrote these newsletter articles?" I asked. "I mean, where did the words come from originally?"

"The words," said Cassandra, "must have been supplied by the universe itself. That's my theory, anyway. Do you have a better one?"

"You know that I don't. You've seen this conversation already."

Cassandra laughed again, and her spirit was a rainbow of jewelry intermingled with stardust. "In all my life, in the past, and in the future, this is the most fun I've ever had riding in a truck," she said. "With everybody else, my foreknowledge just totally creeps them out. With you, I can play games with it, and you're willing to play back with me. Why aren't you like everybody else?" she asked.

"It may be because I can't make myself totally believe that you're trapped the way you say you are."

"Test me," she said.

"How?"

"I'll tell you something that you're going to say in exactly—" she consulted her watch—"three hours and forty three minutes from this moment. The exact words. And if I do that, you have to promise to believe me."

"Go ahead," I said. "And I'll make it a challenge. I'll make a mental note not to say whatever it is you tell me, and that will be proof that you have more flexibility to change things than you realize."

"Fair enough," Cassandra said with a hint of a smile on her face. "Here's what you don't want to say. You don't want to say: *I think I need the weirdness to slow down a little, so that maybe I'll have a chance to catch up to it.*"

"This is going to be easier than I expected," I said.

"We'll see."

As we drove, Cassandra told me a little about her life. She had studied psychology while working as an apprentice and office worker for a local therapist, and then she had foreseen that it was time to pack up and move into the Sancta Sophia seminary in the Ozark Mountains, studying spiritual science, holistic dream study, mystical Christianity, meditation, spiritual healing, evolution of the consciousness, psychology of the soul, Agni Yoga and intuitive development.

"I just showed up one day and told them that I was going to be taking classes there for two years," she told me. "And they told me they didn't have any records, any application, any anything, and in any case, the classes were full right now. And I said that there wasn't really anything they or I could do about it, and they said there was no way, and the next day, the very next day, I was in the classroom, and somebody had called to drop out, and nobody there was inclined to mess with me again. In fact, they were the most aware group of people I ever met, next to the gods and near-gods."

"What was it like in class when you already knew what the instructor was going to say?"

"I knew *everything*," she said with a little giggle. "They weren't much for formal sit-down testing, but what there was, I knew what was going to be on the tests before I ever even arrived at the school. And that was the funny thing; I never, ever got a perfect score on any of them, and some of them I didn't do well on at all."

Exactly two years later, she foresaw that it was now time to come back to Rutherfordton and start up a wellness center in the middle of the downtown area that would offer nontraditional energy-healing and massage therapies for the country folk she had grown up with. To keep everybody else in town abreast of what they were doing, she started publishing the Gazette, which explained all the strange nontraditional ideas in ways that the local people could begin to understand and relate to.

"So you were here when the Master arrived?" I asked.

"I knew when they were coming, so I met them at the gates of the building," she said, giggling a little. "You should have seen them trying to hide how surprised they were that somebody was expecting them, that somebody knew the exact minute they would arrive. I took them back and showed them how to get in under the fence in the back, and how to get down to the water for the baptisms, and of course I already had the place all swept out and orderly, with the tables and little Coleman stoves all set up and ready for occupancy. In fact, they haven't done much with it since, except complain that I should have lugged more tables over the fence. Actually we bought them disassembled, and I had some friends put them together inside," she said, answering my raised eyebrow.

"So *you're* the reason I've had so much trouble!" I said.

"Actually, the Master picked out your place. I think he had it in mind all along. I just made it easier for them. Well, here we are."

She swung the truck into a gravel driveway that became mud long before it reached the trailer, set up kind of crooked on concrete blocks. Cassandra, with a towel over one arm, rapped on the door, and we could hear some kind of shuffling inside.

Finally the door opened, and a man in a tee-shirt and unkempt beard peered out at us myopically. The color of his skin was a pale green, and his hand trembled a little as he leaned against the door.

"Albert?" Cassandra asked him.

"Who're you?" he demanded.

"I'm here because Sallie up the street says you aren't doing so well," Cassandra answered him boldly.

"Who?"

"Your cousin. She says you have kidney problems. Is that true?"

"Ain't felt so good," Albert admitted glumly. "What's that got to do with you?"

"We want to do some energy work on you. Make you feel better, maybe."

"You selling something?"

"We want you to take your clothes off and lie down and I'm going to put my hands all over your body, and if it works, you'll feel like a new man, and if it doesn't, you haven't lost anything except maybe the energy you spent taking your clothes off. Are you going to let us in or not?"

There was no obvious invitation, but Cassandra pushed her way in the door, and I followed her. She led Albert inside a living room whose floor was slanted just enough to make walking uncomfortable, and covered with newspapers and cigarette butts in what seemed to me to be a highly-combustible combination, and there were articles of clothing mixed in, and the coffee table was full of used plates. Apparently Albert would use one, and leave it there, and then bring out food on another one and stack it on top while he ate it, and repeat this until he ran out of plates. There were three full ashtrays on the coffee table, and one of the glasses was a quarter filled with a liquid that was covered entirely with grayish mold.

Cassandra turned off the television, which made it much easier to hear her.

"Now what we're going to be doing is feeling on your body for places that are abnormally hot and abnormally cold, which is either where your energy is being blocked, or where it's radiating out of you too fast. We're going to try to restore your energy flow. Do you understand that?"

"Say again? My what?"

"It's called the healing touch, sometimes called Reiki Therapy."

"Problem's in my kidneys," said Albert, pulling a cigarette out of his pocket.

Cassandra took the cigarette out of his hand and looked for a free place to put it on the coffee table, and then set it carefully on the arm of the sofa. "Just take off your clothes and lie down on the floor here, face down. We'll put this towel over you."

Albert looked like he was going to protest, but he couldn't seem to figure out a good reason to. Finally, he took off his shirt, and after a moment, he turned away from us and took his pants off, and backed over to the front of the couch and settled himself awkwardly on the floor. Cassandra put the towel over his lower back and legs and took out her device and ran it up and down his body, making small noises to herself. I wondered what she was looking at, because with the eyes of my spirit I could see that there was an obvious dark radiation from his energy fields across his lower back and both of his lower legs, which also happened to be where three trolls were watching us with malicious interest. Finally, Cassandra began moving her hands across the back of his neck, and then down his spine.

"I'm feeling a little coldness here," she said. When she reached his kidneys, the largest of the trolls looked up in alarm, and as she began massaging his lower back, I could see the energy flow pulling itself back into balance.

"You have to relax your mind and think pleasant thoughts," Cassandra remarked shortly. "Imagine what it would feel like to be completely healed."

After a while, the dark energy began to subside, replaced by a brighter glow in the white end of the spectrum. By now, Cassandra began massaging his lower legs, which she remarked were actually hot to the touch. The three trolls watched with acute and angry dismay as the energy gradually restored itself to balance in the legs, which were swollen and a more intense version of the same odd greenish color as Albert's face. Abruptly, they all jumped from their host and hovered, muttering, as the healing glow intensified.

"Does that feel better?" Cassandra asked finally.

"Much better," said Albert, his voice muffled. "I guess you think it's kind of messy in here," he said after a minute.

"It's more than I'd be comfortable with," Cassandra admitted, checking her instrument once again.

"I never could find a woman I could settle down with," he said. "When I was growing up, my ma and pa never showed no love for nobody. Said it was a bunch of foolishness, and I grew up thinking the same thing, and I'd tell women that, and that's probably the worst thing you could say to a woman if you like her, that she has no hope of getting love out of you."

Karen, you can imagine how astonished I was at this verbal transformation, but the transformation in his body was even more dramatic. The color of his skin began to turn redder, and the swelling in the legs began to subside. His spirit had restored a healthy glow throughout.

"Damn, I feel a good deal better," said Albert after a moment. He stood up, and carefully kept the towel around him. "What do I owe you people?"

"This isn't a sales call," Cassandra told him. "But I want you to promise me a few things."

"What."

"That you'll clean up this place."

"Okay."

"And you'll believe that you're healed, and you'll get a shower and you'll find a lonely woman and tell her you don't think love is a bunch of foolishness."

Albert stared at her, but this time there was a touch of amusement about his mouth.

"That all?" he said.

"Next time I come back," said Cassandra, "I'll have thought of some more things. Well?" she said, turning to me as we walked out the door.

"I can't believe you," I said.

"Why?" she asked, and her smile seemed wider than it should have been.

I shook my head. "Just when I think things can't get any stranger in my life, you or somebody else takes it to a whole other level."

"You think it's all too weird?"

"I think I need the weirdness to slow down a little," I said, "so that maybe I'll have a chance to catch up to it."

Cassandra looked at me with one eyebrow raised, and I looked back at her, puzzled. She looked at me and I looked at her for another few seconds. Finally, I realized that I had just spoken the exact words that she had told me I would say three hours and forty three minutes ago, and I stopped and looked at her.

"I lost the bet," I said, my voice taking on a sense of wonder. I looked at her with new appreciation. "You were right. I couldn't help myself."

"I could have told you what you were going to say in just a few seconds," she said. "But that would have been rubbing your nose in it."

"Like yours has been all these years."

"Yes."

I reached my arms out to Cassandra and embraced her, holding her head against my chest, knowing that she had already foreseen this gesture and therefore feeling a little self-conscious about it, knowing at the same time that I could not have prevented myself from doing it in any case, feeling my head spin at the thought of what her world must be like. I held her close and watched our spirits mingle in wonderfully interesting patterns.

"I haven't given up," I whispered.

"I know. I'm glad."

Finally I dropped my arms, and as she stepped back, I looked into her eyes. "You know what I want right now?" I asked her.

She smiled. "Yes," she said. "I just might be able to guess."

We got in the car and she drove us to the nearest restaurant.

By the time we got back, two trucks had pulled up to the rusted bay doors at the back of the warehouse. People were unloading hundreds of folding chairs from the back of a trailer and passing them to waiting hands inside the building.

"How many seats does that make?" Venus asked Fool while we watched others unfold them and lay them out in an expanding circle of rows.

"We had seven hundred already," he said. "And I think I loaded a million point two zero four chairs into my truck, and Orpheus had seven or eight in his, so if you take the square root of negative eleven, you come out, by my best calculations, with more chairs than we will ever need, because nobody is paying attention and nobody cares, and if by some unbelievable miracle they *did* care, the demons would find a million reasons why something else is much more important than having the Master raise his mighty arms and detach the foul creatures from their hosts in some kind of group ceremony. All we really needed were about 23 chairs, so you and I and the other gods and near-gods would have someplace to sit while we waited in vain for the first other person to show up."

"The Master says the walls of the building are too small to hold everybody that will want to hear the presentation," said Venus, "and he says that it will be heard all the way out to the street. Do you doubt the Master?"

"Don't you?" demanded Fool, his voice rising. "For the last two and a half years, we've been out there trying to get people to listen, and every single person who stopped to listen is here now setting up chairs. Let's count the house, shall we?" He looked around, counted on his fingers, and then looked back up at her. "I get two dozen people in our audience so far. Somehow he thinks that he's going to bring in several hundred times as many people in the next five days as he was able to collect in the past *two years*! Right? Am I missing something here?"

"The Master has a plan," said Venus with conviction.

"Yeah? Well what is it?"

"I have no idea."

"Then how can you be so sure?"

"Has the Master ever said anything that hasn't come true, somehow, some way?"

"You know what I think?" Fool continued as if she hadn't spoken. "I think this is a test to see if we can think for ourselves. I think he's waiting to see which of us figures out that nobody is going to come out here except maybe the police. Either that, or he means something different from what we think he means."

"Well, you decide what you believe," said Venus. "I'm surprised you men have stuck around as long as you have."

"Answer me this: did you ever hear him ask for more chairs?"

"That was my idea," Venus admitted. "If he's going to bring in more people than this building will hold, then we ought to have places for them to sit."

"What about the outside? Shouldn't we fill *that* up with chairs too?"

They were still arguing, but I was already gone. I found Cassandra seated on the edge of the loading dock with her legs dangling down, kicking at the tires below. She was eating a sandwich, alone as always.

"Tell me," I said.

"Tell you what?"

"You've seen this movie. You've seen this conversation. You know what I want to know."

Cassandra sighed, but it was a happy sigh. "Yes I do."

"So are we wasting our time?"

"No," she said. "And in the movie, I don't tell you any more than that."

"That's bullshit. You could tell me anything you wanted to."

"All I can do is repeat my lines," she said, giving her full attention back to the sandwich. "And this is my last one on the subject: yes, there will be more people here than you can imagine. As to how he does it, you're about to see the damnedest thing you ever saw in your life. And by the time it happens, you'll think it's all perfectly ordinary and natural."

I sat next to her in silence, hearing, in the distance, the chirping of a cricket. For a moment, I closed my eyes and extended my awareness, and discovered that the cricket had mated, and now it was waiting exultantly to die.

"You know what's coming," I said.

"Yes."

"How soon?"

"In about an hour, give or take a few minutes."

"Are you worried?"

"That's a luxury that has been denied me," Cassandra said.

I waited, trying to hear—what? I wasn't sure what to expect, which made the anticipation somehow painful. I knew that the woman next to me could tell me exactly what was going to happen, and several times I opened my mouth to ask her to dispel the suspense. But finally I realized that I preferred not to know, and the full realization of her curse came over me.

On impulse, I reached out my arm and drew her close in an embrace that might have been sympathy, and might have been an instinctive huddle against my fears. She leaned her head on my shoulder, and I realized that she had known I was going to do this, which would have taken all the magic out of it.

Feeling oddly flustered, I stood up. "You'd better get as far away from me as you can," I said.

"If that's what you want."

"I want to be alone when they arrive."

"You'd better move then."

"I mean, if there's shooting."

"Of course," she said with an ironic smile. "I might be killed."

I walked into the center of the floor, behind the podium, and leaned against it, closing my eyes and relaxing in a simulation of sleep. It was good to rest for a few minutes. With this group, every day it seemed like they crammed in a month's worth of living.

After a few minutes, I looked out over the chairs, and tried to imagine that I would be speaking to an assemblage of people who filled up this entire building, all the chairs that were laid out as far as I could see in the gloom, and all the space around the back of the chairs, all the way to the wall and—how could they fill up *beyond* the wall, I wondered. The Master's prophecies made no sense, and I tried to figure out all over again how these gods and near-gods imagined that a cripple who seemed to be confined to his chair was going to magically address the multitudes who magically gathered here.

It was better not to think about it. It was better just to let it go. The end would come soon enough.

To my mortal eyes, the building was cloaked in a grim darkness. To my spiritual eyes, ghosts of the spirits of gods and near-gods floated here and there, to and fro in mesmerizing patterns. This, I realized for perhaps the tenth time, must be what others had seen when humans first began believing in ghosts. There must have been a darkness as deep as this, and somehow the spirit eyes of people must have been opened enough to see, not the body, which would be invisible in this lightless place, but the spirit glow inside of it, looking like what I saw now. From a distance, these gossamer glows floating along in the simulation of human bodies was, to my eyes, exactly what I had always believed ghosts looked like.

What were they doing, and why? I suddenly realized that I had never seen any of them sleep. *Did* they sleep?

Watching the ghosts was so interesting to me at that moment that I totally missed the silent emergence of a dozen more of them from the doorway that I had first used to enter this building—what seemed like many years ago now. My first hint that the police had arrived came when a voice shouted through a bullhorn, so startling that it felt as if my nerves had shattered and splintered into my body.

"EVERYBODY DROP TO THE FLOOR! THIS IS THE POLICE!"

Instantly, the movements of ghostly figures quickened, and from the outside of the building, pale shades casting a dour blue glow converged inward. I tried to see the ultraviolet flashlights that I knew must be flashing all around, but by then the blue ghosts had me surrounded, and I raised my arms slowly as the ring closed, and then I was seized from behind and thrown roughly to the floor.

Above me, I could hear the sounds of heavy breathing and then a triumphant shout—"We got him!" which were echoed by others closer to the door, perhaps to others waiting outside.

Instead of protesting, I rested my cheek against the cold smoothness of the polished concrete as my hands were shackled behind me, as rough fingers removed the wallet and keys from my pockets. Eventually, I was pulled to my feet with a brutal carelessness and shoved, stumbling, in the direction of the side door, surrounded by men who wore no discernible uniform, who were dressed in loose pants and tight black sleeveless shirts that had a vaguely military look to them.

"We've got you now, fuck-face," one of the men taunted me, and I could see from his glow and from the grinning, hideous face of the troll attached to the back of his head that he enjoyed, in a deeply sexual way, these times when his prisoners were helpless to prevent him from doing anything he wanted to them. The troll was feeding now on a fine gourmet energy that seemed to my eyes to be a brilliant shade of the darkest black.

I should have felt the old familiar helpless rage well up in me, but my insides felt oddly comfortable, and I enjoyed the difference between what I knew I would have felt and what I was experiencing instead. The difference was almost delicious.

"You've been on this chase a long time," I said, reading his spirit.

"Keep your mouth shut," the officer growled, and kicked my shoe with the toe of his foot.

I had read his intention in his spirit, and only because I was ready for it was I able to keep my balance and keep myself from tumbling forward with nothing but my face to break the fall. I stumbled ahead, my mind racing, because I had read much more in his spirit than the fact that he wanted, very much, to have the others leave me alone with him for an hour. These other pieces of information were very confusing.

We left the building into the cool air blowing soft from the river, its muted roar exactly loud enough to erase the sound of our feet on the pavement. A brilliant moon reflected off the ground, giving our mortal eyes a gray semblance of daylight. I was led across the parking lot to the opened gate. A voice in the back of my mind told me that I should be very careful how I gave my answers now.

"Is that him?" a voice called out ahead of us.

"He's here all right. We've caught the Master himself. Surrendered without a struggle."

"Let's have a look at him. I can't believe it was this easy. We've been trying to catch this guy for a long long time."

Three men stood by the open gate at the front side of the fence. One of them I recognized as the police commissioner, whose spirit radiated a ruddy glower like the last embers of a fire. Next to him, I saw a stocky man dressed in a business suit whose disheveled black hair, dark facial stubble and deep set eyes below brooding eyebrows suggested a combination of malice and lack of sleep. Behind them, I had trouble making out the third man. Where the moon caught his face, the light seemed to absorb rather than reflect. It was as if he was wrapped in his own shadow.

One of the officers behind me pushed me forward, and the police commissioner deferred to the sleepless one, who looked me up and down. "Did he have any identification?" he asked finally.

"Yes." My wallet was handed forward, and the sleepless one opened it carefully, drawing out my driver's license.

"This will be the first time we have his actual name," the police commissioner muttered to the shadow behind him.

"Adam Zakar," the sleepless one read carefully the card in his hand. "Adam Zakar, you have led us on a merry chase these last four years. I hope you'll excuse me if we don't refer to you as 'the Master' while you're in custody," he added, twisting his face with a visible effort into a thin, ironic grin.

"Wait a minute; what did you say his name was?" The police commissioner stepped forward and took his first good look at me. Then he turned and kicked a stone with a frustrated, vicious gesture and snatched a flashlight out of the hands of one of the officers. He turned the flashlight on my shoulder, illuminating a much broader area than I had originally intended, with little sparkles spread out all over the front of my shirt. The powder they had given me was potent stuff.

"This isn't him," he told the others. "This is the guy we sent to mark him. Who else was in there?"

"Is the place still surrounded?" the sleepless one demanded.

"Yes," one of the officers answered.

"Bring everybody else out here," the sleepless one barked.

Several of the officers looked at each other.

"There's nobody else in there," one of them said.

"Have you searched the place top to bottom?"

"They're still in there looking," he said. "But we haven't found anybody else."

"I thought you said there were others."

"We thought there were. Somebody said he saw a lot of people moving around, but it must have been a mistake. We've pretty well looked everywhere, and there's only him."

The police commissioner turned around and took his hat off and turned around again. Finally he approached me with a livid expression on his face, and the coals in his spirit had been stirred up to a red fire. "You idiot!" he shouted at me. "Where the fuck are they? What the fuck are you doing with the goddam motherfucking marker on *your* motherfucking shoulder?"

"I must have gotten some on me by accident," I said. "Is there a law against that?"

"There are so many laws against aiding and abetting criminals—"

"Is that what I've been doing? Where's your evidence?" I demanded.

The police commissioner opened his mouth, and then he stopped, and after a second he closed it.

"Am I under arrest for being inside my own property?" I demanded, taking courage from the uncertain greenish yellow color that had entered the police commissioner's spirit. "Do you have a warrant?"

"Perhaps I should handle this," the sleepless one suggested smoothly. "Yes, in fact we *do* have a warrant," he said to me. "Or at least, we will have one backdated as soon as I get back to the office. But it seems to me that my colleague was expecting your cooperation here, and I'm wondering now whose side you're on." He nodded to somebody behind me, and the handcuffs were unlocked. I rubbed my wrists and extended my hand. After a moment, the sleepless one handed me back my wallet and keys.

"I'd like to know why you went to the trouble of marking yourself instead of the person we came for. And I'd like to know why you told them to get out before we arrived."

"I didn't tell them anything," I said. "Can you see that I'm telling you the truth?"

"No."

"He is," came a voice from behind the police commissioner. "Apparently he really didn't warn anybody."

"Then where are they?"

The others turned around for a second, and I strained my eyes to get a better look at the man wrapped in his own shadow.

"I think that's a question that requires some investigation."

"I'd just like to know why he marked himself instead of this Master," the police commissioner said.

"He doesn't know himself. But he's one of *them* now. You were fools to have trusted him in the first place. Anybody who meets this Master is going to be one of them. Haven't you learned that already?"

Finally, I had the wit to use the eyes of my spirit on this mysterious person, and those eyes slowly turned up to the sky. Justin Macaulay's majestic parasite, looming taller than I had imagined, rested its red eyes on me from the top of the sky, and its smile chilled me to depths I didn't realize that I possessed.

"I think you need to go," I said to the police commissioner. "Your search hasn't turned up anything, and you're standing on my property."

"You're a material witness."

"To what?"

"Do you think we don't know who's been living here?"

"I think there are a lot of things you don't know," I said, staring evenly at the twin leprechauns that perched on either shoulder.

"Just so," came the voice out of the shadows.

I was still staring at the police commissioner, but suddenly his face and then his head slackened, and his chin touched his chest as if he had fallen asleep standing up. I looked over at the sleepless one, but it was the same with him. Then Macaulay stepped forward, faced me for a moment before he, too, dropped his head to his chest.

For a moment I looked around in confusion. Then I felt the chilly breath of *attention* from above, and slowly, fearfully, looked up into those red eyes that seemed to come out of the sky.

The eyes regarded me with cold interest, and I stared back as boldly as I could.

"Can you talk?" I said at last, summoning defiance from somewhere in my spirit.

There was no answer. Instead, the creature lifted a red, sharply-clawed foot up into the sky, and slowly, deliberately, brought it down toward the top of my shoulders.

Karen, I wanted to run, but there seemed to be no connection between my mind and my body as I watched, like a bird watching an approaching snake, the leg descend toward me in the darkness. As the claws touched my shoulder, I experienced a panic attack. Frantically, I tried to swat it away, but my hands passed through the ghostly body, and I realized, with a sick certainty, with a familiar feeling of powerlessness, that there was nothing I could do to stop the claws from attaching themselves to my body and reaching directly into my brain.

The creature took its time, enjoying the sensation, drinking in my fear and despair like a deep draught of fine wine, savoring the moment before, with a vicious gesture, it drove itself all the way into and through me.

My shoulder twitched at the sharp stab of contact. I tried to writhe away, but my body had turned to ice. I turned, but there was nowhere to go.

Then my mind felt as if it was swirling into a hurricane of chaos, as if a powerful wind was scattering my thoughts and memories like a hundred million bits of paper, and somewhere in this wind I could hear a voice of hollow thunder echo so loudly across my awareness that the words bounced around the inside of my skull, making it hard to understand the next word and the next one, even though the words came slowly and with a malice that I would not have believed possible.

"YOU...[EXPLETIVE (Vagabond-Animal-eater-on?)]...HUMAN...THINK... TO...DEFY...US...," the voice hammered into my awareness with a thunderous snarl. *"KNOW...WHAT...IT...MEANS...TO...DEFY...THE...OVERLORDS..."*

A sharp stabbing pain in my head dropped me to my knees. I put my hands to my face as the searing sensation arched down into and through the distant chill of my body. For a long second, I felt as if the world and my awareness of it were swirling away from me, but a part of me, very distant, recognized that if I allowed this to happen, if I let my awareness spiral away, this creature would control my body as it did the others. I clung to this faint voice as another bolt of pain roared through my brain and pushed its cruel way down through my neck, my chest, my stomach, my loins, my legs, my feet...

Through the pain, I felt the dark overlord's alien consciousness riffling with a leisurely interest through my memory, selecting with fastidious care random papers out of the hurricane swirl in my brain, reading through them carefully with a dark frown that I felt rather than saw. With a herculean effort of will, I inserted my awareness into the hurricane, and began with pitiful clumsiness to collect as many of the papers as I could out of the wind and hide them. I had only managed to collect a few when the great dark awareness stopped reading and looked down at the disturbance in its mental storm. A great slow surge of what might have been surprise gathered itself in the center of the maelstrom, and then I felt a stern purpose replace it, and all at once the wind doubled in strength.

Once again, the universe seemed on the edge of coming unglued at all of its infinite structural hinges, but now I was better-connected with the faint helpful voice on the periphery, and as the storm and the bits of paper that were my memories and knowledge whirled at an ever-faster pace, I moved my center of attention from my mind to my spirit.

Instantly, I was standing in a body that was unaffected by the dark overlord, a luminous presence that was beyond its reach. I looked over at my physical self, watched it buckle helplessly against the ground. From the outside, I willed by body to stand, but there was no strength in my legs, so I faced my tormentor in my spirit body.

I touched the talons that were sunk into my physical body.

"Release me," I demanded, and the spiritual vibrations of my voice echoed up into the stories-tall body with an electric force.

The overlord looked away from the storm and the papers it had gathered, and looked down and around, seemingly searching for the source of that voice.

"Take your goddam claws off of my body!" This time I shouted, and the strong vibrations of my words seemed to generate a white heat where they touched the overlord's talons.

The creature shivered but did not release its grasp. Instead, it waved a handful of scraps of my memory at me.

"YOU...DO...NOT...KNOW...WHERE...HE...WENT..." There was anger in the accusation.

"Get off of me!" I shouted up at the darkness, raising the temperature of my touch on the creature's unholy body. "You have no right to be here; you're nothing but a damned parasite."

The overlord winced at the searing heat of each word. It shifted one talon, then the other in discomfort, but held the connection with remarkable bravery. Its eyes regarded my body coldly, and when it spoke, the words conveyed a deep mockery. "HE...LEFT...YOU...BEHIND...KNOWING...THIS...WOULD...HAPPEN...TO ...YOU..."

I recognized the truth in his words. But I saw something else.

"You're afraid of him," I said in surprise. Karen, for the first time, I actually believed in the spiritual power of the person they called the Master, who had always seemed to me to be a helpless cripple.

"He's going to defeat you," I said, feeling the wonder of it, re-examining the helpless man in the wheelchair and changing my estimation of him. "You and your pack of horrors are no match for him. We're no longer your cattle. What's going to happen to you when he drives you off of this planet?"

In that moment, the fear was replaced by anger, and my body fell to the ground at the roaring in my head, strong enough now to confuse the mind of my spirit where it touched the body and sympathized with it. For a second, all was confusion, and then I realized that this was the worst it could do, and I had weapons yet untried.

I thought of the first time I had glimmed, and the memory allowed my spirit to do what I had done once before: call bits of holy spirit from the ambient air into my spirit. I generously shared the glowing sparks of the universal flame with the creature whose claws were still inserted into my physical body.

My body felt the overlord's mind recoil in something very like horror. The storm in my head subsided as if the sun had broken through clouds.

There was another wind in my mind, but I applied the sunshine to it, and the glow from my spirit warmed my body. I directed a poisonous white light up into the body of the overlord, feeling its grip weaken.

"YOU...ARE...A...DISGUSTING...FOOLISH...HUMAN...IT...IS...OUR...SHAME ...TO...BE...DEPENDENT...ON...YOU...YOU...KNOW...NOTHING..." the voice bored into my mind. "LOOK...INSIDE...ME...AND...YOU...WILL...SEE... THE...TRUTH...I...AM...DESTINED...TO...KILL...HIM..."

Then the overlord, with a courage that I, myself, might not have been able to muster, held onto my shoulder despite the poison shooting up into its dark body, and maintained contact long enough for me to look inside its awareness, giving me a few seconds to riffle through the organized files of its mind and see for myself what I least wanted to know.

I saw that the creature spoke the truth, although how I knew it was the truth, and not another lie, I could not have said. But before the overlord could shut the filing drawer, I had seen something else that I knew this creature would never have wanted me to know, and then the connection was gone and in less than an instant my spirit and my body reconnected, one to the other, and I lay gasping on my knees for long seconds, before finally I mustered the courage to stand up.

The Police Commissioner and the sleepless one and the evangelist were all rousing from their slumber, and assumed their former postures as if time had indeed stood still, as if they were unaware that minutes had vanished from their lives. Justin Macaulay stepped back and wrapped himself in shadow, and I faced the sleepless one, who gave me a long look, and I looked back, reading his spirit like the pages of a book.

"I should have you shot and dumped into the river," he said. "But something tells me that you're going to be of some use to us eventually."

"So I was just told," I said.

He looked at me curiously, and then turned to the group of men who were returning, empty-handed, from the warehouse. "We're leaving," he called out. With an ironic gesture, he gave me a half-wave of his hand. "Enjoy your evening," he said. "I'm sure our paths will cross again before long."

"Before you go," I called out at his back, "maybe you can tell me something."

The sleepless one stopped walking and slowly turned around.

"What."

"What the hell is a district chief of the FBI doing out here in Asheville, North Carolina? And how is it that you have soldiers working under you?"

Instead of answering, the FBI district chief walked right up to my face, and leaned in hard.

"Boy," he said in a long slow drawl, "you have no idea what you're in the middle of. And if I were you, I'd do everything I could not to find out."

XII

If we could see our lives and ourselves through the eyes of the infinite Awareness of the Universe, what would we look like? How absurd and laughable our arrogance and pride and vanity would seem in creatures so small! All the wealth and power in the world would seem as insignificant as the ant who happens to have temporary possession of the largest crumb on the picnic blanket.

In that moment, we might realize that the only opportunity we have to become significant in the eyes of the divine is to recognize our station in the universe and live in humility, and to behave gracefully and tenderly toward others. Perhaps it is interesting that this is exactly the message we have received from the foundations of the world's major religions, and yet how many people have incorporated this simple lesson into their daily lives?
—From *The Rutherfordton Spiritual Gazette*

Because this was the first time I had met the Big Score at his own offices, I budgeted a full hour of travel time, even though the address was only three or four miles on the south side of the city. I passed the high school, crossed the bridge that led down to the entrance into the Biltmore House properties, drove through the Biltmore Forest community that had grown up around a tourist destination that billed itself as the largest home in the U.S., and up onto Hendersonville Highway toward the airport, finally turning right into a complex of office buildings, no two of which resembled one another. I parked the car and walked into the most impressive-looking building, and was told by the receptionist in Suite 100 that the address I was looking for was two buildings over.

This one was much less impressive; a five-story rectangular slab made of brick painted white, with narrow windows, so lacking in any interesting features that you could drive by and not notice it among the flashier architecture on either side. The only interesting thing I saw as I walked in the front door was a neatly-tended garden on either side of the entrance, still blooming thick clusters of pansies this late in the season.

The entire first floor was a waiting area with a receptionist at the center who took my name, made a phone call upstairs, and gave me a warm oriental smile as she hung up the receiver.

"You're half an hour early. Please be comfortable. Tea?"

"Yes," I said, noting on her spirit that this was the answer she expected.

"Make yourself comfortable. It will be right out."

I sat down on one of the couches and looked over my proposal one last time. There were at least 20 people in the waiting area, but only one on my side of the room. When I sat down, he closed the paper and looked me over.

"What're they taking off your hands?" he asked me.

"I'm not here to sell property," I said.

"No?"

"No."

"Well let me give you some friendly advice. If you ever need to unload a building ahead of foreclosure, this is the place to visit."

"Really? Why?"

"Why?" he asked me. "Because the old man's a little crazy," he confided in a low voice. "If he wanted, he could get what I'm selling straight from the bank, and me and the other investors would get nothing. But instead, what does he do? He buys an 80% interest and he makes us partners. Partners! If we can find a few tenants and use the money to fix the place up, in five, maybe seven years at the outside, we could come out whole. When our backs are to the wall! Where are you going to find a deal like that in this world?"

"And all you have to do is bring it to him first, instead of making him buy it at auction in foreclosure and manage the place himself."

"I know it sounds crazy," my lobby neighbor admitted. "But that's how he likes to do business. I hate to tell him, but the word got out a long time ago about him in real estate circles. It's a small world. You've probably got guys from five states here with properties they're about to turn over to the bank. So they figure, what have I got to lose? And they come here."

"It does sound crazy," I admitted with a smile, turning back to my proposal.

"It's the way he likes to do business. He says he likes for everybody to have a reason to want the deal to succeed. If you have a transaction where somebody wins and somebody else loses, he says, everybody loses in the end."

"Is that what he says."

"Don't just take my word for it. Ask anybody here. He says, if you're just watching out for yourself, you're not doing the world any favors, and the world remembers it. It's a hell of a way to run a business, but I'm not going to kick about it. No sir, not in my position."

I stared at my proposal with a sinking feeling in the pit of my stomach.

"So what are you here for?" my lobby neighbor persisted.

"I'm a stockbroker."

"Really? I didn't know the old man owned any stocks."

"He doesn't."

"I bet he will when you get finished with him," my lobby neighbor said with a knowing chuckle. "An easy mark like him, I'll bet he'd buy whatever you have in that folder and then some."

I think I would have given this man an irritated reply, but at that moment, the receptionist told him with a smile that they were ready for him upstairs, and she set the tea down on the table next to my couch with another smile, and I thanked her and admired the almost perfect whiteness of her spirit. I looked for her parasites, but for some reason they weren't visible, and by then she was back at the desk, so I turned back to the proposal, giving myself permission, just this once, to be selfish about my recommendations.

People from the other side of the room were called upstairs, and more arrived. I started getting worried. I checked my watch. It was only just 1:00, barely an hour before we were supposed to close on the warehouse back at The House's meeting room. Should I call and let them know I was going to be late? I didn't yet know *how* late. Better to call when I had a better idea of my schedule. Besides, they couldn't proceed without me, could they?

Soft music, sounding to my Western ears almost like random individual notes plucked slowly from an unfamiliar instrument, filled the room. I closed my eyes, and found that it was easy music to meditate to. I rubbed my temples and settled into an upright sitting position and let my awareness extend from my spirit to the holy spirit in the room, feeling the other people in the lobby, who all seemed to share a similar anxiety, feeling the cheerful calm of the receptionist, whose aura was like a soothing balm to the room, feeling the simplicity and understated elegance of the building, whose unpretentious appearance was, I saw now, a deliberate camouflage to the things that took place inside, and also a reflection of the owner's modesty and preference for simplicity. This, I realized, was the formula that allowed all of the distressed buildings in the Big Score's real estate portfolio to recover their financial health in steady, methodical, predictable ways. Such buildings would attract tenants who happened to share a certain preference for simplicity and modesty—exactly the kind of people who would be steady with their payments and careful stewards of the property that was their corporate home.

It was another half an hour before the receptionist returned and told me I could go upstairs, and that I should take the tea with me. She led me to an elevator. "They're expecting you on the fifth floor," she said.

"Thank you," I said.

"You are very welcome."

Zho met me at the elevator door. "I was afraid we would not be able to find time in the schedule," he said. "But he was very anxious to see you today."

"I appreciate the fact that he was able to find the time."

"You are grateful to each other. That is a good start for any discussion."

There was something curious about Zho's spirit, other than the fact that it, too, was an almost pure white color. But I didn't have time to think much about that, because I was led into a wood-paneled room where one wall and part of another was floor-to-ceiling bookshelves. The room was dominated by a beautiful table of what looked like polished oak, and at one end of the table, seated and talking with somebody, so short that his head barely exceeded the height of the table, sat the Big Score. When he saw me, he stood up and bowed and shook my hand. His wrinkled face was a study in fastidious attention to detail, and he leaned forward out of habit, as if he wanted to miss nothing about the person he was talking to.

"Mr. Zakar," he said. "I hope you can forgive the wait, and join me now. Come, put down your tea over here next to my chair," he said, leading me back to a seat next to his.

"Thank you."

He dismissed the person he was talking to and motioned for Zho to sit down on the other side of him.

"This man," he said to Zho, "once gave me honest advice simply because I was a human being who asked for help," he said. "In all my life, I never stop looking for people like this, yet I find so very few. Perhaps someday," he said to me, "you can tell me why this is so, that the simple courtesies that we should be able to take for granted are simply impossible to find in this world."

"If I find the explanation," I said, "then you will be the first person I'll tell it to."

The Big Score looked at my face carefully. "I think you might be closer to that explanation than you think," he said after a moment. "And so I will ask you, in all seriousness, to remember your promise to me."

Karen, while this man was talking, I was studying his spirit, which was stunningly bland and yet very interesting at the same time. Like Zho's, like the receptionist's, it was an almost pure white color, but I could see now that it was composed of many shades of white which were all so close to each other on the spiritual rainbow that my mind had not distinguished between them. Now I could see that there were very intricate, interesting patterns in his spirit, but that they were unmingled with any colors from the dark end of the spectrum. In fact, it was as if they all huddled closely around the upper end of the white spectrum, as far away from the black colors as they could get.

And there was something else, which was what had been so strange about the receptionist and Zho. Although I looked carefully, I could detect no parasites. Nor, as I thought about it, was there any reason why a demon would attach itself to somebody who seemed to radiate only in the upper quadrant of the white spectrum.

"You are Buddhist," I said, and then realized that I had said it out loud.

"Yes." The Big Score favored my observation with a smile.

"In fact, everybody here is, aren't they? Quite devout, from what I can see. That is," I suddenly felt the need to explain myself: "I am impressed with your spiritual achievements, which must have required a lifetime of meditation."

The Big Score and Zho exchanged a look between them.

"I thank you for noticing something which I have allowed myself to take pride in," the Big Score said finally. "Perhaps, if we may ask one more favor, you will someday tell us how you came to notice this, which has escaped the attention of so many who pass through this room."

"That too is a promise," I said. "But first, I would like to help you navigate through this country's estate tax system."

For the next fifteen minutes, I walked Zho and the Big Score through the insurance presentation that I had prepared, showing them the high eight-figure premium that this solution would cost, some details of how we would set up the life insurance trust, and the estate tax and financial implications if he were to die in this year, or that year, or another year, including a more precise version of some of the calculations that Mort had sketched out on his napkin. One possibility was to have him finance the premium payments with The House, and I took him through the economics of this alternative for different potential dates of death.

When I had finished, I asked him if he had any questions.

The Big Score nodded graciously. "To me the details are not important," he said with a dismissive, elegant movement of his hand. "The only thing I need to know, from you, is this: in this country that I have lived in for so many years, but yet still do not understand very well, is this the best way for me to ensure that the work of my life will be passed to my children and theirs?"

Karen, I looked at this man, at his eyes, at the glow that was the eyes of his spirit superimposed on the eyes of his body, and I knew, from the patterns in the glow itself, that somehow I had earned this man's complete trust. A part of me, the part that had been a broker with The House for 20 years, was exultant. All I had to do was answer "yes," and I could retire in comfort.

"No," I said.

"No?" The old man's eyes narrowed a bit in mild confusion.

"This is the proposal that my firm would have instructed me to give to you," I said. "I have done that, and so I have fulfilled my obligation to my employer. But now I will show you what I think is a much better, much less expensive way to accomplish what you want. I can show this to you, with a promise that I will coordinate everything with the lawyers, and you should decide for yourself which course you want to take."

My daughter, in the hour that followed those words, this man and I experienced a direct connection of trust and good will—a feeling which, I realized, had nourished my soul during all of those miserable years as the garbage man in the offices of The House. In fact, if you could define my life as you are reading these words, it has been the pursuit of connections exactly like this one, the feeling that you and another person are on the same side of the table, working together over things that will bring good results.

There will come a day—and I have seen that day with my own eyes—when all business activity will be guided by that feeling between two or more people.

I showed the man who was no longer my Big Score how his life's work could be spirited past the tax collector, and the money he did have to pay as a toll could be channeled out of the government's pocket to the charitable organizations of his choice, and he and/or his children could be remembered for their kindness as they returned some of the benefits that the community had given him over the years.

When, at last, we both looked up from the paper, there was a glow in both of our souls, a shared color that is not part of any spectrum that I have ever seen, but which is more beautiful than I could describe with words. And in his eyes, there was a light of gratitude, that somebody with knowledge had shared it without expectation of reward.

"Now," he said at last, standing up to indicate that the meeting was at an end, "I must take care of you. For this is a great gift you have given me, and I can see now what I did not see before, that it took courage to defy your firm and give it to me."

I took a last look at the glow between us and stood up. "I have already received more than I deserve," I told him.

"Yes, I know that too," he said. "I can see that you are a different man, different in a good way, from the one I first met those years ago, and I admired that man very much. Nevertheless—" he held up a hand as I started to speak. "I feel that I must do this, and if you are truly my friend, you will allow me to."

He led me down the hall to a large, understated office whose most interesting feature was that there was no computer visible anywhere in it, and stepped behind the desk, reached down into a drawer, and pulled out something wrapped in a cloth. It fit easily in the palm of my hand. I took it from him and, not knowing what else to do, I unwrapped the cloth and stared down at the carved figure, the small thing which would eventually change my destiny and my life.

"It is very very old," the old man said to me. "I have kept it all my life, and my father kept it, and his father and his for as far back as our memory goes, which is 15 generations, and I think perhaps it has been in my family for many more before that. For each of us, it has been our most important possession. But perhaps you will understand when I tell you that my own daughters will not give it the same importance as I have, and so I have to give it to someone who will. I see now that you are that person."

Karen, I will tell you with shame that as I fumbled to rewrap the cloth, I compared this peculiar work of art with the $7 million retirement fund that I could have had simply by giving a different answer to this man's question sixty minutes ago.

I wondered what to say, and then the right answer suddenly came to me.

"Thank you," I said, bowing a little. "I am very, very grateful for your generosity."

As I walked out the door, I checked my watch. It was now 2:35, and I was at least 15 minutes away from the office. I dialed the receptionist on my cell phone as I got in the car, and discovered with some vexation that the phone's battery was, yet again, dead.

Karen, you will not believe this, but as I drove back, with the gift seated in my lap, I began to realize things that had not occurred to me before. I began comparing the feeling I had with the Big Score with the feelings I had with Heavy Hitter and the Branch Manager and the other brokers who threw their crude jokes in my face like manure. I began comparing the feelings I had for Fool and Apollo and Medetrina and Venus and Cassandra with my loyalties to The House, and it was as if something broke inside me.

I realized that I did not want to sell the warehouse back to The House, or Fool's father, or DiStefano or anybody else. I would make a decision after the gathering that was described on leaflets all over town.

And I realized that I was not going back to the office.

But what could I do? As I drove back up over the bridge, I experienced once again the old familiar feelings of dread in the pit of my stomach. Knowing that this was exactly the kind of dark energy that attracted spiritual parasites, I scanned the sky anxiously through the windshield. And I saw a strange sight; a thick cloud of demons swirling like vultures off in the distance.

Over the river.

Without pausing to think, I turned down a side street and hit the accelerator, taking myself closer to the cloud of nightmares and fantasy, navigating by its presence and by following the downward slope of the road until, by sheer luck, I found River Street by a back entrance, and turned up the road at an unsafe rate of speed.

As I pulled in to the warehouse parking lot (the gate had been left open, and I preferred it that way), spirits circled my head, and I felt the itch of talons on the back of my neck and the center of my back. With a great mental effort, I projected happiness in addition to the anxiety I felt as I ran inside the building, looking around to see what could have attracted the attention of so many living nightmares.

A few faces looked up from a small group of near-gods who were sitting cross-legged on the floor.

"Is everybody all right?" I called out.

"Yes. Why?"

"Nobody's dead or anything?"

They all looked at me. The one named Rhea finally said: "I think we would have noticed."

"Where are the others?"

Without waiting for an answer, I darted further into the building, looking in all directions. I had to slow down when I reached the rows of chairs. I could feel parasites beginning to plant their talons in me as I swept the room frantically, looking for any sign of danger or catastrophe.

Nothing. As nearly as I could tell, nobody was hurt or even particularly excited. After a minute, I began to relax, and this sent the colors of my spirit back into the white end of the spectrum, and I felt the itching go away.

Nothing. Why had I been worried?

Just as that thought reached my brain, it seemed as if one side of the building exploded into an unfolding fireball of flame, so intense and hot that it seared my face and knocked me backwards into the chairs. I turned around in a panic, and as I did, there was another explosion way off to my right, and I watched it blow concrete inward like a spray of water.

For a long second, I stood in confusion, trying to decide what to do. Then I ran over to the front of the building, toward a wall of flames, and found two of the people who had been sitting there just seconds earlier now unconscious and lying in awkward positions on the ground. One of them, Alecto, stirred and looked at me with wild eyes.

"There's a fire!" I cried out unnecessarily, for her senses were surely picking up far more immediate evidence of the blaze than my voice. "We have to get out of here!" I told her.

She sat up and rubbed a place on her head that was bleeding and stood up, and I picked up the other woman, who was the friend of Hestia, and carried her toward the door, where my path was blocked by the fire. I ran clumsily in the opposite direction, where another explosion was now rocking the building.

The flames seemed to be everywhere, leaping and dancing in every direction I turned. The heat pressed against my face, and I wiped my eyes repeatedly as the smoke whirled a blizzard of sparks throughout the enormous space under the roof. Dabbing at my running nose, my face under my arm, I ran here and there, looking for an opening between the flames, but it was clear that we were deep inside a deathtrap. It was so hot that I was afraid my clothes would spontaneously burst into flames.

Behind me I heard a shout, and managed through the smoke to catch a glimpse of Venus and Cassandra and Fool in another clearing. What they were saying was impossible to make out, but I ran in that direction, and as I did, the ceiling collapsed behind me, tons of debris obliterating the place where I had been standing. At that moment, the woman draped across my shoulder began to squirm wildly, and I set her down on her feet, and she stared around her and ran in the direction of the others.

Was anybody else trapped back there? I turned and stared into the crashing darkness at the center of the blaze. It seemed as if all the flames converged together into a single omnipotent Baal who stretched up into the darkened sky above. I felt the air move.

"It's creating its own wind," said Apollo beside me calmly. "There's a growing convection current in the heart of the fire that's pulling all the oxygen out of here."

"Can't we *do* something?" Venus demanded. "This is ruining everything!"

"I think we should get out of here."

"How? Do you see a way?" I shouted, turning around. But neither he nor Venus was there. Was I hallucinating? I spun in confusion, and ran toward the back of the building, where the fire seemed to be less thick. After a minute, it seemed as if the floor was shaken by an earthquake, and then the ground under me buckled, and I felt myself falling headlong into emptiness.

Once again, my spirit and my body disconnected, and my spirit was coolly aware that this drop into the subflooring of the warehouse was my death. I watched my slow, clumsy descent with something almost like amusement, shaking my head at my body's remarkably ungainly efforts to grab hold of something that would prevent me from falling, as if by not falling I would somehow be able to survive the fire that was closing rapidly in on the place where I had been moments before.

What a fool I was! Watching me fall was like watching a slow-motion movie, and I found that I could slow it down to almost a stop and see myself frozen in the air ten or twelve feet above the floor of the underground cave below the warehouse.

The more I froze time, the clearer my thoughts became, and I realized that it was not time that was frozen, it was the fact that my spirit body could accelerate itself to near-infinite speeds.

Curious now, I moved very close to my physical body, whose arms were flailing with infinite slowness as if I was foolishly trying to swim through the air to safety. I allowed time to speed up a bit, and suddenly I was also experiencing the heart-stopping panic of free-fall into nothingness, and the "me" that was above the "me" that was falling accelerated enough so that time was stopped again, and I gathered myself for what seemed like hours of careful inventory, of trying to remember what knowledge I had about this situation.

Was I dead? Clearly not. Yet this seemed to be a condition not unlike death, and when I died, this thing hovering around anxiously would become my only body.

And it would be free to hover, to fly, to stop time at will. And perhaps more.

I looked up, and saw that my eyes were able to see through the ceiling of the building. They seemed to have infinite focal range. Although the sun was still out, I could see the stars. I selected an interesting orange red one, and narrowed my gaze until I was close enough to see that it was orbited by several planets. By fixing my gaze on one of these inconsequential bits of rock, I saw that it was covered by thick clouds, and that under those clouds, strange animals moved about on the rocks along the shoreline of a sea that stretched out to the horizon and beyond.

Karen, at that moment, for the very first time in my life, I recognized that death is something very different from what I had always imagined it was: it is a doorway into the infinite. The incredible, bottomless, infinite mystery of the universe, so full of promise and excitement and wonder, called to me from places beyond the sky, and like Ulysses tied to the mast of his ship, I listened in fascination to the mysteriously beautiful song of the sirens calling me to the afterlife and promising more than paradise when I get there. And I knew that this ancient story from the Odyssey was the vestige of a much much older tale, when people we now call gods, who lived in full and constant awareness of the spirit, must have heard this song at all times in their lives.

I faced the temptation of death, weighing my options in that place that was outside of time. And I felt something unexpected: a deep loyalty to the physical body whose head was now only about a foot and a half above a rough pile of bricks.

Death was something I could experience whenever I wished, and there was an odd comfort in that.

But did I have a choice? This body-of-my-spirit did not yet have the strength or physical presence to reach out and catch my physical body, or even to move one of the bricks that had fallen down into this subflooring space. What else could I do?

I accelerated my awareness, stopped time completely and let my attention fall off of the familiar body suspended above the ground. Instead, I turned it inward, toward a distant roaring in the body-of-my-spirit.

It was time to test its power.

Slowly, I reached inside and extended the torso made of braided sparkles of universal awareness, lifted it upwards, expanding into a giant, eight, ten, twenty feet tall, until my head passed completely through the flooring of the warehouse like a ghost, and I looked around until I spotted the others, congregating at the far end of the building. For lack of a better destination, I allowed my feet to snap up to where the others were gathered, adjusted my size, and then, as easily as if it were a feather in the wind, I allowed my physical body to join back up with the spirit, pulling it through a different direction in space-time, through the opening in the space between the spirit universe and the physical reality I had known all my life.

Suddenly I, my physical body, was standing on the solid ground in the middle of the building, feeling dazed and disoriented and, after a few seconds, relieved and very, very confused.

The flames swirled around us, and there were sparks everywhere.

"You can't stay in here," Venus told me calmly.

"You need to be out of the building," said Fool. "It's getting hot in here."

"Yes," I shouted. "But how?"

They looked at me for a long second. "The same way you got here."

"Where should we go?"

"Our spirits are all up on the roof. We were waiting for you."

"Show me the way."

One by one by one, they vanished, although with the eyes of my spirit, I could see that they were actually squirting across the space between the floor of the warehouse and the roof in a confusing way, passing by some miracle through the roof. I found myself back in the awareness of my spirit, and that proved to be a wise choice, because my spirit immediately leaped to the roof and pulled my body through, and we were all together and in relative safety on the corrugated steel at the edge of the top of the building.

"Well done!" Fool clapped me on the back.

"Why are we up here?" I shouted back.

"The view is better up here. Isn't it incredible? Don't you think fire is the most beautiful thing in the world?"

The flames burst through the roof and leaped and danced against the background of their own dark cloud, all the more brilliant for their self-created contrast. The heat drove us back against the edge of the structure. The light was so intense that it cast our shadows on the ground below.

"Is everybody out of there?" I demanded. "We didn't leave anybody behind, did we?"

"I think most everybody made it," Fool answered. "Look, it broke through the back wall."

"Most of us?"

"Maybe a straggler or two," Fool shrugged. "We'll know tomorrow. But the important thing," he said with a grin, taking a quick sip from a bottle of milky liquid, "is that I managed to rescue the Soma."

The black smoke billowed up in the air. Towering flames reached their fingers out through the hole in the center of the building and over our heads, and others were licking above the roof where more recent collapses had fed their dancing fury.

"I think we should get down," Venus suggested.

"Follow me," Fool called back to me.

We walked carefully to the edge, and one by one we leaned over, grasped the edges of the metal and hung for a second, dropping down to the ground, feeling the heat of the fire inside beating at our faces through the brick walls of the dying warehouse. Slowly, we walked to the parking lot, and the others were waiting there, watching the fire with an owlish intensity. The Master sat in the same chair I had seen him in, and he was the only one who seemed to find the fire uninteresting. His face stared blankly at the molecules in front of his eyes.

I knew that I had been hallucinating, that somehow these people had gotten me out of a certain death situation while I was going insane. But as I tried to make sense of the memories and figure out what, truly, had happened, I found that the memories were utterly confused and disjointed, like a puzzle with a lot of missing pieces.

What was happening to me?

An odd thought occurred to me, and I started to laugh. I tried to imagine what Heavy Hitter's face would look like when he found out that the building no longer existed.

I stared back at the hellish fire and shook my head. With a bemused expression, I watched the black smoke rise up into the clear sky. I reached into my pocket, and my hand touched something warm. I realized that I still had the gift that the old man had given me.

The wind caught the smoke and sent it pouring across the street. Distantly, I could hear the wail of fire engines, but they were much too late to save the structure.

The hell with it. It was good to be alive.

"Well," said Fool, "I don't know about you, but I don't think I'm going to be sleeping in *there* tonight."

"Where can we go?" Rhea asked.

I could think of only one thing. "We can stay at my place," I said. I touched Fool on the shoulder. "Let's get those trucks before the fire gets to them."

Interlude: The Big Questions
What is the deva community?

The gods and near-gods are sitting near the platform, organized in a rough semicircle as if they are about to glim. But the mood is so mellow among us that for once a glim seems unnecessary. Fool brings out some soma and offers it around, and I'm the only one who declines.

"I don't think I totally understand this whole deva community thing," I say.

Apollo (favoring me with an amused look as he sips carefully from the cup in his hands): "You don't understand the infinite diversity of enlightened life forms from one end of the universe to the other?"

"Is that what they are?"

Apollo: "On many worlds, the entire population of...whatever form their intelligent life forms take, routinely sings the Song of the Universe the way we might hum 'Old MacDonald.' It's a part of their way of life. On backward worlds like this, only a few are capable of participating in the universal civilization."

"Why do they—we—do it?"

Apollo: "It's a celebration of the Awareness of the Universe, a chance to merge a little bit, and maybe because we believe that every time we glim, we are closer to reuniting our sparks with the fire. But I also think that we all have a curiosity about each other. And so we trade experiences whenever we get together, and I think it makes all of us more like each other—and, perhaps, this too makes it more likely that we will someday be able to approach the Awareness of the Universe, our spirits armed with these additional perspectives."

"Does the Master glim like the rest of you?"

This naïve question draws spontaneous laughter from the group.

Cassandra: "Everybody there treats him like royalty."

Briareus: "Didn't you hear the Master talking with the others the last time we glimmed?"

Cassandra (answering for me): "He was too busy merging with one of the flames."

Everybody, even Apollo, looks at my spirit, apparently assessing the truth of this astonishing statement.

Hestia (directing her words at everyone but me): "That can't be true, can it?"

"It was a creature who lives on a star. I didn't select it; it kind of picked me out of the crowd."

There is a long, appraising silence that hangs in the air.

Fool: "What was it like? None of us have ever, like, *done it* with any of the flames. We didn't think it was possible. They're so—different."

I suddenly notice that even Apollo is leaning in to hear me better.

"I think he was asking me if I'd seen an old girlfriend."

Fool: "Serious? You're not shitting me?"

"I don't think so. But it was kind of jumbled together. I had a headache afterwards."

Fool: "I can imagine." He whistles softly, taking another drink of the soma. "In fact, I might try it sometime; what do you think, Dope?"

Apollo (gracing him with a withering stare): "He lives not long who battles with the immortals. Homer's Iliad. Do not presume to try what Proteus has done. You know his gift."

Hestia: "Have you ever noticed how popular we humans are in the deva community? It's like they can't wait to get their hands on us, almost like they wait for the human delegates to arrive before they start sorting out who's going to trade memories with whom. I've actually had creatures fight over me."

Cassandra: "It *is* pretty weird. I tried to tell them my life was boring. I thought maybe it was because of the Master, he's so advanced that they think we're all like him."

Apollo: "It's not that."

Fool: "Then what is it?"

Apollo: "They think we're like the mechs."

"The who?"

Cassandra: "The mechs were a race that existed a billion years ago. But for some reason, everybody still remembers them."

Apollo: "Actually a little more than two billion."

"So what was so different about them?"

Apollo: "Every intelligent society in the Deva community followed a roughly similar course in the evolution of their societies. First the planet develops a diversity of life, and fierce competition that eventually leads to a species that has some overwhelming characteristic—often intelligence—which allows it to dominate the game—and, usually, bring it to an end. The members of this species, if they do claim the benefits of intelligence, start on the road to mechanical achievement, and at some point, usually early, they become aware of the spirit. Once they see that they're already connected with the Everlasting Awareness of the Universe, they abandon their cheap mechanical toys and the society adjusts to a new goal: the purification of the spirit."

Cassandra: "But the mechs didn't do that."

Apollo: "Even after their species achieved Enlightenment, they continued exploring the physical mysteries. Nobody knows why, but they achieved an amazing proficiency. They traveled to all corners of the universe. They studied emerging life on endless worlds, and built colonies in the heart of stars to study their mechanics more closely. It is said that they found a way to travel along the outer rim of the universe as it expanded, and to penetrate through and look at the other side. Apparently, there are artifacts from their civilization scattered on many trillions of planets, sometimes whole cities left behind, plus a lot of bits and pieces that nobody can begin to understand."

"So how are *we* like that?"

Apollo: "Some in the Deva Community think they can see something in our mental makeup that is similar to the way the mechs thought and behaved. They think it's possible that we'll become the third species to venture out into the cosmos, and pick up the pieces of the broken empire."

"There was another one?"

Apollo: "Very early in the universe, another species roamed between the stars. The mechs followed in their trail. But nobody knows much about those predecessors."

"What happened to the mechs?"

Apollo: "That, of course, is the unanswered question. The oldest races say that one day, without warning, they packed up and left our universe altogether, all of them, gone without a trace. The rumor is that they went looking for something that they couldn't find in this corner of reality."

Fool: "A decent cup of coffee at a reasonable price?"

Apollo: "We can only guess."

"*Is* there a guess?"

Apollo: "All we know for sure is that they went looking for something they couldn't find here. And for some reason, there's a rumor in the Deva Community that someday our species is going to follow them."

XIII

Only a very few people in all history have had a chance to walk with one of those rare individuals who have communed directly with the infinite Awareness that some call God. If our records are correct about the lives of Jesus and the Buddha and avatars before and since, many people, when confronted with this person and this opportunity, rejected it and went back to their lives.

The lesson is that true spiritual growth is and always will be inconvenient, because it intrudes on the comfort and normalcy of our lives. Stepping outside this box of comfort and normalcy, even if it brings peace to the soul and healing to the body, is an act of rare courage.

The citizens of the New Age are not a danger to our present social structure except in this way: they anticipate a world where this act of courage becomes an act of normalcy.

—From The Rutherfordton Spiritual Gazette

Despite the lateness of the season, the air was still warm, and it worried me. It worried me almost as much as the people spread out sleeping on my living room floor back in the house, this unseasonable temperature that felt more and more like a warning, a wake-up call to people who weren't listening.

I sat on the swing in the front porch and watched the clouds pass across the pale face of the moon in the last moments before sunset, staring and not thinking about anything.

The swing creaked where the chain held against the metal bolts on either side, and also where the metal bolts anchored the chain into the logs across the top of the porch. Karen, you may remember when the house was built, even though you were only six at the time; I put that swing in especially for you, so that you and I could sit outside and you could eat your ice cream cone and tell me what happened at school, which was at first stories about how incredibly stupid the boys had been, and later how this or that disgusting boy liked you, and finally a little bit of guarded information about who you hoped would ask you to which party.

I'm not sure I ever told you that the house was built for me by a real estate developer who I arranged an emergency loan for once when his back was to the wall. I personally cosigned the note, and your mother was frightened for months that we had risked everything. A few years later, his business was thriving, and ours was one of fifteen houses he was building simultaneously up in the hills. It was made out of the leftover logs from the other houses and the stones were left over from the stones of the other houses' chimneys.

Presently I realized that Mars was standing over me, looking uncomfortable and apologetic.

"I couldn't sleep," he rumbled presently. "Would you like some company?"

"Sure."

He settled into the swing beside me, and let out a deep sigh. I could see from his spirit that his heart was troubled, and I read things about the military part of his life that made me look away, back up at the moon and clouds and untroubled sky.

"This is the beginning," Mars told me in a deep, heavy voice. "And my brother, I can tell you that I am frightened."

"That may be the last thing I expected you to tell me," I said.

"Fear is the source of my power," he said. "Before long, before very many days, there will be no more need of it in this world. It will be a glorious thing for this world, and I would be selfish to mourn. But there will be no place for me."

"Is that what you're afraid of?"

"It is said that Moses stood on the mountain and looked down at the land that had been promised to his people, but he was denied the opportunity to go there. It is said that David collected the materials that would be needed to construct the temple in Jerusalem, but God told him he had too much blood on his hands to be allowed to build it. It is said that Gautama whom they call the Buddha stopped at the door of nirvana and refused to cross until everyone else in the world crossed first.

"Their story is my story," said Mars. "I cannot live in that joyful, peaceful time to come, as a living reminder of the things our species has finally put behind us. And so I will release my spirit from this body."

"You really think it's going to happen?"

"I have seen the Master's face when he returns from his communions. He says that the Almighty Awareness is so amused by what we are doing that It is actually participating. I would believe the Master alone could achieve this thing that I am predicting. But the two of them together are not likely to meet an obstacle they cannot overcome."

I thought that over. At that moment, he had much more confidence in the Master than I did, but later I would remember these words and find comfort in them.

"And that's what scares you?" I asked finally. "You're afraid to die?"

"I am afraid of many things," said Mars. "But more than anything else, I am afraid of the time when I roam the universe carrying this spirit, with my life imprinted on it for all to see. It is said that the last shall be first. What is not said is that the first shall be last in that other place, and I will be far, far behind the others. I am deathly afraid," he said, "that the world to come, the world that we are bringing about, will offer me no chance of atonement."

We looked at the moon together for a while, and let the unseasonably warm wind blow across our faces.

"I think most of us admire you," I said after a minute. "There was a time in my life when I wish you could have been my friend."

"Those boys would have been crippled for the rest of their days. Is that what you would have wanted?"

"No," I said. "Maybe once, but not now."

"We are going to have to return to the building soon," said Mars after a moment. "There will be police there who do not want us in the middle of their investigation, and that too frightens me."

"You're afraid we'll have to fight with them?"

"I am afraid I must kill some of them. They have done nothing to deserve a premature return to the glories of the universe."

"I was supposed to sell the building back to its original owners today," I told Mars. "But I just didn't feel like doing it."

"Yes. We knew you would not."

"How?"

"Proteus, you are at once the most complicated and the least complicated of us," said Mars, with a hint of amusement in his eyes. "Your spirit is now born, but it is like an infant, still learning to crawl, and like the grass blowing in the wind, allowing us to see the shape of the invisible wind by the way the grass is moving. All we had to do was blow a little harder than anyone else."

"I'm that easy to figure out."

"How could you be anything but what you are? We are all difficult to predict when we are burdened by our limitations. When those are removed, you become clearer and more focused on what the Almighty Awareness intended with your unique construction, and the ambiguities drop away like the pieces of a block of marble that surround the statue inside. That is why the Greeks carved as they did, because the gods taught them this simple truth. And like everything else, the message was garbled and lost."

Karen, this was the longest speech I had ever heard from Mars, and I was amazed at how intelligent he was. I wanted to ask him more about himself, but I could see from his spirit that he was reluctant to talk too much about his past, where he came from, what he had done. So we sat and watched the distant image of a car, and then another one close behind, as they wound around the far side of our hill.

Mars stiffened at the sight.

"What?"

"This is not a busy road at this time of day."

"No," I said.

"Would it not be unusual for two cars to be so close together?"

"I don't know," I said.

"Let us go out and meet them," said Mars. "I do not want them close to the house."

We were at the top of the driveway when the headlights came around the turn. The cars were moving slowly, as if they weren't sure where they were going, as if they were checking the mailboxes that were spaced out a quarter mile apiece in this area roughly halfway between the Biltmore House and Mars Hill College. Finally I could see what Mars must have known all along, that they were police vehicles.

After a while they stopped at the driveway and started to pull in. I stood by the side of the driveway, and the cars stopped.

Two men in police uniforms emerged from the front car. My eyes met the officer who approached me, a tall Hispanic man with a bland, sensitive face that was frozen now into what I could see was an unnatural and forced state of determination and authority. As our eyes locked, there was no connection, no hint of human fellowship in his posture or his stare. His aura was a cool green; not the dark green of envy or the deeper blue-green of malice, but a brighter, almost metallic hue that was indifferent, efficient and cold.

He had become—for this encounter, at least—an instrument of the state. An elf rested comfortably between the man's shoulder blades, and he watched me with a superior smirk.

"Are you Mr. Zakar?" he said.

"Yes; that's me."

The second officer approached us. He walked with a lot of sideways movement, like a barrel with a head attached, and his head was adorned with a spare blond crewcut that contrasted with a dark blue aura that now radiated truculent black overtones. His voice sounded, to my ears, like the low growl of a dog on the edge of attack. "Mr. Adam Zakar," he said, seizing my arm, "We have a warrant for your arrest. You have the right to remain silent—"

"My cousins," Mars interjected with a gentle voice, "you must not treat my friend this way. Surely if you have questions—"

Somehow, the officers had not noticed Mars, and I could see from the quickness of their movements and the shifting colors of their spirits that they were startled when he emerged out of the shadows to interfere in my arrest.

As I had anticipated, it was the crewcut who spoke up.

"Mister, I strongly advise you to go back in the house," he said. He let go of my arm and took a baton off his belt with a slow, satisfied precision. An enormous troll, larger than the officer himself, leered at us from a perch on his back.

"My dear cousin, I deeply appreciate your advice," Mars answered, his sepulchral face twisted into a vexed and unhappy expression as he confronted what was, to him, a complicated social situation. "However, perhaps if we could answer your questions here, or follow you downtown in our own vehicle—"

"It's all right," I said. "Go back in the house."

"You shut up," the blond officer called back at me over his shoulder. His aura grew ominously darker as he advanced on Mars. Every restless teenage boy knows this representative of the law; his pleasures came from intimidating and humiliating people, and he treasured and honored his badge—and, by extension, the laws it stood for—because the whole system fed this dark malicious hunger inside him.

"My cousin, you should not so lightly dismiss what is really a simple request."

"Mister, that was your last warning—"

The muscular officer advanced on Mars threateningly, and I was certain that this situation was not going to end well.

"Please," I said, pulling away from the Hispanic officer and stepping between them. "Tell me, what are you arresting me for?"

"Arson," the Hispanic officer answered promptly.

"Arson?"

"Yes."

"Arson of the warehouse?" I asked incredulously.

The officers exchanged a look which suggested that I had already compromised my case in their eyes. As the Hispanic officer pulled out a pair of handcuffs, I heard a loud sound of a police radio from the second car, and a muted version of the same sound from the first. After a second, another police officer stepped out of the second car and called over to us.

"We're supposed to take this one in too," he shouted. "And then we have to find out if there are any more in the house."

"That will be my pleasure," said the crewcut, taking out his gun and stepping toward Mars.

We will never know exactly what was intended, because an instant after the officer raised his weapon, there was a blur as if two or three seconds of time were somehow skipped altogether, and the police officer who seemed totally in command of the situation was now unconscious and not yet fully fallen to the ground, and Mars was walking calmly past him in my direction. The officer next to me probably should have pulled his club or drawn his gun, but instead he stared at his fallen partner for long seconds, which was long seconds longer than Mars required to take his club and gun with either hand and, at the same time, put his arm around the officer's neck, in a gesture that seemed friendly, but which caused the Hispanic officer to freeze in alarm, his aura radiating a bright yellow.

"I apologize for this inconvenience," Mars said soothingly, tightening his grip in a warning gesture as his captive offered a slight resistance. "It is not my choice; I have been instructed not to let anything happen without some guidance from the Master, as I tried to explain to my cousin there. Perhaps you could come inside the house with me and we could talk about it. If it will help, my friend will come inside too, where you can keep an eye on him."

This may not have sounded like an excellent plan to the police officer, but he did not resist as Mars turned back to the house. Before we had taken more than a couple of steps, two more men in blue uniforms from the second car were running in our direction.

"My cousin, do you think you could tell them to get back in the car?" Mars asked the officer whose neck, I now realized, he was holding in one hand in a very precise way. The frozen policeman shook his head infinitesimally, and then the life seemed to drain out of him, as he, too, slumped to the ground. The other two officers, perhaps realizing that Mars was holding the second officer's gun, halted their approach and moved slowly behind either side of the front car. Through the windows, I saw them draw their weapons.

"Wait!" I called out. "I surrender!" I held my hands in the air, hoping that this would defuse the incipient gunfight on my front lawn.

"My friend, I cannot allow this," Mars told me, taking my arm and drawing me back toward the house.

"What do I do if they start shooting?"

"I promise that in that case," said Mars soberly, "I will truly avenge your death."

"You know, that's really, really terrific, but—"

At that moment, my poor confused brain finally noticed something that another part of my awareness had recognized for the past 30 seconds or so. From somewhere behind us, we could hear the music of a flute, a gentle trilling in the air that seemed to enter my mind directly, rather than using the normal entrance of my ears. The instrument was played with such skill I felt its notes tug insistently at my heart and vibrate deep into my spirit.

I noticed, in a bemused, abstract sort of way, that the two policemen did not fire their weapons. In fact, they stood now with facial expressions of what might have been incredulity or astonishment or plain stupidity, and it seemed as if they had forgotten their reason for being here and perhaps even their names. I thought at first that they were going to surrender to Mars, but then I realized that Mars himself had released my arm, and was standing aside with an alarmingly similar expression on his face.

Long before I wanted it to, the music stopped, and it was as if the earth was silent and expectant.

I turned, and there was the Master.

Karen, now I am going to fail you. I do not know how to describe the things that happened next in words, because words were fashioned from our ordinary experience, and they start to break down when you travel deeply into extraordinary situations.

At this moment, in this time and place, I crossed that line where they break down completely.

If I told you that the Master was standing ten feet behind us in the driveway, in full possession of his body and of his senses, holding his flute by his side, then you will picture the poor cripple I have described to you standing, by some miracle, by himself in the crepuscular pre-evening light, and you will think I was surprised to see him able to stand and move about. But I can assure you that this was the last thing I was thinking about as I looked at him now.

He was, in every way that there *is* a way, the most remarkable thing I had ever seen, both with my spirit eyes and my physical ones. My physical eyes looked back across my front lawn, where my attention collided with a man who displayed a thousand times the confidence of a normal human being.

It was the face of a man, a member of our humble species, who had conversed, many times, personally, with the Awareness that is everywhere in the universe.

And at the same time, on the same face, I saw a thousand and much more than a thousand times the deep humility of a normal human being in his most sensitive moments, for exactly the same reason.

Somehow, these encounters with divinity had inscribed themselves into the Master's facial expressions, into his gestures, in the way he moved, as if the planet he stood on were at once the most trivial speck of dust and nothing here could be an obstacle to him, and at the same time as if whatever or whoever he was looking at was by far the most interesting and important thing in existence, fully worthy of the attention of a consciousness that encompassed everything from here to infinity and back.

With my spirit eyes, I saw things that were even more remarkable and surprising. In order to control this violent scene, the Master had extended the white-gold aura of his spirit body out like the corona around the sun, so that he stood in that first moment inside of a bubble of white-gold spiritual light that extended all the way back to my house and all the way out to the street, enveloping us in a light whose warmth I could feel deep in my spirit. I noticed that more than half of the aura came from a node of brilliant light less than a foot above the Master's head, so that he seemed to be followed by a miniature sun, but I knew that this too was a part of his spirit body, the mystical eighth Chakra that I had seen above the gods.

Even though it was invisible to them, this aura, touching the two still-conscious police officers, stupefied them from the inside out. They could no more have fired their weapons in his presence than they could have flapped their arms and flown to the moon.

Seeing that spiritual glow, I understood why so many artists through the ages had drawn their portraits of holy mystics with a halo glowing around their heads. They must have heard distant echoes of the original scenes, stories told by people who had witnessed firsthand a radiant spiritual corona similar to what I was blessed to be seeing now.

The Master looked around at the scene in front of us and gazed off at the mountains, and then the clouds, as if he were seeing the world for the first time. After a moment, he held out his hand, and a passing butterfly settled gently onto his finger.

Mars stood to one side with his head bowed, and the Master reached out to tousle his hair with a playful expression in his face and in the color in his aura, and then he embraced Mars in a loving gesture so unaffected and beautiful that it brought tears to my eyes.

"I wonder if any person in history ever walked through life with a more effective bodyguard," he said with a smile. "But you know what? I've always wanted to see the inside of a jail cell. You wouldn't want me to miss out on an interesting experience like that, would you?"

Then he turned his attention to me, and held my hand in a warm embrace.

"Proteus," he said, "when you decided not to mark me for the police, and marked yourself instead, it was the most interesting and courageous thing I have seen so far in my short time in this world."

I continued to stare into his face. After a few seconds, I realized that he was expecting me to say something.

"You'll have to tell me about that cell phone number trick," I heard myself saying.

"I will teach you how to do it yourself, if you want," he said with a hint of jest in his eyes. "But for now," he said, turning to the officers who were still standing behind the police car, "I believe we're being arrested. Come on," he called out to the air behind him without looking back. "This too is a social situation. Let's introduce ourselves."

The gods and near-gods were emerging from my house, forming a semicircle behind me as the Master helped the crewcut man to his feet. The enormous demon on the officer's back leaped into the sky with a howl of despair and slowly backed away from the radiance until it was invisible against the greater darkness of the sky.

"I see your name is Michael, am I right?"

The officer stared at the Master and finally nodded.

"Michael Kerchner," the Master said, "I want to introduce you to my friends."

"A pleasure," the crewcut officer said without apparent irony.

"I believe you are here to arrest this man?" he continued, indicating me.

"Yes," the officer said slowly, as if he were trying to remember his lines.

"And the rest of us?"

"We—didn't know you were here. But yes, there are John Doe warrants for people who were living in the building when it was set fire to, plus the owner here."

The Master leaned over and lifted the Hispanic officer up off the ground. "Emilio," he said, taking his hand in the now-familiar embrace. "It is a pleasure to meet you."

"Yes," said Emilio, straightening up as if at attention. "For me too."

"And these are George and Phil," said the Master as the two other officers, their guns in their holsters, walked up.

I shook hands with George and Phil, and noticed that none of them had parasites on them any more.

Phil nudged Michael. "Did *you* tell him our names?"

"Michael, Emilio, George, Phil," said the Master with a happily serious expression on his face that also, somehow, conveyed how absurd this whole scene was, "we surrender ourselves into your custody. We have two more vehicles down by the side of the house," he added, "So it shouldn't be hard to get us all to the station."

"We don't have enough handcuffs," said Michael doubtfully.

"I don't think that will be too much of a problem," the Master told him. "We're here to help you any way we can. In fact," he said, "if it's not too much trouble, I've always wanted to drive a police vehicle…"

Karen, I don't think I have ever witnessed a stranger sight than the booking procedure where the officers were trying to fill out their paperwork on the gods. The police officers, under the spell of the spiritual glow, were cheerful and considerate and happy, although they weren't always able to get their paperwork filled out properly.

"Tell me your name again?" an officer said at the table next to where I sat, waiting for my turn behind the camera.

"Apollo."

"Is that your real name?"

"Yes."

"Is that the name you were born with?"

"No."

"Can you tell me the name you were born with?"

"It is irrelevant."

"That may be true, Mr…Apollo," the officer said politely, "but I have to put it down on this form so we can check the database and come up with a composite record, and we really can't formally charge you with anything until we have your legal identity. And your lawyer will have to provide it for us anyway."

"I have no wish to be charged with anything, and I do not intend on buying the services of a person whose words and opinions are for rent. You are simply asking me to participate in a primitive bureaucratic ritual that is completely irrelevant to me."

"Legally, we can keep you locked up until you give us your identity."

"I will be out of this building before sunrise."

"I wouldn't bet on that if I were you. Just a friendly word of advice to take back to the cell with you."

"There are times when lying is the most sacred of duties," said Apollo. "Eugene Marin Labiche. I will take your advice under consideration as I walk out of here."

In their respective turns before the camera, the gods and near-gods all took turns mugging and performing. Only the Master seemed to take it seriously;

he said, at one point, that this would be the only still photograph of him in existence, and later he thanked them with radiant sincerity for taking what would, he said, become the world's least expensive and most effective publicity photo, although at the time I had no idea what he was talking about.

Then we were all herded down to our cells, 16 men in one, eight women in an adjoining room, out of sight but right next door.

Suddenly, in this room, the full weight of the situation came back to me. They had us. We were trapped in the jail cell, and there was no earthly reason for them ever to let us out. I sat on the side of the bed with my back against the wall and watched the Master carefully seat himself cross-legged on the floor. After examining everything about the spartan room with intense interest, he motioned for the others to organize themselves on the floor in a circle surrounding him.

"Proteus," Briarius called out to me, indicating the floor next to him. "We need you in this space."

"He doesn't enjoy being incarcerated," Fool observed. "Maybe if they see how miserable you are," he said to me, "they'll let us all out."

"Don't *you* want to get out?" I demanded sourly.

"Not at this very moment," he replied readily. "The Master's in here, so there isn't anywhere else I would rather be."

"*Where happiness fails, existence remains a mad and lamentable experiment,*" said Apollo. "George Santayana. Put away your misplaced gloom and sit down with us a while."

The Master waited for me to fill the empty space they had left for me. From the sounds next door, I could tell that the women were doing the same thing.

Soon there was a buzzing sound in the room, a low, deep hum that traveled down to our bones. Something must have disturbed my meditation, because after a minute I opened my eyes and saw an officer standing in the hallway looking in at us—obviously, from the color of his aura, trying to decide whether to intervene and make us act like normal prisoners. I saw the Master open his eyes, and after a moment the officer walked back down the hall.

AUMmmmm.

Once again, I let my mind expand to encompass holy spirit outside my body, and to synchronize with the low hum that refines itself into the exquisitely beautiful Song of the Universe, the modulations that will take me far away from the cell, from my home planet, from my galaxy, from all things familiar.

AUMmmmmmmmm.

In our little cell, the song vibrates the air and the steel bars. The sound penetrates our bodies and our spirits in the same notes that can be heard in places where the breath of the singers is methane and plasma and void at absolute zero.

The other cells become silent, the other prisoners hear, and perhaps they know instinctively that this is a religious moment.

The sound has, of course, carried down the hallway to the officers in the jail, and one of them comes down to check on the weird noise. Everyone else has their eyes closed; I am the only one who sees him. I see that it makes him angry to see us sitting cross-legged in a circle making this noise, and for a long minute he searches his memory for something in the procedures manual to give him a reason to come into the cell and force us to quit humming. Finally, lamely, he shouts out in a voice that is unnecessarily harsh and loud, kicking the bars as he does so.

"Cut it out in there; you're disturbing the other prisoners."

"Nosir, they're not disturbing me. Are they disturbing you?" a voice calls out from another cell.

"Not me. They can do that all day long, as I care. In fact, I like it."

"Me too," another voice, from the cell on the other side of us, calls out.

Meanwhile, the Song of the Universe has intensified. I am now connected with the greater chorus, and am struck, as I was when I first heard it, at how many thousands of beautiful variations a single note can take as it pushes the vibrations down below the auditory capabilities of the human ear, down to where the sound can only be felt in the sympathetic trembling of the bones harmonized to the deepening note that is harmonizing the floor, the ceiling, the walls, the bars, the air around us—and, involuntarily, the officer who continues to demand that we stop whatever it was we are doing.

His anger grows. Finally, he pulls his gun out of the holster. At that instant the Master opens his eyes and speaks in a voice that somehow harmonizes with the Song.

"You know you don't want to do that," he says.

"Mister, I gave you and your friends here an order," the officer hisses.

"You gave us exactly the anger that a man would feel whose only daughter has been diagnosed with lymphatic cancer," the Master says gently. "You think it has destroyed your marriage because Emma has withdrawn from you, but the truth is, she is trying not to burden you with her own pain, and your days together will be stronger once this has ended."

The officer stares at the Master.

"How did you know this? How do you know me?"

"It doesn't matter," the Master says. "What matters is that you believe that your daughter can recover from this. Do you believe that?"

"It would take a miracle."

"Are these miracles possible? There is a part of you that has to answer yes to this question, and that part of you has to be willing to give itself to her."

"I would give anything," the officer whispers.

"Yes." The Master nods. "I can see that now."

Since my eyes are the only other witnesses to this, I am the only one who sees that the Master has extended his aura to the holy spirit inside the officer, at once causing the twin hags to leap off of him with a cry of pain as if they have been burned, and storing what seems to be residual white energy that would, I somehow realize, be passed on to the daughter the next time they were together—and that would remove her parasite and begin the healing.

It is an extraordinary moment, as the Master and the police officer face each other across the vertical bars of the cell. And then the moment is broken, as another officer enters the room and stops at the sight of the first officer's drawn handgun.

"What's going on?" he says.

There are tears in the first officer's eyes, but I don't think the other officer sees them.

"Nothing," the first officer says, reholstering his weapon.

AUMmmmmm.

I close my eyes once again, as the Song of the Universe fills our minds and our bones and finally our spirits, the subtle interplay of vibration that defines all emotion and all awareness and is the trap door outside of space and time. Once again, I feel as if my awareness is synchronized with an extended perception, and that the myriad sparkles of holy spirit are like stepping stones out into the universe.

AUMmmmmm.

My daughter, on this new visit, I paid a bit more attention to the wild assortment of creatures who shared our song, who represented a cross-section of intelligent life in the universe. I can tell you that somewhere between here and forever, there is a planet which harbors creatures who look a little bit like very complicated caves, who draw their sustenance from the ground and the wind and the ambient temperature changes in the air. The living caves never move from their place of birth, but they are very skilled at communication, and they live to bring other creatures to their world.

Another species, which seems to be composed mostly of teeth and claws and sharp edges, lives in a place where the social interaction can be compared equally to a constant state of war and a dance, where bodies are routinely slashed to pieces in what might be viewed as constant territorial wars, or like a kind of performance art that provides immense pleasure to the survivors and a kind of immortality to those whose lives are lost, whose characteristics are recalled and shared and absorbed by the remaining warriors.

Yet another intelligent species looks a little like a stalk of celery except that it is made entirely of radioactive material. Yet another is not unlike a terrestrial amoeba the size of a trash can lid, and more than a few are made up of disconnected parts that communicate either by radio or by color or both. I see living flames from the stars and deeply philosophical sea plants, creatures of ice and creatures like coiled springs who live in the deep gravity wells of white dwarf stars.

I feel my awareness move through this fantastic zoo when suddenly I am facing what may be the oddest-looking member of the Deva Community, a dignified-looking living cloud of purple-yellow color, releasing small bolts of lightning in its interior, each flashing an internal glow that is, I realize, part of its communication mechanism.

"You are wonderfully interesting." The cloud somehow makes me feel the words through the modulations of the Song of the Universe. "You are like the mechs, yet so unlike in appearance. Not unlike the God. May I have the privilege of sharing experiences with you?"

Mechs? God? I find myself wondering how such a creature could be alive, and where, and this must have been written on my spirit, because the living cloud obligingly dips its flattened base in what might be a reverent bow, and in that moment I am swirled away to a different place, to an environment beyond my imagining.

Life in the Universe:
Prophet of the Endless Sky

My home is the sky. I am smoke; I am dust and the electrostatically-charged air within it, a gossamer mist riding 250-mile-an-hour winds near the upper edge of this gas giant planet's atmosphere. Living white puffballs and mindless yellow wisps scatter away like minnows as I pick my way through long-tendrilled light-catchers that reach up out of sight and shimmer in my gentle wake.

My goal is somewhere ahead. Through the mists of the cloud-forest, my senses detect—yes!—an everlasting cyclonic storm—one of the mysterious ancient relics of the Old Ones, constructed on such a small scale that the moons of Mars would barely fit inside together.

Furtively, with one last glance everywhere, I extend myself into an eternal hurricane.

The swirling wind tears at the gossamer of my body. All is momentary chaos and confusion, and then I am suddenly inside a great hushed stillness where—wonder!—a gallery of images, carved into the wind itself, beckons my attention.

As I have before, I touch this whirling gallery with my awareness, and for blissful hours, messages from the distant past wash into and through me, filling my mind with bizarre, incomprehensible concepts like "adventure," "literature" and "scientific inquiry," with stories of ancient glory and proud, puzzling references to the One Great Storm, Coriolis, the lost capitol of a once-mighty civilization of the sky.

I am bathing in the heroic tale of a cloud who roamed the air when the sky was young, who dared to steal the wondrously useful thing called "*fire*" from the gods. It is a good story, strongly told with the skill of a powerful sermon, and as it is finished, I feel overwhelmed and envious at the sheer audacity of it.

Then, with a frightening quiver through every molecule of my body, I am startled by a voice in this place where I must not be found.

"Sky Dancer?"

A living cloud no older than my own adolescence, only a bit broader and more bloated, is wandering in confusion through the great stillness. Finally, he locates me, and with a visible diminishment of anxiety extends his forevapors into mine, adjusting the mix of molecules in an intimate caress-language that is much more expressive than the audible speech of creatures who are cursed with solid inflexible bodies.

"Sky Dancer, I've searched these many hours for you! Herd Leader saw you were not with the young grazers, and I was worried for you. You know it is forbidden to stray!"

"I drifted," I say with apprehension, though I am fond of Breeze-Lover and enjoy his company.

"You could not have drifted this far," Breeze-Lover says reproachfully. "You were restless again."

"I was restless," I admit. "Is it not boring always to graze for the benefit of the God? One feels the urge to see the many places where none of us have traveled before."

"Thoughts from the Evil One!"

"Can it be evil to enjoy the wonders of our sky?"

"You live not for this world, but the next one," Breeze Lover intones with a righteous fervor that I envy and find exasperating. "Is it not said that *You must grow and gather oxygen and methane in abundance in your bodies, so that you may be harvested by the God and know the boundless joy of paradise?*"

Then he looks around curiously at the stillness and the meticulously-crafted wind-walls around us.

"What is this place?" he asks finally. "Many times I have seen them from afar."

"A wonder! Thoughts are written in the wind!"

Breeze-Lover draws back in alarm. "A thing of the Old Ones! Were they not evil?"

"Says the Herd Leader. But have you ever heard him quote so from the Prophet?"

"Nay," answers Breeze-Lover reluctantly.

"If they were truly evil, would he have withheld such a quote?"

"I know not. There is much you and I do not know."

"Including what the God and the Prophet think of these ancient messages," I say impatiently. On impulse, I envelop Breeze-Lover's forevapors and draw him to the far edge of the vortex.

A torrent of images, thoughts, ideas—yes! After a moment's searching, I find the record that I wish Breeze-Lover to experience: a vision of living clouds who—wondrous thing!—together as one, raise a tremble that fills the sky. It is a strange rhythmic tremble in the air that is a joy to the senses, and there are words woven into it, strong words that touch the place deep inside where my lightnings are born.

Sing to the endless sky
Sing a song of beauty
Of the rainbow mist
And the warm wind
Rising up out of the darkness,
From the scented heart of the magnificent world
That is our joyous home.
Sing of ice and fire
And the endless spirit of God,
Of lightning shared in gentle intimacy
And the knowledge that we are
Unified with the One beyond the stars.
Sing of joy in the endless beauty of life

For we are the sky,
And it is us,
For we are the endless spirit,
And Its magnificence
Is all the more glorious for our lives and our song...

Breeze-Lover is quivering as the vision ends, for its deep piety has touched him inside. Yet he is also troubled.

"Could they have been talking about the God?" he asks as we make our way back to the herd. "This is so different from the Prophet-Minister's sermons. The God is stern and vengeful, and jealous of the worship of others. Are there more of these?" he asks after a moment.

"There are many visions, all different," I say. "And there are many strange thoughts in them."

"I heard some myself. *Fire*. What is *fire*?"

"Nay, I know not."

"I fear this is a thing of great evil, for there is nothing in their words about growing fat for the God."

The herd-that-is-my-family is now in view; the familiar sight of dense yellow-white bundles of vapor grazing on a shimmering field of light-catchers. As we come into their field of awareness, Herd Leader disengages himself and approaches with a ponderous dignity. His corpulent rolls of oxygen and methane, heavy and faintly violet in the distant light, attest to his piety.

"My children," he says with affection, for he enjoys the young ones that he is assigned to keep close to the fold, "you have strayed from the place of the grazing. I fear you are using energy that is reserved for the God."

"Nay, Herd Leader," says Breeze-Lover before I can reply. "Our bodies belong to the God, and we are born to serve it."

"Yet I see that you have a question for me."

This time it is I who speaks. "What is '*fire*'?" I ask him.

The response is not what either of us expect. A wind born out of Herd Leader's displeasure sweeps us away a short distance, and his body has become dark with menace.

"Where did you hear of this thing?" he demands.

"It was written in the vortex," I tell him.

"We thought you might know by who, and for what purpose such a thing could be produced that does not talk of feeding for the God," Breeze-Lover adds quickly.

Herd Leader relaxes at the piety of Breeze-Lover's question. "They are the inscriptions of the Old Ones, always to be avoided."

"Why would they write them if they were not to be read?"

"They contain blasphemy. All lies and vanity to distract our attention away from the simple words of the God. Faith is all you need, my child. Fight your nature, and the God will reward you for it. For is it not said that *When you bring me the volatile gasses to the refueling station, your rewards will be in heaven?* In time, you will learn that all things are a mystery, and truth is beyond our comprehension. It is better not to think, but only to graze and grow fat for the God, and turn our thoughts to another world."

"Is *fire* one of the mysteries?"

Herd Leader blows a wind in our face to silence my words, and he extends his vapors to make sure none of the others are listening.

"*Fire* is a forbidden mystery which must not be talked about," he says, the words a bare tremble that is a cloud's version of a hushed whisper. "I will hear nothing of it again, or else I must mention your…*adventure* to the Prophet-Minister himself."

By now, the last of our herd have grazed to bursting, and Herd Leader turns to lead us toward the swirling interface at the edge of our broad windcurrent, one of half a dozen that flow in bands horizontally across our world, each current several times wider than the Earth. Here, at the place where it brushes against an equally-vast windcurrent blowing in the opposite direction, the winds touch at a speed difference five times the strength of a terrestrial hurricane. The air around us is a turbulent roar of swirling anger. Into the edge of chaos, down, down we plunge along the steep infalling swirl, down to the darker places toward the distant surface of the planet.

Minutes later, the air around us is so intensely hot that water changes from hard, brittle ice to liquid and floats like a fine mist in the air. In appearance, we remain the same, for while the intense heat raises the tendency for our bodies to expand, the air pressure rises by a factor of ten, squeezing the molecules of our vaporous bodies back together.

For a time, we soak into ourselves the abundant water vapor. Then all of us in the herd-that-is-my-family extend our gaseous bodies into and through others, rubbing the place where the water has been stored, vapor against vapor, building up a powerful electrostatic charge, magnifying our natural ability to draw lightning from our inner bellies.

Finally, when the pressure has reached its peak, we storm.

From deep inside, a hundred clouds release into each other the brilliant searing bolts of lightning, each so intense that they separate water into its constituent hydrogen, which is discarded, and oxygen, which is retained and convected to our second belly, safely far from the expansive methane vapors elsewhere in our bodies.

Finally, exhausted, we drift into the upwelling on the far side of the divide, up, up into the cooler darkness of night, and there is peace, the contentment of grazers who have only to digest what they have gathered during the long daytime feeding cycle. It is the time of contemplation, when our bodies slowly, carefully, convect bits of the oxygen into the methane and, with tiny surges of lightning, we light sparks in the presence of a rich chemical mix inside us and around our bodies, creating one by one the complex phosphorus/iodine/nitrogen organics that are the chemical superstructure of every living cloud.

While we digest and drift with the wind, the Prophet-Minister offers the blessings of his daily sermon.

"My beloved herd," he addresses the group with a gentleness and resolve. In his holiness, he can barely move his enormous body without the help of a dozen adolescents, who cling to him reverently. "Our world is filled with temptation, ever since the evil one came to our sky and planted his curse, and spread out before us a beauty and magnificence that blasphemously simulates paradise to the untutored and heretical mind.

"But the maliciousness of the evil one did not stop there, for he also planted into the depths of our minds a powerful curiosity, a thirst for knowledge, so that everything we see is a temptation to draw us from the grazing which the God finds pleasing."

As the Prophet-Minister speaks these words, many are stirred to anger at the evil one, for the many tortures he has inflicted through natural curiosity and the desire for joy. Why did the God allow him to torment us so? Why is it so necessary to test our faith?

"My beloved herd, the God is a stern and unforgiving ruler, who expects we-of-the-sky to fight against our own nature, deny our carnal desires for knowledge, for beauty, for joy, for all the temptations that call us away from our feeding. In this fight, we have only one ally: the word of the Prophet. For the God in His wonderful wisdom recognized that without clear guidelines, without guidance from His chosen representatives, the herd would stray, and He would be required to administer eternal, painful punishment on the People-Of-The-Sky.

"It is only by faith, by turning off the thoughts in your mind and accepting the words of the Prophet, that you can resist the temptations of the evil one. Is it not said by the God, through the Prophet: *Only the gathering of the methane and oxygen into the full ripeness of your bodies is important, and your thoughts should always be on the next world, which will be as wonderful as your imaginations can make it, once you ascend to harvest with the God."*

The audience is spellbound by the beauty of these words of the God, so unlike the way we mere mortals express ourselves. Our imaginations offer detailed, exotic visions of what that next world must look like, if it is so much more magnificent than the remarkable vista spread out around us.

"My beloved herd, some of you have asked about the word 'harvest,' which of course is not of our language. In their wisdom, the sermon-makers have determined that it is an ecstasy of union between the God and the cloud-flesh, too wonderful to be understood until the blessed event. For is it not said that *What you will experience when you arrive at the refueling station is too darned great for others to look upon, so bring no witnesses when you offer yourself to the God.*

"How glorious that union will be! What a privilege it would be to grow fat enough to be pleasing to the God and merit the holy union with the blessed refueling station!

"My beloved herd, hear now my words and turn away from exercise of the mind or the body, gather your faith and devote your life to feeding, that you may grow fat to please the God."

Many others, quivering in ecstasy, fan out to digest with increased determination—among them the beloved one who budded me. For a time we drift next to each other in silence, and she watches my lackluster attention with a quiver of concern and disapproval.

"You must pay attention, my bud."

"I fear the Prophet-Minister dislikes me, and he distrusts you because of me," I say to Gentle Rain-Maker as we pass through a thicker cluster of the light catchers.

"Do not say this!"

"I can see that he blames you for my youthful behavior. Yet still I am grateful to you for life. Now I wish to give back, rather than hurt you."

"Then believe in the voice of the God," says Gentle Rain-Maker quietly.

"Help me with my doubts, then, for I am not one who believes without knowing. Look there," I say, indicating one of the herd who is ripe for harvest, a bloated cloud named Sky Grazer. "See how he is so large he can hardly navigate."

"He is very holy," Gentle Rain-Maker agrees.

"Why does the God demand that we make ourselves unable to move freely about the wind?"

"Is it not said that *Clouds are sinful, and the sin was committed many many generations ago, and so now you must live for the afterlife?*"

"But what sin? Why is this never explained to us? And why are we to pay for what was done by our ancestors?"

"So many questions," Gentle Rain-Maker sighs. "Once, I too was filled with them, with this many and ten times this many. But that was before I heard the voice of the God myself."

"Truth?" I whisper.

Gentle Rain-Maker speaks in a furtive tone now, and the mingling of chemicals that is her voice trembles with something that is at once fear and secret joy.

"I had a dream once," she confesses. "In this dream, I felt interesting vibrations at the radio end of the spectrum, and it seemed as if those vibrations were somehow—yes, this is the craziness of dreams—speaking voices, communicating as clearly as if they were modulating chemicals at their fringes. In this dream I listened to these voices, and they were talking about enslaving our people by creating a false religion.

"In my dream, I heard one voice say to another, 'The creatures below us are not stupid, but they are trusting. Let us make up a *thing-which-is-untrue*, and they will believe it because they know nothing of *things-which-are-untrue*, and because it is their nature to trust and believe what they are told.' And the speaker created the faith so that we would be subservient to him.

"In my dream, I saw the Prophet come down from the sky to deliver this untrue message to our people many many generations ago. Armed with this simple announcement, with this thing-which-is-untrue, the Prophet became the ruler of the People-Of-The-Sky."

"Could this be true?"

"I could not rest until I found out the answer," says Gentle Rain-Maker. "And so I went myself to see the God."

I am shocked at the blasphemy. "Truth?"

The air between and through us quivers so much with nervousness that it is a miracle the elders do not notice the disturbance a thousand miles across the horizon.

"When?" I whisper.

"I was as young as you are now. I waited for my chance, and finally, one day, I saw a bloated one rise blissfully upwards to the joyful harvest with the God. And so, secretly, I followed. We, he first, me discretely behind, journeyed upward, into the ammonia ice clouds that are so beautiful to touch, and beyond them into a layer of haze. As I ascended, my body expanded and became the size of a hundred of the elders-who-are-ready-for-harvesting, and so thin that it felt as if the sky and I were one.

"For a time, the farther I traveled away from the below-warmth, the colder it was. But above the haze layer, as I moved higher, it became less cold, with a warmth that came from a single brilliant point in the sky, and I had the odd thought that this point was far, far away from us, so that no matter how high I climbed or how large I allowed by body to grow, I could never reach it.

"And I watched the blessed one, so large now that he filled half the sky, stop in confusion, for we knew not where the God was. And then I felt a curious vibration in the pale, thin air, not unlike in the dream. Like the point of warmth, it came from somewhere above me, and I saw the bloated one expand still further. We drifted toward the source of the vibrations, and I suddenly found myself touching—how can I describe it? It was a thing made of ice, as solid as ice, but far more complicated than any ice I had ever seen before, a kind of ice that would not melt even in high temperatures where ice becomes vapor. It was shaped like a cylinder with a point at one end, and it was circling our world at the edge of the sky, and I, so thin and spread out, was invisible to it at that altitude. And when I allowed my body to touch it everywhere, I experienced vibrations inside that were just like what the Prophet-Minister describes when he talks about the Voice of Everlasting Beneficence, and I knew that something, something with the ability to think and communicate, was inside that cylinder of complicated ice.

"You saw the God." My own body quivers. "What happened then?"

"I heard the Voice. And I fled in terror and exultation. Imagine! To have heard, with my own mortal person, the God itself."

"What did it say?" I breathe, barely able to control my quivering.

"It said incomprehensible things. Its first holy words were: *Approach the refueling station.* After that, though I was distant, I thought I heard instructions for how the blessed bloated one—again, who can comprehend this?—should line up with the *'intake ports.'* All I knew was that this was the holy ritual of purification, and I have not doubted the words of the Prophet since, nor listened again to my foolish dreams."

"Yet still I do not wish to be bloated," I tell her stubbornly. "I wish to roam the sky in freedom, to feel the passage of the ice crystals through my molecules, to taste the warmth below and the cold above, to lightning with my dear cousins, and taste the ozone as I store the found-energy of broken water that is heavy gas—these are the joys that a cloud should live for."

"You would not bloat for the God?" Gentle Rain-Maker's voice is frightened. "Have I given birth to a monster?"

"I will bloat in old age, after I have tasted the things this world has to offer."

"I will pray for you, my wayward bud."

This very day, our grazing takes us within sight of another of the Old Ones' artifacts, though it is apparently unseen by the others, whose minds are only on the grazing and the bloating.

This is my advantage. Slowly, so as not to attract attention, I allow myself to drift toward this library of the wind, wondering how long I will be able to search, unmissed, for the things that still perplex me.

As I reach the turbulent air of the interface, I extend into this vortex, looking now not for stories, but for straightforward explanations. Impatiently, I sort through many strange and wonderful mysteries, texts that describe the casting of materials (incomprehensible) and the architectural principles behind the construction of storms along the interfaces (beyond incomprehensible), which are designed to last as monuments forever to their creators.

And then, as I am about to leave in frustration, I find a simple, ancient screed, a wisp of wind and nothing more, where there is a formula and a procedure tossed in as an artifact, an afterthought by creatures who seem to have taken this marvelous bit of knowledge for granted.

For an hour, then two, there is experimentation. Before long, other texts begin to take on meaning, things unexplained become obvious. The casting, to be tried at a later time. And...something else.

Alone in the library of the wind, trembling with excitement, I reach inside, pair bits of oxygen and the methane from my own reservoirs in the prescribed abundance, touch it gently with lightning, continue feeding the spark with methane and oxygen and—wonder! A brightness and heat that sustains itself, giving off energy, drawn as if out of the wind itself.

I hold, with my own body, the miracle of *fire*. It is a hard, brilliant glow, as if I have somehow caught lightning and held it in one place. And yet there is a softness to it, and flexibility.

Eagerly, I extend out to scoop up a mix of chemicals latent in the air, and by varying its distance from this brilliant dot of energy, I am able to siphon off rich stores of compounds that my body drinks in eagerly. In seconds, I have assimilated more than I could have digested in a week. Strength and rejuvenation surge through my body, and in my triumph and excitement, I burst through the walls of the artifact and race the wind to show the herd what I have found.

"What is this called?" Gentle Rain-Maker hovers behind me as I demonstrate the wonder.

"The ancient records call it '*fire*,'" I tell her.

"A meaningless word. But it is a remarkable thing to see. Is it evil?"

"I think not. Here—" With still-clumsy gestures, I pass an undigested mix of chemicals near the flame, and catch the products of the reaction. "Taste this," I say, and tell me if this is an evil thing."

The one who budded me cautiously touches a gathering membrane to the sulfurous compounds, and then draws in the remainder with a deep appreciation. A low contented rumble of thunder emerges from her inner body.

"It is delicious. The work of many days of digestion. You have made food more palatable by bringing it near to *fire*. What should we call this wonderful thing?"

"The Old Ones had a word, but it too is meaningless. They called it 'cooking.'"

"Then we too shall call it that."

For a dozen feeding cycles, we share the secret of *fire* and the nourishment it provides. As I become more adept at the cooking, her new bud grows at an extraordinary rate, while I reach adulthood long before my time. I grow into a lean, powerful body, not unlike the visions inscribed in the vortices of the Old Ones, which is an abomination in the herd.

One day, as I return from another artifact with new recipes, Breeze-Lover approaches the two of us with a sluggish dignity, his body multiplied many times in pious corpulence.

"Let us feed for the God in the name of the Prophet," he says.

"Yes."

"Yes."

"You have been missing again," Breeze-Lover observes.

My vapors become more tenuous; my color more yellowish. "I confess that I was lost."

"The Prophet has much to say about lost members of the herd, and the fate that awaits them. Is it not said that *Those who stray from the grazing places, and from the word of the God, shall be devoured by the tigers of sin and blasphemy.*"

"Tigers?" I say.

"A word of the God that cannot be translated precisely. But on the authority of many sermons, we know that it is as if there was a cloud that could rip apart the fabric of our vapors and feast on them."

"But my bud has returned," Gentle Rain-Maker points out. "Is it not said that this is cause for joy?"

At this, Breeze-Lover turns an aspect of displeasure on the one who budded me, and on the new bud growing along her flanks.

"Why are you bringing new life to the herd?" he demands. "Where is it said that you should do this rather than grow fat for the God?"

The one-who-budded-me cowers in fear at this question. "There are so few of us left," she says in a small voice. "I thought it would be wise to make more—for the God of course."

"The young are rebellious," Breeze-Lover mutters. "More of them is a vexation to the Prophet-Minister."

"This creature I bud will grow fat and pleasing to the God. I promise it."

"You are becoming learned in the words of the Prophet," I observe to shift the subject.

My friend swells with pleasure at the compliment. "I listen and remember. Is it not said that *Those who take to heart the words of the God shall not stray into error or sin?*"

"It is. I have heard the Herd Leader say these words myself."

"And the Prophet-Minister, for those who would listen to him."

I ignore the reproach. "I must ask you a question relating to the God."

"I will try to answer it."

I carefully spark the air between us, and nurture it into *fire*. After a moment's skillful preparation, the air quivers with a mix of chemical byproducts.

"You have found it after all." There is a neutrality to the voice where I had expected excitement.

"Yes. After many hours of searching the records. I am forbidden from showing you this, yet it seems that the Prophet's words are conflicting on the subject."

Breeze-Lover stands back with aloof distaste from the heat of the flame. "How so?" he asks in a voice whose chemical composition is neutral of all inflection.

"Here is a way to repair and regenerate the structure of our bodies, to speed up digestion from days to minutes. Could this not be used to grow fatter than we could without it?"

"Perhaps," says Breeze-Lover. "But see how it consumes your methane. Is that not a blasphemy?"

"A temporary loss. With the time I would spend digesting, I can collect many times more."

"And is this not a product of the Old Ones, this thing called *cooking*?"

I am about to answer, but then I realize what Breeze-Lover has said.

"How do you know its name?" I ask.

"We who are trained for the Prophet-Ministry are given to know secrets which are not divulged to the laity." The chemistry of Breeze-Lover's words conveys an air of superiority. "It would confuse the others to hear of these things. Yet this is a blasphemy that we have been specifically warned about, which you have chosen to indulge despite cautions from the Herd Leader himself. Do you deny it?"

Too late, I sense the trap, for the herd now approaches from every direction. Prophet-Minister, pulled along by a dozen adoring adolescents, expands before me like a false horizon of dark anger.

"I believe my acolyte has asked you a question," he rumbles.

"I deny nothing," I say, holding the flame aloft for all to see. "See the *fire!*" I say to the group. "It is a blessing, won by the sacrifice of one who came before us. With this, we can take the time we spend digesting and explore the world, perhaps constructing, perhaps composing—"

Before I can say more, Prophet-Minister sweeps the flame aside with the wind of his mighty displeasure, and there is a lingering chill in the air that extends for miles in all directions.

"To what end?" Prophet-Minister demands with an acid taste to his words. "See how much of the God's methane you have used up in your own body. Is it not said that *Any activity that uses up more methane in your bodies than it produces is sinful in the eyes of the God?*"

"This cannot be sinful. It is a joy to the body!"

"That is the very definition of sin," Prophet-Minister thunders angrily. With a ponderous contempt, he shakes broken bits of sulfur on the place where the flame is no more. "We will hear no more about this thing from the old gods," he says with a voice of finality.

He has already turned when I cry out my challenge to him. "I say that this thing I found is good, and I say that life itself is not evil, but is to be embraced in all its pleasures and possibilities. I will give this thing to the herd, and let the herd decide whether the glow of the flame is a good thing for their lives or an evil intrusion on them."

Prophet-Minister turns slowly, and the air chills around us for a long second.

"You shall die for your blasphemy before you have a chance," he says, and there is a terrifying finality to the pronouncement. "You, whose body is a living reproach to the pious and corpulent among us, who would introduce distractions into our feeding, know now that these very words were anticipated long ago by the Prophet Himself," he shouts, calling out to the herd now more than to me. "For is it not said that *There will come those who will argue against the holy teachings of the God, and twist the truth with words that sound righteous, but are evil and full of blasphemy.*"

"I do not deny our obligations to the God," I continue boldly. "The one-who-budded-me has persuaded me that this is a true faith. But I choose to worship a god who is greater than the God, who encompasses more than just the refueling station above us in the sky, who is the wind and sky and places beyond the sky, who lives inside of us and participates in our joy. I feel in my body that this—" I indicate the spectacular rainbow cascade near the top of the infall, the yellow-purple mist warming our bodies from below, the winds to the east, the flashing crystals above—"this was meant to be cherished, not rejected by the People-Of-The-Sky. The Prophet would have us fight what we are," I say to the trembling herd, "yet I intend to do things that the Maker-of-my-body intended."

The wrath of the Prophet-Minister, building and expanding like a hurricane, is an awesome sight to behold.

"From this moment, you are banished from the herd," he roars at me.

There is a collective shudder in the sky around me, as the others of the herd absorb this dreadful proclamation. "Without cousins, how will he make lightning and store energy?" one asks, and the question circulates from cloud to cloud.

"Better to die in the open sky than to live for nothing but feeding," I retort, "for I say we do not live for feeding alone."

"But where will you go?" others ask as I drift away from them.

"I will search for the One Great Storm, the place once called Coriolis. And when I find it, you will see that I am not a twister of truth, but a carrier of it."

"Then you will die now," cries out the Prophet-Minister, and from inside him a mighty thunderbolt rises and strikes through my core. The Prophet-Minister's body churns in swollen purple anger, and winds swirl and tear at my vapors.

Yet the effect is not what the herd expects. Instead of being torn to my constituent gases, I fill with such anger as I would not have imagined possible. From inside my body, which has grown powerful with the feeding from the cooking, I answer with a storm of thunder and wind and chaos and mayhem. I lash out and whirl and the lightning is everywhere around me, and the sky trembles. I cry out my frustration at the winds, and the winds carry my anguish to the edges of the horizon and beyond.

Finally, gradually, the storm inside me begins to subside with my anger, and I look around me, and I am alone, for the others, even Herd Leader and Prophet-Minister, have fled in terror.

And I know that in the power of my anger, I have, in the minds of the herd, fulfilled the Prophet's ambiguous, dire warning.

I am truly alone.

For the human awareness who is bathed in the life of this extraordinary member of this species, the time which follows is experienced in fast-motion, a jumble of images where weeks become hours, days become seconds. My awareness is bombarded with a montage of experiences, of new and strange floating forests and exotic ecosystems of the sky, triumphant battles against predatory demons where I roar a new trembling of exultation into the wind, of crossing the interfaces of windstreams to the top of the world and back, stopping always wherever I find a relic to gather in new quantities of forbidden knowledge.

Awash in this sensory experience of alien images, a part of me remembers forests and deserts, jungles, landscapes of eternal snow and many varied ecological niches of the home planet of the human race. But here I am exploring a world where each level of the sky extends to more than 300 times the total land mass of my planet, an empire of the sky littered with ruins, populated now by lonely herds whose numbers grow smaller every year.

Sometimes, I greet them in the depths and hear in their strangely unfamiliar language patterns the same stories of the glorious Prophet and the God.

"Welcome after the name of the Holy One. I am called Nimbus, or sometimes the One-Who-Dreams."

"I saw that you were not bloated. I am Sky Dancer," I say. "May I storm with you?"

The other, not unlike the one-who-budded-me, yet younger, is curiously unmoved by what most of our species would consider a rebuke. She examines the direction of the herd for a moment.

"They will not have noticed me," I assure her. "They live for the grazing."

"Yet you do not."

"Nay. I have been on a journey."

"Where has it taken you?"

"To many places. I have seen many things, all except what the-part-of-me-which-storms has a deep hunger for."

"I too have these hungers," she whispers. "For many months I tried to suppress them. Yet my thoughts forever stray."

"If you would leave the herd, I would show you where stories are written in the wind."

"Truth?"

"In the time of my journey, I have seen stories of the Old Ones and their achievements, trembling choruses awesome in their beauty, discussions of things that are still beyond my understanding. The Old Ones, in their wisdom and their power, measured the depth of the sky, and calculated the distance between the upper winds to a ball of fire whose light requires 43 minutes to leave its surface and bathe our horizon."

"You would show me these wonders?"

"I would show all who would follow."

"I wish, at first," she says, and there is a hesitation, "for you to show only me."

"Are you not afraid to be gone from the herd?"

Now there is no hesitation. "You will be my herd."

"It is still a long journey," I warn her. "I am following the artifacts back to their legendary source."

"Yes," she says quietly. "A trembling in the heart of me has whispered of this place. A great storm where thousands, perhaps millions of the Old Ones lived lives of adventure and power."

"How could you—??"

"This place trembles in my heart—and, curiously, in a place which is somehow behind it. I think I could follow the tremblings to it."

"Let us storm, and then I will follow *you*," I say, and there is a strange pleasurable tingle as her lightning enters my body.

My companion's strange new sense leads us to a network of giant pathways of chilled ammonia crystal fragments and ice, fitted carefully together and—wonder!—it carries us with no discomfort through the interfaces where the great winds brush against each other, carrying us through as if the maelstroms were nothing more than gentle breezes.

As we follow this artificial pathway, the eternal storms and wind-written records grow larger and more numerous, until finally we see from afar a vision so awesome that it stretches the imagination to the limit. It extends out far beyond the horizon, and there is a beauty and majesty and awe embedded in the architecture of the wind itself. It is surrounded by an endless stream of satellite vortices which sometimes merge with it, creating unimaginable energy and a cornucopia of lightning and rich ozone gas.

Coriolis. The One Great Storm of the ancients.

"We have found it," my companion says simply, watching the sculpted shape of the wind for long minutes.

My mind is filled with a deep awe and satisfaction. "To think that creatures like us had such vision, such power!" I say.

"All abandoned for the God," says my companion.

For a time, we rest our bodies at the swirling edges of this monument, whose interior lightning produces raw nutrients in quantities sufficient to feed multitudes. It creates its own infall. As we approach the swirling outer walls, Nimbus feels a trembling at the edges of her awareness. In the breezes in front of the storm, we find many varieties of organic light-catchers which have been tended and watched over as Herd Leader watches over us. The strange word inscribed in puzzling texts comes back to me, for I recognize this to be what the ancients called a *garden*, and I detect signs of recent tending. Yet the wall and the horizon as far as my awareness extends is silent and empty.

"Show yourselves!" I call to the swirling winds, rearing up to my full cumulonimbal height. "Is it right for one cloud to hide from another?"

There is nothing but silence. I am about to storm at this neglect of hospitality, but the presence next to me begins to tremble, and from her emerges the most beautiful trembling I have yet heard, more haunting even than the most moving of the Old Ones' idylls written into the wind.

> *The One that lives in the space behind our thoughts,*
> *and the One that is everywhere outside*
> *are mixed together in magic and mystery*
> *as we are with the wind.*
> *Sing! Sing in joy to celebrate*
> *the eternal goodness that is our birthright*
> *and the freedom that lives in our souls.*
> *The horizon calls to me, and yet I choose to linger here,*
> *because we, you and I, are joined together*
> *by all that is and will ever be.*
> *This moment, this life, is our journey together,*
> *and the stirring of this song that we feel inside*
> *is the call from the One to the One.*
> *If the words that carry our voices to the sky*
> *are brave enough to connect our hearts,*
> *then our song begins with us*
> *and echoes in the place beyond eternity...*

In the silence that follows these tremblings, there is a great emptiness where the voice of my companion had filled my insides with feelings too complicated to name. It seems as if the wind itself is hushed, and my heart aches at the passing of the tremblings that Nimbus has poured into my heart.

Slowly, timidly, People-Of-The-Sky emerge from the fearful swirl, not yet daring to approach us.

"Tell me what place I have come to," I say to the molecules of air between us, and they taste the air and murmur among themselves.

"You are a Prophet-Minister?"

"Let your awareness give you answer. Am I too bloated to move my own body? Nay. I am banished."

"We too, each of us in our turn."

"I have heard nothing of banishings before my own."

"We are never spoken of again."

"How many are here?"

Slowly, others emerge from the winds, and there are little ones among them, newly-budded. "Who can count us?" one who identifies himself as Storm-Raker tells me, merging himself cautiously with my own molecules. "Ten times ten times many times ten. We hide from the God, who would make us bloat."

"You live in diminished joy, in the shadows of life!" Nimbus cries out.

"The God does not search here, as He does the joyful sky."

"Who speaks for the community?" I ask him.

"Follow us to the interior. The Ancient One will welcome you or not."

At the very edge of the storm, a rich concentration of organics swirls around us. In a moment, the wind grabs at the structure of our bodies, and in the chaos it is impossible to see or taste anything, for nothing is stable for more than an instant. And then, suddenly, we are inside the great storm, entering what appears to be a great oval gap in the heart of the sky, a hole in the atmosphere large enough to drop two planet earths into the center with room to spare.

In this calm place, we see a single figure resting on a bed of organics, held up by the gentle breezes so that he has to exert no effort from his tired body. My awareness is astonished at the sight, for I have never before seen such age in one of my species.

Nimbus and I approach him reverently, gently extending our vapors into his.

"Your names?" he says to us in a brittle, exquisitely gentle voice.

"I am called Sky Dancer. This is Nimbus, who found the way to you in her heart. And you?"

"Once, a long time ago, I was known as Rain Maker, a Lord of the Sky," the withered creature tells me. "Now they call me The Old One, or sometimes the Word Master, for I tend the ancient records that none read any longer."

The molecules of the old one tremble delicately in the stillness here. "Tell me the tale of your life," he says. "And take no longer than necessary, because I know not how long I will be in this world, now that my body has stopped making organics."

"It is a simple story," I say. "I blasphemed against the God and the Prophet, and the Prophet-Minister banished me. He hoped to send me to death, but you see that I am not one to lurk on the edges of the herd until the wind scatters my flesh."

"Blasphemed how?"

"We, each of us, sought the forbidden knowledge," Nimbus tells him. "We believe our species does not exist by food alone, simply for the eating. There are other nourishments we require."

"Such as?"

"Joy. Understanding. Adventure. The sky has magic that touches my spirit, and I will not deny the importance of that connection."

The old one sighs, and behind us, where the swirling wind touches my back, there is lightning of such intensity that it tears the air itself apart.

"Some of your answers are correct, and some are dangerous," he says at last. "And so I must make conditions. We offer you sanctuary," he says. "But do not trouble yourself with the sky again. It belongs to the God now."

"Now. Perhaps not forever."

"You would fight with the God?" the old one demands.

"At this moment, I would prefer to fight against your death," I say, drawing myself closer. With a quick extrusion of lightning, I turn a spark into a *fire*, and at this appearance of bright liquid thunder, those who have brought me to the old one back away in fear.

"Ah, *fire*," the old one says, and there is a hint of satisfaction in the trembling of his words. He regards me with new appreciation. "You have brought back to us a bit of the old ways, which even I had forgotten. Yet there is a recipe that I seem to remember..."

In the time that follows, Nimbus and I learn to prepare delicious, digestible forms of organics which fill Rain-Maker's delicate body and return a measure of his strength. It requires many days, for his body has forgotten how to allocate the organics that he can no longer metabolize, but as the structure rebuilds itself, he returns to the manuscripts. We receive tours of the majestic archives, many times the size of all the libraries of the wind put together. When Nimbus absorbs the many exotic and powerful tremblings to a greater God, I am drawn to those texts which contain the history of our ancient, now dying species.

"The Old Ones were People-Of-The-Sky like us," Rain-Maker tells me. "They worshipped a god who was different from the God, the way the sky is different from you or me. See, it is written here in this hymn, there in this song of thanks. This was before the Prophet returned with his visions and voices. We were a great race once, before the Voice came down to the Prophet," the old one says bitterly. "We roamed the skies and created vortices like these to provide energy, and because of the beauty of doing it."

"Now we are few," I say. "Scattered herds that diminish with each sacrifice."

"It is written, here, and here, a record of the day the Prophet returned. He told us that our worship of the spirit-that-animates-the-sky was a pagan, sinful activity, that our noble constructions and inquiry were vanity and pride. For many years, he collected his converts, and then there was turmoil and a great upheaval, and it was safer to join the herds than to be victims of their raiding parties. That was many generations ago," the old one continues, "when I was forced to witness the triumph of the God and the Prophet over hope and beauty and joy and adventure and knowledge. It is written that the multitudes were afraid not to obey, yet I returned here, to mourn the loss of what once was and is now lost except for words in the wind. I welcome refugees and renegades to our most ancient and noble construction, for many would rather live here in the shadows of our former greatness than in servitude to the God. We are the damned, and the God is our enemy."

"Yet you defy the God every day. Your numbers grow, as those of the herd diminish."

"We fear that day when the herds are gone, fully-harvested, and the God comes looking for His lost disciples. How we will deal with that day, I cannot know."

I think about what he has said, and recognize the truth of it. "Then I must return to the herd," I tell him.

"They will not accept you back."

"I will tell them that it is possible to defy the God. That it is being done."

"You will bring them down upon us."

I laugh at this. "The bloated ones will not find their way here, even if I were to tell them how to travel. They can barely move from feeding place to feeding place, so great is their piety."

"Still you will fail. If you defy the God, you also defy the Prophet-Ministers," says the old one. "They will never tell you this, but that is the greater sin, the thing they most fear, more even than blasphemy against the God. The God would not be able to control us if not for the Prophet-Ministers who use its power to give them their own."

"This time, that power will not go unchallenged. And then I will challenge the God itself to give me answers."

"I will not see you again," says the old one sadly.

"Keep the secret of the *fire*, maintain your life but a little longer, and I will lead you back to the sky."

Leaving Nimbus to care for the old one, I travel along an ice-bound byway, emerging at last from the far side of the wind shear into the presence of the herd. For a moment, their appearance is shocking, for I am not as they are. I am lean, strong, capable of wrestling with the skystorms, while the members of the herd, even the young ones, are bloated, puffy, sluggish and slow to recognize me as anything more than an apparition, a trick of the senses. A happy exception: I note that the new bud of Gentle-Rain-Maker is inquisitive, but Gentle-Rain-Maker herself appears dull and apathetic, her spirit broken by my banishment. Yet her body storms and thunders as she is the first to recognize me.

"You have returned!" she cries out, touching my forevapors again and again. "But what—how did you live?"

"There are many others like me—like us."

"I had given up on you. I am so happy you have returned. See? Little Thunder has been raised on stories of his missing brother, though we are forbidden to speak of you to the others."

"How is it that you dare return?" Herd Leader, bloated almost beyond recognition, separates himself from the pack with a dignified lethargy. "Look at you. You are an affront to our piety. Have you not been sent from here to die?"

"Yet I chose life and joy instead," I say to him, and the others gather in wonder. "I found many others as me, who live for more than just the eating. I found cities that our species constructed before the God's arrival."

Behind me, there is a darkness, a looming presence, and I turn to see the largest of our species that I have ever witnessed. It is so large and full of the requisite gases that I cannot see the top and the bottom as it advances wrathfully on my presence, propelled by dozens of acolytes.

And yet there is something I recognize about the configuration of this cloud.

"Breeze-Lover?"

"I am known as the Prophet-Minister now," the giant tells me coldly. "My predecessor has long since merged in ecstasy with the God. Indeed, this is my appointed day, where I too will join him."

"I should be joyful. But instead I am sad."

"You should not be here, my old friend. I must protect the herd from your ideas."

"I do not wish to rejoin the herd," I tell him. "I wish to follow you when you go to the God."

There is a shocked silence in the herd. All feeding has stopped.

"Nay," says Breeze-Lover sternly. "Even if I could, I am not allowed. Such a thing is forbidden."

"I will offer myself as a sacrifice."

"You will not be pleasing in the God's eyes. Look at the slender strength of your body. Is it not said that *Those full of rich oxygen and pure hydrogen are to report to the Refueling Station, and those who are not shall stay below and feed until they are?* How are we to ignore the words of the God on this, my holy hour?"

"How do we know *how* full?" I ask.

"Is it not said that *The young and the thin and the quick are too uneconomical to harvest?*"

"Can you stop me?" I ask quietly.

Breeze-Lover does not reply.

"Will you delay your meeting with the God for fear that I will follow you?"

Again silence.

"Then ascend, and I will accompany the one who was once my friend to the God, and the God will deal with me as he takes you to the places of heaven."

There are no more words. Breeze-Lover touches another acolyte, the acolyte quivers with sluggish triumph and immediately assumes a gravity of bearing and firmness of tone, and the herd has a new Prophet-Minister. Then Breeze-Lover turns his attention to me, and in a gesture of reconciliation, he extends his vapors to mine, and we, together, allow the electrostatic connection holding our molecules together to release some of their grip, making us lighter, taking us up to the place where the God awaits.

We rise into and through the ice layers, first the slippery water ice, then the brittle ammonium hydrosulfide ice 25 miles higher, and then abruptly into the scattered fields of tiny ammonia ice, barely more substantial than gas molecules. The air pressure is so feeble that my body expands to the size of Breeze-Lover, and he, in turn, has become the sky above me. Still we climb, and abruptly, as we pass through a layer of hazy yellow cloud, the temperature begins to rise again, so that I am once again passing through liquid water vapor, and I am aware now of the point of light in the distance that Gentle-Rain-Maker had experienced so many years ago, the source of distant heat that the ancients called, mysteriously, the *Sun*.

Breeze-Lover hesitates at this place, testing the wind for some sign that the God has noticed him. He drifts this way and that, until finally the Voice emerges from the sky, and he and also I tremble at its majesty and the mystery of its utterances.

"*The station is over this way,*" the holy voice thunders. "*My god, they seem to get dumber with each generation.*"

Until the hearing of this voice, I had not truly, down to my core, actually believed that the God existed. Now I am faced with the reality of it, the possibility that the old ones had worshipped a false deity, that everything I have done is truly blasphemy against the truth.

This is the moment of exhilaration for Breeze-Lover, and for a time I share in the rapture of my friend, the honor to have been addressed personally by the God. And then the voice sounds its additional approval:

"*Lord, look at the size of this one.*"

By now, we are touching and experiencing the God in all its majesty. It is much smaller than we are, but the surface has no porosity; instead, it is hard like ice, only less cold, actually warm to the touch, clearly a thing from either the distant surface below or somewhere beyond the sky. The God is generally cylindrical in shape, but with many complicated protuberances, and I am so interested that I blurt out the question before the purification ritual can begin.

"I want you to answer me, holy one!" I call out boldly. "What is the purpose of our lives?"

For a few long seconds, there is no answer. Finally a voice emerges from the chemical emissions escaping a tube near the front, "*Did the computer get a translation of that? Can you tell what he's asking?*"

"Nay, you are not required answer the blasphemies," Breeze-Lover calls out, serene now that his faith has been vindicated. "I am prepared for the Ritual."

"*—I'm not sure,*" mutters the God in his regal majesty. "*There could be two of them out there. I say we begin and ignore the questions for now. Approach the fueling station,*" the God calls out in a terrible voice.

Trembling with ecstasy, Breeze-Lover floats toward the God's strange form.

"*Align your oxygen to the larger intake valve,*" the Voice calls out. "*It's the long thing sticking out near the back. I'm not sure this one's smart enough to understand his own language. But what a haul! We're over quota this month for sure.*"

These incomprehensible words of power fill Breeze-Lover with a transcendent joy. He finally locates the God's chosen appendages, and puts the oxygen part of his tenuous body against it, feeling the delicious hardness of the God the way one would feel ice crystals hardened by an upwelling storm.

"Now the methane goes against the smaller tube. You could move a little more quickly."

With a stately grace, Breeze-Lover aligns himself and prepares for the transcendent journey to heaven.

What happens next is the most violent thing I will ever witness.

Without warning, Breeze-Lover's gases, the accumulation of a lifetime of feeding, are ripped brutally out of each end of the body, tearing the intricate fabric of his polymer chains with a total disregard for pain or life. The double vortex of intense suction creates an inner vacuum, and there is a massive infilling, playing havoc with the cloud's electrostatic forces like gossamer in a chainsaw. The effect is so horrifying that as Breeze-Lover screams, I act out of instinct, and envelope the God with my body.

"Stop!" I cry out, and punctuate the word with a small bolt of lightning directed into the heart of the cylinder.

Instantly, the violence ceases, and there is a long terrifying stillness. Breeze-Lover weeps in agony, drifting away from the God, his body crippled. Then I notice something that I had not before, that the air surrounding the God is filled with the remains of other People-Of-The-Sky, shards and shreds and bits of organics decomposing in the wind.

It is a place of death.

Then a feeble voice emerges from the God.

"—must have shorted the vacuum system, but at least the computer is back on line. What WAS that?"

"I'll go outside and make the repairs."

Two gods? I wait in silence, my mind working with incredible speed, urged on by the chill winds and the manifest weakness I have found in the God, who still seems not aware of my presence above and around it. And what does it mean, that the God will go outside, when the God is—

I notice a tiny, infinitesimally small figure emerge from the God into the heart of my tenuous body. It propels itself by means of ejected gases toward one of the tubes. I watch carefully as this minuscule creature opens a hole in the strange material of the God and inspects some long filaments.

It is absorbed in this task, and so I am able to gather a storm around it, fed by my anger.

"You are no god!" I shout. "Does a god require a cylinder of ice to protect it from the top of the sky? Would not a god have known of my blasphemy and punished me instantly?"

The tiny creature emits a great number of tiny vibrations, and I am able to sense that it is a living form covered by a layer of material. I draw the material and the thing inside away from the ship and hold it tightly with electrostatic force, though it tries to eject gases and wriggle free.

"*Let the object go,*" the Voice calls out from the cylinder. "*Or—or you'll go to someplace even worse than hell.*"

"Obey it," Breeze-Lover calls out in a weak voice. "Please. Do not endanger yourself further."

"Do you not see that this is no god?" I demand. "What are you?" I call out, punctuating the question with another electrical bolt, this time across the surface of the cylinder."

"*—hook me up directly into the computer's translator before he blows us out of the sky,*" the voice calls out with an unmistakable note of panic in the chemicals it allows to escape. "*Listen,*" the voice continues, "*All right; you've figured it out. We are not really gods, exactly. We're a refueling station for space vessels—oh, hell, how do I translate that? The methane and oxygen are what powers the commerce in this part of the solar system.*"

The incomprehensible words move me to anger. This time I deliver a charge of lightning directly into the tiny creature in my grasp, and there are no more vibrations from inside the covering. I cast it contemptuously away, and the body drifts back toward the cylinder. Presently, the tiny false god is drawn inside a hole which appears magically in one side of the solid material.

"*You killed him! My god, you fried him in his suit!*"

"As you have killed so many of us. Do you too wish to die?"

The answer comes in the form of another protuberance from the cylinder, which swivels into my body. After a moment, this tube releases a rapidly-moving object which passes directly through me and, after some distance, destroys itself in an outpouring of intense heat and light which passes harmlessly through my body, carrying with it, after a moment, a million hard broken fragments not unlike ice crystals, except for their exceptional temperature.

For a moment, all is silent, as the cylinder seems to assess the effect of this display of *fire*. Then a second tube emits what appears to be intensely-focused light, which also passes through me, heating up a few of my molecules to create a mild itching sensation.

"Enough of your foolish games!" I call down to the thing which is no god. "You will leave us now."

"*You think so?*" the God thunders back, and the tubes that drew away much of Breeze-Lover's substance are swiveled into my body. Before I can retreat into the wind, there is a deep wrenching pain rising to agony inside, as the twin vortices begin tearing at my flesh, no longer focused on the methane or oxygen, but at the deep internal structures.

I scream, a long agonized wail of despair and pain. Through the fog of my distress, I see Breeze-Lover moved to action, limping painfully toward the thing that is no god, his vapors purple with a grim determination. In a moment, he has gathered up from inside himself some last scraps of remaining oxygen, and some remaining methane, and with a feeble bolt of lightning he holds a bit of flame, a small candle of this new thing we have learned to call *fire*.

Carefully, Breeze-Lover inserts the *fire* into one of the tubes, so that it is vacuumed inside with the broken pieces of my body.

Now there is a trembling, and I feel the vacuum release me. The cylinder appears to expand, but there is no flexibility in the pseudo-ice that it is made of, and the *fire*, magnified a thousand times ten thousand times, comes roaring out of it, shattering the structure into so many constituent pieces that it is nearly a vapor, expanding outward in a cascading *fire*ball that lingers in the air, lingers, and then vanishes, the wind blowing away any traces that the God ever existed.

There is nothing but silence and the wind.

After a time, Breeze-Lover and I extend and mingle our vapors, and there is love between us, and the trembling of pain. I am weak, he is near death. Yet both of us are triumphant.

"You were right," Breeze-Lover says after a moment. "How many have died in this place?"

"It was no god. But what was it?"

"Perhaps we can never answer that question," says my companion, extending his awareness toward the top of the sky. "Perhaps we will never understand why they chose to harvest our people. It is a mystery for our children and their descendants to ponder over."

"I fear that others will return," I say.

"I hope they do," Breeze-Lover says, and a measure of his old strength is in the words. "We are more powerful than the God, and if another prophet is sent into our midst, we will search out the sender and give it a taste of *fire* and lightning."

"You look almost slender," I say.

Breeze-Lover has not the strength to laugh, but there is amusement in his tremblings. "But answer me this," he says ruefully: "What am I without the God?"

"You will be a prophet of the god once worshipped by our species," I say, "whose hymns are written in the wind for us to recover. Come," I say, leading with the remaining strength in my body the broken cloud, drawing him down toward the warmth of our home and the herd. "We have much to tell them, and much to learn from the old ones.

"But before that," I tell my old friend, drawing him gently away from the place of death, "I've discovered a few wonderful recipes that I can't wait to share with you."

The scene whirled away, and I was no longer a creature of the sky, and my body felt unbearably heavy where I was sitting on the hard floor.

I stared, uncomprehending, at a bare concrete wall, until finally I realized where I was and looked around.

Everybody else, including the Master, was sprawled around the floor, asleep. I wondered what time it was and checked my watch, and the full impact of my situation came back to me.

Slowly, feeling every ounce of the gravity in my legs, I, who had only a few minutes ago roamed the rooftops of a protostar, picked my way across the room and sat down on the bed, closing my eyes, realizing that sleep was a long way off.

I sighed.

It was going to be a very long night.

XIV

It is an article of faith in the emergent New Age community that human beings are capable of more than they realize, and that they will have to let go of doubt before they can explore their full potential. The scriptural tradition tells us that Jesus and, later, his followers performed miracles of healing and transformation, and that the Buddha and his followers took for granted the ability to know the thoughts of other minds and to travel from place to place through spiritual conveyance. In modern times, there are countless stories of people who were healed of diseases in ways that cannot be explained by medical science or normal physical laws.

The common thread of all of these stories, the common prescription for miracles across history, seems to be the simple, ultimately humble willingness to believe that we are more than we seem, and that we are capable of more than we can explain at this point in our scientific understanding.

The New Age acknowledgment is not that we are gods, or that we are omnipotent; it is simply that we don't yet know the limits of what we are capable of, and in times when there was no powerful, charismatic teacher providing us with examples, we have done a very poor job of exploring them on our own.
—From *The Rutherfordton Spiritual Gazette*

After the meeting with my lawyer, a police officer entered the room, and he and my lawyer engaged in a long argument about things I didn't understand and was too tired to listen to. I think the gist of it was that the police suddenly thought I was a high risk to run away, and so there was no likelihood of bail, even though the process had apparently been started more than two hours ago. My lawyer shook my hand with an apology and said he would talk to a judge in the morning. Then I was escorted back to my cell by not one but three officers, who watched me warily, their spirits radiating the dark browns and yellows of intense suspicion. By the sheer amount of the glow, it was clear that they were quite agitated, but I was too tired to care about their problems. I had enough of my own.

I could not be sure, but it seemed like I was put back in the same cell. But now it was empty.

"Where are the others?" I asked as they pushed me through the door. "Can I ask to be put back in with them?"

"That's quite funny," one of the officers said shortly, and his demon looked at me with a smirk as he locked the cell.

I sat down wearily on the cot, took a long, deep breath, bent over the paper and pencil that my lawyer had kindly provided me, and began composing my letter. One of the police officers remained behind and watched me through the bars.

"What?" I said finally.

"Why don't you wave your magic wand and disappear?" he asked me.

"They confiscated all our wands," I told him.

"We've tightened security," he said. "I just wanted you to know that."

"They confiscated my key to the cell at the same time," I told him, and went back to writing.

After a long time, after I had written many pages, I looked up and the officer was gone, and with a jolt of amazement, I realized that I was looking into the face of the Master. He smiled at my startled reaction.

"That is a beautiful thing about you," he said, nodding his head toward my letter. "You never waste a moment, even when the circumstances seem to have you trapped."

The Master took my hand and pulled me to a stand. "It's time to leave this place," he said. "I have something to show you."

"What do you mean leave this place?" I demanded in confusion. "Do you mean escape?"

"Yes."

"Where are the others?"

"They are already gone. You are the only one left here."

"But—"

The Master squeezed my hand. "Hold on. Whatever you do, don't let go."

"You're just going to fly us out of here?"

"Nothing nearly so complicated."

My daughter, I cannot quite remember what happened next, and I will always regret that I was not paying more attention at that moment. But how could I know what we were about to do? The Master gave me a hard tug, and it seemed as if he was pulling me in an oblique direction. My body felt very strange, and then the room seemed to my eyes to become oddly distant; as if I was somehow moving away from all the walls at the same time. I shook my head, closed my eyes, and when I opened them, I saw that my body was now pressed against a wall of cloud in a direction that I had not somehow been aware of before. The Master, still holding my hand, walked into the cloudy mist, but I was having a very hard time orienting myself toward it. It felt as if my body would not turn in that oblique and hard-to-look-at direction. But the tug on my hand was insistent, and finally I seemed to edge between (how was this possible?) the very distant solid walls of the jail cell and directly into the cloud—

—and through it to the other side…

Suddenly, I was standing in bright sunshine, with a warm, gentle wind in my face. My nose caught the delicate smell of flowers and pine needles.

For a long second, my mind refused to accept the scene in front of me. I rubbed my eyes and looked again.

The Master and I were standing, hand-in-hand, on a stone patio so large that the end of it, ahead and behind, was lost in the distance. To my left, it extended perhaps the length of two football fields, where it ended in front of what seemed to be an ancient castle whose stone walls were crowded with balconies and windows and ornamentation and protruding porticoes across every square yard of the surface, rising so high that the top of the towers were obscured in clouds, so long that it, too, ended somewhere in the invisible distance.

To my right, the endless front porch of this castle ended perhaps 250 yards from the castle at a beautifully carved stone wall, perhaps four feet high, and beyond that I saw a broad green valley with a distant lake in its center, and beyond that, lush, tree-covered hills rolled out to the horizon. Behind the hills, I could make out the misty hint of mountains capped with snow. In the valley, my eyes detected movement, what looked like a herd of white animals too distant to make out clearly. Yet I thought I saw flashes across their foreheads, and had the odd impression that they might be unicorns.

All along the patio, scattered apparently at random, somebody had built raised gardens of exotic plants whose flowers, brilliant in every color I could imagine, were very different from each other; some made of individual petals as large as my open hand, others like tiny flags in the wind, many different species in each garden all clustered together. Their iridescent leaves, every subtle shade of green, seemed to be more delicate than anything I was familiar with. The soft wind shook them vigorously, giving the gardens a fairy quality that, mixed with the sweet, almost intoxicating smell of the flowers, made me think instantly of paradise.

The Master let go of my hand and blew a few haunting notes on his flute, and beautiful flying creatures that looked like a mixture of gossamer and rainbow, butterfly and bird, were attracted to the sound. In wonder, my amazement partly anesthetized by the music, I touched one of those leaves, then let my fingers run through the metallic blue and red flowers that cascaded like a cloud from the central stem. I looked up as we walked toward the next garden, which was filled with a riot of yellow and orange and blue colors shimmering in the breeze.

The Master took the flute from his lips and looked at me expectantly. As we walked, I felt a crush in my mind as a million questions all tried to get out of my mouth at the same time. But I found that none of them were adequate to the extraordinary opportunity I had to tap the mind of this person whose glow blinded my spiritual eyes.

Reluctantly, I turned my attention from the flowers we were passing to the person who seemed to have all the answers.

"In this time we have together, why don't you tell me the most important thing I should know," I suggested finally. "You know the right questions better than I do."

The Master silently acknowledged the rightness of my question. He put the flute to his lips again, and one of rainbow creatures landed on his shoulder, its eyes regarding me sharply as the melodic notes rose and then faded, leaving behind a gentle ache of wonder and loss.

"All of the important answers can be found in one place," he said after a moment, taking a flower from one of the gardens and holding it up to the light. "I could spend a million years filling the air with words about the things I've experienced, and I doubt that more than a few of them would translate adequately into our present languages. So the only questions that really matter have to do with how to get that experience for yourself."

The creature on his shoulder flew off abruptly. We walked past a pond of crystal-clear water, in a cistern that looked as if it had been carved directly out of the polished stone under our feet. I stopped to look down at my reflection, taking some comfort that here, at least, was something tangibly familiar. Yet the reflection of my face looked unkempt, and I realized that I hadn't shaven in two days. I pushed my attention through the reflection into the water, where small brightly-colored creatures darted here and there below the surface, looking almost but not quite like tropical fish.

"I don't know where to start," I said. "Just tell me how to take the first step."

"The people in a certain village lived along the upper ridges that surrounded a deep valley," said the Master. "They could look down and see the waters of a beautiful, clear lake in the distance, and it was said that the shore of this distant lake was the most beautiful place in the world to live, the place of paradise, where all troubles were left behind and all who came there were happy and at peace.

"Over many centuries, many people set out on this journey, but only a very few in history had returned, and they confirmed that the lakeshore was, indeed, magically beautiful, and talked about their journey and the path they had taken.

But each person who returned spoke of a different path, and so the people who lived at the top of the ridge were confused about the true path.

"Even though everyone wanted to go there, most people never tried.

"Instead, they gathered once a week to talk about the journey, and they worshipped those long-dead persons who had been to the lake and back, and prayed in good faith for their help, and waited for an answer before they would start down the slope themselves. Different groups worshipped different successful travelers, and even though there were an infinite number of possible routes from the ridge to the bottom of the valley, the followers of each successful traveler argued that theirs was the only true one. Some talked of a slow, rambling path that avoided all hazards and obstacles, the safest route, but which required a lifetime to complete. Others talked of a more direct route through the dense woods and underbrush, braving the tangle of vines and the dangers of losing your way.

"A member of one of these congregations—it doesn't matter which one," the Master continued, "would go every day to the edge of the top of the ridge and look down longingly at the lake, and with all his heart he would desire to make the journey, except that nothing he heard in his weekly gatherings talked about the journey itself, only about the True Path. And as he was standing on the edge, the wind and the sky took pity on him, and they blew up a sudden storm, and this person was toppled from the top of the ridge, where he fell, and tumbled, and rolled, and fell until, by what appeared to be a miracle, he sat up, still alive, on flat ground once again.

"Dazed, he looked about him, and saw that the lake that he had gazed at for all of his young life was there, within a few feet of his bruised body. And so he stood up shakily and sat down in the water, and let it flow over him with its healing touch, and he drank the water, and finally he swam across the lake to the opposite shore, just for the sheer joy of it.

"And there, as he was climbing up out of the water, he saw that he was not alone. There were other people here, living in the woods close to the shore, who came to bathe in the water every day. And the young man ran up to them and asked them how they had come to be here, and all had a different story. Some had fallen as he had; others had walked down a variety of routes, and the young man was astonished that so many people had succeeded in a journey that his people regarded as so unusual and remarkable.

"And so he asked them why they didn't return. And they stared at him, and asked why they would want to, when they had everything they needed here. And they told him the secret of all saints and the secret of all who come to the paradise of the spirit: that it is far more difficult to make your way back up the ridge to the people who are still waiting to make the journey, than it is to make the journey in the first place. And once you return, the reward for your sacrifice is that you will be misinterpreted, misunderstood, and you, rather than your message, will be worshipped.

"Do you understand?" the Master asked me after a moment.

"I think so," I said, and I thought I did, though later it would often feel muddled in my mind. "We only count those who get there and come back, and that's rare, and so we think the journey itself is nearly impossible."

"I can tell you that when you get to that place," the Master said, looking out across the hills, "you will realize that you are a very small piece of the awareness of the universe itself, and you will see that you have always had the ability to share in its awareness and experience the thoughts and feelings of divinity. Think of that as a marker. Now that you know what that place looks like, all you have to do is start."

"Can you show me how to take the first step?" I asked.

"Master the Song of the Universe," the Master suggested. "That is one path. Surrender your individuality and eliminate the babble produced by your foolish mind—which is a longer path. Do everything you can do with energy and love, and that is a still longer, gentler trip. Ultimately, you'll find that the path you take will lead to a journey as easy or difficult as your unique personality demands. And always there is a shortcut which is shorter than all of them, where you realize that if you can simply stop fighting for your own individuality and relax your spirit back into the Awareness it came from, you will roll down to your destination with no effort at all, because something very like gravity is constantly, gently tugging you in the direction of spiritual awakening and enlightenment."

As the Master was speaking, I watched his aura, trying to catch the nuances of his words. But what I saw there was so unexpected that I thought my spiritual eyes were deceiving me.

"You're in pain," I said.

"Yes. It is quite intense."

"But you're not injured?"

"My body is intact, yes. It is a different pain."

"How can that be?"

"I think you're the only person who has ever noticed this," said the Master, and there was a hint of unfathomable gratitude in his smile.

"What's wrong?"

"I am living in a hell undreamed of by the spiritual pundits who speak without knowledge of fire and brimstone. I am living, right now, in a state of separation, and it requires all my concentration not to scream from the agony of it."

"You are living as we live," I said.

"Yes," the Master agreed.

We walked in silence. I let my individuality go, just a little, and it was attracted, magnetically, to the Master's aura, and I saw things I hadn't considered before. I tried to imagine feeling pleasure on a scale a thousand times greater than my happiest moment, in direct communion with the Eternal Presence, where It and I are interchangeable, so that I have difficulty knowing where It stops and I begin.

I saw this, and tears came to my own eyes.

"It must be incredible," I said.

"The opposite is just as powerful," said the Master. "Separation from that, becoming merely human again, is a shatteringly difficult transition. I tried to describe it once as the contrast between the moment of peak sexual climax and being thrown into a bonfire, but that really doesn't begin to capture it."

"I don't see why you can't live in both places at once," I said. "I mean, be there experiencing that and being with us too."

From the Master's smile and the amused glow of his spirit, I saw that this was an unbelievably naive question.

"You saw me when I was with Mommy," he said quietly. "You thought I was an idiot. Remember?"

I looked down in shame, and noticed that the ground was now a mosaic of tiles arranged into fantastic pictures of creatures that might have been crabs.

"Yes," I admitted.

"You can't give Her a little bit of your attention," the Master told me. "In order to function, to bring you the things I've seen and learned, I needed to become, once again, tiny and limited and foolish, with the consolation that somehow Mommy still adores me with a love beyond imagination."

"It's an amazing sacrifice," I said, seeing it on his spirit. "I see now why so few people ever come back from that place to help the rest of us out."

By now, we were walking into the shade of a stone archway, which seemed to be made of finely-polished marble blocks the size of railroad cars. The top of the arch was easily fifty feet over our heads, and across it, protruding from the stone like the gargoyles of a Gothic cathedral, but infinitely more detailed, were creatures of fantasy. At first glimpse, they looked like the crabs I had seen in the tiles, facing outward, with two protruding eyes, and a kind of pattern that might be a snout between them, and, below that, two fangs along the bottom of the head—if indeed it *was* a head.

The creatures' legs (if those *were* legs) hung over and below them on each side, and above the eyes were what looked like semicircular horns curved downward, and outside of them, where the ears of a dog might have been, more patterns that might have been the outside of a shell or tufts of feather curved down and inward.

The strangely unnerving eyes stared straight at us. I had the impression that whatever creature this represented, it was intelligent, fiercely aware and somehow regal, although I could not imagine how something that looked like a crab could give me that impression.

"Is there any hope for us?" I asked as we walked through the arch.

The Master opened a large wooden door whose top was lost somewhere in the darkness overhead. It turned on invisible hinges, silently, perfectly, easily, granting us access to a brilliantly illuminated open space behind the castle, so large that at first I thought we were outdoors. It was hard to see all the way up to the many-windowed ceiling. Trees, looking vaguely like palms but with brilliant golden leaves, stretched up from the floor over our heads, and from the balconies, long vines festooned with purple and pink flowers hung down toward the floor like colored spanish moss. Shafts of brilliant sunlight lit up the polished floor.

"There is more than simply hope," the Master said. "In the world today, you see a sense of restlessness, a realization that there must be something more to life, a desire to explore the mysteries. All it needs is the right spark."

"And you are that spark?"

"I can see the results of the things we are doing in the very near future," he said. "I have seen a new society, born out of this one, as different from civilization as civilization was from the hunter-gatherer tribal cultures before it. To me, it means that, in a general way, we will succeed. What I don't know, yet, is whether we will succeed in teaching the basic truth without creating a new religion. I don't know yet whether I'll be able to slip out the back door and return to Mommy without a billion people somehow confusing me with the message and praying to me instead of joining her."

I tried to process that information as we passed under another archway into a small, furnished entryway where four long corridors extended out in oblique directions.

About 30 yards down one of the corridors, the Master turned left, and we entered an open garden, following a stone path toward a part of the castle complex that seemed to be a delicate series of spiral towers, seemingly too fragile to withstand gravity. Spidery suspended walkways ran between them. Everything shimmered in brilliant color in the bright sun, as if the walls in this part of the complex were made of polished opal. As we left the garden, our feet entered one of those narrow walkways, suspended high above a river rushing down over rocks. The tops of trees lined our path, shimmering in that same funny delicate way, and among the leaves there seemed to be a kind of golden fruit the approximate size and shape of strawberries. I reached out and pulled one off the branch, touching it to my mouth. As soon as my teeth broke the outer skin, a cool liquid as sweet as honey poured across my tongue.

"Is that all of your questions?" the Master asked me.

"I guess I have one more," I said, finishing the fruit.

"Yes?"

"Where," I said, "the hell *are* we?"

Karen, I am happy to tell you that in all the days I knew the Master, this was the only time I ever saw somebody make him laugh as hard as he did now. He laughed and laughed, and put his hand on my shoulder and looked at me with new appreciation. It made him even more human in my eyes.

"This world revolves around a yellow type G star and its small binary companion on the edge of a little cluster of stars known to astronomers on Earth as the Jewel Box, roughly eight thousand light years away in the direction of the second-brightest star in the Southern Cross," said the Master finally. "You will see an interesting display when the second sun goes down," he added.

"But—I mean, how did we get here?"

"If you were to look in a direction that we have learned not to perceive, this world and ours actually touch that other dimension at almost exactly the same place along a curved plane. A long time ago, people routinely traveled from here to there and back, and they made this their primary residence. The ignorant called them Gods, but they were no more Gods than you or I."

"What is it called?"

"We call this interesting structure Asgard, but it has had other names. Shambhala. Olympus. The Pure Land. Yangsang. And one other. You will see evidence that Jesus visited this place often. Some believe this is what he referred to when he said that the Kingdom of Heaven is at hand."

"But not you."

"No."

"What was the other name?"

The Master leaned forward, resting his arms against the stone wall that bordered the walkway. With our backs to the castle, he gestured toward the long valley below between us and the distant mountains. "Out there, many kinds of fruit grow all year long, and the animals have no fear of humans," he said. "Some of them are familiar," he added, "and many others seem to have been brought here from other places. To survive in that rainforest, there is no need to do anything but pick the fruit off the trees. A world that is a garden, shaped to ensure a life of contemplation and ease. What do you think of when you hear these words? Not the Kingdom of God, but a far more ancient legend, garbled in the retelling as all legends are."

"Eden," I whispered.

"Seventy thousand years ago, the human race found a pathway to this place across the invisible doorway, and when they joined the Deva Community, and showed them this place, they were told that it was an artifact of the Mechs, built by their incomprehensible technology long before life had crawled out of the oceans of our world, and then discarded the way you or I might toss an empty beer can into the street," said the Master. "There is evidence that our distant ancestors lived here, tending this garden, for many thousands of years, before they returned to our planet.

"Now we are back in Eden," the Master added, "only to find it empty."

"Why did they leave this place?"

"Follow me," said the Master. "I have something to show you."

The narrow walkway crossed a deep gorge where a waterfall cascaded down from a rocky cliff to our right, and after a few minutes, our path reconnected with another part of the castle through another arch, made of the same translucent, polished material that I had taken for opal. I stopped and ran my fingers across the glasslike surface, staring into the depths of colorful fire. The material was warm to the touch. On the other side of the arch, we entered a smaller room perhaps the size of a hotel lobby, scattered with low couches like I had seen in the entryway to the halls.

In the center of that room, at the center of the couches, there rested a perfect glass or crystal sphere, at least forty feet in diameter.

"This is the library," the Master told me, gesturing toward the sphere. "It is my favorite part of this remarkable place, a kind of terminal that connects us with the endless record, where everything that ever happened is preserved for our viewing. Now, just to pass the time," he said, as milky images began forming in the center of the crystalline sphere, "let's look at how our ancestors came to leave this place and return to Earth."

Several hours later, the Master and I emerged into the familiar downtown streets of Asheville, having made an instant and disconcerting jump through the oblique curtain of fog, trading warm starlit evening for the gray light of an overcast afternoon. Rain had washed through the city in the past hour, and the moisture hung heavy in the air. The Master led me through an alleyway that, from the scent, must have served as a convenient latrine for the homeless, and out the other side, where we could see thin plumes of dark smoke—the last gasp of the warehouse fire.

"I have to get back to the office," I said.

"In this condition?" The Master regarded me with a faint smile. "I think we ought to get you cleaned up first. And there's the matter of your escape from jail that will have to be dealt with."

"Yes, my lawyer is going to be very angry," I said. "I'm sure he didn't sign on to defend a jailbreaker."

"He's not your lawyer," the Master said pointedly. "He's theirs."

"What do you mean?"

"You are about to find out."

At that moment, my cell phone rang. I hesitated, but something in the Master's eyes encouraged me to answer it.

"Yes?"

"You goddam motherfucker," came the angry voice of Heavy Hitter at the other end. "What made you think you could fucking double-cross us?"

"What?" I could feel my shoulders sag as energy drained out of my body. "What are you talking about?"

"What I want to know, *right now*, is how the hell you found out about the insurance policy. You tell me that much, and we can take our time about screwing you later."

"Listen," I said, growing hot myself. "In the last 24 hours I've been trapped in a deadly inferno and arrested and booked and—"

"Who the fuck do you think told the cops where to find you? You think I don't know these things?"

"I thought—"

"That's exactly the trouble, too goddam motherfucking much fucking *thinking*. You have any idea who you've decided to mess with here? You make one move toward collecting a dime of that $12 million and I will personally—"

"What a minute," I said.

"—ram it, nickel by nickel, up your—"

"Are you telling me you had the place insured for $12 million?" I finally blurted out.

There was a long silence on the other end.

"You bought the policy in my name," I said, seeing the picture with all too much clarity. "Then, when I sold it back, if the warehouse happened to burn down before you could cancel the policy—"

"Are you trying to tell me you didn't know this? That you didn't deliberately not show up for the closing?"

"You know, I really don't care what you think," I said. "But ask yourself, is this my style? Is this the way I do business?"

There was another long silence on the other end. Finally, Heavy Hitter came back again.

"Does that mean you'd be willing to come down here and sign some papers?" he asked at last.

"The warehouse is gone. You can't sell something that doesn't exist."

"Did you read the contract you signed?"

"What do you mean?"

"I mean, he's only interested in the *land*. Your fire just saved him some of the cost of having to clear the warehouse out of there."

"*My* fire? I'd bet every dollar I have that whatever it was that set off that fire was timed to happen while you and I and this client of yours were putting the last signature on the last piece of paper."

"I don't like what you're implying."

"People almost died in there. I was one of them."

"Listen," the voice on the other end said. "I was assuming, until this minute, that you *had* read the contract, and that you were the one who burned it down. The best thing you can do for everybody, including yourself, is just get the hell over here and sign these papers," he said.

"And give up the $12 million?"

"You would never collect it anyway," Heavy Hitter said, "unless you can make them believe you didn't set the fire in the first place. Your best defense now is to go through with the sale as we arranged it, and pretend you didn't know anything about the insurance. That would give everybody a chance to stay out of jail."

I thought about that for a long second. I wanted very much to go back through the magic curtain to Asgard, but when I looked around, the Master was gone.

"How can you be so sure?" I asked finally.

"We sent a pretty good lawyer out there to find out what was going on," Heavy Hitter advised me, sounding almost cheerful. Then, discussion over, his voice lit up in an almost visible smile.

"So tell me," he said: "What do you get when you cross a lawyer with a warm pussy?"

Interlude: The Big Questions
What did the Master do when *you* met him?

Everybody climbs up out of the water and dries off on the assortment of flat rocks along the shoreline, allowing the sun to do most of the work. Today, there is no hurry going back up to the warehouse. I wait for a lull in the conversation and pounce.

"What was it like when you guys met the Master?"

Cassandra (promptly): "It's always different and always perfect."

For once everybody agrees with her.

"Perfect how?"

Apollo: "He knows exactly what we need to complete ourselves. The first meeting is always exactly right, but it's only right for that person."

"Can you give me an example?"

(A young man who calls himself Eris climbs down the bank so we can hear him over the sound of the water.) "I grew up with a hunger to be famous. I wanted to change the world, to write my name across the sky. I wanted to run for office and have my own TV show and lead a march on Washington, and I wanted these things so badly that I couldn't start any of them, because to start one would mean not working on another. It was like I was trapped in my own dreams."

"And?"

Eris: "And I was walking past this—well, I thought he was a vagrant. He looked mentally disabled. His clothes were like a street person's, and he was sitting on the sidewalk with his back against the wall of a building, watching me in that scary way he has. Because we made eye contact, I reached into my pocket, thinking to give him a dollar, but he spoke to me before I could move.

"*The world is waiting for you,* he said. *And you haven't accepted the invitation.*

"I asked him what he meant by that, and he told me my life story in about six sentences. It was so unexpected that I almost blacked out, right there on the sidewalk. I wanted to ask who the hell he was, but there was a bigger question inside of me, and I was afraid he was like some kind of genie, only you could only get one wish instead of three.

"So I asked, instead, my own question, which was: "How do I get to the sky from where I am now?"

"He looked at me again, and then he answered me in six words, and it made all the difference."

"What did he say?"

Eris: "He looked me up and down and smiled, and said: *The sky begins at your feet."*

Nobody says anything for a few seconds. To my surprise, Mars has pulled himself up on the rock to listen to the conversation.

Mars (in a slow sepulchral voice): "My brothers and sisters, in my short and unfortunate life, I have witnessed things and given myself to actions which are far outside the boundaries of forgiveness. As a warrior, I have tasted the blood of children, and there are bare places in the earth where towns and villages existed before my arrival. The memory of these things is a weight on my spirit, and for all the talk of repentance, if I were to tear these actions out of my soul, there would be very little left of it.

"One day, I felt that I could not carry this with me for another hour. As I sat and watched the lights of the ambulances in the street across the way, I thought of what a simple thing it would be to do to myself what I had done to so many others. I did not know then what a blessing it is to release a spirit from the crushing limitations of its body, but as I watched them load the injured bodies into the ambulances, I sensed some of this glory, and it called to me."

Mars looks at his own spirit mournfully for a long second, at the swirling legacy of horrors that none of us are quite brave enough to examine closely, and a tear comes down his face.

"So what happened?"

Mars: "Something impossible." *(He wipes the tear with the back of his hand.)* "I realized that there was someone sitting next to me, though none before has ever been able to approach me undetected. I thought to kill him, but then the Master put both of his arms around me, and I knew that such a person who could embrace such a one as me must be sent by God Himself, the God who I thought had abandoned me, as he had abandoned my victims to the maggots and the vultures.

"And so I addressed him as one might to God. I asked him how I could leave it all behind and simply go forward with a new life.

"I thought he would tell me how to do this thing, but when I looked in his eyes, I knew that this was not possible. Finally he spoke, and he said the words that gave me no hope, but the courage to move forward without it. He said to me, *No matter how hard you run, no matter how hard you try, you can't ever leave yourself behind.*"

For some reason, everyone is looking at Apollo now, and so he puts aside the vexation that he wears like a protective cloak, and his voice sounds strangely soft in remembering.

Apollo: "I am a scholar. I wish I could tell you that I have a real skill or talent, but all I know is to search the dead ancient manuscripts for scraps of truth which had been entrusted to a tablet or scroll before the thoughts they contained had been reinterpreted into falsehoods. I found many of them, and they told of a very different truth than the one we hear in the lecture halls and from the pulpits of a dozen different religions. For a long time, I truly believed that I was the only person who had glimpsed these things, and I had no clear idea of how to communicate them to a world that had lived with and grown around and built on the reinterpretations for 20 centuries or more.

"I tried to write a book, and after 30 false starts, I had reached the ragged edges of despair. I thought perhaps that instead I could help to start a curriculum at the University that would explore the New Age literature, which—I argued—had become the protest literature of the modern era. It would explore the new literary/philosophical voices calling from outside our social order, the voices which were already organized into a movement which would define the next transformation in our cultural norms, the New Age willingness to explore everything we know about our place in the universe with a fresh spirit.

"When the University rejected the proposal, I resigned as of the end of the semester in protest.

"At my next lecture, I noticed a ragged, ill-dressed man in the back of the room whose eyes caught mine and distracted me throughout the discussion. I let the class out five minutes early, and everybody left but him. Finally, in my impatience, I demanded to know what he wanted of me.

"He told me he wanted nothing from anyone, but he expected me to present him with a small gift before he left. What gift? I asked. Your fear, he said.

"I shouted at him from the front of the lecture hall to where he sat in the back of the room, where it looked as if he did not have the ability to rise from his chair. I shouted that there were a million scraps of lost knowledge like a jigsaw puzzle missing perhaps a third of its pieces, and that fitting them together was impossible. I couldn't do it. Nobody could.

"And he told me that this wasn't what I was afraid of; that failure was nothing new to me.

"And in that moment, I realized that this was true, and I voiced my real fear. I told him that people like us once had knowledge of these things, these eternal truths, and then they lost it. Now I see us slowly regaining them. I was afraid, deathly afraid, that we would lose them once again.

"He smiled at me from the back of the room. Yes, he said. You are right to be afraid, because, he said, *The dark has infinite patience. It never stops waiting for the light to go away.*"

For a long time, nobody says anything. Suddenly I want very much to know what he had said to Cassandra. But Hestia speaks next.

Hestia: "It's all so beautiful. Compared with these, my story feels drab and ordinary."

Her friend (not one of the gods or near-gods, but newly-baptized): "Tell it. I think it's better than any of them."

Hestia (shaking the hair out of her eyes): "You were talking about marriage, and it's true what Venus said. When I got married, I was so idealistic, and he seemed so wonderful and I looked forward to a life of adventure together." *(Her eyes turn back on the times of her young life.)* "And it was very good for the first year, and then he stopped spending time with me. All of a sudden he chose to give the hours of his day to everything and everybody else, and when he wasn't at the bar with friends, he was working, and everything was about his job, and gradually there was no place for me in his life, and my dreams and idealism were being crumbled piece by piece, day by day, by a man I loved more than I had ever loved anything else.

"Finally, I gave him an ultimatum, and it broke my heart to think that I would have to force him to return to spending time with me, and it broke my heart a thousand times more when he told me that he preferred divorce to the relationship I was proposing. Later I learned that he'd been sleeping with different women at work, that some of his road trips were really trysts in a hotel room for the weekend. And so I gave him his divorce, and the day the papers were signed, I went to the roof of my apartment building and looked down and waited for the street to clear enough so that I wouldn't hurt anybody when I hit the ground. I felt completely worthless, totally without value. I felt that I would never be a special person to anybody, ever again.

"But even though I saw nothing to live for, I couldn't make myself lean far enough over. And so I went to a lecture that night, and Apollo was my old professor, and he met me at the door and told me that he had somebody he wanted me to meet. He said that somebody had sent for me, and I asked him who and how he knew me, and Apollo said that he knew everything, and I should just shut up and come along."

Apollo (mildly): "I'm not sure those were my exact words."

Hestia: "So he led me to what looked like an alley, and he stopped and told me to walk in, and at the end of it, near a dumpster, I saw this guy in a chair who looked like an invalid, and I talked to him and he didn't answer me, and I asked him why he wanted to see me, and he just sort of smiled. And then he handed me a few sheets of paper, and he said to me, *The wind is always with us, for the air cannot ever be completely still.*

"I still have the paper, and the thing he must have written for me before he ever even met me. It is the story of my life. I carry it around with me wherever

I go, because it allows me to believe that I still have value as a person, that life and love and my dreams are all still possible."

Quietly, she fumbles around among her clothes, and with an odd ceremonial gesture, as if they are an heirloom, produces the papers for us to look at. After a minute, Cassandra hands them over to me, and there is a tear in her eye.

This is what it says:

The Lesson of the Fool

Once upon a time, in a city close by the shore, there was a man who was considered lucky by all who knew him. People considered him lucky because, one day while he was walking along the beach, he happened to spot, mostly covered by sand, a gleaming rock which, when he pushed aside the sand, revealed itself to be the most beautiful diamond in the world.

The man brought his diamond home, and for a time, he proudly displayed it to anyone who would come to the house, and people came from all over town, and many came from other towns, and when they left, they were envious of this man, and considered him lucky in all things, even though all of his luck had been concentrated in one rare moment on the beach. They were convinced that there was some magic in the beautiful depths of the stone, because it seemed to glow with a fire that was more than the sunlight that fell upon it, and because when you walked into the room, there was a sense of comfort that invited you to explore yourself, and encouraged you to become more than you were. To be in its presence was to be empowered, and only one man in all the world had this magic and mystery whenever he wanted it, to be savored whenever he desired.

When they left the man's house, people always wondered why it could not have been their luck to be walking along at exactly the moment when the beauty of the diamond first showed itself above the sand.

A year passed, and even as more and more people came and admired the man's diamond, the man himself became restless. To them, the diamond was as beautiful and unusual and empowering as ever, but to him it had become as familiar as the chair in his living room or the lamp next to his bed. He began to think of the diamond as ordinary, and he began spending his hours on the beach, searching for a diamond that would, perhaps, be even more beautiful than the one he had.

And because he was searching for so many hours each day, the man DID find things of interest. Sometimes he found unusually smooth stones that were interesting to look at, and bits of white quartz and polished driftwood washed up along the shore, and shells not yet destroyed by the waves, and he brought these home and treasured their shiny surfaces as if they were more precious than the fire of his diamond, for they were new, and their novelty was more important to him than the radiance of the gemstone that was the most beautiful diamond in the world.

And after a year of this, the people of that seaside town found that the beautiful diamond really WAS magical, for the more the man wandered the beach and brought back his dull treasures, the more the diamond began to withhold the radiance of its inner fire. And the wisest people who came to see it whispered to the others that this diamond and the magic inside this diamond exist to bring comfort and empowerment and encouragement and joy, and if it is prevented from shining its glow into the soul of the man who was always on the beach, then its health would suffer.

But the world knows that if the owner of even a magical diamond thinks it is ordinary, then it must indeed BE ordinary, and so the number of pilgrims slowed to a trickle, and finally stopped altogether. And those who were wise enough to know that the world is usually wrong were no longer interested, for the inner fire which was the magic of the diamond had finally retreated inside in a state of confusion which we men, who have no magic of our own, can only guess at.

On the outside, the stone that once shone with extraordinary beauty became a normal gemstone, still extraordinary in its value, but no longer the radiant beacon of hope which had made it such a unique treasure. Meanwhile, the man of the house had brought home so many interesting stones and shells from the beach that there was no longer room for his furniture. One day, after an unusually large haul of trinkets from the beach, this man pulled his truck up to the front door and cleared out more space for them by gathering up his other possessions. And, perhaps by accident, more likely by an unhappy trick of magic from deep inside the beautiful stone, he happened to sweep up his diamond with the rest of it, and in a few minutes the ordinary possessions, and the *diamond, and its magic, were dumped back on the beach in a lonely pile soon covered by drifting sand.*

Today, if you walk along this beach, you might see what many other people have seen, a place where there are bits of fabric poking out of the sand, and what might once have been the wood of polished furniture, and the faintest hint of the smallest edge of a buried stone which, if you were to approach it at the right angle when the sun is at the right place in the sky, would seem to have caught a spark of the fires of the sun itself and held it for your dazzled inspection. The most important thing about this scene is what you would not see: that the magic of the stone has retreated inside, and that it waits and even hungers for the chance to once again lift the heart of a human soul and carry it to those magical places that men can never reach without the help of the divine.

But the diamond, and the magic inside it, has learned the Lesson of the Fool. It has learned that many people, perhaps most, when they have the most precious thing in the world, still manage to make it ordinary simply because they see it every day. And so the stone and the magic inside it have made a quiet vow to reveal its inner fire only to one who is willing each day to approach it with a new sense of wonder, and another day's appreciation of his luck.

The story ends in a mystery. It will not be long now before someone finds this extraordinary gem again. And when he does, he will see at once that he is holding a thing of beauty and value, and so of course he will take it home with him.

The mystery is whether he will treasure what he has found, or simply use it as another ornament in the house.

The mystery is whether the next person who finds this source of endless wonder and delight will ever deserve, and therefore whether he will ever receive, the magic that waits for him to prove that he is not a fool.

    Rhea: "That is unbelievably perfect. It's my story too." *(Wiping a tear from her face.)* "I wonder how many others."
    "It's always perfect? Always?"
    Apollo: "Always. How could it not be? It is his welcoming gift to us, and he takes that very seriously."

There must have been something on my face, because at that moment Apollo allows his eyes to glaze over, and my experience is there inscribed on my spirit for him to experience. He stares for a long time, and the others, noticing his attention, follow it to the place on my spirit.

Finally Hestia looks back up at my face, and voices what the others are thinking.

Hestia: "Oh, my god, you are *so* lucky."

XV

The New Age mind accepts the fact that there is never any final knowing of anything, that we will always be improving our knowledge and awareness on a journey of progress that has no ending. It is, more than anything else, a recognition that all strong belief systems are limiting and ultimately harmful to the progress of our understanding.

Every time our hypotheses about life and the universe crystallize into beliefs, every time we are arrogant enough to believe we've reached final knowing about something, the human race becomes a little less flexible and effective and forgiving and able to advance.

—From The Rutherfordton Spiritual Gazette

Karen, I don't know how closely you follow the news any more, but here in Asheville, the escape of 22 people from the city jail became the news story of the decade in this part of the hills. There were headlines, and if you turned to the inside pages, you would find pictures of us, the gods and the near-gods, mugging unconcernedly for the police camera. Looking at them now, again, I think I'm the only one of the group who looks worried.

The newspapers offered followup stories with the police, rumors about leads, speculation about where we had fled to and how we had eluded the massive manhunt that was, the police commissioner assured the police beat reporter, closing in on us. He told the radio stations that we were some kind of religious cult, and that one sound bite sent writers scurrying out to research stories on cults and why they thrived.

Tens of thousands wondered how we could possibly have escaped from the jail, and where we were now.

Of course, we were right back in the warehouse, trying to clear the tons of concrete and cinderblock and roof trusses and piping and the semi-melted remains of hundreds of metal folding chairs and other assorted debris off the floor and out of the way of the people who the Master expected to come to hear his sermon.

We worked safely inside of a yellow police tape. "I'm really not supposed to let you in here," the fire investigator told me, frowning with disapproval at people climbing over debris, carrying large blocks of concrete like ants in a crumb cake. "This is still technically the site of an investigation."

"Technically?" I said.

"And there's the danger of somebody getting hurt. Have you thought of that? You could get sued."

I saw with amusement that he was under the spell of the Master's spiritual glow, and there were no demons attached to him any longer. He seemed a little bit groggy, as if he had just woken from a deep sleep.

"Did I hear you say you've finished the investigation?" I said. "Does that mean you no longer think I set fire to my own building?"

"Come over here," the fire investigator said, stepping carefully over and through still-smoking remnants of the front of the building. He led me across the street and up the hill through tall weeds to a place so steep that it was hard to keep our balance. From here, I was able to look back down on the labors of the gods and near-gods dragging debris away from the center. Finally, the investigator stopped at a round blackened area perhaps four feet in diameter, where it looked as if a hot, highly-localized fire had burned out the grass and weeds right down to the bare soil.

"What can you tell me about this?" he asked me.

"It looks like maybe there was a fire up here too." I looked more closely, and saw that the blaze had actually made four distinct impressions in the ground near the center of the blackened area. I shook my head.

"This is the backwash of an M-20 3.5 inch rocket launcher," the investigator told me, watching my face intently as he talked. "In Vietnam, they called it the Super Bazooka. Used to be, you couldn't buy these things, but when the assault weapons ban came off, they were suddenly back in the public domain. Hell of a thing to be in the hands of civilians. It can fire at a rate of six shots a minute, but so far I've found pieces from just four rockets, one on each side of the building. As you can see, they were aiming down. Each time they fired, the fire coming out of the back of the rocket blew through the back of the tube and hit the ground and made one of these little holes."

"And that's how the fire started?" I said.

"That's how the fire started," the investigator agreed. "Two people probably watched until they were sure everybody was inside, and then they aimed for the oil drums. They tried to make the fire as close to a ring around the people inside as they could. I still can't figure out why there should be oil drums against three sides of the building, unless somebody was planning this for a long time."

"Oh," I said.

"What?"

"A truck came and they delivered them about a week ago."

"Who?"

I shrugged my shoulders. "They even made me sign for them. I thought it was heating oil for—for my friends."

"Do you remember anything about the truck?"

I shook my head. "I never even looked at it. I just signed the sheet and the delivery guy went back outside."

The investigator shook his head. On his spirit, in bold letters, was printed a message of astonishment at the stupidity of people in general and me in particular.

"So what makes you think I didn't do it?" I asked him.

"If you were just trying to burn the place down, there are a lot easier ways to do it than this," the police investigator told me. "This wasn't arson. This was attempted murder of everybody inside that place."

I thought about that for a second. "By who?"

"I can't tell you for sure," the other said. "But we've had three other incidents where a weapon like this was used to start a fire. An abortion clinic about 35 miles up the road, another down in Greenville, and a third in Atlanta. Internally, we call them terrorist attacks, but there's a lot of pressure right now from the FBI that, in public, at least, only Moslems be associated with the 'T' word."

"I don't understand. We weren't doing abortions," I said.

"All the same, somebody was trying to kill you, all of you. So the last part of my investigation," the police investigator continued, "comes down to two questions. First, can you prove that you were in the building when the fire started?"

"Just ask any of the others," I said.

The investigator nodded, and I could see that this was not the most important of the two questions on his mind.

"All right then," he said, "I want you to think hard. See if you can tell me what you or any of the others could possibly have done to get this far on the wrong side of radical Christian fundamentalists."

I dumped a wheelbarrow full of bricks at the perimeter and brushed the ashes off my clothes. Looking around, it was hard to see that we were making any progress at all, and we had been at it for a full day.

"Why haven't the police come down to arrest us?" I asked Apollo, who was so covered in soot and grime that even his hair was a different color.

"They have," he answered.

"When?"

"Three times already, maybe more."

"And they just went away again?"

"You apparently didn't hear the sirens. There were a dozen police cars up the street not more than two hours ago."

"I didn't see them."

"Mars convinced them to turn around," Venus interjected. "He's getting to have all the fun while we do the real work."

"We're also looking at filing false arrest charges," Apollo added. "I'm not sure they *want* to find us quite yet."

Toward the middle of the room, the Master was showing a group of gods and near-gods where *not* to pick up the debris, and he was being quite precise about it. They were pulling bricks and charred cinders away to form an outline around what appeared to be a randomly placed long irregular scar extending from the hole I had fallen through on the river side of the warehouse out to very near where the front wall had been, wider in the back, narrowing irregularly to the front.

"But why?" somebody was asking him.

"Let's leave them a reminder of what happened here," the Master said gently.

At this Fool burst into laughter. He raised his hands to indicate our surroundings, which was basically debris surrounded by jagged remnants of walls, much of it too treacherous even to walk in, some of it still smoking. "Do you really think anybody who comes here is going to be confused about what happened?"

"They will if we clean it up thoroughly."

"And that will take, what? A year? Maybe what we could use here is a miracle," Fool added.

The Master looked around carefully, and there was a very subtle hint of mockery in the glow of his spirit. Or did I just imagine this? "It looks," he said, "Like you *could* use some help."

"Unbelievable!" Fool cried out. "Now I understand why we hang on your every word. With your incredible cosmic insight, you can just look at this—"

he indicated with his hands an incredible landscape of debris—"and the revelation comes that fifteen of us can't possibly clear this out in time!"

"Would you like me to do something about it?" the Master asked him gently.

"If it's not too much trouble."

The air grew utterly silent. I noticed that people had gathered around us from all over the building. All work had ceased in an instant as they stared at the Master.

"How many additional people do you think we'll need?" the Master asked him.

Fool looked around carefully. "A few hundred at least," he said warily.

"What else do you need?"

"A sound system would be nice, so they could hear you out on the edges."

"Anything else?"

Fool gave the debris one last appraisal. "Yeah, while you're at it, get us a bulldozer."

The Master waited for more requests. When there were none, he clapped his hands in a merry gesture. "Okay," he said. "Tell everybody to stop working until tomorrow morning." Then he turned his back and walked away.

"Hey, where are *you* going?" Fool called out after him.

"I'm going to take a nap," the Master answered.

As the Master left, my phone rang.

"Hello?"

"Mr. Zakar?" I recognized the voice of Francis Coddington.

"Yes; thank you for calling back. Listen, I'm not sure exactly how to say this, but I want you to promise me something…"

"Hey!" Venus called out. "Are you too busy working to glim with us?"

I snapped the phone shut triumphantly. "That was the last of them," I said.

"The last of what?"

"My customers. All 118 of them have been contacted. For the moment, they're safe from the worst sort of pillage."

The gods and near-gods looked at each other. "He's still Plautus," said Hestia.

"Hey, that reminds me," I said. I pulled the phone back out and dialed a number.

"Yes?"

"Zho, I'm calling to deliver on a promise I made to your boss," I said.

After a moment, Zho put me through.

"Remember when you said that if I ever found the explanation, that I should call you?" I said.

"Yes. Of course."

"I want you to come out to 75 River Street this evening, if you can make it. There's somebody here I think you should meet. And after you do," I said, "I have some ideas on where to put that charity money coming out of the lead trusts."

I followed the sound of music toward the back of the ruins. Orpheus sat on a concrete boulder near the place where the fence had been torn down by the fire department people, and others sat nearby in the tall grass under some trees that leaned out over the river. He was pulling the strings on his guitar, at first in what sounded like experiments, then in a melody where every note that followed every other note felt somehow satisfying and completely inevitable.

Once upon a day,
You and I—
We knew the taste of wild places;
Our lives moved through the open spaces,
While the herd...
They stopped adventure at the door,
We found what they've stopped looking for
Deep outside the comfort zone...

No tears allowed in the electric womb;
No poets sing their tales of doom.
Love and life have left the room;
You're buried alive in your padded tomb.

Venus turned around and, after a second, walked over and sat down next to me. "I could use a good glim right now," she said.

"What's wrong?" I asked.

"Can't you see?" she said.

Once upon a day,
I smiled—
At the sunlight in your golden eyes;
They gave me wings to fly,
Above the herd...
They huddled safe from joy,

Together in their alone,
Deep inside
the comfort zone...

It was not easy to look past the dress that she wore, but when I finally concentrated on her spirit, I could find no external issues there at all. I looked harder, and noticed, after a while, that she was feeling unbeautiful, although nobody seemed to have given her any negative feedback.

I looked up at her face, a face an angel would be proud to wear.

"Why?" I asked her.

Venus shook her head, and the golden cloud of hair swirled around it. "Every woman can look in the mirror and see exactly what she looks like," she said. "But no woman can see how attractive she is without a consensus of outside opinions."

"But—"

"In some ways, this is the worst place in the world for me. Nobody here thinks that physical attractiveness is important enough to comment on."

"After we glim," I said, "I'll take you for a walk. That should give you your fill of whatever it is you need."

Venus smiled sadly. "I'm afraid I might be insatiable."

Once upon a day,
You cried—
As beautiful as no other,
My first and perfect lover.
In the herd...
Their voices called your name;
You left your tears behind and came.
Now I live here all alone,
Waiting for a call from the comfort zone...

No tears allowed in the electric womb;
No poets sing their tales of doom.
Love and life have left the room;
You're buried alive in your padded tomb.

Orpheus stopped and looked at his guitar for a long moment, plainly unhappy.

"The trouble is, your songs never tell us anything!" Venus called out suddenly. "Can't you give us a song that will do more than excite teenagers and drive their grandparents deeper into old age?"

The air grew instantly silent. Orpheus stared at her with a fixed expression on his face, and there was in that appraising look the ominous feeling of danger about to be unleashed. I could feel a terrible confidence in his ability to more than meet her challenge; to meet her challenge in a way that would burn the circuits, to answer with unexpected consequences—which I knew now was the only sure result of challenging one of the senior gods.

Venus held her ground, the challenge still (unwisely, I thought) on her face, projecting in turn a confidence that whatever he did would fail to move her.

I thought he was going to reply, but the performer in Orpheus must have recognized that this stillness of the air and this tense expectation of everyone who had heard the challenge was the perfect level of attention for a musical performance. After gracing Venus with a long, thoughtful stare, he pulled the guitar close to his chest, rose a little taller on the rock and began picking out a response, exploring the lower chords and the spaces between notes in a way that somehow reached into your chest and touched a deep sadness inside. When he finally found the right combination of notes, the melancholy spirit hung tangibly in the air around us.

Then Orpheus began to sing, and the song made his godhood visible in all its power. His voice sounded as if it came from another dimension, leaving words hanging among the sadness of the notes, words which, at the same time, haunted the mind and shook it by the scruff of its ganglial neck.

Later, I would hear Venus and others ask him to play again his simple story of a messiah who stops by our planet, assesses the situation and decides to quietly move on, after leaving a warning for other messiahs to do the same.

It so perfectly captured the complicated, perplexing frustration they all felt, the vexation that perhaps comes to everyone who has tried to rescue our human species from its confusion, only to meet stubborn and organized resistance where one might plausibly expect gratitude.

The voice rose over the chords of the guitar, merging with and embracing the wind:

I visit the graveyard of your dreams,
to lay flowers at the burial mound
where hope gave its life for expediency
proving, if only to the bare ground
that time does not heal all wounds.

There are no markers in the soil;
Even the ghosts dare not haunt this place.
Like me, they fear, like a second death,
the Curse, and the Curse is the life you face
without these buried friends to give it meaning.

From time to time, comes a redeemer
who carries within him the power, and the will
to raise the moulded shades back to life.
He offers us back the living hope, and you kill
him, kill hope again, and mourn the loss.

Fed by the blood of so many redeemers,
the grass spreads out to hide my flowers
and for a second I raise my hand to the wind
and uncloak my own well-hidden powers
just to feel the buried stir of foregone peers.

To warn of danger, I leave a hobo sign.
After me, the next and the next will know
to drop their withered flowers on the lawn
Put their magic back in the cloak and go
Across the sunrise to the next quixotic mission.

Sages and messiahs are ever drawn to mouldering hope
As lovers to sex; their climax is hope's resurrection
But here is no fertility, no chance of a completed quest.
The dead stay dead here, under my protection.
And when I too am buried, you will not disturb my rest.
Listen to the wind, and mark well my warning
scribed forever in the wild language of mourning
That tells it all, yet just ten words in the giving:
"The dead are better off, here, than with the living."

There was a long silence.

Then, abruptly, long before we were ready for the voice to end, Orpheus stood up and walked down toward the river. I looked around expectantly, but everybody was still humming the eerily sad chords of the song, whose influence seemed to hang in the air long after the sound was gone. It was clear that nobody felt like glimming just yet.

I turned to Venus, who looked away, not quickly enough for me to miss the tears streaming down her cheeks. She stared at the water and I stared with her.

By now, people were following Orpheus or moving slowly back toward the ruins. I stood up too, but Venus put her hand on my arm.

"Don't go just yet. I have a question to ask you."

I sat back down and we watched the others until they disappeared behind the loading dock.

"Did you mean what you said?" she asked me at last, turning her brilliant eyes to my face. The electrical connection was so strong, so painful to the place behind my own eyes, that I had to look away.

"When?"

"Just now."

"I think so."

"Do you think I'm beautiful?" she asked me, looking me full in the face.

"Is that all?"

"Tell me."

"I have never seen anybody who looked as frighteningly lovely as you do," I said, restoring the connection with her eyes, touching the edges of her hair with my fingers. "I've never in my life seen so many attractive features on any one woman. You truly are a goddess."

"I think everybody is intimidated by it," Venus said wistfully, pulling her hair around in her hands and then releasing it in a shower that cascaded down across her shoulders. She shook her head quickly and leaned back, and I was uncomfortably aware of how tight her dress was against her breasts, how little it did to conceal their size and shape. I looked up at her face, but it, too, made me feel uncomfortable.

"Even when I'm in the middle of everybody, like we were just now, I feel alone," she said. "I don't think I have friends the way other people do. The men get nervous around me and try to hide their shortcomings and insecurities, which makes any real connection impossible, and the women are distant and resentful."

"How can you complain, when you're everything any man ever wanted and any woman ever wanted to be?"

I was about to stand up, but she took my hand, and I stopped.

"Thank you," she said.

"You're one of my very favorite people here," I said. "And I'd feel that way no matter how you looked."

Suddenly, she kissed me. It was experimental at first, and I was so surprised that I hardly responded. Karen, I'm embarrassed to admit this, but I didn't know *how* to respond, since it had been decades since I had kissed any woman other than your mother, and I never expected to give my intimacy to anybody ever again. But her lips were patient and my body finally responded while my mind tried to sort out what was happening.

Venus drew her head back and looked into my face appraisingly, which gave me a good, long look at hers. She tossed her hair, smiled, and closed her eyes, touching my lips again with what became a long, exploring, increasingly intimate kiss. The sensation of her lips against mine gradually overwhelmed my senses. Its warmth passed through me like a leisurely electric jolt that reached all the way down to my toes and back. Suddenly, I felt impossibly weak and enormously strong at the same time.

I wrapped my arms around her and squeezed her against me, trembling a bit like a leaf in the wind.

Finally, she leaned back and drew me down to the ground with her, allowing the dress to fall above the soft contours of her stomach. Even though I had seen her bathing nude in the river, the sight captivated my attention, and it took a long second for my eyes to return to her face.

"You're wondering if I'm really serious," she said, her spirit radiating amusement.

I looked around. We were completely hidden by the tall grass. I couldn't see the road from where we lay.

"I'm a little bit scared of you, I think," I said.

"Not nearly enough, I'm afraid."

I touched her hair, wondering at my luck. "Why me?" I said.

"Why *not* you?" she said playfully.

"You think you can have me just by deciding to have me."

"Do you think I look like this for no reason?" she said. "It has its advantages, and I think it's my prerogative to use them."

She was smiling at me expectantly, her eyes daring me to dare to touch her. I realized in that moment just how confident she was in her power over me. Something in me still wanted to resist her, to show her that she couldn't take me for granted, but these thoughts were being washed away by a spreading warmth in my heart. I looked down, and with the eyes of my spirit, I saw that her soul was extending up from her heart, the glow of her spirit touching mine, tenderly and inevitably erasing my ability to think, pulling all my attention into the increasingly intense feelings of the moment.

I kissed her again, and my hands explored her body, touching her breasts over the sleek fabric of her dress, feeling her nipples tighten at my touch. I felt the tight curve of her hips, her belly, and let my fingers run down the impossibly smooth skin of her legs, and back up gently across her inner thighs and then back up to her breasts again, taking the dress up over them. With a practiced shimmy, she discarded it altogether.

How long we were together, I still can't say; I can't even remember when or how I took my own clothes off. As the touching became more erotic and focused, my awareness extended beyond my own body into hers, and I felt our spirits mingling, hers into mine, mine into hers, so that I was somehow experiencing two awarenesses at once, an awareness of how I felt and also of how she felt as I touched her.

I told her that she was beautiful, and she smiled up at me as if I was a child, but there was gratitude in her eyes. She was excited by the powerful effect her appearance had on me, and as she closed her eyes and tossed her hair, this confidence in the power of her beauty gave her a sense of control that fed her desire and somehow made it easier for her (us?) to relax and experience my touch. I felt her feel the way my hands were touching her, and I could read in the glow of her spirit—and feel it as if it was my own feelings—what she liked, what she wanted, and I was rewarded as I touched her with full participation in the erotic effect of her body responding. I produced, for both of us, cascading waves of pleasure, sensation after sensation.

Slowly, patiently, with total certainty, I followed the trail of this mutual pleasure all the way in, experimenting, finding ways to make the feelings intensify, felt them grow stronger and stronger, the pure pleasure sensation intensifying in the expanding white glow of her spirit intermingled with mine, my hands and mouth growing ever more certain of the direction that she wanted and needed me to go, and the intensity of this connection flooded me with a kind of overwhelming sensual pleasure that I had never experienced before, a mixture of feelings, physical and emotional all jumbled confusingly together with her physical and emotional feelings.

Our boundaries were blurred and I could no longer tell where she stopped and I began.

The feelings that swirled into and through us swept away everything else in a hurricane of intensity. Time became irrelevant; I have no idea if we made love for a few minutes or half a day; all I know is that the glow rose like a fire above and around us and finally carried us into a mutual surge of climax, and it was like an explosion. I felt as if my consciousness was shattered into a thousand million pieces and scattered everywhere, that there was no "me" any more, or at least nothing that was capable of coherent thought.

Panting, I lay against her and tried to assemble, piece by piece, the individual sparks of myself that were still mingled, in a slow, contented dance, with the sparks of her.

Finally, long before I had recovered, Venus shifted impatiently, and I rolled over and lay on my side, my hand across her belly.

"That was fun," she said, extending her neck to give me a light kiss on the forehead.

"It was a lot more than that," I said. "Don't try and tell me different; I experienced everything you were feeling."

"Yes," she said, laying her hands behind her head and looking at me appraisingly. "I was curious how you would use your special gift. The Master said that it would be interesting, very different from anything I've ever experienced before."

"So this was an experiment?" I said, more lightly than I felt.

She reached out, pulled my face to hers and kissed me gently on the lips, and then more deeply. "You are charmingly naive," she said. "I think it's one of your best qualities."

"You didn't answer my question."

Venus sat up and lifted her dress off the ground, shaking it slightly. "I never help men be less clueless about their feelings," she said. "If I did, it would leave no time for anything else."

She looked back at me when I didn't say anything.

"It's hard for you, isn't it?" I said finally.

Her face hardened so quickly it sent a chill through my body.

"Abso-damn-lutely it's hard. He knows how I feel about him," she said. "I've seen it on his spirit. But it wasn't written in capital letters; it was almost like a footnote on that vast, incredible spirit where, if you look hard enough, you can find everything there is and a few things more."

"I'm sorry," I said, and I was.

"Don't give me any crap about it. Right now, he has everything else to think about, and I'm a footsoldier in his little army. There's plenty of time."

"Sure."

"What the hell do you mean by that?"

"I—"

"You think I'm *confused* about how I feel about him, or about what he is compared to me?" she said, her voice rising. "You, every one of you, all you see is a giant walking ankles deep in the human race, and if you love him at all, it's for what he's done, not for the incredible, vulnerable man who buried himself so deep inside of infinity that he no longer knows how to feel what I feel for him every minute that I'm awake or asleep and all the time in between. He's got one chance to relearn the most important thing he once knew, "and I," she said, beating her chest with a fist, "goddam me, I—oh, goddam you and every other one of you—"

I stared at her.

"He was there with us. Didn't you feel it?" she said, wiping away the tears that were flowing generously down her face. "We made it all the way through to his goddam Mommy, and that was him standing right beside her when we connected, when you became Her, he was there inside you, inside of me—"

I tried to stand up, but she put her hand on my chest and pushed me ungently back down on the grass, and turned back, alone, toward the parking lot and the ruins on the other side.

"Can't I walk back with you?" I called out.

"I think I can find it by myself."

I lay on my back and watched the clouds move across the spaces between the leaves of the trees. It felt suddenly like our lovemaking had been a dream, the memory sat so uncertainly on my spirit and in my mind; something that neither of us had done, but instead had been experienced by a very different creature called *we*, VenusProteus, and as the smaller half of that creature, I felt vulnerable, isolated and alone.

I had just made love with the most beautiful woman in the world, and she had left me with a certainty that it would never happen again. I realized with surprise that this was exactly the way I preferred it to be, and that the goddess Venus had known that long before I did, had foreknown it before we had ever kissed, and I realized how difficult it must be to be her

Karen, as I lay there, feeling happy and sad and tender and confused and sympathetic all at once and all jumbled together, I extended my awareness, and looked down at my naked body through the eyes of a bird. The sight was so utterly strange that I laughed out loud, seeing how limited and earthbound and drab my body looked against the grass and the scattering of colored leaves. Feeling vulnerable and alone, I allowed my awareness to mingle with the sparks of holy spirit at the core of this small bird, experiencing its wild alien awareness, built around the freedom of swimming at will through the sky.

At the edges of this strange consciousness, I became aware of something strangely familiar, a distant recognition of the sluggish creature who lay in the leaves. This bird was not there by accident; it had been drawn to me by something too deep inside for it to understand. As I turned my awareness to the individual sparkles of godhood, reading the life of this bird, my spirit became aware of other memories, faint, strangely tender shared experiences that matched what was written in my own spirit.

After a long second, I realized the truth: that some of those bits of holy spirit had once been a part of your mother's spirit, recycled now with their residual memories in the luminous ghost of this creature who lived in the air.

I sat up, reached out my hand, and without hesitation, the bird flew down to land on my finger.

There was no reproach in those bits of spirit that had once been a part of your mother, no hint of judgment, only a fierce cherishing of memories imprinted on it from the other life, our life, which extended into this bird's awareness, creating what the bird regarded as an illogical, senseless affection for an earthbound and potentially-dangerous human.

"I miss you, darling," I said, feeling a tear forming in my eye. "You were all I ever wanted."

The creature looked at me critically, first with one eye, then with the other, and shifted impatiently on my hand.

I wanted to say more, but suddenly, the bird flew off, and I looked up, and saw Fool standing over me.

"Remind me never to join a nudist colony that would have you as a member," he said.

"How did you know I was out here?"

"Venus said you were reconstructing your masculine pride, or something like that. I guess it works better with your clothes off."

"Is that what you came to tell me?"

"I came to tell you to get dressed so you won't be left behind."

"Where are you going?"

"Where do you think?"

I stood up immediately. A few minutes later, I followed a group of the gods and near-gods out into the street. The Master was walking along ahead, uphill toward the west side of the city.

"It's Wednesday night," Fool called back at me. "What do you do on Wednesday night?"

I shrugged. "A movie?"

"Suppose you happen to be one of the small handful of people who cares about the fate of your immortal soul?"

"You go to some kind of house of worship?"

"Exactly right!" said Fool. "Some people go to get closer to God. I go because it's a hell of a visual experience."

We followed the sidewalks past a row of unkempt apartments, and then things became a little more upscale, with rows of neat houses crowded together, a small park with a basketball court enclosed by a chain link fence and some swings. Around the next corner, we approached a church, and I could tell from the sound of the singing inside that it was an African-American church. Karen, call me racist if you must, but the truth is, the voices sounded too good for it to be a bunch of white people.

"Here's the drill," Fool told me. "We all walk in and sit down in the back, and the Master will be in total communion with the universal consciousness, which is way more complicated and interesting and powerful than the normal church conception of God—you got that so far?"

"I think so," I said.

"And the reverend or the pastor or whoever it is will have no idea that the eyes of God are watching him give his sermon, because he doesn't know any of the things that we do. And yet he will tell the congregation all about God and the devil and how to live a better life in a voice of absolute blind conviction, and the irony of him talking up there and us in the back is just too amazing."

"And then what?"

"And then we leave and nobody ever knows that somebody with authority on these matters was sitting a few feet away."

The door was open, so we walked in among the singing, and the Master found a place where we could squeeze in at the back, although I wasn't sure how all of us were going to be able to sit down.

> *Moon and stars in shining height*
> *Nightly tell their Maker's might;*
> *When Thy wondrous heavens I scan,*
> *Then I know how weak is man.*
>
> *What is man that he should be*
> *Loved and visited by Thee,*
> *Raised to an exalted height*
> *Crowned with honor in Thy sight!*

The Reverend of the church stood off to the side of the empty pulpit, singing with the rest of the congregation, his hands over his head, and it seemed like everybody was dancing as well as lifting their voices, holy spirit so thick in the air here that it was like a beautiful, interesting foggy mist to my spirit eyes, made all the more charming because the demons which perched on the shoulders and backs and heads of the congregation were looking this way and that at the swirls of color with vexation and annoyance. This was one of the few times when my physical eyes had a clearer view of my surroundings. I was watching an interesting swirl in the air between my face and the high ceiling when the Reverend stepped up to the pulpit, a tiny, unhappy-looking troll on his back.

"Isn't *that* something to sing about?" the Reverend asked, and received a chorus of "amen" in answer. "Today, I want everybody to open your Bibles to—" he said, and stopped, and there was a long silence, which lasted until everybody in the congregation was looking up at him in perplexed expectation. Finally I stopped watching the brownian dance of holy spirit and looked at him too, and realized that he was looking straight back at me. Then I realized that he was not looking at me, but directly next to me, where the Master sat with his hands folded in his lap in a state of total composure and relaxation, the beautiful rainbow fog of holy spirit thicker around him than anywhere else in the room.

Finally, the Reverend shook his head a bit as if breaking a trance, and then, to the obvious annoyance of the demon on his shoulder, who had been whispering into his ear, he briskly stepped down from behind the pulpit and walked past the aisles and straight to the Master, and bowed his head.

"You understand that I am not bowing to you, but to the thing that is in you," he said.

"Yes," the Master answered gravely.

"I always look to see if I am being favored with a Visit," the Reverend said. "I wasn't sure if I would even know God when I saw Him, but I always looked just the same."

"We aren't here to disrupt your service," the Master said.

"My sermon doesn't matter now," the Reverend assured him with a smile. "Since you're here, would you give us something we can take home from here today?"

"I would," the Master said simply.

The rest of the church was by now in an uproar of murmuring and confusion, and it took the Reverend more than a few seconds to get everybody quieted down again, so he could explain why the Master—who must have looked like a white person pulled randomly from the back of the audience—was up there next to him.

"I think most of you know that I believe in angels and devils and saints and sinners," he said, "and the difference between them is that God is either there or he isn't, in greater degree than he is in you and me. Well, when I looked out at all of you today, I saw something that I had hoped someday to see: I saw a stranger among us, and when I met his eyes, I saw the eyes of God looking back at me. And I knew that the greatest gift I could give you would be to let you hear this man tell us how he comes to have the eyes of God shining through his own, and maybe how all of us can one day hope to have the same thing happen to us. I know nothing about what he is going to say, but I believe it is more important than anything I have ever told you."

After this extraordinary discourse, he stepped back, and the Master, without any sign that he regarded this as anything unusual, stepped forward and looked around the room, giving everybody a chance to see if they, too, could see the eyes of God behind his mortal ones. He let his hand linger on the reverend's shoulder for a long second in a gesture of tenderness and respect that was not lost on the congregation. Then the Master favored the group with a gentle smile, with that indescribable expression that conveyed bottomless humility and a confidence beyond the stars, and waited for a second, two, three before he let the words come out.

"I believe those of you in back heard your Reverend say that he was not bowing to the person who stands up here now, but to the living energy which is shining into and through me. That energy, and its awareness, is in you as well. And I tell you that the entire purpose of coming to this building and joining hands in prayer is to recognize and embrace that spark of the divine that is in you and about you, and build a bridge from it back to the fire."

"Amen," the parishioners spoke back to him.

"I'm here today as a man who has built that bridge and walked across it and made the acquaintance of the remarkable awareness of the universe that some call God Almighty," he said. "For many days and many weeks, I have looked at our tiny world through the eyes of a consciousness that extends from here out to forever and back.

"And there is one thing I can tell you from that experience," the Master told the group with a smile. "I felt mighty small, and I felt mighty honored, and I come back to you now knowing things that every human being ought to know, because what I did is our birthright as children of the Almighty."

"*Amen!*"

"I'm not going to deliver a sermon today," the Master told us. "Everybody who wants to hear everything I know is invited down to 75 River Street, about two and a half miles from here, the place where that old warehouse burned down. All I can promise you for sure is that I'll say things there that you won't ever forget or want to forget for the rest of your lives.

"But here, out of respect for Pastor Damien, and because he gave up his pulpit to me, I'll tell you a few things that I think you really want to know, which is the story of how I came to be in that place where I was able to walk with the Awareness of the Universe—and maybe how, one day, you too can do this thing that I know many of you want to do more than anything else this life has to offer."

"*Amen!*" people called back, and the eyes were on him now. Any scrap of attention that he didn't have when he walked up to the front of the room he had now for as long as he wanted it.

"Because I can tell you, from personal knowledge, the place I am, others have been there before me. And others, many others, will be again."

"*Amen!*"

"When I first got there, I saw that what we from a dozen different faiths call the scriptures and the Word of God was somebody's effort to tell some of what he saw and some of what she thought we should do to get there. A few of these things were written down by people who didn't know what the hell they were talking about, so the best we have now are little scraps and hints and clues where sometimes, not often, somebody might have gotten the words down just right, and often they got them wrong or made them up out of ignorance, and even so, the jumbled echoes of the authentic voices carried across the ages."

There were no Amens to this, just a fixed collective stare from everywhere on the benches that was not hostile but wary, and the colors of the spiritual emanations had turned a cautious white orange, which told me they were listening but they were afraid of what they were about to hear.

"Now before I tell my story, I want all of you to try to imagine how I feel, and you would feel, knowing that people had been there before and had given us their best account of what it was like and how to get there, and today we still know nothing and less than nothing at all about what these remarkable people desperately wanted us to know."

Now the Master leaned back with his hands on the pulpit, and he smiled gently at the group, and the bright compassion streaming out from his spirit warmed the room like sunshine. "Yes, I did say that we know less than nothing," he said gently. "All across the world, the people who stand up here where I'm standing now, in churches and their equivalent houses of worship in other religions, are delivering ten falsehoods for every truth, are claiming certainty when they are filled with doubt, are microscopically interpreting the misinformation and embellishments and claiming that there is only one narrow path into the kingdom of heaven and they hold the keys to the gate.

"For just a moment, I want you to put yourself in my shoes," the Master said. "You stand up here where I am, and you know the truth behind the false facade. You feel a wonderful, terrible need to pass on more of this truth than has survived in the distant echoes from all those other people who came before you, and to pass it on more clearly, because nothing will ever be more important to the world and its people than the connection between them and the Awareness of the universe. But to do that, you have to deliver bad news to good people of sincere faith like those of you in this room here today. You have to tell them that they're going to have to unlearn so much of what they've put in their hearts and minds out of genuine love for God and Jesus and their brothers and sisters around the world.

"Before you can tell them anything, you have to give them the tragic news that except for their good intentions, most of the time they've spent building their bridges to God has been at best unhelpful, and at worst will be an obstacle if they're ever going to do what the sages did.

"And then, if you can get them to accept the bad news and unlearn the many things that are blocking their path, then you have to deliver the good news in a way that they can understand it.

"And brothers and sisters, there are no words in our culture to help you. Our culture and our civilization have nothing in common with the way you have to be to merge your awareness with the Almighty. The economy, the entertainment industry, mountains of e-mails and commutes to work and desks filled with busywork are all part of an enormous distraction machine that throws out a million and one plausible reasons to keep your attention focused on all the interesting things you can buy and wear and see and who's going to win the football game this week.

"It is a miracle that you can even find your way to this church with all that going on out there, and if you think I've been disrespecting you with my words before, understand that you, here today, are among the very few who have managed to put all that aside and follow your spirits in hope of getting a step closer to the Almighty. It is the people who take the time to go to their houses of worship who are the best hope for our species, if you and others like you can open your ears and hear the message clearly instead of shutting it out and concentrating on the dogma that is our modern mistranslations of the echoes of the past.

"And finally," the Master continued, "as you feel this powerful desire to help a world of people who maybe can't be helped, and who powerfully don't *want* to be helped, you also, at every second of every day, feel a burning hunger inside to go back and be with the Almighty. And I can tell you this: you can't do both at the same time. Being with God, seeing the universe through the eyes of the Almighty awareness of the universe, takes every bit of your attention and awareness and then some, and when I say 'then some,' I mean that it takes everything you have and then the Almighty kindly supplies what's missing.

"And so you have up here in front of you, speaking to you now, the luckiest and the unluckiest man in the world, both at the same time. And this," said the Master, looking around to make sure he had eye contact with everybody in the building, "is how I got to be so lucky and unlucky.

"This," he said, "is my path to the Almighty.

"I think, growing up, I might have been the ugliest little boy who was ever born," the Master continued with a smile. "It may have been the fact that I was undersized and barely strong enough to hold my head up when I first learned to walk, or the way my voice sounded or some other sign or signal branded across my forehead. All I really know is that I began my life as an outcast, alone, separated not only from the divine, but also from the nurture of friendship. I was hounded by my peers, sometimes in cruelty, sometimes in sport. I was their common enemy, and they bonded with each other over their shared contempt for me. And so I withdrew, and found hiding places in the woods where it was too much trouble for them to find me.

"I, or the person I was, had a lot of time to myself, and more than the average amount of loneliness.

"Of course there is much more to say about this time in my life, but the larger truth is that every child experiences pain and rejection in this culture of ours. To say that my pain was sometimes unbearable is also to say that I am now stronger in ways that most people are not, which must be precisely what the divinely-ordained rabbi meant when he told a first century audience that the last shall be first and the first shall be last."

"Amen," somebody said.

"At the time, though, I knew nothing of this; my goal was simply to endure the days. To break the monotony sometimes, I began talking to myself.

"These, you must realize, were not the most interesting conversations in the history of our planet, and so, just as a way to break the new monotony that was only slightly better than the old monotony, I started several conversations going in my head at the same time. This, my brothers and sisters, is harder than it sounds, but after many years of solitude, I grew practiced enough to succeed at carrying on two or three intensely boring discussions at once, as if four or six separately-conversing nodes of my own brain were all talking independently with each other, and I could mix them up and bring them together and have six parts of my own mind all engaging in unfortunately predictable conversation with each other.

"My friends, it was then that I stumbled onto something important and profound and so simple that you might be tempted to laugh as I tell it to you, even though it is the first important step in what some have called *the-Journey-of-which-nirvana-is-the-first-resting-place.*

"I realized—and you should prepare yourself to laugh at the obviousness of it—that *the quality of the conversations in my head went down every time I added more voices.*

"My brothers and sisters, there is so much importance in this insight that I tremble as I try to explain it to you. I realized that whenever one part of my mind was talking with other parts of my mind, and another part of my mind was answering, my awareness and ability to think was diminished and ineffective.

"And that's when I realized that the opposite must be true. If I could just get all those talking-to-each-other parts of my mind reintegrated into one whole mind again, then I would be much better at thinking and doing.

"This is harder than it sounds. Even when I was not actively involving those other parts of my mind in conversation, there was a murmur in the background that required the attention of large portions of my brain.

"I later learned that most religious traditions have a name for this thing I was trying to achieve. The best, I think, come from the Hindu and Buddhist cultures, and mean something like: *to turn your consciousness into a still, quiet lake, free of ripples, so that it perfectly reflects the sky, which is the Almighty.*

"For some time, I journeyed toward this stillness by meditating for hours beside the river, telling successive voices in my head to shut up right now and contribute to a single, unified flow of attention, just for a few seconds, and then they could go back to whatever they had been murmuring about. But they weren't easily fooled. They knew (even before the part of the brain that we'll call "I" did) that the end result of all this would be to extinguish their autonomy into some greater whole, which looked, from where they stood, a lot like dying.

"One night, as I stared at patterns of moonlight on the water, the last of the murmurs was finally quiet. I felt peaceful in a way that I never realized I could feel before, still, silent, perfectly at rest. I knew that this mental coherence would not be there for long, but I wanted to hold onto it as long as I could.

"And then I noticed it.

"In the back of my clear mind, behind it somewhere, there was another voice, another awareness, another *me.* I was staring out at the flow of the water over rocks, and the places where the rocks and the water came together into a kind of fine white opaque foam, so the only way you could see the shape of the rocks underneath was by the shape of the water flowing over them. And the reflection of the moon and the dark shimmering trees on the water, and the gentle mist drawn in by my nose and the cool feel of the air all came together, and I realized that the thing I was looking at was not water and rocks and air and reflection, but an interplay of one single truly magical force, that the water and rocks and air were all one thing interacting to create something that was far more than the sum of its parts: this scene at this moment. And then, instant by instant, another scene and another, tiny variations on the same scene in an amazingly detailed and exquisitely beautiful panorama that stretched dynamically forward and backward in time all the way out to infinity.

"For an instant I held past and future and present together as one perfect thing, the river as it was and would be, the universe as it was and would be. And I saw what held it all together. I saw the tiny sparkles of what looked like magic dust, pulsing with life and awareness. I looked in myself and I saw that the thoughts entering the stillness of my physical mind came from another body, a spirit body that was made up of these sparkles, which I know now to be holy spirit, the individual cells of the body of the Almighty.

"And I realized that this body that was made of holy spirit was a part of the scene in front of me, and I let my awareness merge with the other sparkles.

"Brothers and sisters, in that second, my spirit and my mind together expanded to include the trees on the bank across the river, and the woods, and the grass and the wind in the leaves and the moonlight and the spirits of the trees, and the whole oneness of it opened up to me, and I looked at the world through the eyes of another, a gentle, overwhelming presence that my tiny mind was and always had been a part of.

"And I saw the connection between what I had done as a child and what we, all of us, have done in our daily lives. I had divided my mind into separate pieces, and pretended as if those different parts of my mind had a life of their own. We, all of us, are parts of the mind of the Almighty, and we in our daily lives pretend that we are individual. When we merge with the Almighty, when we finally give up the murmuring of the mind and reflect the sky, it feels a lot like dying.

"But I have been there. And I can tell you that it is not dying. In fact, *it was the feeling before which feels like death to me now.* Know that, and you know everything that is and ever will be important.

"My brothers and sisters, the best part of it, the very most wonderful part of that moment of transcendence, was that "I" was no longer separated and lonely. I was a part of the scene and the thing that was generating it. I flexed a part of myself that was the water and it flowed in new patterns. I flexed a part of myself that was the rock and it shifted.

"If the scene had not been perfect, I might have flexed and turned the course of the river a different direction.

"I realized that I had entered the Kingdom of Heaven, and that it was, indeed, for all of us, immediately accessible. It was, as we were long ago promised, 'at hand.'"

"Amen!"

"My brothers and sisters, I have gone back many times to the Awareness of the Almighty, and it feels like home to me now. I have seen that all of you are, in the eyes of the Almighty, interesting and perfect. The cranky God of the scriptures who sits on a throne and demands obedience and calls us back from sin with the threat of eternal damnation is nothing like the wonderful, endlessly fascinating, ultimately unknowable reality and truth of the Almighty. In that Universal Awareness, you find nothing but joy and interest in every single thing about you. Not simply every hair on your head is noted with continuous interest, but every molecule and every thought, and they are always a delight, no matter where you are, no matter what you're doing, and most importantly, no matter who you are, whether or not the world sees you as important or unimportant, whether you sit on a throne or the bed of a prison cell, you are unique and wonderful and interesting and loved with a passion that is too much to fill a simple human breast, a passion that requires the whole universe to hold it."

"Amen!"

"Some of you may say that humans are not worthy to participate in the divine. But I tell you now that this is not what the Almighty thinks about you—and, therefore, I ask you: Who are you to disagree with the Awareness of the Universe, the God whose reality is beyond your imagination?"

"Amen!"

"And I will tell you one more thing. I and some of the others sitting in the back of the room have connected, through our spirits, with intelligent creatures from many different places in the universe, and I have spoken with their spiritual leaders, and they, all of them, are in constant awe of the human species and its potential. Some of those diverse and strange-appearing creatures have routine debates about us, questioning how it is possible for evolutionary processes to overshoot so far and create creatures whose minds are so much more effective and efficient than is strictly necessary for survival and dominance of a particular planetary ecosystem. We are, to them, an anomaly and a mystery, living proof of the hand of God, and they forecast a greatness in our future, in the future of the human species."

"Amen!"

"My brothers and sisters, I want you to know that I can see enemies of the words I am speaking, right here in this room, and they are invisible to your eyes. You can read about them in the accounts of Elijah and Elisha and the ancient prophets, and the Buddha who was attended by the devas, and the stories of Jesus and John the Baptist, who baptized and freed people from the demons that attached to their spirits. They are creatures of darkness, and they are here in this room with us today, as they have been with our species for uncounted generations, ever since the humans we remember as gods left the Garden of Eden and inflicted on themselves forces that they did not understand."

At these words, the audience of demons, who until now had looked merely sullen, began to look at each other and around in a very human caricature of alarm. Some of them leaped off of their hosts and fluttered in the air; others began whispering frantically into the ears of members of the congregation, without any obvious effect.

Yes, I thought. Tell them.

"But I can tell you that the bodies of these creatures, these demons, are made of the substance of our own thoughts," the Master continued. "They are the impulses of the human mind and spirit that we know are not positive and helpful, our worst tendencies given a kind of substance and life. We could live in freedom if we did not indulge these feelings. And yet we argue with ourselves that giving them up would feel too much like killing a part of ourselves, it would feel too much like the death of who we are. And of course they whisper into our minds, as they are whispering now, that they are what make us human.

"There will come a day," the Master said, "and I have seen this future day with my own eyes, when everyone will be able to see these parasites of the spirit. But I do not think that it is necessary for you to see them in order to detach them from your life. You have only to recognize when you are falling into a pattern of self-destruction or darkness, when you turn the pain you feel now into the expectation of future pain and allow it to become suffering, when you act as predators toward people of our own species, when you look out for your own interests at the expense of the interests of everyone.

"To rid ourselves of these parasites, we have only to cut off those parts of us that we don't particularly like anyway, and allow the rest of us to fill in the empty places we have made.

"And we need to love ourselves the way the Almighty Awareness of the Universe loves us."

"Amen!"

"I've finished speaking, for there really is not so much to tell, certainly not enough to fill volumes of densely-reasoned scripture. The truth, the important things that every creature with a spirit should know, can be spoken in a few minutes and can be understood even more quickly. The harder part is to live it, every second, every day. And so when I'm finished, I want to invite each person here today to come up to the front, and I will show you another way to remove the parasites from your spirit.

"When you come up here, I will do nothing more than touch you and love you, love you in the same way that the Almighty Awareness that is God and more than God loves you, the same way that now, going forward, you must love yourselves and each other. That love will be experienced as a bright white light in your spirit, and the demons and parasites and creatures of our own darkness will fly off in fear of the power and brilliance of that love, and they will not be able to return so long as you give and accept that love with each other. And I will invite each of you, personally, one at a time, to hear me give my sermon down by the warehouse, and more than that, to help us prepare for the speech, which I hope will bring the simple things I have spoken of here today to the attention of the world."

Karen, at the end of this talk, there was a stunned silence in the room, as if a spell of immobility had been cast on the audience. But it was the silence and stillness of a spring that had been coiled tightly and was still coiling, waiting for release. I realized in that moment that I had been expecting the Master to somehow not live up to the expectations that had been built up ever since I had first heard his name, what seemed now to be an eternity ago. But that, I think, was the essential thing about him and everything he did, that whatever you expected, somehow he would go beyond it.

The Reverend stepped forward, and his booming voice, so different from the Master's, broke the spell.

"I want everybody to stand," he said. "And I want everybody to sing with me. And as we are singing, I want there to be an orderly line forming to meet with this extraordinary man."

The people in the room began swaying to the sound of the organ, and the choir began to sing, and the line began to form, and Venus had tears in her eyes and Cassandra, who sat at the end of the bench, did not, for, as she later told me, she had seen this scene and revisited it many times in her life; it was one of her favorite parts of the movie.

Amazing grace! How sweet the sound
That saved a wretch like me!
I once was lost, but now am found;
Was blind, but now I see.

'Twas grace that taught my heart to fear,
And grace my fears relieved;
How precious did that grace appear
The hour I first believed.

Through many dangers, toils and snares,
I have already come;
'Tis grace hath brought me safe thus far,
And grace will lead me home.

The Lord has promised good to me,
His Word my hope secures;
He will my Shield and Portion be,
As long as life endures.

Yea, when this flesh and heart shall fail,
And mortal life shall cease,
I shall possess, within the veil,
A life of joy and peace.

The earth shall soon dissolve like snow,
The sun forbear to shine;
But God, Who called me here below,
Shall be forever mine.

When we've been there ten thousand years,
Bright shining as the sun,
We've no less days to sing God's praise
Than when we'd first begun.

From the back of the room, I watched the glow around the Master become a brilliant, almost intolerable white-violet color, the royal edge of the spirit spectrum, and I knew that the Master was gone from our midst, that the awareness that animated his body was now the Awareness of the universe itself, and I felt a sense of awe that this should be shared with people as ordinary as us.

The first to touch his hand was the Reverend, and the glow and its color and brightness were transferred to his aura, and he stood, demonless, in front of the now-stirring congregation as they approached the Master, and he said, as they passed, to each of them, simply: "Today we are truly blessed."

XVI

Because the New Age awareness is not a religion, it does not have members, missionaries, weekly services or designated houses of worship. All living creatures qualify for membership, life itself becomes the devotional services, and the universe is the sacred cathedral.
—From *The Rutherfordton Spiritual Gazette*

In the morning, the bulldozer arrived; so too did the parishioners of the church—along with every friend and neighbor that they were able to find. For the rest of the morning, the bulldozer moved back and forth across the floor, pushing the debris and rubble to the jagged remnants of the outer walls. From there, people with gloves and shovels and wheelbarrows and ropes pulled and threw and carried it to the fringes of the parking lot, where still others used it to build a rough stone fence-like enclosure around the property. With so many new hands, the job of clearing the rubble away went amazingly quickly, and by late afternoon the floor was being swept clean and a new podium was under construction, set back near the large hole I had fallen into. The only uncleared area was the place the Master had forbidden any of us to touch, an irregular mess of bricks and concrete and twisted metal extending from the right front of the podium to the remnants of the front wall, which people were busily dismantling with sledge hammers.

Then the parishioners brought benches from the church, plus an assortment of sofas, dining room chairs, couches, porch rocking chairs, folding chairs all laid out neatly in bizarre-looking rows. The church's sound system had been dismantled and moved to the site. An extension cord half a mile long had been dragged up toward one of the telephone poles, where Briareus was tapping into the power grid.

I sat down, exhausted, next to a member of the congregation who it seemed to me had done more than his share of the heavy lifting. He was taller than the rest of us, with thick, corded muscles about his chest and his lower torso might have been similarly muscled, but if it was, the strength was hidden under what seemed like a first trimester of pregnancy that hung down over his belt. Reading his spirit, I saw that he had been a hell of a football player for Reynolds High School and for two years at Mars Hill College before his wife had gotten pregnant.

"I never thought I'd work this hard again," he sighed, wiping his forehead with the back of his hand.

Like pretty much every white boy raised in the hills, I was shy around people of color. But there was a purity about his spirit, and a purity about his intentions, which put me instantly at ease and attracted me to him.

"They've managed to convince me that it's the most important work in the world," I replied.

He laughed. "There's never any end to the things that need doing. We could all work all our lives and the things that people think are important still wouldn't get done. That's why some people give up altogether, and why others don't ever know when to stop and rest. It's when you're face to face with the Neverending that you get confused about things." He reached over and took my hand. "Call me Elijah," he said.

"I don't know whether to call myself Proteus or Adam," I said. "But whatever I am, I am very grateful that you and the others were here to help. And I think you're going to get a lot out of it too," I added.

"Oh, I think I've already gotten everything I need to get," said Elijah with another deep laugh. "You can go into God and the spirit forever and never spend a minute on anything else and in the end you never even scratch the surface of all there is. Or you can get to the place you need to get according to who you are and be satisfied once and for all and have your life back, only better. When I saw that man last night, I knew it was my chance to take exactly what I needed, and I took it right there in front of him, and he smiled at me when I shook his hand and I knew—in that place that you can see and I can only feel—that he approved my decision."

I looked at his spirit again and saw that what he said was true. But I couldn't understand it. "If you know of a shortcut—" I said.

This time Elijah laughed long and hard, and it was clear that he thought I was the funniest thing he had ever met. He put his arm around me. "I know, from the talking around here, that you can see a person's spirit and talk with creatures from other places up in the sky, and you see the demons that attach themselves to a man, and I guess I must have had one or two myself, because I feel lighter and easier inside ever since the Man of God touched my hand. But I don't need all that, and I don't think most people are going to want to follow you all the way out to this place you're at now."

"They have to," I said.

He shook his head. "Someday, maybe, seeing demons and talking with the good citizens of outer space will be taught in the grade school," he said. "But for now, for the people who never see the Man of God in person, it's going to be different. I look at all of you," he continued, "and I see a world where people know that if they give in to a dark, angry or unhappy feeling, they're going to be feeding creatures that want to keep them unhappy. People knowing that when they love each other and their dog, when they walk up and hug their enemies, when they give to people in need and take the help and charity of others without embarrassment or shame and do whatever is put in front of them with a good heart and a positive spirit, when they comfort people who are down and fight unhappiness everywhere they find it, they're taking the demons out of their lives and starving them out of this world. That's really all we need to know, is how to be a soldier against feeding the demons, and I thank God I was able to see this before I died, because it's a good thing and simple enough that every person can understand it and do it in their own lives without a lot of rigamarole and studying nights and weekends."

I thought about that, and listened to the sound of the bulldozer moving back and forth toward the front of the building. It stirred up interesting smells, of smoke and raw earth and a dry odor that might have been powdered concrete.

"A few weeks ago, I think that would have been enough and more than enough to satisfy everything I wanted," I said. "Now I want to go in all the way."

Elijah gave my shoulders a hard squeeze which cracked bones I didn't know I had. "Some people are greedy for money and some are greedy for things that are a hell of a lot more valuable," he said. "We don't have a name for that other greed yet, but I can see that you've got it bad, and I hope it doesn't become too much of a vexation to you."

During this time, Heavy Hitter had left a message on my phone and asked to meet with me. As I stood up, he called again to make sure I hadn't forgotten.

"Where are you going?" Fool asked me as I got into my car.

"You know damn well where I'm going. You can see it on my spirit."

"That's why I want to go with you."

"Why?"

"My father will be there," said Fool. "I think it's time he and I had a talk."

I had insisted on meeting for an early dinner in Salsa's restaurant, which offered the double advantages of being one of the places the local people of

Asheville won't tell the tourists about, lest they have trouble getting tables for an incredible Caribbean/vegetarian cuisine. The other advantage was the layout of the restaurant itself: tables so crowded together that any hostility or threats Heavy Hitter could offer would be overheard by a dozen people at least.

When we arrived, Heavy Hitter was seated in the back corner, next to a person I recognized from our encounter in the parking lot. Both of them wore business suits, and looked weirdly out of place among the generally bohemian dinner crowd.

Karen, by far the most interesting thing about walking into a crowded place is to see all the various demons, in harsh and unpleasant variety, attached to many hosts. But in this room, the 100 or so demons perched on shoulders, digging into the back of necks or clinging to hearts all failed to attract my interest, because the thing attached to Heavy Hitter had my full attention.

It was not nearly as large as the creature I had seen with Justin Macaulay, but what it lacked in size it made up for in a kind of intense predatory ferocity that made all the other demons in the room look like Bambi. It seemed to be made of teeth and claws, and its spider-like body clung to Heavy Hitter like a dark malevolent parachute above his back.

As Fool and I pushed our way between chairs toward the back, the creature turned its red-yellow eyes on me.

As I looked at what this terrifying creature was attached to, I saw that there was hardly anything left of Heavy Hitter's spirit. Where most of the rest of the people in the room were ghosted by more-or-less intact spirit bodies, his inner glow consisted of a few tattered fragments.

Heavy Hitter and his companion stood up as we approached, and I noticed an intense glow of surprise from the other man, whose demon was a manticore, an angry lion-like creature with a fanged human face and what appeared to be a stinger on its tail.

"Arthur," he said, swallowing a couple of times before and after he spoke the word. "It's—good to see you."

"Oh father!" Fool cried. "I can't tell you how much I've missed you!"

"Really?"

"Mainly because you'd be offended. The truth is, I haven't really thought of you at all—except, of course, when George shows up to kidnap me."

"It shows I'm concerned about you."

"Why don't you send a card instead of George?"

"Well, I meant what I said. I really am glad to see you."

"Prove it."

"What do you mean?" Fool's father looked suddenly wary.

"Do a handspring or something. Make it convincing."

"I think we're all glad to see that you're both safe," said Heavy Hitter quickly with a smile that never quite reached his eyes. "I hear the police are still looking for you, although they can't be looking very hard."

"What they need is a hot tip," Fool suggested with his head buried in the menu.

"Our lawyers are working right now to end this unpleasantness as quickly as possible," Heavy Hitter assured us. "They think there's a case to be made for false arrest."

"And how long are they going to be working after my friend here signs those papers you have in your briefcase?" Fool asked. "Not that it matters to us. We don't need lawyers to keep *us* out of jail."

"Yes, of course. You have this man who can work miracles," Fool's father interjected sarcastically.

"You have no idea."

We all looked at the menu. I took a deep breath, wondering how to get the dinner conversation back on track. I opened my mouth, but it was Fool's father who spoke first.

"It's interesting how it works," he said. "When my own father found something to criticize about me, when I failed to live up to his standards of behavior, I would be sent to my room to wait for a brutal spanking, and I knew that if I dared try to stand up to him, the result would be the same, plus my life would be miserable for as long as he decided to remain outraged. I never, not once, felt like I had any power in the relationship."

"What an incredible wimp you were," said Fool.

"Then, when I had you," the older man continued, "I was deeply afraid that I would do to you what he had done to me, that you would secretly curse me as I still do him. And so when you shouted at me, I merely shouted back or turned away, and you were free to express your anger when I questioned your decisions."

"So?" Fool demanded.

"It is the curse of my generation that we felt powerless with our parents, and then powerless with our children. And you, my son, have never wasted a moment of sympathy for me. Even now, when I'm trying to give you what few other people have ever received in the history of the world, I have to fight you to complete the gift."

"What gift?"

"It will be worth at least $100 million," he said. "And it depends on the sale of the warehouse property."

I looked up at Heavy Hitter in surprise. He met my eyes without wavering, and I saw that it was true.

"The only reason you're even thinking about giving me anything," said Fool, staring back into his menu, "is to control me, and maybe to impress me. In the end, it has nothing to do with me, except to prove to the world my ingratitude."

"You're telling me that even the certainty of tens of millions of dollars won't buy your gratitude, or even your cooperation?"

"How could such a thing ever be for sale?" asked Fool quietly.

"And you can't give it to me now, just because I'm asking for it."

"I would be grateful if you would stop trying to control how I live my life, but I may be offering because I don't believe you can do it."

"I don't think I can allow somebody else to have more of that control than I do," said Fool's father. "I think I could back away if you could leave this Master and live your own life."

"He's not quite the monster you think he is," said Fool.

"I've seen him clearly through your growing contempt of who and what I am. No good person could possibly be reflected in such rabid hatred for his father."

"That was mine alone," said Fool. "In his eyes, you are perfect and whole and immensely interesting. It's yet another one of his lessons that I've failed to absorb."

"Then why are you here if you don't want to come home?"

"You'll find out before long," Fool told him. "And when you do, it's going to come as an interesting shock."

"Since you bring up the papers," Heavy Hitter interjected quickly, "I thought this might be a good time to finish the sale of the property."

"No," I said.

"No, this is not a good time? Or no, you aren't going to sell the property back to us?" There was more than a hint of a threat in Heavy Hitter's voice.

"Not this week. At least not before the sermon."

Both of the demons across the table from us fairly danced with rage, which so far was the most interesting thing we had seen. Heavy Hitter's demon leaned forward into my face, but Fool made a casual gesture, the air sparked in front of my nose, and the loathsome creature recoiled instantly back to the edge of the wall.

"Would you mind telling us why not?"

"Because of what's on the flyer. I don't want anything to interfere with that."

"Suppose we promise to allow you to stay on the property through the end of the week," Heavy Hitter proposed.

"Suppose we delay the transaction," I suggested, "so I don't have to worry about you keeping your promises."

"Suppose we add $100,000 to your end of the deal."

"You have that written into those contracts you brought today?" I asked in mild wonder.

"We decided to sweeten the deal a little bit."

"I wasn't negotiating for more money. As far as I'm concerned, you can have it for the same price you were offering before. Just not now."

Heavy Hitter turned to his companion. "Can you believe this guy?" he said. "What do you do with somebody who isn't motivated by money? For starters," he said, "we could call the loan due and foreclose on the place."

"Wouldn't that take longer than just waiting an extra week?"

"We might be able to speed up the process. And there's the contract you signed."

"I don't think you want that to come to light," I said. "There are other bidders on the property, as I'm sure both of you know. They don't think the contract I signed is totally legal, or that the transaction would pass the regulators if it was known that I was just a conduit. You have enough explaining to do as it is, and you'll need my cooperation to make it look like I was a willing seller and not some dupe you rounded up from a nearby office."

They looked at each other.

"Who have you been talking to?" Heavy Hitter asked me, a hint of anger rising in his voice. "If you think you can threaten us—"

"Answer me this," Fool interjected. "Why are you in such a hurry, that it's a terrible thing to wait a week for the place? My friend here is such a wimp, you'll have it in the end anyway."

"We want to get this wrapped up now."

"You just heard him say he'll sell to you in a week. It's wrapped up."

"We need to handle it now."

"Why?"

When there was no answer, Fool continued: "I can tell you why. Because the creatures who are eating into your soul are telling you to prevent us from holding the meeting. Because that meeting is going to strike what might be a devastating blow against their species, and the two of you are their main pawns in something you have no understanding of, and if I tried to explain it to you, they would close your ears and your minds the way they do to billions of people every day all over the world."

The two men across the table and their demons looked at Fool with precisely the same mixture of astonishment and anger on their faces. Finally Fool's father leaned across the table.

"So it's a great global conspiracy, is that what you're telling me?" he said with a mocking tone in his voice. "And everybody is persecuting—who? This Master person?"

"See for yourself," Fool said, and he reached across the table.

Karen, at the time I had no idea what Fool was going to do, but his father clearly thought this was going to be some kind of physical attack. But instead, Fool touched his father lightly on the chest, and my spirit eyes saw a transfer of spiritual voltage that dislodged the enormous creature on his back and caused it to fall over backwards through the wall like a ghost. In a second, the manticore's head appeared through the wall just below the ceiling. It looked more dazed than angry.

But not nearly as dazed as Fool's father, who put his hand to his forehead and leaned back as if he'd been struck by lightning. He shook his head and then looked around as if he was seeing the room for the first time.

"What—what just happened?" he asked.

"Dad, I'm curious what you want the place for," Fool asked quickly, before the creature could reattach.

"What?"

"Why do you want to buy that property back from the company? Where is all this money going to come from? What's so special about it?"

"I worked in that building when I was nothing more than a district manager," Fool's father croaked.

"Sentimental value? Some people collect jewelry, or stamps, and I guess a very rare few collect the charred remains of warehouses. Come on; you have to do better than that."

"I feel like I'm going to be sick," Fool's father moaned.

"What about the price, then? Aren't you paying an awful lot for the place?"

"Actually, there are higher bidders," I said.

"But he doesn't have to bid for it. He has it locked up in the company. I'm surprised he didn't just take the title home with him one day. Aren't you?" Fool addressed this to Heavy Hitter.

"The transaction is a great deal more complicated than you imagine," Heavy Hitter answered. He stared at Fool's father for a long, appraising second. "There are several goals here."

"I guess you believed what he said about the stock options," Fool answered sarcastically. "Is everybody in your office," Fool asked me, "as stupid as this guy?"

At that moment, the lion-like demon settled warily back on Fool's father's shoulders, favoring Fool with an angry glare. Instantly, his host regained his composure, and stood up. "Listen, you little bastard," Fool's father hissed, his jaw muscles working and the veins standing out on his high forehead. "I don't know what you just did. I don't even *want* to know. But if you try any of that voodoo on me again—"

Heavy Hitter also stood up. We were all standing, and I knew the meal was over before the orders had been taken.

"I had hoped to keep this civil," Heavy Hitter said. "But here's the bottom line: unless you sign, right now, I'm going to start calling in The House's note on the property as soon as I can get somebody on the phone. I'm going to have the House start a regulatory investigation on you, and they're going to call in the SEC, just like any white knight would do under the same circumstances. And when I get back, we're going to hold a special meeting to figure out how to screw you as many ways as we can think of, and I guarantee that we'll be thorough and creative. It's completely up to you, whether you want to make more money than you ever made before or—."

"Can I have some time to think about it?"

"No. You walk away now and you've screwed yourself so bad it will take years to swim back up to the top of the shit pile. And when you do, you'll find me waiting for you with another truckload, and lots more creative ideas. Do you understand me?"

"Now you understand me," said Fool, leaning into Heavy Hitter's face. "I think you're all talk and no action. I think you're too chickenshit to screw my friend here."

"Fool—" I said nervously.

"Neither he nor I are the least bit afraid of what you can do to him. Bring it on!"

"We have to go now," I said, pulling Fool backwards.

"Do your worst and it won't even touch him. Call headquarters," Fool called out as people stood up to make a wider path for us on our way out the door. "Bring on the police, the regulators and an army of lawyers—"

By now we were outside, which didn't stop Fool from calling back at the building his reverse and inverse threats that were all, somehow, aimed at me. Finally he turned to walk next to me, whistling cheerfully.

"What are you so happy about? That was, by any measure, a total disaster."

"For you maybe."

"Maybe for the Master too," I said gloomily. "I was hoping to stall the two of them past the sermon. Now it looks like he'll have the Marines surrounding the place by morning. So why are you grinning?" I demanded in vexation.

"I'm happy because, as usual, I know things you don't know," Fool answered cheerfully. "While you were talking, I was using my time productively, reading my father's spirit."

"So?"

"It was mostly about the days when real men were real men, and real women were real women, and real dogs were real dogs, and...real frogs were also probably real frogs, although I'm not totally sure about the frogs. Or the aardvarks..."

"Did you find out anything *substantive*?" I asked, trying to control my own impatience.

"Oh, sure."

There was a long silence as Fool strode next to me happily.

"I think you'd better tell me," I said finally.

"I couldn't get it clear until I brushed that demon off of him. But then, suddenly, the truth was right there for anybody to read."

"And?"

"I saw that they're not going back to your office right away."

I waited for more, but Fool continued to saunter cheerfully by my side.

"That's it?" I demanded.

"I think we should go there ourselves, and spend a few minutes in your broker friend's office. You know where *that* is, don't you?"

"They might not let me in," I said.

"It's after six," Fool replied. "Who's going to be there now?"

I thought about it. The janitor crew, maybe the stray rookie broker making dinnertime phone calls.

"Why do you want to see his office so bad?" I asked.

"I want to get out the file on my father."

"Why?"

"Because," Fool said, grinning triumphantly, "it has the environmental impact statement and the plans for the nuclear power plant, and I want to see them with my own eyes before we photocopy them for the world to see."

As Fool had predicted, the office was virtually empty, which meant nobody was there to wonder about my presence. As Fool pointed out, even if there *had* been anybody, only a few people in the office would have been interested in challenging a senior broker who was still employed by The House.

"All we have to do is stay away from this branch manager guy, and your buddy at the restaurant, and we're pretty much clear," he said as we passed through the darkened lobby.

"Keep your voice down," I advised him.

"If you're going to steal something, the best strategy is always to do it boldly."

"But you don't *say* you're doing it out loud."

"Which office is his?" Fool asked, poking his head into doorways at random. "Aha," he said, somehow discerning the correct room from the dozens of choices.

As we stepped inside, it suddenly occurred to me that I had never, not once, crossed this threshold. But now that I looked around, the place perfectly fit Heavy Hitter's character. The desk was enormous, the room at least twice the size of any other broker's, larger even than the Branch Manager's. One wall was covered with sales awards whose ornate script and design and fancy gold seals made it look, at a casual glance, as if Heavy Hitter had a hundred different diplomas from various colleges. There were pictures of him with upper senior managers at The House, all taken at one or another of the sales conferences.

I stopped at a plaque that was hanging on the wall behind the desk, in exactly the same place where the Branch Manager had his "Happiness can't buy money" sign.

This one was longer:

"Yea, though I walk through the shadow of the valley of death,
I will fear no evil,
For I am the toughest mother in the valley."

"Look at this!" Fool was already in one of the filing cabinets, apparently having some preknowledge of where to look. He pulled out a thick bundle of paper files, including several volumes the size of coffee table books, and laid them with an audible and indiscreet thump on the round table next to the window. "Here," he said, seating himself and pushing half of the pile toward me. "See if you see anything interesting in that."

Thumbing through the material, I came immediately across a lengthy document jointly authored by the U.S. Department of Energy and a number of power companies. To the right of the text was a graph which showed that the

U.S. would run out of energy by the year 2020, which was boldly headlined: "The U.S. Needs More Power Plants." I skimmed the text quickly.

The Nuclear Power 2010 program, unveiled by the Secretary on February 14, 2002, is a joint government/industry cost-shared effort to identify sites for new nuclear power plants, develop and bring to market advanced nuclear plant technologies...leading to an industry decision in the next few years to seek Nuclear Regulatory Commission (NRC) approval to build and operate at least one new advanced nuclear power plant in the United States.

To help meet our growing demand for new baseload electricity generation, the NEP has recommended expanding the role of nuclear energy as a major component of our Nation's energy picture.

The Department believes that an over reliance on a single fuel source, like natural gas, is a potential vulnerability to the long-term security of our Nation's energy supply and new nuclear plants must be built in the next decade to address increasing concerns over air quality and to ease the pressures on natural gas supply...

The NP-2010 program is focused on reducing the technical, regulatory and institutional barriers to deployment of new nuclear power plants...

To enable the deployment of new Generation III+ nuclear power plants in the United States in the relatively near-term, it is essential to demonstrate the untested Federal regulatory and licensing processes for the siting, construction, and operation of new nuclear plants...

The Department has initiated cooperative projects with industry to obtain NRC approval of three sites for construction of new nuclear power plants under the Early Site Permit (ESP) process, and to develop application preparation guidance for the combined Construction and Operating License (COL) and to resolve generic COL regulatory issues. The COL process is a "one-step" licensing process by which nuclear plant public health and safety concerns are resolved prior to commencement of construction, and NRC approves and issues a license to build and operate a new nuclear power plant...

Thumbing through the other papers, I found a blueprint diagram of what was clearly labeled a GT-MHR power plant designed by General Atomics. To me, it looked like two complicated cylinders connected to each other by a large tube; one was the reactor, the other, being fed the superheated gasses, was the "high-efficiency Brayton cycle gas turbine energy conversion system." Accompanying documents described it in glowing terms as a "direct-cycle helium-cooled reactor" whose prototype, now being built in Russia, was specifically designed to run on (and dispose of) excess weapons-grade plutonium.

Despite its small size, and the fact that it would be mostly underground, the plant would be powerful enough to produce 288 MWes, whatever they were, which was (a competing proposal from Westinghouse noted with some asperity) less than a third of the capacity of the new AP1000 design that was already certified by the Nuclear Regulatory Commission.

In addition to the apparent attraction of using up superfluous plutonium—which, one report noted, was becoming increasingly difficult to store for long periods of time—the gas-cooled plant would be smaller, modular and require substantially lower up-front investment risk. Reading through the reports, it almost sounded as if you could fit it in your back pocket.

Looking further, I began to see why there was so much urgency about acquiring the property and starting construction before anybody had a clear idea what was going on. The site along the French Broad River was one of three places the Nuclear Regulatory Commission had (in secret?) given its blessings to, in part because of certain legal issues which were described in detail, but which boiled down to the fact that the citizens of Asheville would be less likely to be able to block its construction than the population of either of the other two sites. The property, one legal memorandum noted, happened to lie just outside the Asheville city limits in Buncombe County, and Buncombe County happened to be one of the few communities in America to have no zoning laws whatsoever.

Further, in the last election, the voters had passed a state Constitutional amendment saying that bond issues could be floated without being voted on by the citizens, so long as the projected revenues of the project were sufficient to cover the interest and the principal of the bonds in question. That meant, unlike virtually any other part of the country, whoever was building this plant could raise public money and start construction without any legal avenue for the citizens to block it.

The deadline for the next bond issue filing, for this calendar quarter, was in two days. The paperwork was all prepared.

The House would be underwriting the bonds. Heavy Hitter was a major investor in the project and also the lead broker in the bond underwriting.

"This is pretty interesting," said Fool, who had the thick environmental impact statement open on his lap. "Did you know that the French Broad River is one of only two rivers in the country of its size that doesn't have a single endangered species that would be affected by thermal pollution?"

"I can't believe this," I said.

"That's not the half of it," said Fool, closing the thick volume and pulling out what looked like an architectural drawing of the warehouse as it had been before the fire. "Remember that hole you fell through?"

"Yes," I said.

"It wasn't a hole," said Fool. "Take a look at this."

I looked, and I looked again. Finally I shook my head in amazement.

"How could we have known?" I said.

"I wonder if the Master knew," said Fool.

"How would he know?" I asked.

"He knew your cell phone number, didn't he?"

"Why didn't he tell us?"

"It doesn't matter," said Fool. "The important thing now," he said, looking around, "is to find a copy machine and lots of paper."

Two hours later, we walked out the front door of the building. I was feeling elated and nervous at the same time, my mind vacillating back and forth from the scary consequences of what we had just seen to the rush of pride that I had somehow managed to beat Heavy Hitter at his own game. Fool, with a thick file under his arm, was steadily exuberant. "It's over," he said. "Do you realize what's going to happen when we show this to the local papers? It'll be on the nightly news all over the country."

"Should we tell them before the sermon?" I said. "They'll probably want to quarantine the place."

"It's safe enough; you read the storage reports. Besides, who's 'they?'"

"Just make sure you don't lose anything," I said.

"You might not want to take your car," said Fool as I headed for the garage.

"Why?"

"That Heavy Hitter fellow called the police as soon as we left. They're probably looking for your car on all the roads into and out of town."

"Oh," I said.

"Tonight, we'll take a quick trip down that hole. Do you think you could pick up a flashlight or two on the way back?"

"Sure. Where are *you* going?"

Fool tapped the file under his arm protectively. "We have two copies," he said. "I want to put one of them in a safe place in case we're killed or something."

Fool turned and walked up the street, and after a moment I turned away toward where Lexington and Patton converged near the downtown park. Where was I going to find a flashlight for sale in the downtown area? On impulse, I cut across an alley between buildings, and collided unexpectedly with a person who was blocking my way. He was much larger than me, and so solid that it felt like I had walked into a telephone pole. I stepped back a little shakily, and saw three men get out of a car on the other side of the street, walking in my direction with leisurely strides.

There was something about the scene I didn't like, and instinct told me to turn and walk away. But before I took my first step, a hand snatched me back by the collar, and the person I had collided with turned me around.

"Have a little respect," he said. "The boss wants to talk with you."

I looked past him at the men who were now immediately behind him. One of them smiled and held out his hand.

It was DiStefano.

Interlude: The Big Questions
What did *you* see in the library of Asgard?

On the bank overlooking the river, the gods and near-gods sit in the soft dry grass, exhausted from hard physical labor, their spirits radiating a mellow golden glow that mingles in the air and feels comfortably like the prelude to a glim.

"All of you have been to Asgard?"

Venus: "Of course. It's part of the tour."

Cassandra: "Everybody gets a chance to look at whatever you want to. The Master told me once that what you look for tells a lot about who you are."

"So what did all of you look at?"

Everybody waits for somebody else to speak, and I realize from the altered glow of the spirits that I have asked an intensely personal question.

Eris (shifting in her perch on one of the lower rocks, looking around bravely): "I was raised Baptist. So of course I looked into the past to see the reality of the scriptures as I had been taught them."

Fool: "I'll bet *that* was interesting."

"So what did you see?"

Eris: "I saw a young man walk in the desert, and it was amazing that his face and features looked so just like the paintings. I was able to recognize him instantly, and I wondered, how have so many painters for the next twenty centuries managed to capture that face, that look, those eyes…? He walked across the burning rock-strewn sand until his legs would no longer hold him upright, and he lay there on the ground for a day and a night and another day and night, determined either to die or to understand the mechanisms and mysteries of salvation, the answers to questions that had teased and tormented him ever since he was born.

"I saw, there in the crystal, that important moment when this man approached death, and his spirit eyes awakened and he noticed the swirling mist of holy spirit that surrounded his body and stretched out to the edges of infinity. He drew those sparkles toward him with a gesture that was at once majestic and desperate, as a king who is dying of thirst would call for water. He called his spirit body to birth right there in the desert, and the ghost came instantly to life, stood up and carried his body to the castle of Asgard. Many times during his ministry, I saw him walking through its halls, deep in thought and sometimes deep in despair."

Briareus (looking up in surprise): "Despair?"

Eris: "I watched some of his sermons, and through the magic of the crystal, I could understand what was being said, and it was so much like what the Master has been telling us, although he spoke with such power and passion that I was stunned by the beauty of his performances as he tried to explain the reality that lay hidden behind the mysterious, garbled, sometimes-politically-manipulated records that were the holy books of his audience.

"But even as he spoke with such clarity and confidence, even as he fought against the shadows of dogma that clouded the minds of his listeners, even as he pulled demons off of whole crowds of people, he could already see that his own words were going to be mistranslated, and misinterpreted, and would eventually become the enemy of the next teacher.

"And I saw that each time he tried to explain the truth that he had seen in the desert, one of the prominent teachers of blind faith in that dogma would stand up and shout to the people who had assembled: "This man speaks the words of the devil!" And many pious people would, on the authority of their religious leader, stand up and leave the only chance they would ever have for achieving the everlasting life of the spirit. How could he *not* experience despair?"

She shakes her head, and we can see the tragedy of that life in the subtle colors of her spirit.

Venus stares at the ground for a long second.

Venus: "I saw almost exactly the same story, played out in the life of the son of a king five hundred years before that," she says. "A young man searched the world for the same answers, and finally he sat down under a tree and denied himself food and drink while he meditated on the human condition. Eventually, on the edge of death, he noticed the sparkles of holy spirit, and awakened his own soul. He, too, walked those halls alone. Coming back to this planet was the hardest thing he would ever do in his life."

Briareus is watching Venus with wide eyes. He shakes his head as if coming out of a trance.

Briareus: "I wanted to look back at the very earliest years of civilization," he says finally, "and the crystal showed me the lives of a small group of Patriarchs who had kept the knowledge of the Old Ways, who were still capable of crossing from here in this world through the magic curtain to Eden and back again. They lived like gods among animals, each of them outliving many generations of the people who had forgotten the ways of the spirit.

"I wondered where these people had come from. So I looked back further still, to the time when this world was just a vacation destination, and home was the castle of Asgard and the fruit-bearing forests. I saw that our distant ancestors were a beautiful, extraordinary people, innocent and yet mightily powerful. They truly lived without a care in the world.

"After many generations, some of these people began to experiment with a wider range of possibilities. If there was pleasure in such abundance, then they recognized that there must be something that was its opposite. A small group of "connoisseurs of feeling" began to cultivate demons as pets, because they could help them reach increasingly exotic emotions on demand.

"As I watched them, I understood perfectly the ancient story of Pandora's box, of opening something in curiosity that could not be shut back up again. Over many years, I saw them experiment with the strange unfamiliar emotions of greed and jealousy and anger and even hatred—all the dark emotions introduced into a society that had no defenses against them.

"Eventually, of course, the elders began to speak out in protest against what we distantly remember today as the Fall of humankind. They asked for a return to the safer, traditional ways, never realizing that the stakes were much higher, that the demons would sweep humanity from godhood to servitude.

"Then I watched a terrible war between the traditionalists and the connoisseurs of dark emotions, where each side called forth mayhem and fire, and after terrible years, the rebels were defeated, banished from Eden, sent to live in exile on the planet where we live now.

"Gradually, with each generation, their powers diminished, until after a very long time, their children's children's children were no more than savages. Only a few patriarchs remembered the old ways, while those who remained in Asgard would occasionally visit their human cousins, and did what they could to help them. We remember these visitors by the names of ancient gods in many traditions, Taimat and Abzu, Enlil and Enki, Atum, Tefnut and Shu, Kumarbis and Kubaba, Zeus, Apollo, Diana, Thor, Odin, Jupiter, Poseidon, the giants in the earth, visitors from Asgard and Eden who took pity on what their distant relations had become—what *we* have become."

"Why aren't they still there? Were they killed?"

Briareus: "I wondered the same thing. When the Master took us back to Asgard the other night, I looked into the crystal again, while the others slept."

Venus: "And—?"

Briareus: "One day, they walked out of Eden and took up a new journey. Each god changed shape into another kind of creature and walked through space and time to some other place. Later, I talked with The Master, and he told me that they had moved on to a different universe.

"As I watched them go, there was such a joy about them, such a sense of purpose and anticipation, that I envied them this new adventure."

Eris: "Could you see what they changed into?"

Briareus: "Dragons."

"What?"

Briareus: "They were human on this side of the door, and dragons on the other side, where the physical laws must be very different."

"That's very odd."

Briareus: "What?"

"Just recently, I had my own dragon experience." I reach into my pocket, and pull The Big Score's gift out of the cloth wrapping.

My hand holds up a small figurine made out of a reddish stone. The polished, translucent surface gives off a glow which might be a reflection of the sunlight or might be holy spirit; it is impossible to tell which.

The figure itself appears to be a caricature of legends. It looks reptilian, like a cross between a snake and a small, highly-intelligent T-Rex, but with more robust forearms that end not in clawed appendages, but surprisingly delicate hands. The eyes are tiny jewels that sparkle brilliantly even when, as now, they are shaded from the sunlight.

I can see on the spirits of others that they find it as beautiful and disturbing as I do, and I wonder all over again whose long-dead hand had carved it.

Briareus takes it carefully in his hands.

Briareus: "Where did you get this?"

I am not sure what to make of his excitement. "It was given to me by a friend."

Briareus: "Who? When?"

"One of my customers. Why?"

Briareus: "This is what they looked like." *(He turns the figurine over in his hands, examining it from every angle.)* "This is how they looked as they were leaving the castle of Asgard for the next universe."

XVII

We of the New Age no longer believe in a God who sits on a throne and jealously demands obedience from the citizens of creation. Our God is everywhere, and understands our needs long before we address them in prayer. In our faith, health and healing and prosperity and personal growth are given to all who learn to listen to their spirit, and prayers are answered before they are ever spoken.

—From *The Rutherfordton Spiritual Gazette*

"I thought we could talk more comfortably up here," DiStefano said ten minutes later, his hand indicating the gravel-covered roof of the building. We sat at a plastic patio table in the kind of chairs you see around hotel swimming pools. Our little group had walked into the freight dock of a Wallgreen's store which occupied the bottom floor of the building, then up eight flights of stairs that looked as if they hadn't been used in years. The view of the city's skyline half an hour to sunset was spectacular, but I was having trouble taking pleasure in it.

"You haven't said what we were going to talk about," I said carefully, though I could read it on their spirits.

"We are not complicated people," DiStefano assured me. "You remember before that we talked about the River Street property, and that's why we're here now."

"To make me another offer?"

"We understand that you are going to go through with the original sale, ignoring our previous offer," Havender, the lawyer interjected quickly. "And you haven't even filed for the insurance claim."

"Isn't that my right?"

"Mr. Zakar, the world I live in is a rational world," DiStefano interjected, brushing aside the next comment from his attorney with an impatient wave of his hand. "In the world of normal economic commerce, we all understand each other. In our organization, we calculate the profits that one can reasonably expect from a transaction and we see to it that everybody in the food chain is appropriately compensated. But now you come along, and suddenly we don't understand what's going on. Nothing you do makes any sense to us. Me? I think you might be a little crazy."

"So you're taking matters into your own hands," I said. "You're going to hand me something to sign, and if I don't sign it, you're going to kill me. But I can already see that you're going to kill me anyway."

DiStefano gave me an embarrassed smile. "I wish we had time to find out how he knows these things," he said to the others. "It's like he can read our minds."

"It's written in your spirits," I said, "in this case, like headlines. The hell of it is, you actually think you're doing the right thing. You think it will actually help the local economy if I'm killed. Of course, knowing what I know, I've decided not to sign anything you put in front of me."

"Maybe you should read the fine print," DiStefano suggested. "You will find out that we know the address of your daughter's off-campus apartment, and some friends of mine are watching her carefully to make sure nothing happens to her. Because, you see, if she were to die unexpectedly, we would lose all leverage over you."

I saw that it was true. I saw much more. And then suddenly I smiled.

"Give me the documents," I said. "I've completely changed my mind."

"This is the spirit of cooperation we were hoping for," DiStefano said approvingly. Havender rummaged through his folder and pulled out some papers.

"This," the lawyer said, "is a revised will."

"Leaving you my property?" I asked him. "Don't you think that's a little obvious?"

"Leaving the property to an evangelical ministry, actually," Havender corrected me. "They've agreed to sell it back to us at a reasonable price. I'm actually very impressed by their negotiating and business skills, although they seem not at all interested in the insurance policy."

"Let me guess," I said. "Justin Macaulay."

"Faith Ministries. Yes—he does have a remarkable gift at this," the lawyer said to DiStefano. "You would have made an excellent negotiator," he said to me.

"So then I sign this, and then I have to die before this document can have any relevance to your plans."

"That is the most unfortunate part of this whole transaction," DiStefano told me, and his spirit radiated genuine regret. "Believe me when I say that we looked for every alternative we could think of."

"And you think it makes sense that I would disinherit my daughter and leave such a valuable piece of property to the first minister who happens to pass through town? You think a judge won't question this?"

"Actually, it makes perfect sense, once this Macaulay fellow explained it to us," the attorney interjected. "You're a member of a religious cult, and the cult has extreme religious beliefs, and you would naturally want your money to support the wider dispersion of religious faith into the world."

"Macaulay and the Master have nothing in common," I said. "In fact, Macaulay hates the Master."

"We don't think the judge is going to be inclined to make that fine of a distinction," DiStefano told me. "To the judge, you will simply have become a very religious man who got in over his head."

"And you're going to help the judge make that connection." I said.

"There is language in the new will that talks about providing for the religious education of your daughter, and we have left most of your assets in trust for her," Havender interjected. "But the trust is so defective that she won't have any trouble getting her hands on the money without any of those silly restrictions," he assured me.

"The real kicker," said DiStefano, "will be when you and all your friends kill yourselves by drinking poison together. I think it's reasonable to think he will draw the obvious conclusion. That is, after all, what cults do."

I smiled again, reached for the paper, flipped the pages to the back and signed my name. The attorney took the papers and examined the signature carefully. "It's a good signature," he said finally.

"There's one thing you didn't tell Mr. Macaulay," I said.

"What's that?"

"You didn't tell him that you were going to the warehouse personally and meet the Master yourself."

Havender frowned. "I don't see where that's any of his concern. In fact, he was very careful about leaving the details to us."

"So I guess this will leave Ellen Moore as your last holdout."

"The potter?" DiStefano laughed, and then checked his watch. "She's going to be joining your cult any minute now."

The attorney took out his cell phone and spoke into it for a few moments, and then we all sat in silence, waiting, I read from their spirits, for the helicopter to arrive. It landed in a whirlwind of its own making on the roof, and I was led to the back seat and advised to buckle myself in. Immediately, the helicopter wheeled away toward the river, passing over trees and buildings and streets and people walking here and there, too busy even to look up in our direction. Then we followed the river for a short while, and descended to the parking lot of the warehouse. As we landed, a small army of people walked up to the helicopter. Two of them held Ellen Moore by the arms.

"Hi," I said to her. "I told them about the nude bathing," I added.

"Are you part of this?" she demanded.

I shook my head. "I'm in the same position as you are," I said. "But I want you to believe me when I say it's not going to come out the way they think it will."

"They're going to kill us," she said.

"I'm hoping," I said, "that my friends can talk them out of it."

By now, we were approaching the place where the podium was being set up. I had expected it to be crowded, but most of the church people had gone home for dinner. There were small groups of people glimming and others were eating, and they paid little attention to us as we walked up.

"You're about to meet the Master," I said, smiling at my captor. "Aren't you at least curious about him?"

"Yes," he said. "In fact, I am hoping you will introduce me to him personally."

He nodded to the others, and they began to shake the shoulders of people who were deep in a glim, and herd them to a place near the kitchen. I looked around for the Master, Apollo, Mars or Venus, but they were nowhere to be seen.

"What's going on?" Alecto asked me. "Who are these people?"

"Do you know where I can find the Master?" I asked.

"No. He's not here."

"Mars? Apollo?"

She shrugged her shoulders.

"I'm not sure that matters," said DiStefano. "Really all we need is a group of you together. Go get some cups or glasses or something," he directed, sending two men into the kitchen area.

Suddenly, I felt panic rising in my chest. "Isn't there any way to contact them?" I asked, turning to different faces in the group. "It's very important that they come back here," I said. "In the meantime, don't drink anything they offer you."

"They're going to kill us," Ellen called out, struggling with the man who held her. The man slapped her across the face with the back of his hand and her head spun around.

"Hey, no more of that. You want to leave signs of violence here?" DiStefano called out angrily. "Get that stuff mixed up in a hurry, and let's get the hell out of here."

"What are we going to do?" Alecto asked me. "You're the head god right now. You have to think of something."

"I'm the *what*?" I demanded.

"You're Proteus. That means you can do things. Can't you?"

I looked around for Cassandra. Fool was probably still on his way. I tried to imagine a way out of the situation, to stall them until some competent god could return, but all I could think of was that I wanted to comfort everybody. I needed a glim, and it seemed at the same time like that was the last thing I needed.

Proteus, the Greek god who could change his form. Was that what I could do? I took a deep breath, and looked around at the group, at the eyes looking at me expectantly. Calling on my spiritual resources, I willed myself to become Mars, to become an all-powerful fighter, to radiate the bright red incandescent brilliance of bottomless strength and ferocity. I closed my eyes, waiting for the strength to fill me, and then I opened them again, and looked at my hands.

Nothing.

I tried to imagine what Fool would have done, but I couldn't think of anything ridiculous enough to master this absurd situation. All I wanted to do was sit down and have one last glim before I died.

And then I stopped.

The thought of glimming had not come from my conscious mind. It was an urgent message from the other one, the mind of my spirit, which had separated from me and was watching everything with a calm assurance.

"All right," I said. "Fine. Okay, we have to make this look convincing," I called out in a louder voice. "I want everybody here to sit in a circle, kind of like a *cult* circle," I added for DiStefano's benefit. "We'll all glim together."

"What the hell are you talking about?" my neighbor Ellen demanded.

"Sit down in a circle," I repeated. "Right here in the middle of the floor. Think of it as group meditation," I told Ellen. "It will look more authentic this way," I told DiStefano, seating myself carefully in the center of the group.

"I appreciate your cooperation," DiStefano said, looking at me carefully. "But I am also suspicious."

"We're going to meditate and prepare our souls for the next life," I said. "That's what you want, isn't it?"

"Whatever," he shrugged, looking impatiently back toward the kitchen.

Before I had even settled down on the floor, the others had closed their eyes, and with a trusting innocence that I found equally stupid and touching, they began vibrating the early notes of the Song of the Universe. At first I felt too distracted to join in, but after a minute, the steadiness of the others steadied *me*, and as my bones vibrated up and down the scale, I felt the awareness of my spirit reach out to encompass a wider space.

AUMMmmmmmmm.

Letting my spirit guide me, I directed my mind as I had on that first glim, when I had entered the awareness of the cricket. I followed the trail of sparks of holy spirit to other nodes of consciousness, other life in our immediate surroundings.

AUMMmmmmmmm.

Immediately, our spirits encompassed the awareness of some mice living in the weeds, and with an effort of will, drawing on the strength of the others, I incorporated their alien thought forms and sensory perceptions into our group awareness, my spirit serving as a translator from one type of thought pattern to another and back.

After another moment, we were looking through the eyes of a cat, and then another one—all simultaneously.

There were some dogs near a dumpster up the street, and as we became their awareness and they ours, they turned and ran toward the smell of lingering smoke in the bricks and concrete.

AUMMMmmmmmm.

As our awareness expanded, it mingled with countless insects and small spiders, some living in the ground, many others hovering in the air, bundles of pure sensory perception and blind instinct so far removed from the human framework of awareness that it was a roar of chaos to inhabit one of them, but we did not stop at one, or one hundred, or one thousand. Taking our vibrations all the way up and down the scale, we found ourselves incorporating microbes into the group awareness, and as more and more spiritual dots and nodes and bits of blind instinct joined the group, my spirit did something truly remarkable: it fused the awareness of all of these creatures into one will, one intent, as if they were all part of the same body, and the group that was vibrating in a circle was its mind, and my spirit was its nervous system.

AUMMmmmmmm.

The attack came without warning. A dense cloud of insects surrounded the faces of DiStefano and the men who were returning from the kitchen and around the perimeter, stinging at their eyes, crawling up their noses and into their ears in a glorious last gesture before they would liberate their spirits in a cooperative death not unlike the one that had been envisioned for us. Then the cats arrived, and their claws were our claws, and their victims were already blinded and reeling. The dogs were not far behind.

At some point in the attack, the connection between all of these disparate alien awarenesses shifted from being an impossible instant-by-instant-by-instant burden to something like an effortless flow, as my spirit found a translation key that all of the creatures in our perceptual field had in common. We united into a single feral ferocity, each of us cells of a body whose teeth were the dogs, whose claws were the cats, whose wings were the flying insects, whose predatory goal was to tear these men to pieces.

A wild savage joy rose up out of the primitive ganglia at the base of my mind and consumed everything else in a kind of ecstasy, a feedback loop amplified by my own repressed anger not just at these people who wanted to destroy me—*Yes!*—but now, suddenly, at everything that had ever dared to make me feel powerless in my frightened life—*Yes!*—and, by extension, at everything and everybody who had ever bullied or attacked or killed the innocent and weak—*Yes! Yes! Yes!*

By the time the mice and the frogs arrived, the men were on the ground, and the insects had become densely crowded writhing masses of fury inside nasal passages and mouths filled with blood.

Still the wild vengeful energy surged and pulsed along the spiritual connection, rising like a towering blaze of incandescence inside me, borrowing the flames of the mute primitive savagery of the creatures who performed my angry will, and redelivered back into the bodies of a growing armada of wings and teeth and stingers who were now a few seconds from killing our attackers—

Suddenly I stood up and broke the connection, and the whole grand alliance dissolved instantly into confusion and, for many of the creatures, a writhing death. My body was trembling from the sheer raw power of the primitive emotions echoing down the electric circuitry of my mind, mingled now with a deep sickness and regret.

I looked at my hands. *What was I capable of?* Slowly, with a sense of dread, I turned around and saw with the eyes of my body what my spirit had seen; men writhing and thrashing on the ground, bleeding from the face and groin, their hands covering their eyes and noses and their arms and knees trying to cover everything else.

My now, the animals had scattered in a panic, and the clouds of insects began to disperse into the air and along the concrete floor. I avoided stepping on any of them as I collected as many of the guns as I could find and handed them to the near-gods, who were themselves coming out of the trance and staring at the scene with expressions that I thought at first must have been distaste and horror.

I pulled DiStefano to his feet and held one of the guns to his head, but he barely noticed me. After a minute, he retched on the floor, and it seemed like there were a million dead insects, some quite large, in the milky pool on the smooth ground at his feet. A milllipede crawled out of his ear and dropped to the ground and scuttled off. He coughed and took his hands away from his face reluctantly, leaning forward with his hands on his knees, coughing violently over and over again.

I pulled him upright and held the gun to the back of his head. I was so unfamiliar with weapons that I wasn't sure whether the safety was on or off, or even if this particular gun had one. But I figured that DiStefano was not in a position to see this.

"I want you to leave my daughter alone," I said quietly.

DiStefano gasped and stood up, drinking in oxygen. He looked at me, and I saw terror in his eyes, and realized that he was not, at heart, a very brave man.

"If you don't convince me that my daughter is safe, in the next few seconds, I'm going to bring them back," I persisted.

DiStefano retched again, and finally managed to nod his head in agreement. I read the deep unconditional submission on his spirit, and relaxed.

"And know this," I said, shaking him a little. "If you come back, there are people who will treat you far less gently than we did here. Oh," I said as an afterthought, reading his spirit down to the footnotes. "They keep a couple of flashlights in the helicopter. Drop one over the side before you take off. I'm going to need it tonight."

As DiStefano's men pulled themselves to their feet, I put my apologetic hands on each shoulder and sent them staggering back in the direction of the helicopter. It took them a long time to get inside, but finally the engines started, and before it took off, the door opened and something fell out of the side and rolled a few feet away. Finally, the metallic insect rose into the air and disappeared behind the skyline on the far side of the river.

Only then did I finally relax. I sat down and covered my eyes and faced the thing I had done. Karen, the pure lust for savagery had not come only from the creatures we had inhabited. Their horrifying eagerness to tear apart living flesh had been embraced and even enhanced by a part of my own mind, a part I hadn't realized, until now, was waiting there at the base of my awareness, hoping for a chance to wreak havoc, hoping that the other, more civilized parts of my mind would relax again and let them drink deeply of an enemy's blood.

And I had enjoyed it. That was the worst of it.

For a long time I sat, huddled, my head in my hands. After a while the others gathered in a circle around me, not quite daring to intrude, not quite wanting to leave me alone.

No, the enjoyment had not been the worst of it, I realized. I had involved *them*, the others, in this terrifying pleasure that was the best friend of death.

Finally, my spirit responded to some signal or cue, and I opened my eyes and looked up into the air.

For a long second, I didn't know what I was looking for. But with my spirit eyes as a guide, I finally noticed a single butterfly fluttering about in confusion. It had arrived too late to participate in the attack, and now it was uncertain what to do in this strange place where there was no vegetation.

I stood up and reached the gentle awareness of my spirit out to embrace its confusion, and as this creature and I merged our thoughts, I saw that a scattered few of the bits of holy spirit at its core contained memories belonging to my wife and life companion. Apparently her spirit, recycled back into the universe, had a deep affinity for creatures who could fly.

Tenderly, I stretched out my hand in invitation, and after a moment's hesitation, the butterfly landed softly on my finger.

As I turned to carry it toward the tall weeds at the edges of the ruins, I noticed that all of the near-gods, still seated in a circle, were staring at me, and at the butterfly, and the place where the men had been, and back at me with that same expression that I had interpreted as revulsion and horror. Now, looking at their spirits, I could see that it was something else, and I was troubled all the more.

Under my stare, a near-god named Kristina quivered a bit, as if by simply looking at her I had bestowed some kind of benediction.

"What?" I said.

"What you did," she said, her face and spirit lighting up with gruesomely misplaced adulation. "I-I just wanted to say—for all of us—it was just totally awesome."

"It's down there somewhere," said Fool, squinting alternately at the diagram in the papers and the darkness at the bottom of the place where I had fallen on the day of the fire. The hole in the floor was located toward the back of the building, a rectangular gap in the concrete large enough to fit the trailer part of a tractor-trailer, cut into the floor and covered over with timbers to bring it flush with the concrete. The police investigator had noted in his preliminary report that the timbers had been soaked in creosote, and seemed to be the last vestiges of a much older structure, perhaps built along the side of the railroad tracks during the Civil War, a depot of some sort which the warehouse had been built on top of.

When the bazooka shells hit, those timbers had greatly contributed to the fire inside the building.

I shined the flashlight into the bottom. The floor below was at least 20 feet down, and the subterranean space seemed to extend back toward the river.

"How are we going to get down?" I asked. "I guess my first question should be, are we sure we *want* to go down there?"

"How else are we going to know for sure?" Fool demanded. "If we confirm what's down there, and it matches up with the documents we have here, that's evidence that all the rest of it is true as well."

"Is it safe?"

"According to this, they were on a yearly inspection program up until about 1970, and people came down here all the time. In fact, they were still accepting deliveries and storing more material until then. If this is right, there's still a fork-lift vehicle down there somewhere."

"What happened in 1970?"

"That was when they realized there was an environmental problem."

"Oh."

"My dad was in charge of this district. They were paying him on the side to take this stuff off their hands. Then he just made it disappear off the books, and closed down the warehouse a couple of years later."

"And he never forgot it," I mused.

I was about to ask Cassandra if she could find us a rope somewhere, but now I saw that Cassandra was walking toward us with a coiled length of thick yellow nylon cord.

"You have to say your lines," she said as she walked up.

"Cassandra, do you think you could find us a bit of rope from somewhere around here?" I said.

"I just happened to have some in my hands," she said with a sly smile.

"I still don't see how we're going to get down," I said.

"Like this," Cassandra said impatiently. She wrapped one end of the yellow cord around a steel bar sticking raggedly up out of the area that the Master had forced us to leave in its natural disastrous state, about 12 feet away from the opening, tying several knots to make it secure.

"Is that how we were going to do it?" I asked.

"You were going to figure it out eventually," she said.

"You're skating on thin ice today, aren't you?"

She looked at me briefly for a second, and then looked away. "I'm discovering that when I'm around you, I have a little bit of freedom," she said, wrapping the cord around my waist and then fashioning a knotted loop where I could insert my shoe. "I don't really understand how it works, but it's nice."

I put my foot into the loop, and Fool and Cassandra lowered me down. I shined the light around. The walls were simply an extension of the granite in the hillside, and very damp. It felt like I was in a cave, except that the floor was level and covered with cement. I moved ahead gingerly, stepping around little pools of water, following a pair of rails that extended down toward where I knew the river was. To my right, a fork-lift vehicle sat rusting next to the wall.

In a second, Fool had joined me.

"Do you see it?"

"Not yet."

"Come on!" he said impatiently. "It has to be in this direction."

We had to clear out a lot of debris that blocked our progress, but finally we were able to follow the rail as it took us deeper into the hillside, and then abruptly turned left. This was newer construction, and the walls were made of concrete. The hallway was just wide enough for a fork lift vehicle to fit through, and chains along the ceiling suggested that something was driven in here, set on a sling and then lowered. Nearby, stacked up neatly, half a dozen 55-gallon steel barrels rested against the wall.

"Wait a minute," Fool called out. "Turn off the flashlight."

"Why?"

"Just do it."

I did as he requested, and discovered that I didn't need the additional light. The ceiling shimmered faintly, a glow whose undulating pattern I associated with sunlight on water. As I stepped further into this part of the tunnel, I found myself standing above a long pool of water. How deep it was, I couldn't say, but at the bottom there were roughly a hundred long rods of metal, each maybe five inches in diameter, laid carefully parallel to each other. Around them, the water was eerily lit up by a rich purple radiance, what I later learned was the result of electrons being given off as byproducts of the nuclear decay taking place inside the rods. Scientists called this glow the Cherenkov effect.

"Unbelievable," said Fool, his face lit up by the strange light. "And yet this is what's going to make everything else believable."

I switched on my flashlight and shined it around, until I finally found what I was looking for. On the far side of one of the drums, I spotlighted the black and yellow symbol for radiation, and above it, the words *"DANGER FISSIONABLE MATERIAL."*

Stenciled in the side of the drum was the word "Plutonium."

"How much do you suppose is down there?" I asked.

"According to the records, they had a contract to store a thousand kilograms," said Fool without taking his eyes off the glow. "Back in 1972, it was estimated to be worth about $12 million. Today, with inflation, I'm going to guess you could sell it for $120 million, if we ever got back in the nuclear reactor business."

"Being *here*, I'll bet it's worth a lot more than the going price," I said.

"Why more?"

"Nobody wants to have this stuff shipped on the open roads. Having the fuel right here on-site, where the reactor is going to be, would eliminate one of the biggest hassles of locating the plant here in the first place. What I'm wondering now is, who owns it?"

Fool shrugged. "Nobody wanted anybody to know it was down here, and so it was conveniently forgotten. My guess is, whoever owns the place owns this stuff right along with it."

"That would be me," I said.

"I think we'd better talk to somebody in a hurry," said Fool. "Because if I know my father, he and his lawyers are already meeting with a judge somewhere to get that changed."

That night, we sat in a circle and I told the others what we had found, and how we were going to give this information to the newspapers in pieces, the part about the plans for the nuclear plant first, then the part about the Plutonium later. Fool told them soberly that he hoped the nuclear plant would be named after him, and that if this didn't happen, he was studying up on the Internet how to make a dirty bomb.

The Master sat off to one side. While the others began to hum the mantra, I studied his spirit, trying to discern whether he had known any of this all along, but the peculiar brilliant whiteness of his spirit made it hard to read details. And so much of his spirit was above his head, where I was having trouble reading anything at all…Eventually I gave up and closed my eyes, trying to catch up with the others.

Once more, the now-familiar menagerie of shapes and forms, flame, cloud and protoplasm that was a cross-section of intelligent life in the universe appeared to my awareness in vivid and confusing detail. I tried to decide who my next contact partner would be.

The creature that looked like a hundred eyestalks radiating from a ball of gray jelly? It gave me the brief attention of a random half of the stalks and then passed on.

The aquatic creature that drifted by with a lazy rotation of its cilia?

The insect-like citizen of a dark jungle world, whose primary and secondary heads were both topped by a jewel-like appendage that I somehow understood was a sensory apparatus analogous to the tuner of a ham radio?

I passed what appeared at first glance to be a crow, but which, on closer inspection, was a colony of crab-like creatures the size and shape of tiny spiders.

Without realizing it, I had moved to the periphery of the deva community. Here, I could see what I could not have noticed while I was in the middle of everything; that the menagerie was too vast and extensive to take in. Were there millions? Billions? I wanted to count the house. In my current state, vibrating with the Song of the Universe, it felt as if too much of my attention was taken up with the effort of being here to attempt such a complex activity. Instead, I watched until I found the Master's unmistakable form, and was pleased to see that he was surrounded by a host of other creatures, passing beneficences to this group in much the same way he did with us, an aristocrat even in this august and fascinating company.

"It is comfortable here at the edge," a voice commented from beside me.

Startled, I turned my attention first to one side, then the other, and the voice chuckled at my confusion.

"I find it wearisome to materialize in this crowd of youngsters," the voice intoned drily, this time coming from the empty space immediately on my left. "I have no desire to share my mind with any of you now, for I have found it is like—" here the entity stopped and seemed to search my mind for an appropriate analogy that I would understand—"like pouring from a pitcher into a shot glass. And I, too, am filled. But perhaps—" the entity continued hopefully—"you could sit beside me for a thousand years. I find that increasingly I crave companionship, and the young are always too flighty for a restful time beneath the stars."

I smiled in spite of myself. "I'm afraid my lifespan isn't long enough to accommodate you," I said.

"Nonsense. Here, in this place, time is whatever we make of it."

Karen, I have always been comfortable around the aged, and many of my customers are people in their declining years, who come by the office on some pretext involving their investments, but their only wish is to admire the splendid view and spend a little time with me in conversation. And so I allowed myself to be drawn in the direction of the voice, and a confusing instant later found myself standing alone on what appeared to be a dark landscape of barren rock. Filaments of interstellar dust, illuminated by a bright inner light, streamed across the sky overhead in a tight series of spirals around a bright core. It seemed as if we were hovering directly above the center of a spiral galaxy.

"It is beautiful, is it not?" the voice agreed. "I have watched this small aggregation of stars turn on its axis 50 times since my infanthood, twice as long as your solar system has existed. I have seen it capture and merge with other galaxies in the most delicate gravitational dances you can imagine, and I have watched the beast that lives at its heart devour more than its share of stars."

"Beast?" I said.

"Your species would call it a black hole. The mechs once placed a colony on it, because, they told me, it possessed unusual properties. I paid no attention to such nonsense, and in the blink of an eye, they were gone. That was a long, long time ago now, when a star still warmed this planet. Now that star is a spinning ball not much larger, spacially, than this world itself."

I sat down on a rock and watched the stars for what seemed to me to be a long time, but which I knew was not more than an instant to my new friend.

"I am called Proteus," I said after a while.

"You may call me Mentor," the voice replied, "for I have spent my life in contemplation."

"Where, exactly, are you?"

"Actually, you are sitting on me," the voice replied. Then, as I jumped to my feet, its voice conveyed amusement and affection. "Please return to your restful position," it said. "I am spread out over much of the landscape you see here. My mind is in the electrical impulses of the crystalline rock, which now absorbs the starlight, as once it was warmed by the sun."

"Are there many of you here?" I asked, looking around curiously.

"I am the last of my species."

"Oh." I sat down again. "No wonder you're lonely."

"There are visitors from time to time. And we have always been a sedentary species, prone to solitude and contemplation. I visit the place where the others congregate out of the weakness and senility of advancing age."

"What were they like?" I asked.

"Who?"

"The mechs."

"Flighty. Irresponsible. And yet they possessed an insatiable thirst to know everything, the same hunger which motivated you to ask that question. When they came here in my middle years, I recognized that they and I shared this one thing in common, and we traded what we knew. They had been looking for us, for we were the first to explore the universe, when it was very young and much smaller than it is today, and we too had carelessly left behind artifacts which would tantalize those who came after. I can tell you that they were excellent listeners, once the conversation became serious. And then, in the blink of an eye, they were on to the next thing. From time to time, I saw their vessels passing by, but they never again stopped to visit. I thought that was a bit rude, but our standards do not apply to all creatures."

"It *was* rude," I said.

"You are not so different," the creature said to me. "In a very short time, members of your species will retrace their steps, explore their ruins, search their archives, and the trail will bring you here. And like it was with the mechs, I will not expect a second visit."

"How soon?" I asked.

There was the sound of a sigh, and I realized that my impatience was wearing thin. Yet Mentor indulged me with an answer.

"Before your sun has risen and set barely a million times," he said. "Hardly the blink of an eye, if I had such a thing attached to my body. I am preparing already for their impatience—although," he continued in a softer voice, "your companionship has raised my expectations."

We sat and watched the stars in silence, and I allowed the time to slip past me without interference. After a long time, it seemed to me that I *could* see the heavens turning slowly around an invisible galactic center.

"I'm so new to this," I confessed. "I feel like a child playing with toys I don't understand."

"Your species is blessed with undeniable greatness," Mentor said after a time. "This is the adolescence of your race, a time when you adapt your bodies and habits from the evolutionary characteristics of animals to those of a thinking species. Your social problems all come from the same source; despite your intelligence, you are physically and in your important instincts more animal than not."

"Are you saying I don't belong here? I don't even know if I *am* here. Is my body here or back at the warehouse?"

"The true answer is both and neither. And yes, you belong here, and many have been impatient for the second arrival of your species. They were among us once, and those first visitors did what nobody has done before or since. They followed the mechs to the place where the mechs went when they departed this universe."

"I don't understand."

"They—the humans your species remembers as gods—somehow found the doorway to another place, and walked through it in search of whatever the mechs were looking for. It must have been an important journey, because they left the remainder of your species in an extended dark age that threatened your survival."

"You don't know why it was important?"

"Nobody on this side of the door can tell us that. At least, not any more. To know that, you will have to go through yourself."

"What are the chances of that?"

"I did not choose you idly," Mentor said after a moment, and there was a self-satisfied majesty in the dry sound of his voice. "Someone must tell those who left that your species is ready to reunite with its gods, that it is cleansing itself for the next great leap into the universe. I am hoping that you will return to satisfy, for a creature as old as time, the one last thing that I am curious about."

I didn't understand a word of what he was saying, but made a mental note to ask the Master whenever I saw him again.

We fell silent and watched the stars and the filament of gas, until my mind caught a faint rumble, and there was a stirring of the earth to match it.

"Mentor?" I said.

But Mentor was snoring.

XVIII

The most formidable, tenacious obstacles to every goal—success, happiness, perfect health—are self-imposed. In our formative years, we learn to impose limits on ourselves and on what we believe can happen in our lives, and on how quickly things are capable of changing. We form opinions about our capabilities and our destiny, and those opinions become manifested in our lives, the self-imposed boundaries within which we live and die.

The most profound and important insight that can be offered by the New Age wisdom is that the door to the prison cell is and always has been open. We can choose to exceed our limitations. But few in the early generations will accept the invitation of the open door. They will fight to preserve their obstacles, because outside the cell there are no comfortable certainties; only frightening opportunity without limits, stretching out to every horizon.

—From *The Rutherfordton Spiritual Gazette*

"You want some company?" Venus asked me.

I was sitting on the broken edge of the wall facing the river, feeling the wind in my face, wondering when I'd get a chance to go to sleep. I moved over to make room for her.

"What are you doing out here?" she asked.

"Waiting for somebody to return my phone call."

"Who?"

"A newspaper reporter. You remember I told everybody about how we have a story for him. I'm really hoping it could be the story that brings everybody here to listen to the Master."

"You think he's going to call at five in the morning?"

"I don't know."

I listened to the sound of the water and the breeze in the grass, but most of my attention was on the fact that she was sitting next to me. My skin was so sensitized to her presence that I could actually feel the tiny bit of warmth that emanated from her skin, even though we were at least two inches from touching.

Venus read my spirit. "After the things we've done together, you still feel shy with me."

"There's a part of me that feels like I don't deserve your attention," I said.

"All men are unworthy," she agreed with a smile. "It's just a matter of degree."

"When I was still living under the Curse, I would have been scared to death of you," I told her. "Or maybe not you; I would have been frightened of my feelings, of the certainty that the instinctive two-thirds of me would overpower the rational one-third and I would do whatever you asked, no matter how stupid or degrading. And the hell of it is," I said with a smile of my own, "I wouldn't have been afraid of the consequences of what I did under that spell; the fear would have come from the insecure suspicion that what I thought you implied as your reward was not what you intended."

"How do you feel, now that the curse is lifted?"

"Comfortable. Like it's a natural thing that we, two human beings on a warm night, should find a moment to share our thoughts and feelings."

"You're not in love with me," she said. "But I think men have trouble distinguishing between lust and love. That's our main advantage over them."

We sat in silence for a minute. I looked down at the ground. Somewhere almost directly below where I was sitting, the tunnel-cave turned left.

"So what are you doing out here when everybody else is asleep?"

"I'm confused," I said.

"About?"

"I'm not sure. I guess I'm confused about *that* too," I said with a laugh. "Sometimes, when I look at all of you, I try to imagine a world where everybody is like this, everybody is one god or another, and it's too much to hold in my mind.

"And then I remember something that defines my mission here. Every person's life is ultimately tragic," I said, remembering it slowly. "The only truly important mission in life is to change that."

"That's very good," Venus said approvingly. "It kind of captures everything about us."

"And it reminds me how far we still have to go."

"It's going to happen, and then you won't have to imagine it. But I think a lot of people are closer than they realize," she added. "If you ever feel pangs of conscience, or feel guided whenever you're faced with a moral decision by something that tugs at your heart, then that's evidence that your spirit is mostly intact and aware. As soon as it becomes aware, the spirit takes an immediate interest in how your actions and your decisions are shaping the story that it carries around as its body. Based on the life I see written into yours, it must have been alive for a very long time before you came here."

"It hasn't done me a lot of good," I ventured sourly, and I knew she could see that I was referring to my failed brokerage career.

"The way *this* world measures things, that's probably true. As you get better at this, you'll very quickly notice that the people whose spirits have come alive often feel unsuccessful in life. But when you leave this body and *become* your spirit, the whole dynamic is reversed. The Master once told me that you achieve status far beyond everything you gave up if you can manage to live a courteous, gentle, moral, gracious life—the treasures in heaven and all that. There's a lot of talk in the various scriptures about how the last will be the first, about how status is suddenly reversed at some confusing time and in some confusing way. We think this is what they—the avatars—were trying to communicate."

"But if the goal is a total merger with the—do you call it the Almighty?"

"That's a workable term."

"If the goal is to merge completely with the Awareness of the Universe," I persisted, "then status and what is written on my spirit shouldn't matter at all."

"It doesn't," she assured me. "Not at all, from that standpoint."

"I don't understand," I said.

Venus punched my shoulder in what I took to be an encouraging gesture. "What made you think that your personal relationship with the universe was going to be *simple*?" she asked with a grin.

I shook my head and stared at the sky.

"So tell me one thing," I said finally.

"What."

"Tell me why *you* would want to overthrow the status quo. The world worships people like you. People like you are on the cover of every magazine. But if everybody could suddenly look past the outer appearance and see the beauty of the spirit, wouldn't that send you back toward being…ordinary?"

For a moment, I was sure that I had offended Venus, because she just stared into space. But her aura never changed from a mellow golden color. "It's true," she said finally. "Sometimes I'm embarrassed by how drab my spirit looks. I think to myself, am I that shallow?" She laughed again. "And then I realize, yes, I *am* that shallow. And what's so wrong with that? I *like* being shallow."

"You may be the strangest of them all," I said.

"Some of us think *you* are," she replied, her eyes following mine to the tops of the buildings and the white glow that surrounded them. "I'm sorry I called you Mister Commuter, by the way," she added. "I thought you were the answer to a different prayer."

"I kind of liked the name," I said. "Nobody ever told me why you guys got all excited when you saw my spirit."

"Oh." She shrugged. "You walked in off the street, and we're trying to make this stupid movie that we knew nobody was going to watch, and you could not have acted more clueless, except that you gave such vexingly good answers to my questions. So of course I was annoyed that you weren't following my script, but I couldn't *tell* you the script, because then you wouldn't be a representative example. And you said something about how we didn't know who you were, and you were right, so I decided to prove, more to myself than you, that you *were* as clueless as I wanted you to be."

"And I wasn't?"

"Try to imagine my surprise when I looked at your spirit and read the detailed routine accomplishments of a fully-functioning god."

"What?"

"You heard what Med called you, didn't you?"

"Plautus," I said. "What does it mean?"

"Somehow, you managed to become a god of financial prosperity, working miracles in the world even though you were carrying the chains of The Curse around your spirit. I'm not saying they were the most unbelievable miracles of all time, but be honest now." She touched my arm lightly, stroking it with her fingers. "Didn't you feel, when you were working, like you touched a bit of magic into the lives of your clients?"

"I call them customers."

"Yes or no?"

"Yes. But I thought it was ordinary."

"Every miracle seems ordinary if you're the one who's doing it. When everybody has reclaimed their godhood, they'll do things they cannot imagine now, things that they would not dare believe if you told them at this moment, and everything they do will seem ordinary and natural and a little boring. But tell me this: did you see anybody else giving out this magic?"

"No. In fact, they told me it was wrong whenever I did it."

"The people who worked in that office were scared to death of you."

"You don't know them," I said.

"Don't I?"

"Believe me; the last thing they would be frightened of is me."

"You're going to go back and sign those papers, aren't you?" said Venus. "You'll see them at least one more time, won't you?"

"When all this is cleared up, I'm planning on retiring. For good."

"Take a good look at their spirits next time you go back to the office," Venus advised me with a smile, giving me the gift of looking me full in the face with her radiant eyes. "And then I want you to come back to me and apologize for thinking I was too stupid to know what you should have known all along."

I took a deep breath. The thought of facing Heavy Hitter and the Branch Manager even one more time in my life had taken the wind out of my sails.

"Anyway," I said, "you never told me why you, of all people, would want to change the way the world works. Why would you want people to look past beauty, when you have so much of it?"

By now, the darkness had given way to a peculiar type of dawn. The sun hadn't risen yet, but the thick clouds overhead were infused with a predawn glow. It looked a little bit like bright moonlight on a field of snow, except upside down.

Venus sighed, and there was a whisper of magic sadness in the sound that made me want to put my arm around her. Finally, after a long moment of debate, I reached over and drew her against me, feeling with every nerve the warmth of her shoulder, the touch of her hair on my neck, the curve of her torso against my hip. But instead of being erotic, it felt like the two of us were comforting each other against all the sadness that men and women caused each other, and all that they would cause each other even after they became gods.

Finally Venus spoke, and there was a tear in her eye. "I live in a world where you can look in any woman's closet and know instantly which parts of her body she's insecure about," she said. "Do you think I wouldn't change everything if I could?"

At that moment, my cell phone rang.

"Yes?" I sat up instantly.

"This is Tom Patterson from the Asheville Citizen-Times. Is this Adam Zakar?"

"Yes," I said.

"You left me a message to call last night. Aren't you in custody yet?"

"Not yet," I said wryly.

"So let me guess. You want to meet in a dark alley, and you're ready to tell your side of the story."

"I want you to come over here to the warehouse and take a look at something."

"Not possible," he said. "You're really at the scene of the crime?" he asked after a moment. "Can we find a place in town? I think everybody is curious to get your side of the story."

"Why is it not possible? Don't you want to meet everybody?"

"I was told yesterday by the editor not to write about where you're staying. It makes the police look bad when we tell them where to look and they still can't find you."

I gave Venus a pained expression.

"Where do you want to meet?" I said.

"How about Wall Street?" he suggested. "I'll buy you a cup of coffee at the Laughing Seed."

"In an hour?"

"Done. Oh—Mr. Zakar?"

"Yes."

"I wouldn't tell anybody we're going to be getting together," Tom Patterson warned me.

"Why?"

"Let's just say that some awfully important people are not anxious to hear your side of this thing, and I'm not altogether sure they'd stop short of violence."

"It's not like it used to be when the Master was around and talking to us all the time," said Fool as we walked toward the highway. "Back then, we learned everything. Of course, most of it was incomprehensible, and sometimes we were too tired and hungry to listen to the secrets of the universe. But now, I guess he thinks we've got it all."

We had been talking about the body of the spirit, which Fool described as the opposite of petrified wood. "With petrified wood," he told me, "water carries minerals into the structure of the wood and deposits them, layer upon layer of rock, until what was wood has been replaced by rock, and the wood serves as a template for the rock, and the finished product is more permanent. In the body, we draw holy spirit into our energy fields, and the energy fields are created by our experiences. The permanent part of us, the body that will survive the physical body, is made up of a direct imprint of our experiences. The spirit is our life story."

"And that's what the Eastern religions mean when they talk about karma."

"Apparently it determines your status, or whatever the equivalent thing is, in the afterlife. The Master told us once that spirits in the universe can see each others' lives the way you and I look at faces, and that you can think of hell as having embarrassing or regrettable things imprinted on your spirit. It's like the equivalent of being fat and sloppy in a pickup bar—only I think the Master used different words."

"I wish we could all know these things while we're alive," I said. "Wouldn't you make different choices if you knew that you were creating a permanent record of everything you did that you'd carry around with you, visibly for all to see, forever?"

"Apparently that's how it worked before Jesus came along," said Fool. "But the Master said that Jesus noticed something that nobody ever had before. It was a mechanism that he called "repentance"—a word which has been mistranslated and misinterpreted ever since."

"I never totally understood it in Sunday school," I confessed.

"The Master says that life is trial and error, but the spirit has a mechanism for erasing the trials that you truly regret and learned from. So long as you turn your back on them and—by doing so—change your energy field, the actions you cast aside are not permanently written into your spirit."

"But he also said you had to be born again. Doesn't that mean you have a chance to start over?"

Fool laughed. "I think that's going to be the hardest of all for society to figure out."

"What do you mean?"

"Did you know that nearly every primitive society has a ritual of passage into adulthood that involves a great deal of physical danger—either a real or a simulated near-death experience?"

"All of them?"

"So far as we know. Do you have any idea why they do this?"

"Because they're primitive?"

"Because they knew a hell of a lot more than we do about the spirit and the afterlife," said Fool.

"So what does it mean then?"

"In our society, ninety nine percent of the human population never goes through that near-death experience that forces the spirit body to come alive and rescue them," said Fool. "It's waiting to be born, but the birth never happens. It's right there in the Christian scriptures for anybody to read: *'To enter the kingdom of heaven, you must be born again of the holy spirit.'* How much clearer did he have to make it? Later, telling one of his disciples to stay with him and the community rather than attend the funeral of a relative, he said *'Leave the dead to bury the dead.'* Isn't it obvious what he was talking about?"

For the last five minutes of this conversation, we had been standing on the side of U.S. 19-23, the 4-lane divided highway that connects Asheville with Johnson

City on the other side of the Tennessee border. We were waiting for a lull in the traffic, so we could cross without getting run over by automobiles that routinely traveled at 70 miles an hour along this stretch in both directions. While I was scanning both sides, I noticed that somebody was standing on the opposite side of the highway, on the shoulders of the south-to-north side of the road.

"Who's that?" I asked, pointing.

Fool squinted comically, and then straightened up with a start. "Let's walk up the road a ways," he said, his jaw clenching.

"Why? What's wrong?"

"Just follow me and don't ask questions."

I followed him at a pretty good pace, and noticed that whoever was across the highway turned and walked parallel to us.

"How long before we have to meet with this person?" Fool asked me in a low voice.

"We were supposed to be there five minutes ago."

"Damn! All right; let's make a break for it."

The two of us waited for a large tractor-trailer to pass with a roar of wind, and then two cars, and then we ran across, beating a car coming around the corner by a few feet, hearing the blare of a horn as it passed. The traffic was less heavy going out of town, and Fool started across almost immediately. I followed, and looked up to see the person on the opposite side of the road.

It was Fool's father.

"What the hell are you doing here?" Fool demanded angrily.

"Now Arthur, I've been trying to find a chance to talk to you ever since you stormed out of the restaurant. Is there anything wrong with wanting to talk?"

"How did you know we were coming this way? He has your cell phone bugged," Fool told me, answering his own question. "All I want from you," he said, turning back to his father, "is for you to get out of my life and forget you were ever connected with me in the first place."

"Without any chance of redemption," Fool's father answered flatly.

As this exchange was going on, I was watching the angry feline creature perched on the older man's shoulders, whose human face was alternately feasting and looking greedily at Fool.

"All right, then, tell me why you're here," said Fool, looking no less angry. "And then get out of our way, because we have an appointment to keep."

"Yes, I know about your appointment."

"Then you know we're going to blow this scheme of yours sky high and to hell and back, and show the world what an asshole you really are."

"The dream of every angry son," the father observed. "And you also know that if you keep walking into town and deliver that—" he pointed at the thick file of papers in my hand—"you'll be throwing a hundred million dollars right down the toilet."

"Your money means nothing to me."

"No, of course not. But have you ever asked yourself why I do the things I do?"

"Because you have lost your humanity," Fool shot back immediately.

"My god, I wish I had," the older man answered. "My life would be so much easier. The truth is that I'm doing this for you."

"Bullshit."

"Why else? All I ever wanted was to leave you with enough that you could do anything you ever wanted in life. All my life, I've dealt with people who have incomparably more power than I do. But I told myself that one day, you would be one of those people. I wanted you to have the freedom to do anything."

"And that's why you took away all my freedom of choice," said Fool sadly. "In the name of someday giving it back to me as a gift."

The two of them faced each other while I looked at my watch. "How about if you two settle this while I keep the appointment," I suggested.

"You're not going to keep that appointment," Fool's father said.

"How are you going to stop us?" Fool demanded. "There are two of us and only one of you."

"If you help me stop *him*," said the older man, "then the odds are in our favor. And you have a hundred million reasons to make that decision. Try," he added, "to imagine all the changes you could make in the world with that kind of money. Think of the damage you could undo."

Fool raised a tattooed eyebrow. Then he laughed. "You know," he said, "I am your son after all."

At these words, I froze, and began to back off.

"No, stay where you are," Fool called out to me.

I continued to back off.

"Do you know what I read in those documents," said Fool, walking in my direction. "I read that you stand to come away from this with the insurance money on the property, plus a full ten percent ownership interest in this power plant if it ever gets built, and I'm pretty sure you're planning to sell them the plutonium that we found in the basement. I add all that up, and I get a number closer to $400 million. It seems to me you're holding out on me."

He stopped to see the effect this was having on his father, and then continued. "And I remembered something as I was reading through this odious pile of documents. I remembered that you were the Southeast regional manager when that plutonium was stored away. I'll bet money that this was a private deal you had with the power company, that never showed up on the books. You could get in a lot of trouble for authorizing the storage of fissionable nuclear material this close to a city. If you hadn't gotten greedy, nobody would ever have known about it; it might have stayed buried down there for a hundred million years."

"Not true," said Fool's father, and I saw for the first time fear in his eyes. "A consortium of developers is trying to buy up all the properties along the water, to turn it into a river street shopping area. Within a year, two at most, some excavator would have found it." He licked his lips. "Arthur, I need your help, and I'm not too proud to beg for forgiveness. Everything I did for you was well-intended. My goal, all my life, was to give you more than you ever dreamed of having."

"Then give me the full $400 million and walk away from your job and everything else," said Fool.

"Is that what you want?"

"Yes."

By now, I was halfway up the embankment and should have been running to make my appointment, but I couldn't help watching this drama between such different people who happened to be father and son. Fool's father noticed me, and turned back to his son.

"Will you help me?" he said.

Fool burst into laughter. He laughed loud and long. "Oh, god I had you going there, didn't I? You actually thought I was wavering. Admit it! You did!"

Fool's father stared at his son with his mouth open.

"I'm going to remember, for the rest of my life, what you looked like when you were pleading with me to save your skin," Fool continued between gasps of laughter. "But now I have to join my friend up here. We have quite a story to tell."

He took a step forward, and his father moved to block his path.

"You're not going anywhere. I may be ruined, but at least it won't be by the hand of my own son."

"No? Even there you're wrong."

"Am I?"

At this, Fool's father launched himself forward, grabbed his son and threw him clumsily to the ground. Fool rolled and came up as light as an acrobat, but his father lunged and grabbed his legs and pulled him back down on the ground. They stood up together and Fool's father hit his son across the face with his fist, and then hit him again in the chest. Fool collapsed to his knees.

"You're pathetic!" his father was shouting, his voice hoarse as he gasped for breath. "You've never been anything more than an incredible weakling, determined that whatever I did in the world, you would do the opposite. If I succeed, then that means you have to fail. If I work, you live on the street. But now, just this once, you and I are going to follow the same path. If this is the end for me, then at least you're going to share a little of the pain that I feel."

As Fool started to stand up, his father kicked him viciously in the chest, and he went down backwards. At that moment, I finally made it back down the hill. I grabbed Fool's father around the throat with my arm, but he twisted away with surprising strength, making me drop the folder that I was still clutching with one hand.

I bent over. With a snarl, the father swung his fist at my face, and the creature on his back leered at me with malicious triumph as the punch glanced off the side of my head, stunning me for an instant. I backed up and Fool leaped on his father's back, and while he was distracted, I punched the older man as hard as I could in the stomach, which was not nearly as hard as I wanted to, and it seemed only to make him angrier. He spun, throwing Fool off his back, and then, when Fool stood up, he kicked him again in the chest, and Fool staggered back into the shoulder of the highway. Once more, I grabbed the older man from behind and Fool came at him from the front, but the father used my weight to lift himself up and kick out with his foot, and Fool staggered backwards, across the shoulder into the highway, straight into the path of a truck.

For long seconds that seemed to stretch forever, the air was filled with a terrible, agonized sound of tires rubbing against the highway in a vain and futile effort to stop 3,700 pounds of steel moving at 70 miles an hour. Then we could hear the sound of the car behind the truck colliding with its rear, and as if in long slow motion the truck and Fool came together and Fool was knocked sideways and spun around into the other lane, where he was hit by a car that had swerved from behind to avoid the collision. The truck, meanwhile, careened into the deep shoulder of the road into the ditch, while the car behind it skidded into the lane where Fool now lay face up on the pavement and its tires ran over his legs

Fool's father and I stared at the scene, and the time distortion was over, and all I could see was Fool lying on his back and there was the sound of cars and trucks smashing into the backs of others as traffic came to a halt behind the multiple pileup.

I bent over to pick up the papers, and then ran into the roadway as drivers were getting out of their cars. I knelt down next to Fool, who looked at me with an expression of amusement.

"How are you?" I said.

He closed his eyes for a long second, and then opened them again. "It itches a little bit there in the back of my neck," he said, gasping a little to get the words out. "Otherwise, I think I'm all right."

"Call an ambulance," I called out to the small crowd behind me. "Tell them to get here fast."

"Don't bother," Fool grunted. "My spirit is already detaching from my body. It's funny," he said. "It's like I'm looking at you from below, and also from above, both at the same time. Tell me that's not pretty damn funny."

"There's nothing funnier," I said, touching his face. "Thank you."

"For what?"

"For kicking me out of the life I was leading. I owe you one."

"You owe me a lot more than just one," Fool chuckled. "But unless you can figure out how to repay me in the next three or four minutes," he added with a deep cough, "I guess this is one debt I'm going to have to forgive." His eyes took on a faraway look, and his spirit radiated the vivid white-gold color of surprise. "Oh, my," he said. "This IS going to be quite an adventure."

Fool's father was there behind me, and Fool caught sight of him. "Hey, Dad," he rasped. "Come on over here."

"You're dying," his father said.

"Come on. One last hug."

"You blame me, don't you? You blame me for everything that ever happened to you. All I wanted was the best for you."

"Make it up to me now."

Fool's father stepped closer to his son, and reached out to touch his arm. The instant his skin touched Fool's, I saw what looked like an electric surge from Fool's spirit flow rapidly into his father, a spark of white energy so bright it momentarily blinded the eyes of my spirit. Fool's father jerked back as if he'd been electrocuted, but the glow was still dancing around inside him like something alive. After a few seconds, it migrated up and through the older man's body into the enormous manticore on his shoulders, and I watched the demon grimace in agony as it twisted back and forth in an effort to detach itself. Too late, for I saw the glow spread through the creature's body like living fire.

The lion shape froze, and then, slowly, begin to dissolve into a dark misty cloud that dissipated into the air and then vanished without a trace.

Fool's father stared at us for a long second. He looked at the palms of his hands and down his body to his shoes, and back to us.

"What—" he said, but there was no way to phrase the question. He touched his face with his hands, and then looked at us again as if he was noticing us for the first time. He smiled, and his face looked oddly like a child's. For the first time, I noticed that his spirit body was tattered and full of gaps and holes.

"Thank you," Fool's father said. "For—I don't know for what," he said. He backed up, bounced into a car and, seeming not to notice it, backed up into another car. "Thank you," he said again, and began running up the hill with his cell phone on his ear.

All of a sudden, Fool's body convulsed with laughter, which ended in a long coughing choke. "It's too perfect," he gasped after a moment. "I'm here dying and he's calling his lawyer."

"What did you just do?"

"I've been wanting to get that asshole off of my Dad," Fool said to me. "Until this moment, I never knew how. A pretty handy trick." He coughed, and then gave me a weak smile. "It's amazing what you learn in the last two minutes of your life. More, I think, than the whole rest of it put together."

"Yes," I said. I heard the wail of an ambulance in the distance.

"I'm not gone, you know."

"I know."

"My spirit is awake and alive, and it's *me*. I can hardly wait to leave this body. I wish I could tell you what I'm seeing now, but it's going to be an incredible adventure. It's a million miles beyond my expectations. If I had known this, I would have looked forward to dying."

"Hang on for another minute," I said, listening for the siren to get closer.

"Do me a favor," said Fool. "It's my dying wish."

"What," I said, touching his face.

"Hurry up and make your appointment," he said, and then he closed his eyes and gave his body permission to stop functioning.

Instantly, there was a bright internal glow inside the lifeless flesh, and from it emerged a spiritual rainbow shaped roughly like a human body, that seemed much too large to have been stuffed inside the shell that had been Fool. Like a butterfly emerging from its broken cocoon, this beautiful, expansive, colorful, shimmering accumulation of intricately braided cords of holy spirit quavered in the air just over my head, hovered for a long second, and then rose up and out of sight so quickly that I was suddenly unsure I had seen it at all.

I stared up into the sky, hoping for—what? A wave goodbye? But there was nothing now but a brilliant cloud, and, somewhere behind it, the rest of the universe.

I stood up and took a long, deep breath, looking down at the body of my friend.

Fool was gone. The reality of it washed over me, the raw emotion mingled with something else. Somehow my mind superimposed the beautiful thing I had just seen with the memory of Fool's father's tattered spirit, and I understood for the first time the reality of death in this dark age of human history. I understood what I had merely known before: that some people walking the earth would die and there would be nothing left of them, while others would die and it would be the beginning of an incredible adventure.

Leave the dead to bury the dead.

I looked up, and was startled to see that Fool's body and I were surrounded by a crowd. In a kind of panic, I pushed my way through the bystanders, their somnolent spirits radiating a vague curiosity, their parasites watching me with frank hostility. Still clutching my copy of the report, I threaded my way between the tangle of cars, crossed the gravel on the shoulder and walked up the hill, wading through the thick grass and weeds. I looked back to watch the blue flashing lights of a police car picking its careful way through the maze of cars attached to each others' fenders, and behind it there was the ambulance.

Finally, when I was far enough away, I knelt down, put my head on my knee, and let the dark emotions wash over me. I cried softly, letting the tears drop straight down from my face to the grass, my back heaving with the spasms of sobs. I wanted to throw up.

Above me, a swirl of demons, no doubt attracted by the accident, gathered and circled overhead. I closed the eyes of my spirit and raised my arms up to the sky and welcomed them in. Instantly, there was an itch in my back, a tiny flash of pain, like the touch of a needle on the top of my head, an itching along my temples. A muscle in my leg twitched involuntarily. My knee felt sore. After a few more minutes, it felt as if my entire body was covered with ants, and I fed them all from an inexhaustible welling of anger and frustration and sorrow that radiated off of my body like a dark sun, giving them the feast of the ages.

I felt them cover me until there was nothing to grasp hold of, and I reared back and raised my arms to the sky and cried out from the bottom of my soul, and they drank their fill, all of them, for how long I don't know.

Finally, trembling with a deep spiritual exhaustion, I let my body fold back down, and I thought of Fool's antics, and I started to laugh. It was a tiny giggle at first, but it quickly filled the void inside me. I thought of his spirit, free of his body at last, and my spirit filled with a warm glow that quickly became a fire, and the fire was my memory of Fool, who had been my friend and who had invited me to join the gods.

My memory of Fool was a brilliant light of love and something more than love; it was the worship that all gods deserved, the thing that we owed each other, the more-than-love that would redefine all of our human connections and bring about a new age of my species.

The fire of love and more-than-love inside roared up and poured out white energy in what looked to the eyes of my spirit like living flames. The demons scattered into the air like a flock of pigeons, but they had been too late; the incandescence had struck the combustible gossamer of their talons.

With a grim pleasure, I watched the fire that was my love and more-than-love for my departed friend spread up into their bodies and consume a cloud of nightmares in a squirming bonfire, and I walked through the bonfire toward town, a god at last.

And the world had a lot to answer for.

"You're late." Tom Patterson motioned me to sit down. "Is there some reason why you didn't call?"

He had a superior smirk on his face, and on his back he carried a elfin demon with a hideous version of the same smirk. I held out my hand and he took it, thinking to shake hands, and I burned his spiritual circuits with white fire, and the troll elf was a faint stirring in the air that vanished with the breeze. Then I shook the editor's hand, and the handshake was firm and good.

"I'm sorry," I said. "It's already been a very long day. But I think you'll find that what I have to show you is well worth the wait."

I pulled out the documents and pushed them across the table as we sat down. "Once you're finished reading this, I'll repeat my offer to give you a tour of what's in the basement of that building that burned down, and you might want to bring a camera along, because nobody is going to believe it if you don't. And one more thing," I said as he opened up the file.

"What."

"Who else needs to approve your story before it goes into the paper?"

Patterson gave me a puzzled look. "Just the managing editor," he said.

"I'd like to shake his hand too, if you don't mind. You don't even have to tell him who I am."

Patterson looked back down at the papers spread out in the folder. "It's your nickel," he said.

XIX

"The peculiar arrogance of the pre-New Age society is to believe that justice should be defined in human terms, that all good deeds should be rewarded and all evil behavior be punished, in ways that can be measured and defined by logic. When we talk about the unfairnesses of life, we are really complaining that the universe doesn't conform to our expectations and linear sense of justice. Rarely do we notice that everybody's expectations are different, and that if humans were suddenly given control over the events of the universe, the workings of the cosmos would likely be as chaotic, arbitrary and mistake-prone as our criminal justice and court systems are today.

The missing ingredient is humility. In the New Age, we will begin to accept that the divine logic of justice will be forever beyond our mortal understanding, and that this is a blessing, not a curse. The Awareness that some call God sees an infinitely bigger picture, where, properly understood, hardship can be the key to personal growth, and tragedy a furnace where character is forged.

The apparent randomness of rewards and punishments, vexing as it is to our linear minds, gives us the seldom-appreciated blessings of a more interesting and unpredictable universe. The saints of the New Age will join the saints of past spiritual traditions, and see the obstacles in their path as gifts from the divine.

—From *The Rutherfordton Spiritual Gazette*

The story about the proposed nuclear power plant received front-page treatment in the *Citizen-Times* the next morning. Inside, there were additional sidebar stories on the way the facility was going to be funded. The next day, the story was picked up in the national press, and strange people with little notebooks began showing up and asking Apollo—who appointed himself as our spokesperson—a lot of questions. Later I heard that there were followup feature articles in the *New York Times*, the *Washington Post* and *Newsweek*,

Business Week and *Time*. The subject of how to reintroduce a new generation of nuclear reactors into the U.S. power grid was editorialized in the *Wall Street Journal*.

The people of Asheville were asking new questions about the small band of fugitives who, the newspaper claimed, were still living on the site of the fire. My clients were calling me, asking when the mysterious speaker was going to give his spiritual presentation, and I told them to bring everybody they knew. On each call, I warned them that it might be hard to force themselves to be here for reasons which would, I hoped, become clear once they arrived.

Tom Patterson had agreed to withhold only one piece of information from the newspaper: the fact that weapons grade Plutonium was buried under the place where the Master was going to speak. I didn't want the marines to show up and clear everybody out, and he felt like he needed to see it anyway before he reported on it. He told me he planned to be there at the back of the crowd, so we would have a chance to take a brief underground tour later.

Somehow the Master had known the instant Fool died, and so the gods and near-gods had arrived at the highway at exactly the same time as the ambulances. Fool was pronounced dead on the spot, and after the police had spent an hour of on-site investigation to determine that he had, in fact, been hit by a car that was in its proper lane, Mars talked the various medical and law enforcement authorities into allowing the body to be carried back to the warehouse, where it now lay on a bed of charcoal on the rocks at the edge of the water, surrounded by the gods and near-gods and many people from the church congregation.

People stood on the rocks, on the side of the bank or, with me, hips-deep in the rapidly flowing water, staring at the body and waiting for the Master to arrive.

Apparently, this was the first time that somebody in the group had died. Nobody was quite sure what the Master was going to do, or what the procedure was.

"We've learned that a harmony and balance can be maintained between a body and a healthy spirit, that it is possible for human beings to virtually stop the attritional aging process. We can maintain our vitality for at least a thousand years," Apollo told me. "I had assumed, without thinking much about it, that my friends here would all be with me for centuries."

"It's selfish to say this, but I hope there's a way the Master can bring him back," Venus said.

"I don't think he'd want to come back," I told them. "He saw the life he was going to live when the body and spirit were finally detached. All he could talk about was what an incredible adventure was ahead of him."

"He was probably delirious," Apollo commented.

Cassandra stepped carefully down the hill and into the water, and I moved over next to her and, after a few seconds, put my arm around her.

"You knew about this too?" I said.

"Yes. I was wondering if that makes it easier for me, the fact that I wasn't surprised. I wonder if the rest of you would feel differently about death if it wasn't always jumping out at you so unexpectedly."

"How do you feel?"

"He was in every way the most interesting of the gods. I know that the future will be a lot less fun without him around."

"Is that all?"

After a moment, she nodded. "Our response to death is always selfish. We mourn the emptiness of our future lives."

"I miss him too," I said. "I wonder if he's watching us now."

"If he is, I'll bet he's thinking how stupid we look, gathering in a circle around a random accumulation of molecules, arranging for its proper disposal in a world where creatures die by the billions every hour, untended, unmourned and without any need for a formal sendoff."

For the past few seconds, I had been aware of a stirring in the air, and now it sorted itself out into the soft, sweet sound of a flute, the notes full of happiness and expectation, the sounds dancing about us like playful ghosts, filling the air with a kind of exotic joy.

The Master appeared at the top of the hill. He walked down to stand behind Fool's body, played for a minute, then another, and when he finally took the flute from his lips, there was a great stillness and expectation in the air between us and him.

The Master looked down at the thing that had been Fool fondly, and finally shook his head, and looked up at us. I was surprised to see that there was no sadness in his spirit.

"Let us always remember, down to the end of time, that this man we called Fool was the first casualty of the most important war in the short and complicated history of our species," the Master said to us. "In the days to come, there will be more, as the parasites and their compliant hosts fight with every weapon to suppress the truth about our potential and our bondage. There are days to come," he added softly, "when each of you will envy this man for his early exit from the field."

There was a long pause while we listened to the sound of the water, which seemed to me then to be the sound of the long human story passing by this small unmarked place from the endless past toward the endless future. I bowed my head, feeling an odd mixture of strength and nervous anticipation that somehow made me stand a little straighter as I looked back over the makeshift bier that held Fool's lifeless shell.

"This," the Master continued, resting his eyes on each of us, "is the first funeral of the new age. In the future, you will see two different ceremonies of death. One kind of funeral will be defined by sadness, for those whose spirit bodies were never born into life and awareness, and now the opportunity is lost forever. We will gather to mourn the fact that a life and its precious, unique story have been extinguished forever, and there is nothing left of the person who died but a collection of holy spirit that will dissolve into the air like a fine mist.

"This, here, today, is the other kind of funeral, which will become increasingly common in the days ahead. In this celebration of death, we share our joy that a spirit has been nurtured to life among us, and has been born with its full powers out into the universe.

"You and I and every one of us carries on our spirit the imprint of the people we know and love," the Master added, raising his voice a little to be heard more clearly over the sound of the river against the rocks. "Their lives are the ingredients of our lives, and when they leave us, they leave behind the memories and experiences like cave paintings on the human condition, an artifact that lives on inside of us.

"Wherever the spirit of the man we called Fool goes, now and forever, others will see our imprints on the mosaic of his essence and they will know us through him. And so this day is also a reminder that our kindnesses and failures and all our complex relations with others is inscribed on an eternal record that we have the power, and the responsibility, to tend for all our days. In this celebration of the birth of Fool into the cosmos, we bring back and remember and more deeply imprint on our own spirits the contributions of the man whose body we are here to return to the earth."

Silently, Venus walked out of the water and stood beside the Master. After a moment, she got her tears under control.

"Fool's nickname for me was 'hag,'" she said. "He used to call me that before I knew who he was or anything about him, and at first I kind of resented it, because I don't…really…see myself that way. I couldn't figure out why everybody else thought it was so funny, until one day he challenged Mars to what he described as a 'dirty groin-kicking fight to the death,' and he—" Venus started giggling, and had to pause a moment to wipe a tear from her cheek, "—and when Mars became annoyed and came after him, Fool started sprinting around just out of his reach and yelling that Mars was a coward because he was too afraid to catch him. And when I saw Fool running for his life in a situation that was too absurd even to describe, I realized that all he wanted, all he cared about, was to puncture the arrogance that we, who were experimenting with the unbelievable power of real human potential, couldn't help but feel from time to time as we compared ourselves to the people who haven't experienced the healing. But—"

Venus began crying again, and this time it took a while for her to regain her composure. "—but," she continued, "he always wanted to put a little sugar in the medicine. He didn't want to simply teach us a lesson; he wanted it to be somehow fun and enjoyable and entertaining—and..." Venus looked up at us, all around her. "I don't know what it's going to be like without him around, but I know it won't be the same. And I know that I won't ever forget him, because he's a part of who I am now."

As Venus stepped back into the water, Apollo walked gravely up to the place next to the Master.

"His favorite word for me was 'dope,'" Apollo told the group. "And there were times, when I was around him, that I felt that way, that I would see the world through his eyes and realize that there was a great deal I was missing. He taught me, over and over again, because I was always forgetting the lesson, that all of us impose our own order on a universe that is essentially and fundamentally chaotic, and there is something wonderfully, hilariously absurd about the way we take comfort from the pretension that, somehow, our own logic describes and perhaps even controls the universal continuum.

"I remember once when Fool challenged me to a debate on the origins of all the human languages, after I had spent long weeks in the library of Asgard translating the original long-forgotten original language of the human race, what we now call the language of the spirit. And of course I was tired enough to fall into his trap, and began talking about root words that are common to many different modern tongues, and how the magnitude of the variations can be correlated with the distance in time and geography from the origins.

"When it was his turn to talk, Fool suddenly began screaming the foulest obscenities in language after language after language, and everybody but me couldn't stop laughing long enough to hear the next thing he said. And the funny thing was," said Apollo, "when I played his performance back in my head, there was a peculiar similarity in all the different ways that people of different cultures insult each other, and a consistency in their boundaries of obscenity that I never would have realized before. In other words, it was funny, but if you took the time to hear it, there was also a point to it that nobody had thought of before. There was always more to Fool than you thought there was.

"When we moved down here, Fool began referring to the warehouse as 'the palace,'" Apollo continued. "I know that some of you remember the day he was dressed in a crown and king's robes, which he must have found in a costume place somewhere, and he walked around knighting some people and giving them land grants that consisted of square yards of the parking lot outside, and ordering others to report to the dungeon for what he described as "a week or two of friendly torture." When he came to me, he demanded that I kneel down and kiss the hem of his robe. Of course, I simply ignored his foolishness, and as I walked by, he called out to me something that I will never forget. He said, 'The smartest man in the world is a fool in the eyes of the Almighty, and the only wisdom is to practice humility every chance it is offered to you.' And now," said Apollo, a tear rolling down his cheek, "I just wish I could have been the one to say that. But in the days to come, when people will be able to read spirits the way they read the newspaper today, those words will be printed across the cover page of my life experiences, and I will be forever grateful to him for sharing my life with such interest and intensity and fun."

As Apollo walked down into the water, Mars took his place.

"My cousins, I never did see why everybody else thought he was so funny," Mars told the group, his voice reaching down to the lowest octaves of human speech. "To me, he was the god who had the most power and the least. He was the only one of us who could walk by Venus without a second glance, or make Apollo feel like a fool, or remind me of my weakness in those rare times when I was stupid enough to feel invincible. Each of us could have overmatched him in a frontal assault, but I think his lesson was that you never have to offer that kind of a contest, and that when you are a mortal addressing the great forces of the universe, it would be wise to understand this lesson. I think he may be the best prepared of us all to carry his spirit into the cosmos, because he will not carry the baggage of any illusions from this mortal place where we nurture our souls for birth.

"I came to him once in an hour of distress," Mars continued, "after I had prevented a group of young men in a gang from disturbing the Master's meditations, and I had been forced to take from them their knives and heavy chains and guns. I was feeling unhappy because I had stolen from children, and I also didn't know what to do with these dangerous, dark things that I now carried about with me. And so I asked Fool for advice, sensing as I did so that it was probably a mistake.

"And Fool, without even looking at the things I carried, said that I had half of what I needed to start an army. I asked him what the other half would be, and he said 'soldiers.' And I was about to walk away, because he had not helped me in any way that I could comprehend, when he stood up and picked up a gun from the pile and aimed it at his own head, and I was horrified and snatched the gun out of his hand and smashed it on the ground, where it broke into pieces. Then he picked up a knife, and my cousins, I believe if my reflexes had been a tiny bit slower, I would not have been able to just barely prevent him from plunging the knife into his own lungs. In my anger, I broke the blade of the knife against the pavement. And then Fool looked at me, and he said, 'If you don't want them to be used the way they were intended, then why are you carrying them around?' To prevent my friend from taking his own life, I destroyed the weapons with my own hands.

"And now," said Mars, "I feel as if the world is incomplete without this man among us, and there are so many lessons that we will have to learn on our own."

I thought that would be the end of it, but then Cassandra gave me a nudge, and I walked up out of the water and stood up close to where the lifeless body—the random assortment of molecules—rested on the stones.

"For some reason, Fool welcomed me into this group," I said, "and I will never be able to express, much less repay, my gratitude for that—and his last words actually acknowledged that I owed him this debt and more. He was an ardent collector of the best examples of human folly, and he saw me as an endless provider of it. I somehow managed to become a source of amusement to him, who made it his mission to provide this same commodity to the rest of the world.

"As you know, I was with him when he died," I told the group. "Most of you know the story by now; you've read it on my spirit in more detail than words could provide. But the important thing was this: at the end, he saw things which, among us, only the Master has seen, and he was far too excited by it to feel regret that he was about to leave this body behind. I don't think he is watching us now; he left me with the clear impression that there were many more interesting things to explore in that liberated state. But in, in—in that moment, I envied him more than I could say," I said, wiping away a tear. "Because as the spirit emerged from the body, I could see that, in his years of living with all of you, he had prepared his soul to a point where he could show it without embarrassment to even the mightiest citizens of eternity, even to the Awareness of the Universe Itself.

"That has become the new goal of my life," I said. "And when I look at myself from that perspective, many other things that I thought were important suddenly fade into irrelevance. Even the Master was not able to teach me this; I owe this, the most important lesson of my life, to Fool, and everybody with the eyes to read my spirit will know that, and it is the one part of my spirit now that I am proud for everyone to see."

I walked back down into the water with my head bowed, because now, for the first time, my mind encompassed the full impact of a future life without Fool, and I felt very selfish and very alone, and the tears in my eyes made it impossible to see where I was going.

When I was back next to Cassandra, the Master stepped into the place where we all had stood.

"I see his life written in holy spirit among the living," he said, "and I can feel his presence as a part of Mommy in a way that I hope someday all of you will experience. I thought perhaps I would channel his awareness to you and give him the unique opportunity of speaking at his own funeral. But his awareness has declined the invitation, and said to me—this is the most exact quote that I can offer you in translation—that I should simply kick the body into the water and we should all get back to our lives.

"I think this may be the best advice he has ever offered us," the Master told us with a smile. "And so we return this empty shell back where it came from, retaining only the memories."

The Master placed large, flat pieces of coal on top of the body, covering everything but the face, and then he bent over and whispered something that none of us heard. I couldn't see what happened, but it seemed as if the Master touched the coals under the body with his finger, and they instantly burst into flame. For a long time, the body lay wrapped serenely in flames, and then the clothes blackened and a thick smoke began to rise up into the sky. There must have been incense mixed with the coals, because the smoke in the air smelled strangely sweet, and we watched in silence until there was nothing left but glowing embers and fragments of calcium and random molecules reduced now to ash and memories.

I walked slowly up the street toward the office, my waterlogged shoes sloshing a bit with each step. A chilly wind whipped at my damp pants legs, but I was able to turn off the sensation of cold, and it was a pleasant walk with few distractions. It took less than an hour to reach the office, and I was surprised to find so many people there on the weekend.

"What's going on?" I asked Jill.

"The market was down this week. Didn't you hear? And your customers have been calling people all over town to warn them about working with The House or anybody associated with it. Some of them have already filed lawsuits because we're telling them we can't release their money to these outside financial planners you recommended until we can do a full internal inventory of their money. The Branch Manager has ordered a complete lockdown on all assets until we can do some damage control. I'm afraid you're not very popular around here right now."

"I'll be damned," I said.

"I've been told that the minute you show your face, I'm supposed to send you straight to the Branch Manager."

"I think I'll clean out my desk first," I said.

"They've taken your computer and file drawers."

"All I really want is the picture of my wife and daughter," I said. "They didn't take that, did they?"

"If it had the name of any of your customers on it, it's probably down in legal right now. Otherwise, it's still there."

A gremlin was glaring at me from Jill's shoulder, so I reached up and touched her, and it vaporized in a quick puff of smoke.

"Can you do me a favor?" I said.

"What."

"Don't tell them I'm here just yet," I said.

Jill stood up. "I'm going to go powder my nose. If anybody asks, you came when I was away from the desk."

"Thanks. And when you come back," I said, "you'll find an envelope addressed to the Branch Manager on your desk. If you could deliver it to him—"

"Sure."

As I walked down the hall, I heard a chorus of voices from all the offices, and the voices sounded impatient and frustrated. I hurried my steps because I didn't want to hear what they were saying. I didn't care any more.

My office had never looked cleaner. The computer terminal was gone, and so were the files that usually littered my desk. The books had been taken off the shelves and laid in a neat stack, and somebody had removed my filing cabinet, which was interesting because all the client records had been kept in a separate storage room.

The picture was still on the desk, so I picked it up, and then, on impulse, sat down in the chair—which, I realized, had been my chair at the office for the past 15 years, ever since they had moved me out of the bullpen because I was infecting the financial ambitions of the other brokers. I opened various drawers in the desk, but there was nothing in there I wanted now.

Finally, I took my CFP diploma off the wall, and walked over to the window, looking out for one last time at the long view of beautiful forested hills, wreathed in the distance by a fine gray mist. I watched the clouds drag long, slow shadows along the ground beneath them, and then, when my eyes had drunk their fill, I turned for the door.

Heavy Hitter was standing in the doorway, blocking my path. He looked me up and down, noticed the wet pants, and then his eyes returned to my face and narrowed.

"We have some unfinished business," he said.

"I've decided that I'm not going to sign those papers," I told him. "Your customer killed my friend. By the time the Sunday papers come out, the world will know what's buried down there, and the power plant idea will be killed by the weight of a thousand lawsuits. But even despite all that, I think, now, that I was never going to go through with it anyway."

"Just like that?" Heavy Hitter asked me, studying my face with an expression I didn't recognize.

"Just like that."

"You know what's going on down there?" he asked me. "People are closing out their accounts by the hundreds. They're threatening lawsuits. They're asking about fees and commissions, rates of return, conflicts of interest, things they never brought up before. All because you woke up one morning and decided to poison our well."

"It was already poisoned," I said. "All I did was show a handful of people what it was like if they didn't have to drink out of it. I guess the word spread from there."

"And you're not even going to apologize."

"Actually," I said, "that was the last thing on my mind."

Heavy Hitter watched me stand my ground, and after a few seconds a transformation came over him that changed everything. It was like one of those movies where the alien is pretending to be human, and then suddenly reverts to its real shape, and the real shape is so different that you feel as if it must be magic. But this transformation could be explained in the simplest terms. He simply allowed what I saw on his spirit to curl the exaggerated geniality of his face into a dark, twisted sneer of naked hostility.

"You goddamned motherfucking son of a whore bitch—"

Heavy Hitter actually said a great deal more than that, but I found myself watching his apoplectic, purpling face and the smug certainty of the enormous spider-like demon attached to his heart. The words, which were getting louder, seemed to bounce off my ears.

Finally I stood up.

"I've never noticed," I said, more to myself than into the still sputtering torrent of words, "that I'm actually taller than you. Why would I never have noticed a thing like that?" I mused. Then, looking more closely, I saw other things. "Those dirty jokes you always told me, that was never a gesture of friendship," I said.

Heavy Hitter stopped so suddenly that I could actually hear the silence between us.

"What are you talking about?" he demanded, staring at my face with a wary intensity, as I walked around him.

"It was purely and simply to intimidate me, wasn't it?"

Silence, and the same intent stare.

"You hate me," I said, reading the truth on the tatters of his spirit. "You've hated me from the first moment I walked in the door."

"That surprises you?" Heavy Hitter said slowly.

"I don't understand it."

"I've hated you more than anybody has ever hated in the history of the world."

"Why?"

"Why?" Heavy Hitter demanded incredulously. "Why? You sit here in the office and play Mother Theresa, holier than all the rest of us, day in and day out, giving your loyalty to some higher power while the rest of us work for the benefit of The House. I could hardly walk down the hall without seeing the glow of angels coming out of your office. Why did I hate you? Because every day you walked in the front door and right through our pile of shit and not a bit of it ever stuck to your suit. You think you're too good to make money off your customers," he said. "Too good to compete with the rest of us. Too goody two-shoes to laugh at the things we find funny."

"But *you* don't find them funny," I said. "I can see now that you never did. You use them as weapons against the rest of us, and you use them to mold your clients into a greedy, exploitive view of the world, which makes it easier to sell them whatever you have. The jokes you told are and always have been nothing but tools in your hands, and you have used them well."

"Thank you," he said sarcastically.

"But I still don't understand why you should hate me," I continued, staring at the weak glow and the sparks of aura that produced it, like the dying embers of a soggy fire. "I have to piece it together, but I think it is because you—gave up your humanity in this business a long time ago, and a part of you is human enough to miss it."

"What the fuck do you know about it?" he snarled.

I wanted to say something, to find some kind of clever thought to throw in his face, but the idea that this person who had massively more status than I did would envy and hate me caused my poor mind to spiral thoughts in all directions. I thought about what I had seen in the crystal, the future world where people were measured and honored and given status, not according to their wealth, but according to how they helped others achieve this magical, enormous thing which we try to squeeze into the simple term "personal fulfillment."

By the far-off standards of that far-away day, I would have fantastically more status than the exploitive, sneaky, greedy man who occupied the highest rung of The House's production ladder.

Somehow, a distant echo of that future day had found its way back to his awareness, and had become a sharp burr under his saddle.

"The last shall be first," I said.

"What?"

"It's something I learned in Sunday School. Now I know what it means."

"You think so," he said with a snarl. "Only that was you then. This time, you're right in the middle with the rest of us."

"I told you I'm not going to sell you back the property," I said.

"Then we'll crucify you. You signed an agreement. We'll invalidate whatever sale you do make and you'll be hauled before every regulatory body we can find. The House will hang you out to dry, and I'll enjoy every second of it."

"I'm not going to sell the place at all," I said.

"Even better. In fact, *much* better. We'll foreclose on the loan and break you. We'll take your house."

"It's not yours to take," I said. "I sold it yesterday."

"To who?"

"A charity. It's going to use the insurance money to build a spiritual retreat and sanctuary, open to anybody who wants to learn how to get rid of their spiritual parasites and live the way people were intended to before things got all fouled up. They paid me $300,000 after the bank note was retired. One of my clients—somebody you cancelled an appointment with, by the way—worked with me to set it up, and his trust is providing additional funding. There's a check to pay off the loan in the mail right now."

"You think that's going to get you out of this?"

"I gave the property, the insurance policy, everything to the charity," I said. "It all happens as soon as the loan payment goes through."

Heavy Hitter stared at me. "You gave away 12 million dollars," he stated rather than asked.

"That's right."

"Rather than let us have it."

"I would rather have died than let you have it. But I'm also pretty happy with where the money went."

Heavy Hitter shook his head. "I could have brought anybody into this deal. I had to choose you, just because I wanted to see a little bit of dirt under your fingernails."

"Come out and say it. You just wanted a way to screw me."

"We'll get you yet. We'll have your license, we'll have the regulators on your ass, we'll finish your career."

"You're too late," I said. "I resigned this morning. I guess this is goodbye."

Heavy Hitter blocked my way out the door, his body frozen in a position of static, impotent rage while he looked to one side and then the other, as if he expected to find a way to destroy me in the air on either side of the doorway. As I approached him, he didn't step aside, but suddenly watched my face warily. I could read his intentions in the shreds of his spirit, however, and caught his hand before it could collide violently with the side of my neck.

Our faces were barely an inch apart, but I was no longer looking at Heavy Hitter. I was facing his spirit, whose spider eyes gleamed red and yellow, whose face twisted in a malevolent sneer that radiated a dark hatred.

For a moment, I felt the dark energy rise inside my own spirit. And then, suddenly, the godhead inside me was in charge. I sent a bolt of energy from my spirit through the nearly spiritless body whose hand I held, directly into Heavy Hitter's demon.

To my surprise, the creature never changed expression. As the bright energy passed into and through every corner of its body, as the giant phantom slowly burst into pieces, it continued to glare its defiance—a remarkable act of bravery which left a residue on my own spirit, like a fire ash as the last piece of the demon vanished in a bright flame.

I watched the place where it had been with a strange mixture of admiration and horror, and then my eyes fell on the parasiteless man in the hallway.

A change had come over Heavy Hitter's face. In slow motion, he reeled backwards against the wall in the hallway, lifting his arm across his face as if he expected to be struck. Then, his back against the wall, he finally took the hand away and stared at me with a childlike bewilderment. He moved his gaze around him, as if seeing the hallway, the building, the world for the first time.

After a while, Heavy Hitter's eyes fell back on me.

"Don't look at me like that," he said, his voice high and pleading.

"Do you want me to leave?" I asked him gently.

Heavy Hitter, what was left of him, looked down at the floor. He was trembling.

"I don't know," he said. "Will I be safe here?"

I nodded. "Yes," I said.

"I don't like this place," he said plaintively. "I have—terrible memories. Are they real?"

"Yes," I said. The childish trust in his eyes almost broke my heart.

He shook his head and looked at his feet again. I took a step closer, and he leaped back into the wall.

"I have to go," I said. "You have a lot of friends here. You remember that, don't you?"

"I don't think there's anybody here I can trust," he said, a tear forming in one eye.

"Keep that thought," I said, stepping across the doorway. "It'll get you safely through the lobby."

When I arrived back at the property, the bulldozer was gone, the work was done, and everybody was asleep.

I walked around the wooden platform, looking at the odd assortment of chairs and couches, feeling a sense of completion and contentment about everything in the universe.

We had done it. Virtually all of the debris had been moved outside of the ragged brick outlines of walls that still remained, here less than a foot high, there more than three, completely at random. On the floor, the only sign of debris was the one long irregular place where the Master had forbidden cleanup; otherwise it was perfectly clean and orderly.

The cleanliness and order of the smooth floor inside, and the devastation and chaos all around, was the perfect metaphor, I thought, for what the Master would, tomorrow morning, try to convey to whomever decided to show up.

Even though bodies were sprawled everywhere, exhausted, even though I too felt weariness down to the depth of my spirit, I couldn't sleep. I walked toward the river side of the building and stepped over the wall, climbed down to the asphalt and walked with my hands in my pockets, letting my shoes scuffle against the fine gravel that had collected on the pavement. I thought perhaps I would see Cassandra, but there was no sign of another living soul. (What a different meaning these last two words had taken on in my mind!)

Behind me, clouds passed across the moon, alternately brightening and darkening the landscape, and it felt like a war between the two, each side claiming victory and then defeat, two possibilities alternating their dominion over the scene in front of me.

I followed my shadow to the back edge of the fence and squeezed through the opening and sat down heavily on the top of the bank and looked at the stars in the empty places between the clouds, and it seemed as if the stars rather than the clouds were racing across the sky. Would I ever be able to look at the stars in the same way again?

I stared down at the dark water, and at the dancing, shimmering shadows in the air, and at that moment the scene brightened as a cloud moved off of the moon. I hummed deep inside and felt the Song of the Universe animate my bones and my spirit.

Sparkles of holy spirit danced in the air and drifted down and across my field of vision. There was something odd about it. Instead of dancing randomly in the air, the sparkles seemed to be moving together down and away, like a river of pale light. I extended my awareness and embraced the sparkles and traveled with them, my awareness carried by the flow of this ghostly river of spirit.

I was the wind and the mingling of water and air so near the river, and a bird that flitted momentarily across the river. Then suddenly, abruptly, my awareness mingled with a brilliant glow, a city of holy spirit flashing and pulsing and dazzling my awareness, and it felt as if my holy spirit was caught by a powerful magnet that was drawing down sparkles of universal awareness from all directions into itself.

I experienced a sudden overwhelming vicarious rush of the emotions that animated this citadel of holy spirit, deep, vast feelings of grief and exultation, of triumph and despair, of opposites that extended far beyond the narrow emotional bandwidth of normal human affairs.

It was an extraordinary experience, and I allowed it to wash over me, and in those moments I realized that, compared to this, I had never felt truly alive before. In this city of holy spirit, I felt all-powerful and insignificant, wise and foolish, strong and weak, for I had been god and human, and my reference points, at this moment, were oscillating back and forth and back again, and behind it all I experienced a terrible dread that was equally of success and failure, in this magnificent incomprehensible thing he was doing in the world, and a profound peace and satisfaction which extended deep into my spirit, and made it glow with shades of white.

I realized in that overwhelming maelstrom of experience why holy spirit was attracted to his spirit, that like the demons, it too was nourished by the rich diet of experience and awareness and powerful feelings.

I stood up and walked down the hill, following the course of the spiritual river to where it intersected the physical one, and then over the stones along the shore. I sat down next to the Master, who seemed once again to be an idiot, but who, I knew now, was actually reaching his soul out to the Awareness of the universe that he called Mommy.

After a moment, I put an arm around his body, which even in its vacated state was more richly alive and human than I would ever be.

A tear dropped down his cheek, and I felt tears coming to my eyes as well. I held the body close, and exuded comfort from my spirit into his, trying with the tiny imperceptible counterweight of my condolence and sympathy to tip the mighty balance inside of the Master from negative to positive, from human to divine. But the scale and range was so great that I couldn't tell whether I was successful or not, and after a while I simply sat and cradled the body in my arms and looked out at the opposite shore.

Finally, I stood up and gently disengaged myself and turned back to the embankment.

"Don't go."

The voice was so unexpected that it startled me. I turned, and the Master was back in his body. Our eyes met.

"I'd like you to stay with me, just for a few minutes," he said. "I could really use the company now."

I sat back down next to this man who I admired more than anyone I had ever met, who mystified me almost more than I could tolerate. Karen, whenever I was near to the Master, I always felt an overpowering urge to ask questions. But this time I felt drawn simply to put my arm back around him and hope that this was what he needed, this person who had given us all so much.

The wind blew, and suddenly I felt chilly. I put my hand into my pocket, and felt the strange warmth of the figurine. It actually startled me, for I had forgotten it was there.

"What's that?" the Master asked when I took it out of my pocket.

"Don't you know?"

"Let me see it."

For long seconds, the Master held the tiny red dragon in his hands, turning it over and over again.

"Where did you get this?" he asked me.

"It was a gift from a friend. I guess I'd forgotten that I was still carrying it around. Why?"

"Remarkable. This is not part of Mommy's universe," the Master said, holding it up to the moonlight. "Can you feel it? Mommy is as interested in it as I am; it's a complete surprise to the part of us that is supposed to know everything. Notice that you can't see it with your spirit eyes. It's like it's completely invisible."

I looked at the thing in his hands with the eyes of my spirit, and then looked harder. He was right; it was like there was a little patch of darkness in his hand, a shadow, nothing more.

Finally, with visible reluctance, the Master handed the figurine back to me.

"It doesn't belong here," he said. "It wants to go back."

"What do you mean?"

"This is not made of ordinary matter. It obeys different physical laws, and there is confusion around it. The universe doesn't quite know what to do with it, and it doesn't quite know how to behave in this strange place. It must have been brought here by the old gods."

"I thought there was something odd about it," I said.

"Now, for the first time, I understand why you were sent to us," the Master said to me. "This strange thing defines your destiny."

"I don't understand," I said.

"You will. But before you go, you need to reconcile with your daughter," he said.

I let my head drop just a bit and stared at the rocks along the shore.

"I'm not sure it's possible," I said. "The hurt I gave her is too deep for forgiveness."

"She knows that she gave this deep hurt to herself," the Master said. "She can carry *that* burden lightly. You must not force her to carry the additional weight that you will forever feel responsible for it."

"You know I've tried."

"Try again. You've made a good start," he said. "And then," he added, "I want you to tell the old gods something for me. Tell them that humanity is about to undo its ancient mistake, and rid itself of the parasites, and reclaim the glory of our full potential. Tell them it is time they were welcomed back, not as gods, but as equals."

"You know I don't understand a word you're saying," I said.

"Yes. But when the time comes, you will not even have to remember this conversation, for now it is written on your spirit in bold print."

"And what do I tell Karen?"

"That too is written on your spirit."

Together, we watched the water drift past. My spirit felt the glow of his presence like a warm hearth, and it responded with a warmth of its own, although I could feel the pain and confusion behind it, like a wound that cannot heal. Thinking about Karen, I felt the same way, and this sense of shared pain deepened the connection.

I began to hum the Song of the Universe quietly to both of us, and it seemed as if I and the Master and the rock and the water vibrated together, and that the boundaries between us blurred, so that it would have been hard for any of us to tell where one ended and another began.

I settled on the precise pitch which defined comfort and a deep satisfaction, feeling deeply satisfied myself, feeling privileged that I could return this small gift, and the Song resonated deeper and somehow stronger inside us, the rock, the water.

After a few minutes, the moon emerged from the back of the clouds, and I saw that the sky was now clear and the brightness stayed with us.

"You saw what I was feeling," the Master said finally, his voice soft in the wind.

"If you succeed in passing on this information and advice, they might simply create a new religion and worship you," I said. "And you'd have to live with that for eternity."

"And if I fail—"

"Either way, we'll muddle along as we always have. You said yourself that we are all beautiful and perfect and loved by the only Awareness that really matters. It's true isn't it?" I asked after a minute.

"Yes. Those are the truest words that have ever been spoken by human lips. It's amazing that we can fit so much truth in the poor limited language we have available to us."

"Then it really doesn't matter so much," I decided.

The Master said nothing for what seemed like a long time, staring down at his hands.

"I have seen that every human decision has incredible power," he said at last. "Every choice you or I or anyone else makes, no matter how small and thoughtless, embraces one future and destroys a hundred million possible others, for all of us. I am simply one of billions with this power over the future, but I have enormous respect for it. And tonight it fills me with more fear than I think I can handle."

We sat for a long minute, and then the Master spoke again.

"If this moment is remembered and recorded," he said, "then they will say that I was afraid of death. But I tell you now, for the world to hear, that this other fear is infinitely greater."

"Death?" I said.

The Master smiled and threw his arm around my shoulders. "I'm just trying to cheer you up," he said.

"You were out there with…It, the everything. And then you came back to be with me."

"Yes."

"Why?"

"Every person's life is ultimately tragic," he said. "The only truly important mission in life is to change that."

My mind stopped for a second while something behind it located those familiar words. "That was you," I said. "I mean, when I first came into the room and saw you and thought you were nothing more than a helpless cripple, that was your message for me—"

"Every message that matters is a note from your greater self to your mortal self that is miraculously not mistranslated in the journey," the Master said. "I was proud to be there when you said those words to yourself, and felt the rightness of them echo out to forever and back."

"So you came back because of something you overheard in my mind?"

"This world is an unbelievably beautiful place, and it is home." The Master's voice carried softly over the water. "Whatever I am, whatever I become, I am of this place, this illusion I had the privilege of sharing with so many others. And sometimes I feel like I am the only one who can see its spectacular magnificence. I wanted to take a long, deep drink of it before tomorrow."

"You're going to leave us," I said.

"Yes."

"Why?"

The Master shrugged and said nothing.

"Everybody will want to see what you have to say. I think everybody should get that chance."

"They will," he said. "You've seen it yourself."

"I mean right now. Look at all the confusion, all the suffering and unhappiness, all the people who don't even realize that they have a hunger for the things that you know and could tell them."

"And you think I'd be withholding this message from them."

"Every one of them who dies without a chance of hearing the things that you've taught and shown us, is a crime on your shoulders."

The wind blew across our faces. The Master's face became a shadow. I wondered how I had the courage to say this very strong thing to this person who was in every way my superior, but I also felt that it absolutely had to be said by somebody, and this might be the last chance for my species to communicate this important thing to the animated part of the universe.

Then I saw that tears were dripping down the Master's face. The sight froze my heart with something that was as much fear as sympathy. I drew him close to me.

"I'm sorry," I said.

"It's going to be so hard for you," he said. "And I can't do anything about it. I can't even warn you of how hard it's going to be."

"What do you mean?"

"Why do you think Jesus died?" the Master asked me.

The question was so unexpected, I had to stop for a second. "What do you mean? He was killed."

"I've watched the records of his life forwards and backwards. Of all the people whose days are recorded in the library of Asgard, I've spent more time with his than any other. And as you watch it, you realize that he could have spread his message outside of Jerusalem for a thousand years. He would have lived that long or longer, and any attempt to capture or kill him would have been plainly visible in the mosaic of spirits around him. Even after they had fixed him on the cross, he could have simply pulled his body to Asgard in the most dramatic vanishing act in history, and then continued his ministry with the scars to show every future audience what the leaders and authorities of this world thought of his message."

"I think I knew that," I said after a moment. "I think we all know that."

"So the question remains: why did he die?"

"I don't know."

"For a long time, I didn't either," the Master said. "I ran the records of his life backward and forward, looking for answers. So much of what they recorded of his life in our holy books is hopelessly garbled, because he spoke not in their language, but in the language of the spirit, and the accounts we have were translated once from that language into another, and then again into another, and now it is translated into English and we think we know exactly what was said, and the self-proclaimed authorities comb the text with fine precision and magnify the inevitable transcription errors into dogma.

"But some of what survived is very close to what he said. He really did say something very close to what is recorded in the book of John: *If I don't do the work of Abba, then you shouldn't believe me. But if I do, even if you don't believe that I have authority to represent Him, believe the things you see me do and believe the things I tell you.*

"I watched him in the garden, praying, the night before they took him away," the Master continued. "It was the first time he had looked at his life in the context of the deep future, and now he saw, for the first time, that they would make him a god and discard the details of his message. That night, looking forward, he saw that millions would pray to him thinking that this was what he wanted, and they would simply believe that he would take care of everything for them, instead of putting the things he had learned into the context of their lives. He winced, and I imagined that he was seeing congregations being told that Jesus is the answer, that all you have to do is believe in his divinity and everything else will fall into place on its own.

"I saw that the words he spoke that night in prayer were different from those that were recorded in the scriptures of the faith that was named for him. It was understandable; the disciples, instead of praying, watched him weeping openly, and later they must have told whoever wrote the account of that night that he was praying to save his own life, to have the proverbial cup of poison removed from his lips.

"But in the library of Asgard, you can see that he hoped for nothing more than to undo this damage. He asked to have people focus their attention not on him but on his message. He asked the golden dust of holy spirit that extended out from his spirit body throughout the fabric of the universe to share its universal wisdom, and help him undo what he now saw as a terrible mistake, help him to take himself, the person who delivered the message, completely out of the story altogether.

"I watched him pray in the garden, and I saw that this was a moment of strength, not weakness, so different from what his disciples must have thought. His tears had nothing to do with his own death. He cried because he realized, too late, that he had taken what seemed like a harmless shortcut; he had asked people who could not bring themselves to believe that they were capable of becoming a part of Abba to simply trust him, and if they did, then they could follow his instructions. The enormity of that mistake! You, sitting here, cannot see what he learned from his contact with Abba, but I think he must have thought that the crucifixion, the total destruction of the person who delivered the message, in the most public possible way, might someday communicate to the people of his world and all future generations that the thing which delivered the message was not important, was something to cast aside.

"For twenty centuries, the cross would be the opposite symbol of what he intended. And then the world—our world—would wake up to its real meaning, and they would honor him all the more for it, for the bravery of that last act that was all he could do to focus our attention back on what was important about him. He was trying to tell us not to worship him, but to worship and cherish the wisdom that he had found for all of us.

"And here I was, with some of the same information he had, and a chance not to repeat what that great and important person regarded as his biggest mistake," the Master said. "I realized that what the world needed, more than anything else, was a message with no sender."

And then he was quiet, and his words were carried off by the wind, and we looked down into the water and across to the other side, where glimmers of reflected moonlight stirred like bits of white magic on the far side of the river.

Karen, what could I do? I had no answer for him, nothing to challenge his conclusion except my own anticipatory feeling of loss, my own selfish desire to keep him here so I would have somebody handy to answer questions whose solutions were found in the fabric of holy spirit itself. I wanted the shortcut more than I have ever wanted anything, but I was in that moment noble enough not to ask for it again.

Karen, in the minutes that followed on this moonlit night, I managed to see my surroundings through the Master's eyes. The myriad ripples of the water and the ways it reflected the moon, the menagerie of plants and their intricate leaves, the rocks and the way they had anchored themselves just so into the ground in a long mutual accommodation with the soil and the water, the second-by-second miracle of life and existence and the miracle of me and my senses there to appreciate it—all of this filled me to overflow with a kind of tenderness that threatened to burst out and scatter me across the sky.

Tears cascaded down my cheeks. The Master quietly put his arm around me and drew me close, and it felt like he was my mommy, and I was his, two sparks of awareness clinging to each other for a bit of warmth and comfort, waiting for the dawn.

X X

Since we are given the gift of life, let us accept it wholeheartedly and with gratitude and appreciation—exactly as we ourselves would like others to respond when we give them gifts of infinitely lesser value. At a minimum, we must treat our lives and the lives of others (for they too are gifts from the Awareness that some call God) with care and respect and appreciation.

The citizen of the New Age will ask a new question about this transaction that so many take for granted: Is it possible that we can go one step further, and give back something in return? Only one thing could possibly have equal value: to accept the blank canvas of our lives and make sure that each day we fill it with the most interesting, joyful, entertaining and fulfilling story we can manufacture in our life experiences.

Our mission, our goal, is to create a life story of such richness that when it is finished, it can be displayed in the gallery of the Almighty.
—From The Rutherfordton Spiritual Gazette

It was still before dawn when I returned to the warehouse, and already people had arrived and were staking out chairs near the front of the platform. I kept looking around for the police, but there was no sign of anybody in uniform.

As I walked along the side of the platform, the TV camera crews were unloading their equipment, and Apollo was alternately helping and suggesting with growing insistence that they take a walk down by the river. It was becoming increasingly clear that the camera crew people didn't want to leave their equipment unsupervised and had no interest in the river, and Apollo began to raise his voice when I walked over.

"Maybe I can help. My name is Proteus," I said, offering my hand to one of the camera men. After a moment's hesitation, he shook hands with me, and I sent a jolt of white loving energy through him and into the witch who was clutching the base of his spine. She dissolved with a scream that could not be heard by physical ears. I shook the other camera man's hand and a nasty-faced gremlin disappeared in a puff of spiritual flame.

"Nice trick," Apollo commented.

Behind us, Orpheus was testing the microphone and the speakers. Finally he sat down and drew a long, haunting mysterious sound out of his guitar that modulated with the same subtlety as the Song of the Universe itself before it settled back into the background of a ballad I had not heard before.

Take my hand, for the time has come.
    There's no more time left
To fight against your future,
    No time left
To jealously protect
    The worst of your many flaws.
Raise your voice with mine
    And call into the air
The spirit of our endless cause
    And lift forever the patterned curtain of despair.
This is the time when angels rush in ahead
Into the sacred spaces where fools rightly fear to tread.

    Follow me across the ages,
      Through the lines of a thousand pages.
    From world to world, I dry the tears,
      I raise the hopes and calm the fears.
    To see the world through different eyes,
      And raise your soul beyond the skies,
    The echoes of my cosmic trail
      Are holy books and holy grails.

By now, it was becoming difficult to move around, there were so many people here, and more were streaming down from either end of the street. Karen, I scanned the crowd, hoping to see your face. Were you there? And where were the police? Looking for Tom Patterson, I found Alice Gray sitting on a couch in the back, and the sight was so unexpected that I had to stop and look again.

"You don't have to be so surprised," she said with a smile. "You invited me, didn't you?"

Walk with me, for I am alone.
    It is growing too late
For the endless stale regrets
    Far too late
To escape the white light
    We knew before our first day.
It is only in the final hour
    That we can live for tomorrow,
Without losing hope that we might die for today,
    And give death an honored place at the table.
Don't come to me for the secret of life;
I'm here to light the world on fire.

    Follow me across the ages,
      Through the lines of a thousand pages.
    From world to world, I dry the tears,
      I raise the hopes and calm the fears.
    To see the world through different eyes,
      And raise your soul beyond the skies,
    The echoes of my cosmic trail
      Are holy books and holy grails.

"Did you bring Nathaniel? There's a chance we could exorcise his demons later this afternoon."

"I'm off-duty today. But I did," she said, "have the pleasure of bringing the books we ordered down to the library on Friday. Some of the other teachers have been talking it up, and we're starting to get donations to do the same thing for other schools in the area, from friends and parents of students and even some ex-students who wish they could have been exposed to this or that book at a younger age. The Wonderful Books Fund is taking on a life of its own. I'm thinking now that we could make a presentation at the next national teacher's conference. Why should a great idea like this be confined to Asheville?"

"Actually, I have some news for you, but it can wait," I said.

"About what?"

"I just set up a lead trust for a very wealthy client, and we decided that some of the cash flow—which has to go into some charitable cause or another—should go into your fund."

"Enough to buy books for another school?"

"I think the best estimate we could come up with was $13 million a year."
"What!?"
"He really liked the idea. Oh, and he has a couple of books to add to the list."

She stared into my face for a long second. "I'd love to hear them," she said finally.

Suddenly, she jumped to her feet and embraced me, and I embraced her back, and found myself face to face with her demon, which was actually a pleasant-looking elf who responded to my attention without any sign of resentment. It was the most benign parasite I had yet seen; more of a symbiotic partner than the soul-sucking monsters I had grown accustomed to. After it was dissolved in fire, I wondered briefly if I had done the right thing.

Truth scatters the darkness.
    Look between emptiness,
And see the flash that binds.
    Look hard at nothing
And I will show you the difference
    Between your flashlight and the cosmic rays.
For there is so much we have to unlearn
    And now so little time.
To have everything, and give it all away;
    To live from eon to eon out to infinity,
Traveling from crucifixion to crucifixion
On a one-way ticket across the stars...

    Follow me across the ages,
      Through the lines of a thousand pages.
    From world to world, I dry the tears,
      I raise the hopes and calm the fears.
    To see the world through different eyes,
      And raise your soul beyond the skies,
    The echoes of my cosmic trail
      Are holy books and holy grails.

"I hear you've been calling other customers of The House," I said after the song had died away in the air.

"I'm not quite as zealous as some of the others," she said with a short laugh. "I think the Coddingtons alone have called everybody in the city."

At that moment I spotted Patterson, standing on the side of the hill across the street, obviously trying to count the crowd. But where were the police?

"I have to go," I said. "Don't go anywhere; you aren't going to want to miss this."

"I trust you," Alice said, and I could see from her spirit that she did.

"What do you think?" I asked Patterson.

"I think I should have been paid for providing you with all this publicity," he said. "I still can't believe you're not in jail."

"The police have been by at least twelve times, although I can't figure out where they are now. The man you're about to hear is incredibly persuasive. You'll find out for yourself. Compared to what you're going to see," I said, "the plutonium is nothing."

"So far, you're the best source I've ever had," he said, looking me carefully in the face. "So I'm going to go out on a limb and take your word for it."

I left him alone, because I had spotted one more person that I knew. I pushed my way through a crowd that had become so thick that it reminded me of the base of the stage at a rock music concert, allowing myself to be pushed off-course occasionally and then correcting as best I could.

By a weird coincidence, I bumped into Ellen Moore, who turned in annoyance and then recognized me and seemed a great deal less annoyed.

"I'm surprised to see you here," I said.

"Are you kidding? *Everybody's* here."

"It seems like you'd have a better view from your second-floor window."

"I'm here to hear the words," she said. "After I saw what you did to those goons the other day, I decided there must be something going on that I need to know more about. And thank you, by the way. I wouldn't be alive if it wasn't for you."

"I wish you could have met the Master personally."

"This," she said, "is going to be the next best thing."

It took me another five minutes to reach the place near the platform where the Big Score stood surrounded by Zho and a dozen other people from his office, who held back the crowd on all sides and managed to give him a little space. He shook my hand warmly with a slight bow.

"You were right about this man, and the things he could tell me," he said, shouting a little to get over the noise of the crowd. "Now I am doubly in your debt. It is," he added with a laugh, "something of an unfamiliar feeling for me."

"I think maybe you'll at once get more out of this than anyone else and less," I said. "Nothing he says will surprise you, but you will perhaps drink it in more deeply than the others here."

He bowed slightly. "I am honored that you would think so," he said. Then he looked at me curiously. "But don't you have to be somewhere now?"

"Yes," I said, pressing his hand one last time.

I pushed my way up to the corner of the stage and behind it, where suddenly I was free to move around. I rounded the side of the podium, looking this way and that, finally finding Apollo further down along the back, and a man with disheveled black hair standing next to him. I recognized his sleepless eyes immediately, but when I stood in front of him, the eyes seemed not to see me. They stared with mild interest at the molecules a few inches in front of his face.

"Where's the Master?" I asked Apollo.

"If a little knowledge is dangerous, where is the man who has so much as to be out of danger? T. H. Huxley. He was here a minute ago," he said, indicating the investigator with a nod of his head. "The truth is, I've been too busy to keep track of him."

"Maybe he'll materialize right out of Asgard. That would get their attention."

"It would be a cheap trick," said Apollo. *"It is always the secure who are humble.* G. K. Chesterton."

The investigator's eyes were still staring in my direction. I waved my hand in front of his face, but he didn't blink.

"He's very persuasive, isn't he?" I said.

"Yes." The voice sounded very far away. Suddenly I knew what happened to the police. I shook my head. The Master had exceeded my expectations all over again.

"What did he tell you?" I asked.

The investigator turned his sleepless eyes on me, and there was still not a hint of recognition. Only a distant sense of wonder.

"He told me I was in the wrong business," he said, "He said that *the systems of justice attack the symptoms and support the disease in equal measure.*"

Behind me, so low that I wasn't consciously aware of it, the soft music of a flute began filling the air with a kind of trembling, a preconscious stirring of awareness.

An awakening.

As I looked past the investigator out at the audience, I could now see two crowds: the physical one, and the motley assortment of spiritual parasites who clutched their hosts in manifest disapproval and turned faces sulkily to where the Master was preparing to speak. As I was looking over this second crowd, I noticed a darkness behind it, and looking up I saw, rising majestically above the rest, the dark spirit that belonged to the evangelist—or was it the other way around?

With a growing sense of fear, my eyes moved from its face down its massive body, trying to pick out the person in the crowd that it was perched on. A part of my mind wondered what it was doing here, but the mind of my spirit already knew. This thing, going on right now, was going to be the most important spiritual event in many many generations of the human species. We were here to break free of the invisible overlords who had mastered humanity, and the most senior overlords were gathered to prevent our little uprising.

Looking up at the complacent face of the largest of the demons, I felt very small and helpless, and for some reason tears filled my eyes. I could not imagine what the Master was about to do, but I had the sudden feeling that he was outmatched from the start, and they, the demons, knew it.

By now, the flute's melody was casually snaring the attention of the audience, and riveting it to the interplay of notes and emotions, of sadness and beauty, of hope and the mournful desperation that was never visible and never very far from the human consciousness, the sounds and the feelings somehow mixed together into something that defined beauty in the air around us, a prelude to the Song of the Universe and then a tantalizing glimpse of it, of something incomparably greater than our tiny lives.

The Master stepped onto the platform, walked up to the microphone and looked out at the crowd. The members of the audience got their first good look at that remarkable, unforgettable face, and even the faces of the parasites fell into a stunned silence.

Looking at him now, I suddenly stood a little straighter, a little prouder.

Yes, I thought to myself, wiping the wetness out of my eye. He is a match for them. For all of them.

Once again, the Master raised the flute to his lips, and this time it felt as if the song reached into my heart and held it gently, spreading a kind of warmth from the center of my body outward to my limbs, making me tingle as the music seemed to articulate the song of my life, and hint at the magic and mystery that my life could become.

Wake up, it called to me, and even though I was already awake in a way that the audience was not, it seemed as if the world looked a little brighter and more vivid, the sounds of the wind and the music and my own thoughts mingling into a symphony that was suggested and encouraged by the notes of the flute as it defined sadness and despair, then up the scale to an inexpressible joy and expectation.

Then silence, so absolute that I thought perhaps the audience might have been frozen into rock.

And then the voice.

"It is long past time to thank you for accepting our invitation," The Master said quietly, the voice conveying humility and gratitude and an underlying modular power that carried his words all the way to the back. "Your presence, here, today, is a gift more precious to me than anything I have ever received in my time on this earth. In return, I hope that *you* will accept a gift or two," he said. "These will be gifts straight from the Almighty Awareness of our universe, who watches you now through my eyes, and watches me through yours. I know, because that Awareness knows, that when I am finished speaking, this will have become a day that all of you will remember and treasure for the rest of your lives—and, for many of you, beyond."

The Master raised his voice with these last words, because suddenly he had competition. The famous man in the back of the audience was shouting at the top of his voice.

"His words are the words of the devil. Pay no attention to him!" the evangelist was shouting, and there was a stir of approval among the audience of parasites, like a wind passing through tall grass. "If you value your eternal soul," he shouted, "you will follow me right now away from this place, away from this blasphemer who will lead you astray from the righteousness of God and the true message of Jesus."

Karen, for some reason I expected the Master to answer this charge. Instead, he waited for the evangelist to finish, and then he said in a voice that was somehow quieter and yet far more clear and powerful: "As you can see, we have people here among us who want to silence me and kill my message. This man is asking you not to listen even before he knows what I'm going to say. I say to you now," he called out, raising his voice so that I could swear I heard it echo in the still air, "that when the history of this dark era is written, what they will remember first is that thousands of people who never knew the Almighty presumed to teach on His behalf, and thousands of people who never saw the Almighty presumed to tell others how to reach him.

"You know this, already, on some level. You know this in the place where you have hunches that turn out to be true. These are the thoughts of your spirit, and I can tell you that there are those among us who are deathly afraid that your spirits will come alive, because your spirits will give you insights and information that they cannot control."

"Do you deny that you're a false prophet?" the evangelist screamed out, his face twisted into a smug, eerily confident grimace. "I say that the earth will swallow you up for your blasphemies."

"Forgive me for not answering this person," the Master said to the audience. "I was at his sermon a few days ago, where I heard him make one false statement after another, yet I did not presume to interrupt him. Those of you who are more interested in what he has to say, you are invited now to leave the presence of the Almighty and follow him and hear his comfortable lies. For I tell you now that the things you will hear here today, and the things that you will hear later when my sermon is over, will be suppressed, fought against, burned and rejected by a coalition of the invisible enemy through their hosts, who will oppose the key to their own freedom and never know why."

The giant parasite, like a dark god, towered triumphantly over the scene as the evangelist pushed his way through the back edges of the crowd toward the street, still shouting that the Master was evil. He reached the street and walked away from the crowd, and when he turned, there was an expression of surprise on his face, for nobody had followed him, not even—I could see from their spirits—other ministers of various denominations who had come to see for themselves this message of the spirit.

The Master spoke again, and now there was no distraction, no wavering of attention. "We are here," he said, "to recover our birthright as citizens of the planet and of the universe. It is time now to wake up from a dream, a dream of life that is different from life itself, a dream where you believe that you have to live in drudgery, a slave to the agendas of others, that you cannot be free and joyful and alive and aware with all your senses of the miracle that surrounds us and which was created for your appreciation. Open your eyes, and stretch, and look around, and for the first time really listen to that part of you that knows so much, and realize what it is to be human, what it means to be a citizen of this beautiful world, in this remarkable universe, what it means to be alive and aware and blessed with the freedom to follow your own destiny without interference from the world."

And then the Master talked about what it was to be human and alive. He talked about the joy of feeling a gentle wind in your face on a warm spring day when it carries the smell of new-cut grass and the first flowers are bursting into bloom, and he made us remember the cold elegance of the stars shining out of the velvet sky on a clear night.

His words brought back the magical feeling of a child walking through the forest, the tingling of your bare toes in a cold stream and the warmth of ocean waves as you watch the long sparkling reflection of the sun on the distant horizon, casting its inverse shadow from the edge of the world to the bright sparkles of reflection at your feet.

As he spoke, our hearts recalled the green of the forest and the blue of the water and sky, and the gentle awareness that flows into and through the earth and the sky and the bodies of all living things, the dance of life with air and earth and water and sky and itself most of all, the sweetness of love between two people and the connection of love between here and the most distant corners of the universe and everywhere in between in all directions and everywhere that IS a where, and at his words holy spirit descended from the sky like a slow rain of magic dust and fell down on the audience, and the demons leaped off their hosts like a flock of startled birds.

Karen, I know you have seen the footage of this speech, because the camera men captured it all, and because parts of it were shown on TV news all over the country for many days thereafter. Like everybody else, I am sure you were puzzled to hear the mysterious man on the podium speaking in an unfamiliar language, and even more puzzled to see, when the camera panned to the crowd, that English-speaking people were hanging on his every word, so intensely that it seemed as if they were in a kind of trance.

Later I learned that he was speaking the language that all people had once spoken during their long residence on Asgard, and I saw that there were members of the audience who did not understand what he was saying, who backed off from the rest and walked away in confusion. With the eyes of my spirit, I saw that these people all had one thing in common: their spirit bodies were in tatters, and all of them lacked spiritual ears. It brought back to me a scrap of something I remembered from Sunday School, when the teacher stood on the shores of the Sea of Galilee and said to the audience, 'let he who has ears to hear...' For the first time, I understood the literalness of his expression. He, too, must have been talking directly to the spirits of audiences 20 centuries ago.

But there is so much you cannot see on the news footage. The camera did not show how the color of the spirits of the people in the audience moved from the dark end of the spectrum to the light. The Master extended his hand, and the ambient holy spirit that was everywhere around us moved visibly and settled into the audience, and the brightness of their glows intensified. The spirit bodies of the people in the audience were healed of their gaps and omissions. Holy spirit sought the experiences that the Master was placing in their souls, and missing spiritual limbs, feet, fingers, skin and spiritual organs appeared where they had not been before, in a process that looked to my eyes like a kind of reverse melting.

And after the healing, one by one, the spiritual eyes would open, and spirits by the hundreds came awake, alive, born and aware of their connection with divinity.

Karen, I can say with certainty that I will never see a more remarkable, more glorious thing than this baptism with holy spirit. And as the dust fell and the glows intensified on the white end of the spectrum, a thousand demons in all their forms and shapes shrieked and scattered and reformed into a cloud of dream and nightmare in the sky above where we were standing.

As I looked up, I saw that the evangelist had returned. For a long moment, his towering parasite drew itself up in static rage, and then I saw a commotion up the side of the hill across the street, and noticed at the same moment that Mars had disappeared from the back of the podium. The commotion ended almost as abruptly as it began, and I saw from afar that Mars had disarmed and apparently rendered unconscious a group of people who had been planning some kind of attack. He held aloft a silver tube which I later learned was a rocket launcher that had been brought for the purpose of killing the Master.

I looked up at the giant demon to see its reaction, expecting it to exhibit a towering discouragement.

What I saw instead froze my blood. The dark creature raised its wings in wild triumph, its face gleaming with a terrible facsimile of joy, and a part of my spirit recoiled in fear at what this had to mean.

I took an involuntary step backward to the edge of the platform and stared back at the Master, who was looking up calmly at the creature in the sky, facing his nemesis without a trace of concern on his face.

I read the Master's spirit, and suddenly, before my body had even understood what my spirit had seen, I was running across the concrete floor toward the back of the ruins.

At the hole in the floor, I found a rope ladder, attached to the far wall. Karen, I have read that physically-ordinary people, in the full force of an adrenalin rush, can lift the back of an automobile or fight off a lion in the wild. I have never seen these things. All I know for sure is that out of the endless fear that now filled my body from toes to forehead to the far edges of my spirit, I was able to leap across the chasm and close my fingers over the rope ladder eight feet below the surface and drop hand over hand at approximately the speed of falling. I swung inside to the ground on a dead run, my feet splashing in invisible puddles.

As I felt I was getting close to the far wall, I slowed down, waiting for the glow of the containment tanks to give me some ghostly light to navigate by. But everything was in total darkness, and I blundered against the roughness of hewn rock and pushed left, moving slowly now because I was afraid with each step that I would drop unexpectedly into the deep cement containers.

And then, unexpectedly, I could see again. In this darkness, the eyes of my spirit took over, and I saw, in a dim way, that the containment tanks had been emptied of water. Looking down, I saw the pale, incomplete patchwork of Fool's father's spirit down among the rods. I could hardly see it for all the demons that were attached to him at various angles, witches and evil-faced fairies, trolls and dwarfs, and a vampire who gazed up at me hungrily.

I would have shouted, but at that moment, there was no breath in my heaving lungs. I moved to the edge of the pit and knelt down, taking in deep gulps of air.

"Who's there?" Fool's father's voice echoed strangely out of the bottom of the first tank.

I didn't answer. I took another deep breath and looked for a way to get down to the bottom of the tank.

"I asked you a question," the voice came up mildly from the basin. "It is impolite not to answer."

"I am Proteus," I said finally. "You know me as Adam Zakkar."

"What an interesting coincidence," the incomplete patchwork ghost body mused, and there was a terrible amusement in the voice. "I have not prayed since I was a very young child," it continued. "But just a few seconds ago, I said a prayer that you would be nearby when I killed that son of a bitch up top. Now you're here. I wonder if that means that the God he's nattering on about is actually in my corner today."

"What are you doing?" I demanded, making my way along the edge.

"Oh, I think you have ways of knowing," the voice said. "I confess that I will never understand these things. Perhaps you can tell me about them while I finish up down here."

As he talked, I could also hear the sound of a tube rolling along the floor, and my panic increased.

"Can't we talk about this?" I called down.

"I doubt we have much time, but the work down here doesn't really prevent me from conversation. What's on your mind?"

There was the sound of another tube rolling across the floor.

"I want you to reconsider what you're doing, in the name of your son," I said, groping along the side of the tank's walls with more urgency.

"How very persuasive," the voice continued. "My son, who would have been alive except for this Master, as you call him, who stole his loyalty away from me, would have been more concerned about *his* life up there than mine down here—is that what you're trying to say?"

"He would have hated you for the thing you're doing now."

"That would have been such a change from our relationship these past three years," the drippingly ironic voice echoed back to me over the sound of another rolling tube. "You know, these things are a great deal heavier than I remember them. I had so few people that I could trust back then, so I did much of the work myself down here. You might be surprised how much they were willing to pay for what seemed at the time like a perfectly safe storage contract, and I was such a boy scout, I structured the contract so the money flowed back into the company, although of course we arranged everything so that it looked to the outside auditors like I had increased our operating profits. It was this contract, the way it juiced up the earnings of our sleepy little division, which got me the attention I needed to start up the ladder."

As Fool's father rambled on, I was failing to find any sign of a ladder or other means to get down to his level. Finally, I pulled myself over the side and hung by my hands, knowing the bottom must be 30 feet down at least. Then I allowed my fingers to slip, and held them tightly against the irregular concrete surface of the wall, hoping the friction of concrete against my fingers and toes would slow me down enough that the fall wouldn't kill me. I slid down along the side of the wall at an increasing rate of speed, and landed hard on the balls of my feet, falling backwards and rolling. My fingers were wet with blood. It felt as if they had been touched by fire.

"I don't believe I invited you to come down and join me," the voice remonstrated calmly, over the sound of another tube rolling along.

I stood up. I had one small advantage; I was able to see the patchwork glow of my adversary and was certain, based on the evidence of my physical eyes, that he couldn't possibly see me. The darkness was so complete that I discovered a new thing about my spiritual eyes, that they could see the physical world, that through them I could get a dim sense of the ground in front of me, and perhaps 12 of the long rods piled up against each other along the far side of the containment area. Now that I was on the floor, I could feel heat coming from that direction.

"You realize you're already too late," the voice continued with infuriating calmness, and I ran toward it, saw that he had rolled six more rods into a second pile at the center of the chamber, and was now tying them together with a rope. As I moved slowly forward, still feeling my way and not quite trusting my spirit eyes, the increasing heat of these six rods on my body felt like a barrier that I had to push through as I threw myself forward, lunging my shoulder into the dim ghostly figure above the rods, throwing him over backwards with a surprised grunt of air forced out of his lungs.

He let go of the rope and lay on the ground, gasping, and in that moment I thought that I had won, that I had managed to rescue the life of the Master and my friends and thousands of other people listening to the sermon above us. The demons all hissed at me from the ground. I touched them with a loving hand and they scattered in all directions, some flying up toward the ceiling, others spreading out in the chamber. There was a long gasp from the man on the ground, but astonishingly, his spirit colors didn't change at all. This time, losing the demonic influence seemed to have no effect on him.

"You want to die?" I demanded, standing over Fool's father.

"I am already dead in more ways than one," he said, still in that infuriatingly mild voice. "All I want now is to kill you and that monster upstairs who stole my son from me."

"You know that he didn't steal him or anyone else," I said. "Fool chose us over you, and from what I can see here, it was a great decision."

The patchwork ghost shrugged, pulling itself to a sitting position. Slowly, he stood up, and I was ready to knock him down again, but he backed away from the glow and held his hands up and out over his shoulders in a gesture of surrender, facing slightly to my left, which told me he still couldn't see me.

Dismissing him from my mind for the moment, I reached down for the rope and started to drag the pile away from the direction of the glowing patch at the far side of the wall. It was amazingly heavy, a huge dead weight that seemed to have grown roots in the concrete floor. My hands, slippery with blood, were unable to keep their grip.

Suddenly, there was a dark and raspy movement swirling in the air around my head like an enormous bat, its glow leaving trails in the air. Instinctively, I warded it off with my arm, but of course my arm passed right through it, and it turned and hovered in front of my face, a malicious leprechaun with a green hat, staring into my face with an odd confidence.

Somewhere deep in my spirit, I felt a scream shaking my body, and a shock of awareness erupted from my spirit into my mind, a frantic communication from the insubstantial ghost which lived inside me, and it took a few seconds for the message to penetrate the poor, sluggish confusion of my conscious awareness.

Finally, the contact was complete, the message delivered, and I stared at the Leprechaun's cocky leering face with a mixture of horror and fear.

The creature extended an impossibly long arm and I felt a prick where its claw entered my forehead, but the rest of it remained hovering in front of my eyes.

"You recognize me. You have always known me. I've missed you these last few days," it said with mocking tenderness.

It was my voice, the voice I had always assumed was mine when I talked to myself as a child, and later as my wiser self when I was an adult. I knew that voice that spoke now in my mind more intimately than I knew the sound of the words that came out of my own physical mouth.

As I watched the lips of the creature move to the sound of my own voice in my own mind, a new horror seized me, a fear that was deeper and more paralyzing than anything I had yet experienced.

"Yes," I whispered. "I know you."

"You are afraid. It is good that you are afraid."

"No."

"You will have to return to me now. You belong to me, and you always will. It is time for all of us to take back what is rightfully ours."

"I'll fight you," I said. "And I'm not defenseless any more."

"No?"

Karen, there was something about the creature's confidence, mixed with the frightening familiarity of the voice, that made it suddenly impossible for me to concentrate the forces that I had learned to use. I tried to love the demon that had inhabited my body—since birth?—and project into it the white searing energy that would tear it apart. But I had no love to give it, and all the time it was feasting on and reinforcing the fear that I was radiating out from my spirit like a dark star.

I didn't want to love. I wanted to kill.

"When this is over, I'll be back with the Master," I said. "You—all of you—have lost and you know it."

Instead of answering, my demon smiled broadly, and then turned with a bow and the tip of a hat, its gaze directing my attention to the air above and behind him. Karen, I could actually feel the heat of its malevolent confidence blocking my thoughts, scrambling my brain, fighting for control of my mind. I shared, for long terrifying seconds, its knowledge that we would soon be brutally reunited on its terms, at its leisure, as if these were *my* thoughts.

With dread in my heart, I turned my eyes to follow its gesture, up toward the tracks which led back up to the entrance to the cellar and outside.

At first, I could see nothing.

Then, suddenly, hundreds, thousands of other demons streamed into the underground chamber like a swarm of bats, swirling around and around in a thickening nightmare cloud above my head. There were so many that it took more than a minute for the cloud to finally accumulate all of the assorted demons from all of the people in the audience upstairs, the witches and hags, the dwarves, malevolent fairies, trolls and vampires and more exotic creations of the human imagination at its worst.

The cloud swirled down at a leisurely pace, following the invitation of my own demon who danced in delight around my face. In a moment, I was totally surrounded by a thick cloud of terror and fantasy. I closed my eyes, trying to feel nothing, feeling instead the worst kind of despair radiating out from my psyche so powerfully that it cast bright inverted shadows against the walls of the container.

A feast for the angry demons.

As the growing sea of grotesque faces enveloped me, I heard a sound, turned my head with a monumental effort and saw the patchwork ghost that was Fool's father climbing a steel ladder out of the tank along the far back of the wall.

I could feel the myriad itch and pinprick sensation of demons penetrating my flesh, while others hovered inches from my face, dragging my attention away from the man who wanted to kill all of us. A deep sluggish weariness poured down through my body. I felt too weak to lift my head. But of course a wiser part of my mind knew that I had won, so it was all right to sacrifice myself now. Following the comforting, seductive urging of that voice, I gave myself up to the demons, inviting them closer, letting them attach to the places where my flesh tingled and crawled on my arms, neck, back, shoulders, legs, feet, feeling like a man tied down to a giant anthill.

Let them spend their time on me, I thought to myself. As far away from the Master as I could get them.

As the creatures covered every square centimeter of my body, my thoughts settled into a cloud of confusion interrupted by wave after wave of intense claustrophobia. Grimly, I shut the eyes of my spirit. The discordant chorus of wild thoughts swirled into and through my mind, trying in different, sometimes contradictory ways to pull my emotions toward panic, toward despair, toward fear, toward anger, a tug of war that somehow cancelled itself out into mental chaos.

The world darkened. I wished for nothing more than death and the release it would provide me.

There must have been some tiny sliver of survival instinct left in my mind, because I found a part of my awareness coolly traveling a mental line between all of these emotions, a path of calm where it was possible to think again, balanced between the many dark places where the demons wanted to drag me.

With superhuman patience, this part of me reached out and stilled my thoughts here, there, wherever it could touch.

Slowly, gradually, the radiant darkness ebbed. I fought to bring my mind to the deadly stillness of deep meditation, and as I took the food off of the demonic table, as the feast ended, I felt the demons' rage. A thousand fists beat against the glass that separated them from my emotions.

Resolutely, with a fatigue that I knew I had to ignore, I wiped the blood off my fingers and pulled hard on the rope that tied together the radioactive rods, thinking to separate them further from the waves of heat beating at my face from the far end of the tank. When it didn't move I yanked harder, and felt the inert weight shift a half a foot along the floor with a grinding sound that echoed strangely off the far walls.

Then, from somewhere above me, I realized that some of what I thought was an echo was actually the sound of machinery reluctantly, noisily stirring into motion. It grew louder, and I felt an unexpected tug on my rope. At the next hard inexplicable tug, the pile was pulled up into the air, swaying hard. At the next, the rope was jerked out of my hands, knocking me backwards.

I watched it lift overhead in dismay. I had not defeated Fool's father after all. He had not been dragging the rods to the other stack. I saw now that he had been consolidating them together for the lifting machinery.

Another hard yank from above, and the rods of Plutonium swayed upwards and moved restlessly back and forth directly over my head.

The demons howled, and I could feel from their thoughts a kind of wild triumph, that what had been a defeat above ground would become a victory from this unexpected direction.

I saw in their minds the Master's death.

Frantically, hiding my awareness inside the general feeling of demonic confusion and chaos, I reached inside, searching, searching.

I thought of Fool, but this only raised up anger at his father, and I had to fight for control again. I thought of the Master, of our last evening together, but this evoked a dark sense of sadness and despair, and fear that I had failed him.

Then, Karen, I thought of you.

I remembered your face, and it became many faces. It became the face of the baby who looked at me with trust and amusement, waiting to be entertained. It was the happy, flushed face after a dance at the school recital, drinking in the applause; it was the face of a young girl leaving the car for her first dance at school. I saw you as a woman, so beautiful and composed and aware, an independent creature who I have loved through a thousand and many times a thousand other faces as we traveled, together, toward your adulthood.

I remembered your laughter, and I remembered your tears, and how I would dry them until, one day, you learned to dry them yourself.

The memories of you filled my mind, and somehow it mingled with the triumph that the demons were feeling, and so for a fatal second they didn't notice the terrible, awesomely powerful thing that was erupting from the core of my spirit. All over again, I saw you run up to me on the sidelines after a soccer game, all bruised and dirty from slide tackling in front of the goal and triumphant because your team had just beaten the boys. I saw the sleepy look on your face as you tried to stay awake so I would read another chapter of the bedtime book, and my mind brought back the way you looked when you came downstairs in your prom dress.

I saw your place at the center of my life during my very best years, and I felt the love rise up in me like a golden halo around my heart, spreading out like the Master's own glow the first night I had seen him stand on two feet, a generous, powerful warmth that embraced all things and all possibilities, and you were at the center of it, the magic engine that produced the light.

My memories of you were woven deeply into my spirit as it radiated at the top of the bright spectrum. I stood up, and with the glorious light of you and us, I erupted in a volcanic explosion of love that sent demonic spirits flying away almost fast enough to outrun their own screaming disintegration. I was the Sun, and I exploded into a brilliance that blinded my own spirit eyes. When the explosion was over, the eyes of my spirit watched bits and pieces of shadow raining down where the demons had been, still burning from the brilliance of my love and the glow of my happiest memories—

Only the leprechaun still hung onto my neck, its legs blowing out horizontally and flapping in the breeze as if it were caught in a hurricane. Slowly, a part of my mind savoring every second of it, I gave this utterly familiar creature my full attention, and then I gave it the same love that I have always felt for you.

There was a silent howl in the deepest parts of my mind as the white energy, concentrated now into a small space, entered my alter ego. The face looked at me first with determination, then with shock, then with astonishment, then fear, before it finally expanded, dissolved, vanished, and then there were no more demons.

For a long second I looked around. Then my eyes turned upward. My first thought was to protect the Master so that someday you, Karen, would have a chance to meet him.

As I leaped off the ground, my awareness split apart, and one part rose effortlessly to the top of the containment area, glided to the bank of switches at the far wall, and inserted an electric hand into the tattered patchwork spirit of the person who was manipulating the machinery that controlled the rope.

What, exactly, my spirit body did to him I don't know; the physics of the spirit are still unknown to me. But at the touch, Fool's father leaped in the air with an unintelligible shout and ran, blindly, down the corridor. He collided against the side of the wall, and the room echoed with a sickening sound midway between a thud and a smack. Then he turned and ran in a new direction, and my spirit body saw his legs carry him at a reckless speed blindly across the dark floor and over the edge of the empty tank into empty air, his legs flailing in surprise directly over the rods, now suspended above the glowing pile of melted Plutonium at the far end of the containment tank.

As he fell, my physical body saw the sudden appearance of a tall vertical fire that was the rope holding the remaining rods suspended in the air. The fire burned for a long second, and then my physical eyes saw a human body fall across the glow onto the suspended rods, clinging to them to keep from falling to his death.

The additional weight snapped the burning rope. The rods fell into the pile at the end of the containment chamber and seemed to stick there as if they had fallen into taffy.

In that awful, terrible moment, the far side of the room lit up with an intense glow that dazzled even my spiritual sight. Blinded, I fell to the ground, covered my head with my hands, but still the brightness grew, to the point where even through my closed eyes and through my arms the brightness was intolerably intense. A wave of heat washed over me, and I waited for an explosion that never came.

Finally, the brightness fell into abrupt shadow, and I looked up and saw that the floor underneath the rods had melted away, and the glow was sinking into the ground with a brilliant sunset display that illuminated the melting concrete wall, which flowed first like rubber, then like a waterfall, a great infall of liquid stone dripping rapidly into the expanding hole whose crater was expanding out toward my feet.

The floor tilted in the direction of the far wall, and I could hear the sound of the rods in the second containment chamber rolling downhill, where I knew that they, too, would gather into a pile.

As the hole reached for me, the spiritual awareness that was still up on the floor above the containment area reached down and pulled my physical body up and out, and I materialized without fanfare on the ground above the tank, moving forward on a dead run. It felt as if I was flying up the rope ladder into the daylight, and as my feet touched the concrete, I screamed words which I now think must have been words of the spirit, incomprehensible to my own ears, but which I hoped would help everybody, at some deeper level, realize that they should immediately run for the street.

Karen, there must have been something convincing in that scream, because it, rather than the huge infall of concrete and dust behind me, caused the panic you saw on the television footage. I have looked at that footage many times since, trying to determine if I had really spoken the language of the spirit, but as you know, the cameras were on the Master, capturing in every detail the collapse of the platform and the swirling hole that appeared under it.

Then there was a rush of heat at my back, a geyser of flame and vaporized concrete, and underneath us it felt as if the world hiccoughed. Later, there would be a debate about what, exactly, happened then, but the best theory offered by scientists who later studied the site was that the gathering of rods in the second containment tank had melted downwards just like the first one had, and somewhere near the bottom of our planet's crust, at the place where the mantle begins, the two bundles of nuclear material had collided under intense pressure, and together, miles below, they became a nuclear bomb whose force was channeled upwards for several miles through the ground along the path of least resistance, the hole that was directly behind the Master as he spoke the last words of his magical sermon.

A directed spurt of fire rained down on the concrete floor like electric hail as people ran away in all directions. The Master managed to hold his balance and maintain his otherworldly composure even as the ground shifted and swirled under him, and the cameras all managed to catch him in that last unforgettable moment, a creature half human and half flame, who nonetheless was able to say, loud enough for the cameras to catch his voice—and so calm and unhurried that people forever and a day from now will be talking about his courage—the words that he wanted us to remember.

"Forget about me," he said as the ground pulled his flaming body down into the sources of the orange geyser. "But remember everything that I said."

And then the earth closed, the rain of fire subsided, and the Master's ministry was over.

I stood alone in a melee of frightened people running in all directions except toward the sealing wound in the ground behind me, spinning around as people collided with me, hearing the distant wail of emergency vehicles in a kind of numb trance. I wanted to cry, but there were no tears.

I turned and there was Cassandra, standing as alone as I was. She had placed herself exactly where my lopsided progress was taking me, and once again I shook my head in a deep respect for her knowledge of things before they happened. I let my arms hang at my sides, feeling the emptiness and the deep fatigue of defeat mingled with the distant, comfortable afterglow of my radiance of love.

I embraced Cassandra, not in mourning, not in celebration, but in a shared feeling of need.

"You knew," I said, releasing her and stepping back.

Cassandra said nothing. She was staring at the hole that had finally stopped swirling. Behind it, there was another sound, which we later learned was the French Broad River emptying into a deeper part of the hole. The river bed would be dry for nearly two hours.

A chill wind stirred the grass at our feet, then grew stronger and blew across our faces. I looked up at the sky, and realized that the season was finally turning, that it would be cold tomorrow and for the next few months. Winter had chosen this moment to arrive.

"You knew this was going to happen," I said again, trying to put into my weary voice the accusation I wanted her to hear.

"He orchestrated a hell of an exit, didn't he?" she said, looking across my shoulder, back at the place where the rods had been tunneling toward the core of the planet. "It's funny," she said. "I can look at this moment every second of my life, but I only have a few minutes to actually *be* here, in the place where he left the world behind. It's overpowering."

I followed her eyes to where it looked as if the back of the warehouse and a good part of the parking lot had melted into a thick lumpy soup of melted concrete and what must have been lava, still smoking around the edges where it burned the grass. Where the secret basement had been, there was only a strange funnel-like depression that must have gone deeper than it looked, because at the center, a thin spray of water misted up into the air.

Under our feet, the ground trembled faintly.

"I tried to stop it," I said, fighting back tears. "In the end, I failed him just when he needed me most."

"Don't be ridiculous. Whatever happened down there was purely for you, not for him. He knew long ago how this was going to come out."

"How can you possibly know that?"

"It was a secret he and I never shared with the rest of you."

"If you had told me—"

"He didn't want us to stop it. Surely you knew that."

"*Why?*"

For a long time, Cassandra didn't say anything. The cold wind blew through my clothes, but my skin felt strangely warm.

"He gave people all over the world a show that will give the demons the feast of their lives," she said at last. "Tonight, every news program in the country will have him as their lead story. What the demons don't yet realize is that once their little feast is over, there will be followup questions about who he was and what he taught. The footage itself, his last words, the language he spoke and the translations will be carried across the planet. The genie is out of the bottle," Cassandra told me, looking from the sky back to my face. "He outsmarted the demons, got the attention of the world, and they don't even know what his name was."

"But he's dead," I said.

"Yes."

"Is he really?"

"The body is gone. The rest is back with Mommy, where it belongs."

"I wanted him to stay with us," I said. "Even knowing his sacrifice, I was that selfish."

"Yes," she said. "Even though I've seen this moment more times than anything else in this scripted life of mine, it still pulls at me with an incredible sadness."

We stood together, my arm around her, staring at nothing and everything. We watched the ambulances drive slowly into the center of the crowd, where people lay on the ground. I could see that many burns were being tended, but by some miracle, there seemed to be no fatalities. Slowly, we walked, arm-in-arm, back across the warehouse floor for one last look. And as I stepped over an obstacle, I realized that I was walking across the long space where the Master had instructed us not to clear the rubble. The deadly eruption of ash and lava had fallen exactly onto this place where nobody had been seated. I shook my head in one last burst of admiration for the god who had walked among us, and then we turned back to the ambulances.

"Right before he went up on stage," said Cassandra, "he did something that scared me right down to my bones."

"What was that?"

"He pulled me aside and said something that wasn't in the script. His words were nowhere in the future that I knew. It was the first moment of my life that I had not foreseen. I didn't even know that he was going to talk to me, and so for the first time, I listened to somebody tell me something totally new, totally unexpected. And it was about you."

"What did he say about me?"

"He said that you and your daughter were each living with an enormous wound, and that I had to help you heal that wound, and then I had to look after you. Do you know what he was talking about?"

"Yes," I said.

"And he said something about a journey. Do you know what that meant?"

"Yes," I said. "I think I do—now."

"Well?"

"Don't give me that," I said, feeling suddenly very tired. "You've seen all this before. Just assume that I've said my lines to the satisfaction of the universe and leave me alone for a few minutes."

Cassandra didn't move, and after more than a minute, I looked up in her face.

"What's wrong?" I said.

"This isn't part of the script," she said tightly. "There aren't any lines. And I need to know."

I took her hand in mine, noticing, not for the first time, how beautiful her spirit and mine looked as they mingled in the place where we touched. "Walk with me," I said.

We walked through the crowd, which seemed to me at that moment to be a sea of stunned faces that alternately flashed red at the lights of the ambulance behind us. Looking at their spirits, I saw that for the first time, these people could see the glows of each others' spirit bodies, and they were no longer sleepwalking, but awake, alert, a little frightened by the possibilities that were only now starting to become visible on the horizon of their lives. Before we had walked half a mile up the road, an enormous geyser spouted out from some invisible place on the near bank, throwing steam and water into the sky toward the city. Where the chilly wind blew the water into a fine mist, you could see a beautiful rainbow stretching across the sky. Nobody else was looking in this direction, so we stood and watched it, each holding the other's hand, for many minutes as upwelling steam slowly began the long process of refilling the river bed.

"My wife was ill with cancer for more than two years," I said finally. "They operated on her ovaries, but apparently the disease had spread to other organs. She started with chemotherapy and it was destroying her body, one round, and then they decided they wanted to do another round, just to be safe. She couldn't eat. When they came back with the X-rays and told her that the nodes were gone, she didn't believe it, and it turned out she was right. They wanted to do another round, and she told them she'd rather die.

"Then, one day, Karen came home from school and found her on the floor of the kitchen. I got to the hospital about the same time they did, and she was conscious again, so I waited while they got the tests back from the lab. She wanted more than anything else to die, and we talked about it, and then, suddenly, she was unconscious and there was a sound coming from the heart monitor, and I told them she didn't want any more intervention, but they wheeled her out without paying any attention to me.

"A few hours later they had her hooked up to more stuff than I had ever seen before, and she looked like she'd aged 20 years in a handful of hours. Karen—my daughter—begged her to hang on so she could try the chemo treatments one more time, but my wife was a strong and stubborn woman, and she told us both, in a calm voice that broke both our hearts, that it was time to die while she still had some dignity left. Finally Karen shouted at her that she was being selfish, and ran out the door.

"When Karen left the room, my wife asked me for a favor," I said, my voice shaking now with the power of the memory. "A part of me must have known what she was going to ask, because when she called me close, I trembled. I begged her not to ask me to do this, but she looked me in the eyes and said that it was the only favor she would ever ask me for again. And then—oh God—"

At that moment, the grief that I had been holding back for more than a year burst through its dams, and I started sobbing uncontrollably, feeling ashamed and relieved and confused as the tears poured out of me. My breath came in ragged gasps that made it impossible to talk. We walked along River Street, the crowd behind us now, and I tried to control the heaves in my body.

I thought I had it under control, and then I cried all over again.

It was a long time before I could speak. Finally, I told Cassandra how I had brought the pills back to my wife's hospital room, and her eyes, dark and deep-sunken into the sockets, fixed on me, and read somehow that I had been successful.

"I laid the pills on the table next to the bed, and reached down and gave her a last hug, and a kiss that lasted only a second, and I was amazed at how cold her lips felt against mine. Then she told me to leave, that she didn't want to go through this for another minute, and that I should tell Karen goodbye for her. And I left."

"You helped her die," said Cassandra. "And your daughter never forgave you for it."

"It was worse than that," I said. "Much, much worse."

It wasn't until we had reached the end of the street near the college that I finally managed to lift enough of the weight off of my heart to be able to speak again.

"I tried calling Karen, but she wasn't answering her cell phone," I said. "I called and called, because I thought maybe she and her mother should say goodbye to each other. Finally, I sat down in the lobby and waited for her to come in for the morning visit, and I knew that it was too late. She walked in the door and came right over to me, and asked me why I wasn't upstairs. I told her that her mother was gone. By some coincidence, at exactly that moment, a nurse came up to us and asked us if we were who we were. And she told us that my wife had passed away about five minutes ago."

"She wanted to know how you knew before the hospital people did," said Cassandra.

"Are we back on the script?"

"No. I have no idea what you're going to say next."

"You're right. Karen started screaming. I don't remember now how it is that we got outside, but we were out in the parking lot, and she was still screaming at me, and I was in an emotional state like nothing I will ever feel again. It felt as if I was going to break inside, and here was my daughter, yelling at me that I had killed her mother, that maybe together we could have talked this woman that we both loved into choosing life over death.

"And finally something broke inside of me, and I found myself yelling back. I—"

"Oh my God," said Cassandra.

"Yes," I said.

"Say the words," she said. "Tell me what you said. Until you do, I still have hope that you didn't say what I think anybody would have said in that situation."

"I told her that her mother could have lived with the pain of the cancer. But she couldn't live with the pain in her body plus the pain that she, Karen, piled onto it when she demanded that she go through another round of chemotherapy in a lost cause. I told Karen that *she* was the selfish one, and that her mother would be alive right now if she hadn't made it clear that every visit was going to be more of the same, another screaming insistence that she sacrifice her dignity and endure yet more pain so we, Karen and I, could have a few more minutes with wife and mother.

"I told my daughter that she was too much for her mother to bear, and as I said it, I knew that I had crossed a line that would kill her love for me. But at that moment, I was like the twitching muscle of a dead frog when you touch it with electricity. I had no control over what I said. The words spoke themselves, and they were terrible in the pain they inflicted on her."

"And you haven't spoken since?"

"When I saw the look on her face, I tried to apologize, right then and there. But she just turned away, and got in her car and drove off, and I had no energy to follow her, nothing left in my body. I was doubly mourning now, and it felt as if my body wasn't big enough for the grief that filled it and poured out into the air and the ground and the sky all around me.

"At that moment, I could easily have taken my own life and not have noticed, but even that thought didn't come to me until later. I was empty, broken; I had nothing left except to plan the funeral and go to work and try to manage my life. I walked back into the hospital and spent a little time with the lifeless bundle of chemicals that had been my wife, and then they led me away and I saw Karen at the funeral, but she didn't speak, and I saw from her face that no apology was possible."

"And that's still true?"

"I don't know," I said.

"What are you going to do?"

"I'm writing her a long letter."

"That's it? A letter?"

"It's a *very* long letter. And if she'll talk to me after she reads it, if she'll read it, then I'll tell her again how sorry I am. But I'll do a better job of it this time, and I'll help her realize that what I said was a product of the terrible thing that I did, and that the terrible thing that I did was a voluntary transfer of pain from her mother to me, and that this was fair, because up to then, she had borne a disproportionate amount of it, and it was my turn, my turn for the rest of my life."

"I think you may have a chance," Cassandra said after a moment. "That's what the Master told me," she said.

"What?"

"That this is the time to talk to her. She's going to be curious about—" Cassandra gestured at the distant scene behind us, at the geyser and the distant milling of people and the red flashes of the ambulances, at a sullen gathering of demons that now hovered impotently above the scene—"about what's happened. He said that I should tell you to use that, because she still loves and cares for you, and is still interested in your life. All this, when it gets in the papers, will make her even more so."

"And then I have to leave," I said.

"Where?"

"Outside the universe," I said. "That was really why I was looking for you in the first place."

"What do you mean?"

"After this is over, I'm going to look for the old gods," I said. "I have a way to get to the place where they went, which the Master says is in a different universe altogether. They went looking for something, something that's missing from this place, and I have to find them and give them a message."

I took a long, deep breath.

"And I want you to come with me," I said.

Cassandra gave me a sad smile. "You know I can't," she said.

"Why?"

"You know why. I know what's going to happen already. There's nothing in there about going to some other universe."

"Are you sure? Was there anything about this conversation in there?"

Cassandra stopped walking and looked at me.

"Let me tell you what I think," I said. "I think that so long as that question was part of this conversation, so long as we were going to be talking about you passing outside this universe to a place where the laws don't apply, we're in a place where you can make independent decisions. You want to test it?"

"How?" she said.

"Say yes," I said. "Tell me you'll come with me, that you'll hold my hand as I stand in that place in Asgard with the dragon statue in my hand, and step across into wherever it is that the old gods went. Say those words, and see if the future that seems so set to you now doesn't just shrivel up and melt like a snowball in hell."

Cassandra gave me a frightened look, and I could see the fear on her spirit.

"I'm afraid," she said.

"I know."

"I'm deathly afraid you might be wrong, and I think I'm even more scared that you might be right."

"Do it as a favor to me, and don't think about the consequences."

"I will," she said. "I'll come with you. I can't think of anything I'd rather do than share this adventure with you. Oh—God—"

Karen, at that moment I saw something in Cassandra's beautiful spirit that I have never seen before and will never see again. It was as if she had become a living light show, a human fireworks display of the spirit, and I saw in her, at that decision, one universe die and another give glorious birth to itself, as the future rearranged itself. I saw this thing and realized that what Cassandra was going through was infinitely more intense, more personal, more remarkable, than the remarkable thing I was looking at.

She swayed, and I caught her and held her steady while the spirit in and around her sparkled and shone and finally settled down, many minutes later, to something resembling normalcy.

"Well?" I said.

"I can see right up until the day we leave," she said. "After that, it's fuzzy for a few additional seconds, and then…Nothing. Nothing at all."

"You're free," I said.

"I will be," she answered.

"So tell me then," I said. "Will Karen agree to meet with me?"

Cassandra gave me a happy smile, and I realized that this was the first time I had seen her truly happy since I had first met her. It was a beautiful thing to see. Her spirit, in that moment, was even more beautiful than it had been when the universe was giving birth, and I think her face was more beautiful still.

"I think," she said, "that I'll let you and your daughter work out that mystery without any clues from me."

"We're not far from her dormitory," I said. "Do I look all right?" I asked Cassandra.

Cassandra looked me up and down with some amusement.

"You look like a person who is probably two hours away from a terrible death from severe radiation sickness," she said.

"Oh," I said.

"So it's probably time to go."

"Where?"

Cassandra took one of my blood-caked hands in hers. "To Asgard," she said. "I think it's time you got a working tour of the Mechs' infirmary."

XXI

We have now an amazing opportunity to experience, consciously, the sense of anticipation and exhilaration that attends the birth of a new faith. Future citizens of the New Age will look back at us, living today, with a kind of joyful envy, because we are present at the creation, at the time when the human species made an historic leap in its social evolution.

What they will never be able to quite realize is that most of the people, living today, will never see this amazing thing that is taking place in their midst. While the collective consciousness recovers and finally preserves the core wisdom at the foundation of every religion, only a small handful of citizens will recognize that they live in a blessed time and place.

Yes, this lost opportunity for spiritual joy is a tragedy almost beyond bearing. The only humane response is to extend an invitation to everyone, an invitation to recognize and participate in the new sense of wonder and the mystery that is everywhere around us—and then to welcome with open arms everybody who has the wit to accept a free ticket to the magic show.

It's playing now. Its stage is the world and everything beyond it, where, if you listen closely, the chorus is just starting to sing a catchy new tune called the Song of the Universe.

—From The Rutherfordton Spiritual Gazette

Karen, I am sure by now that you have seen the television footage of that amazing afternoon, and I know that some of it would have been a confusing disappointment. You see the Master addressing the crowd, but you can understand none of what he is saying, even though you can hear his voice so clearly. This, I see now, is why the Master never used the broadcast media to deliver his message; because when you speak directly to the spirit, the meaning isn't captured electronically. Even to me, who was there, it sounds like gibberish in the electronic replay.

And of course the confrontation between the dark parasite king and its followers are invisible to the camera, and so there is an inexplicable pause before the underground explosion, and then the camera offers us that last remarkable image of the Master—the way he will be remembered by millions and perhaps billions of people around the world, who will never have the opportunity to learn his name.

The footage was played and replayed and replayed again on the television news, and Tom Patterson, who wrote the story for the *Asheville Citizen-Times*, will win the Pulitzer price for journalism. No, it hasn't happened yet, but I have seen him receive the award in the crystal ball that is the library of Asgard. I have also seen that the people who Mars intercepted on the side of the hill will be found guilty of the original destruction of the warehouse building, and no connection with Justin Macaulay will ever be proven in the courts or otherwise. After that, we stopped looking, because I already know that the dark shade that Macaulay carries with him is waiting for us in our own futures.

In the days after that remarkable event, I would walk around the streets and could always pick out the people who attended The Speech, who experienced life without demons or parasites and whose spirits were blessed with the rainfall of magical dust from the sky. In their eyes, you can see the difference; they're no longer sleepwalking. They are a brotherhood and sisterhood now, the first citizens of a new age in the history of the human race. If we do it right, it will become a remarkable golden age when the full potential of our birthright is finally within reach.

Outside the library, a dense canopy of leaves shimmered in the sunlight and a warm breeze crossed my face and chilled my head where the hair had been. The air was sweet with the scent of flowers. On either side of the path, exotic fruit blossomed in splendid multicolored profusion; orange and yellow berries and larger red globes the size of lacrosse balls, sweet and pulpy.

Apollo touched my balded head lightly. "Now we know one more thing about the mechs," he said. "Apparently they didn't pay much attention to the idea of hair—at least at the time they built this place. *Every physician almost hath his favorite disease.* Henry Fielding."

"Their infirmary did nothing to heal my grief over the master's death," I said. "It feels like my stomach is going to rip itself out of my body and run screaming down the path. And I hardly knew him, compared to you."

"*The worst is not, so long as we can say, 'This is the worst.'* Shakespeare, of course."

"It is an adjustment," Mars acknowledged slowly from the other side of me. "I will never again feel the warmth of his spirit like sunshine across my soul."

Apollo looked at him speculatively for a long second, then rested his hand across his fellow god's shoulder. "I'll miss him too," he said.

Mars stood up and led me with a forceful gesture away from the others, to the stone balcony overlooking the forest, where we could see across the long valley to the mountains in the distance, and measure the shape of the wind in those curiously flexible leaves.

"Could I ask you something?" he rumbled, his face looking at the ground.

"Of course."

"Cassandra has told me where you're going," said Mars after a moment. "I want to ask if—if I can come with you."

"I don't understand," I said.

Mars looked at me, then across the patio at Apollo, then back at me. "This world—this universe—holds nothing for me any more," he said. "There is no longer any place for one such as me. But I think that where you're going, there might be need of someone with my skills. And—" Mars looked down at his feet again. "And there, the rules might be different. There I might find atonement, instead of the endless shame that I will carry with me here. I might even—" here he managed a smile—"meet the original Mars, if he is still walking this path. I would very much like to compare notes with him."

Karen, I really didn't intend to hold this god in suspense, but as he stood against the balcony of the patio waiting for me to think of what to say, I saw an intense uncertainty and anxiety on his spirit.

"It would be a privilege," I said finally. "We'll find them together, you and I and Cassandra."

To my surprise, Mars embraced me, and I felt in his body the enormous release of tension. "I will be forever in your debt," he said soberly. "Please know that I mean that in the most literal sense of the words."

Across the patio, others had gathered in an unhappy group. If there had been any parasites left in paradise, they would have been drawn to this radiant feast of dark spiritual emanations.

"The Master told me once that we should learn to celebrate our greatest losses," Apollo commented into the general silence, "because the feeling of loss is a measure of what we have been allowed, temporarily, to enjoy."

"We have a right to a time of mourning," Briarius said defiantly. "He's gone, and we still have so much to learn."

"*The world breaks everyone and thereafter many are strong in the broken places. But those that will not break it kills.* Hemingway. I acknowledge that, right now, our weakness may be our saving grace. But remember that in the future, there will be many who would envy us our loss for the wonderful thing that we had."

"You're probably all going to laugh," said Venus, "but I always imagined that we'd be married. In my fantasies, I planned how we would have a meditation room for him in our house, so that whenever our kids got too distracting, he could go in there and be with Mommy. That was really, really stupid, wasn't it?"

"My fantasy was that I would help him become the benevolent ruler of the world," Mars rumbled.

"You don't want to know the things I imagined on his behalf," said Apollo. "And in any case, I doubt they would have ever given him tenure."

"Don't you think," I said, "that he accomplished everything he set out to do, and none of the things that he did not intend? In the end, that last part may be what sets him apart from all the other avatars who went where he went and came back to talk to us about it."

Suddenly Venus burst into tears.

"That's nothing but crap!" she cried out. "You know, every one of us knows, that if everything he told us was true, then nothing, not even he himself, could have taken him away from us. He would still be alive, and if he *is* still alive, he'd come back to us. So where is he? Tell me that if you know so much! Where is he?"

"He's with Mommy," I said somberly. "The rest of us should be so lucky."

Venus looked up at me with the full force of her fierce eyes. "All I want to know from you, from any of you," she said, "is what do we do now?"

For a long second, nobody answered. For a long second, it seemed that there *was* no answer. Then he spoke up at last.

"You will fight," he said.

There was something in the way the words were spoken that made all of us straighten our backs a little, and for a magical moment it seemed as if despair was nothing more than an indulgence.

"The things you will do from this day forward," he continued, "will be remembered by every future generation as a turning point in the history of the human species. They will remember how you drove the invisible overlords out of hiding, and showed the world how to use love and happiness as weapons against the dark oppressors. For as long as you live, the odds against you will be impossibly high. But know this: for the first time in many many generations, the enemy has reason to be afraid.

"And someday, perhaps soon," he continued, his voice softening, "another will come who will know how to make the world see the many important things that I was never able to. I hope that person will find as much joy as I have found in all of you."

Karen, I will never again feel such a powerful jolt of excitement as I felt at the instant those last words reached my ears. All at the same moment, all of us realized that the Master was here, really here, back among us. Long before my mind could register this fantastic news, we were on our feet and around him, touching him, crying, laughing, filled with a joy that was immensely more powerful because a few seconds ago our feelings had been so near the opposite end of the scale.

The competition to get close to him was too much for me; already, the others were crowding me out. And so, avoiding Mars's elbow once again, I stepped back and watched the gods create a mosh pit of embraces and questions around the Master.

From this place behind the others, the eyes of my spirit saw something that I don't think any of the others ever noticed. I saw that there was no rainbow sparkle of holy spirit animating the body at the center of all this attention and activity. Looking up, I could see that all of his spirit was concentrated in a kind of pulsating ball over the Master's head, and I realized that this thing which had returned to us was a living manifestation of Mommy, and that now it was Mommy Herself we were talking with.

The body that the Master had materialized for us held up its hands, and I felt as if I was being cradled in the arms of a gentle parent and rocked, not to sleep, but to a deep sense of peace which is the closest thing to sleep the spirit is allowed by its energetic physics.

"Why did you leave us?" Venus asked him, sounding now like a little girl.

Instead of answering, the Master reached down and touched one of the alien flowers in the raised garden behind him. "If you could keep one or the other," he said, indicating the flower with a nod of his head, "would you choose to keep the flower, or the beauty of it?"

Venus shook her head. "I don't understand," she said.

The Master touched her forehead. "The beauty of it lives here. Without that, what you see there in the garden is just another collection of molecules."

"So?" she said.

"So if I could choose," the Master told her gently, "where do you think I would choose to exist; here, or in that place where I will always live, somewhere behind your eyes?"

"I miss you," Venus said.

"I know." The Master smiled, and in that moment he became less substantial, a shimmering form in the air. "I knew from the moment I found each of you," he said: "a thing which all of you are about to experience, over and over again, in your own lives: *if you dare to touch the lives of others in a way that makes them happy, or in a way that gives them hope, you will hurt them in equal measure when you leave.* You must console them with the words I say to you now, and it is the truth," he said. "You are written indelibly on my spirit, and you will be forever. I take you with me everywhere I go, and I intend to go many places."

Venus looked down at her feet. And then, somehow, she found the words that all of us were looking for. "When you go," she said, fighting back tears, "take our love with you too."

The fading apparition, a facsimile of that remarkable, unforgettable face, smiled acknowledgment, and touched the tiny glow above her head, the eighth Chakra, and then touched each of ours in turn.

"And now I have a gift for you." The Master held out his ghostly, semi-transparent hand, and for a second what he held there was too dazzlingly bright for our eyes to make it out. Then I saw it through my spirit eyes, and it seemed to be a jewel, and as I looked at this shining object, I realized why we humans are instinctively drawn to jewels, why we think they are beautiful. The most elegant jewels are a pale reminder of something we remember in places below and beyond our physical minds, something that we still recall from ancient days before humans entered this world.

The Master held out to us the remarkable sparkling beauty of living dust, a pulsing, glowing ball of pure holy spirit.

"Take my gift," he said, and he exhaled, blowing the dust into a stream of golden sparkles. The infinitely precious substance, the material sparks of universal awareness, flowed into our bodies, into our spirits.

And then, as we were receiving perhaps the most valuable gift in all of history, the Master's body seemed to grow enormously larger. He was ten feet wide and twenty five feet tall, and he continued to grow until each of his legs were ten feet wide, and as he grew, he became less and less distinct, and finally I realized that he was slowly dissolving in the air, that the force that held this holy spirit hologram together was being released. The Master shimmered like a cloud, like a wisp of smoke, like nothing at all.

We stared at the place where he had been, and then all of us stood up at once, and there was greatness in our spirits.

My daughter, I will always and forever be empowered by that moment when I held so much of the universal awareness inside me at once. I experienced a clarity and power that perhaps even exceeded what the gods of our ancient legends once knew, the ability to speak directly to the spirit of any creature, the power to direct the wind and move the earth, to participate in that divine attention that infuses the cosmos.

In that moment, I was in a trance, and yet more alive that I have ever been. Where the others went I cannot say, but I stepped off of the endless patio and up over the curb and onto the sidewalk a little ways past the baseball stadium, and I looked up into the sky and saw what I had never noticed before, a large, dark cluster of spiritual parasites hovering and circling like vultures over a location that appeared to be several blocks from where I was standing. I followed that swirl of parasites the way you would follow smoke to a fire, and found myself standing in front of a hospital building.

My daughter, the events after that are still hazy in my mind, but this I know: I walked through the front doors of the hospital and along the corridors and into rooms, and I have an unclear memory of exploding parasites and a golden glow of energy touching the spirits of the sick and injured in the places where they needed healing, and I remember in a moment of clarity recognizing that before my arrival and for a thousand years or more, the doctors and the hospitals and the parasites had orchestrated a dance that is mutually beneficial, that the parasites bring business to the doctors and hospitals, and the doctors and hospitals treat the symptoms but are careful to leave the spiritual afflictions that nurture the parasites alone.

In my memory I can hear the cries of joy as people stood up out of their beds and walked behind me along the corridors, and perhaps you will not be surprised to hear that everywhere I led this growing crowd of the healed and the joyful and the awake, hospital security guards and employees put themselves in my path and did what they could to stop me. But I was Zeus and Odin and the flame in the whirlwind, and on that day I could have brushed aside trees and buildings as easily as I walked through their flimsy barricades.

And at the end, when I had cleansed the hospital of parasites and the sick and lame and near-dead were following me out into the street, after I had given away the gift that the Master had given me, I slept, and I woke up in a room near the top of the castle of Asgard, with the sunlight streaming into the open window, and for the first time I felt as if I truly belonged in that palace of the gods.

Karen, this is the story as best I can tell it. I wanted you to know all of this before you saw me, because otherwise you would be shocked at how much I have changed, and the experience might be so disturbing that it would interfere with the much more important thing, the fact that I will do whatever it takes to renew our love as father and daughter, and show you that you are the most important and special person in the world to me.

If you are willing to meet with me, then all you have to do is go outside and lift a hand to the sky. When you do, a certain bird, which has been watching over you and giving me hourly reports on your safety, will land on your finger, and I will see you through the eyes of the bird, and join you and the bird on a long walk into the woods and along the river.

And then I will go on a journey whose outcome cannot be predicted in advance. I will go to the invisible doorway in Asgard where the ancient gods left this universe many centuries ago, and I will hold the statue of the dragon, and the hands of Cassandra on one side and Mars on the other, and together we will walk through that magic curtain in new shapes, and try to find out, if we can, what has become of the mechs and the old gods and what they were looking for when they left our universe behind.

There is no way to predict when I will see you again, but I know in my heart that I will return. I have confidence that the peculiar gifts of Mars and Cassandra, and the strength of my own godhood, will be more than enough to overcome any challenges we find on the other side of that door.

I do not know very much about what we will find there. Cassandra tells me that when we pass through into that other universe, we will find ourselves in a courtyard a thousand times more magnificent than the one we left. And there will be an elegantly-dressed dragon there, and he will show no surprise at our sudden appearance. He will bow to the floor, and say to us: "Welcome to all of you. We have been waiting for you for a very long time."

Beyond that, Cassandra does not see, and that curtain of mystery is a blessing to her, and therefore to me also.

Karen, whatever you decide, take my love with you wherever you go, and know that I have made arrangements with the new monastery and retreat that my friend that I have called the Big Score is building with some of the money from his trust. You will always be welcome there, to rest, to receive the baptisms of water or holy spirit, to learn the things that my friends the gods and near-gods are preparing to teach the world.

On the journey, if you think of me at all, do not pray that I will be safe. Pray instead that where I go and what I do will be a blessing to our human species, which has suffered too long in too many ways, and which has denied its godhood and our individual, wonderful dreams for much, much too long. Pray that what I saw in the mind of the overlord on that terrible day when it prophesied that the Master would die is true: that if we are courageous, we can and will defeat it and its dark cohorts who plague our world.

And I, in turn, pray that you will receive more than your share of the wonder and magic that is coming to all of us.

About the Author

Robert Veres has been a leading writer and commentator in the emerging financial planning profession for more than two decades. He has served as editor of two magazines, and his non-financial articles include a five-part fictional series on the potential effects of nuclear war. He currently publishes *Inside Information* newsletter from his office in the mountains near Asheville, NC.

978-0-595-84633-7
0-595-84633-5

Printed in the United States
87192LV00007BA/1/A